COPPER
Hell's Handlers Book 4

Lilly Atlas

All rights reserved. This book or any portion thereof may not be reproduced or used in any manner whatsoever without the express written permission of the author except for the use of brief quotations in a book review.

Copyright © 2019 Lilly Atlas

All rights reserved.

ISBN: 1-946068-29-2
ISBN-13: 978-1-946068-29-3

For everyone who fell in love with Copper and Shell back in Zach's story. Thank you for waiting for them!

Other books by Lilly Atlas

No Prisoners MC
Hook: A No Prisoners Novella
Striker
Jester
Acer
Lucky
Snake

Trident Ink
Escapades

Hell's Handlers MC
Zach
Maverick
Jigsaw
Copper

Audiobooks
Audio

Join Lilly's mailing list for a **FREE** No Prisoners short story.

www.lillyatlas.com

Enormous, commanding, and hotter than sin, Copper is the only man Shell has ever wanted. Even as a young teen, when it was impossible and taboo to capture the attention of a grown man, she longed for him. For years, Shell clung to the dream of turning eighteen and finally being noticed by the Hell's Handlers' rough and gruff president. But the universe had other plans, and she was forced to make a horrible choice. A choice that altered the course of her life forever, sealing her fate and ensuring the dream of being Copper's ol' lady would never materialize.

Sixteen years his junior. Daughter of his MC's former president. Single mother whose deadbeat sperm donor doesn't provide an ounce of support. Loved as a younger sister by every man in the club. The list of reasons goes on for Copper to stay away from Shell. Problem is, he's been hot for her for years. Copper finally gets some relief when she moves out of Tennessee, but once she's back, all those reasons to keep his distance grow weaker by the day.

Unable to fight against his own judgment any longer, Copper finally claims Shell for his own. But once again the universe steps in, revealing secrets with the power to destroy them both.

Shell will do anything for Copper, even tear out her own heart and confront the most agonizing parts of her past. But will she be too late to save her dream? Will she be too late to save Copper?

Table of Contents

Prologue	1
Chapter One	9
Chapter Two	20
Chapter Three	28
Chapter Four	38
Chapter Five	45
Chapter Six	52
Chapter Seven	62
Chapter Eight	71
Chapter Nine	79
Chapter Ten	86
Chapter Eleven	94
Chapter Twelve	105
Chapter Thirteen	116
Chapter Fourteen	127
Chapter Fifteen	136
Chapter Sixteen	149
Chapter Seventeen	160
Chapter Eighteen	168
Chapter Nineteen	181
Chapter Twenty	191

Chapter Twenty-One	203
Chapter Twenty-Two	218
Chapter Twenty-Three	228
Chapter Twenty-Four	243
Chapter Twenty-Five	253
Chapter Twenty-Six	260
Chapter Twenty-Seven	269
Chapter Twenty-Eight	279
Chapter Twenty-Nine	289
Chapter Thirty	297
Chapter Thirty-One	307
Epilogue	319

COPPER

Lilly Atlas

PROLOGUE

2010

If they caught her, there'd be hell to pay.

Absolute hell.

Michelle didn't even want to imagine the level Copper's anger would climb to if he discovered her trailing after him and his men in the dark woods behind the clubhouse well after midnight.

The fury would be epic.

Biblical.

She may be a fifteen-year-old kid, but she wasn't an idiot. Sneaking out of her home, pedaling her bicycle across town to the clubhouse, and lurking in the shadows until the men emerged was not only dangerous, it was reckless—and probably pointless as well.

She wouldn't be able to see a damn thing when the guys finally stopped trekking. But she had to be here. Had to find out if the club had really captured the man who murdered her father.

Four sets of heavy-booted feet tromped through the woods, making no effort toward stealth, thankfully. Shell wasn't exactly mouse-quiet herself, but the noise from the determined group drowned out her leaf-crunching steps.

She shivered despite the down jacket engulfing her body. Mid-January at the base of the Great Smoky Mountains was pretty freakin' cold. Lucky for her, it hadn't snowed in the past few weeks.

"Fuck, it's dark out here. Wouldn't be able to see my own damn dick. We almost done with this romantic stroll through the woods?" That was Maverick's voice. Easy to distinguish because ninety percent of the nonsense out of his mouth was laden with snark and sarcasm. As one of the newer patches, he was making a name for himself with his wit and constant inappropriate humor.

"We have a fucking flashlight, you big baby. Suck it up and keep walking."

Zach. Another new patch.

Clenching her teeth in a fruitless effort to stem the chattering, Shell stole on after the men she considered family. Loved them like family as well. Loved them more than the majority of her flesh and blood relatives, if she was honest.

The further into the woods they ventured, the more confident Shell grew in her guess of their destination. The guys had to be headed to The Box. Thoughts of what that meant sent a different kind of shiver racing down her spine. Growing up in the MC, Shell had heard countless rumors about The Box. How the club kept a giant underground torture chamber filled with hundreds of Handlers' enemies from years back. How it was about a mile out into the woods behind the clubhouse. How the walls were coated with blood and faded screams echoed through the dungeon. The Honeys loved to gossip and guess precisely what went on down there, and each tale was more gruesome than the last. By the time she was twelve, Shell had heard stories of prisoners having limbs sawed off, eyeballs plucked out, and dicks clamped in a vice. Half of what the club girls said couldn't be believed. At least that's what her mother told her when she was nine and asked what a blow job was and why she overheard a Honey using it in reference to her father. Since that day, she'd always tried to take what they told her with a grain of salt. It's not as though the men actually shared any club business with the women who were little more than whores.

The truth was probably a watered-down version of the legends, even if the Honey bragging about blowing Shell's father had been telling the truth. Turned out the man had been with nearly all of them at one point or another. Something every fifteen-year-old girl wanted to think about. Regardless, The Box existed and wasn't a place anyone wanted to find themselves.

After another five minutes of wordless journeying through the woods, the men suddenly came to a dead stop.

Michelle darted behind the nearest thick-trunked tree. She held as still as possible, not even daring to breathe. Too bad her heart was pounding so loud it could be heard a mile away.

Had the guys noticed her? Did they suspect they had a stowaway? Could they hear the rattling of her frozen and terrified bones?

This was by far her stupidest idea ever.

"Bring him out to me," Copper said.

Shell would recognize that voice anywhere. That Irish brogue belonging to the six-foot-five, tatted biker who starred in every teenage fantasy she'd ever had. His name decorated a diary hidden deep under her bed, scrawled over and over with spritzes of cheap perfume and lipstick kisses. If anyone ever found it, she'd die on the spot, but so far, her secret was safe.

"You sure, brother? Wouldn't it be easier to do this shit down in The Box?" Rusty asked.

Shell frowned. Younger by ten years, Rusty was Copper's brother and a huge jerk. There was no other word to describe him. Okay, there were a few others, but despite their extreme sailor-enviable mouths, the guys got on her case every time she swore. Sick of them always nagging about ladies not cussing, she avoided using any kind of foul language in front of them. Kinda like she avoided Rusty at all costs.

"I want him out here. I want him to feel the air, see the stars, smell the clean scent of the forest. He needs to realize everything he's never going to have the chance to experience again. He needs to feel what I'm taking away from him. I want him to experience one last flicker of hope that we'll let him live, right before I slit his fucking throat."

Shell swallowed. Though she couldn't see his face, she imagined Copper stroking his beard, deep in thought as he plotted someone's demise. There were stories about that, too. About the lengths Copper would go to protect his club. His men and their families.

But now she had a front-row seat to the horror show.

"You got it," Zach said. There was some rustling, then silence that seemed to drag on for hours but was probably only minutes. Everything appeared darker, longer, more intense when outside in the hours following midnight.

Finally, footsteps crunched over leaves again, followed by a grunt and a thud. Shell blew out a silent breath and peeked around her tree. Someone had lit a lantern, illuminating a small clearing in the woods. A man knelt on the ground, arms bound behind him with Copper, Maverick, Zach, and Rusty circled around him.

Back to her, she didn't have a view of Copper's face, but she sure had a clear line of sight to the man on the ground.

Reaper, they called him. Because of the number of men he'd sent to their graves. Those were rumors Shell believed. She'd seen the dark-eyed man in action. Her insides quivered at the memories, and she sucked in a soundless, trembling breath.

This was why she'd followed the guys into the woods when she should have been home snoozing away in preparation for school in the morning.

Reaper was the man who'd killed her father five years ago.

Earlier that afternoon, she'd been at the clubhouse helping some of the ol' ladies prepare dinner. Tasked with letting the men know their meal was ready to be devoured, she'd wandered toward Copper's office only to hear Reaper's name being tossed around in conjunction with plans to head to The Box in the night.

Her mind and body had frozen until the noises from Copper's office alerted her to the men mobilizing. Then, she'd scurried back to the door of the kitchen and pretended to emerge just as they did, feigning her ignorance.

Even by the dim glow of the lantern, it was apparent the eyes staring up at Copper held no remorse. No fear. It was as though life, even his own, held no value to him. Almost made her wish the men would keep him alive and in pain a while before ending him. Most might find it sick. Most might wake with nightmares after watching someone die, but Shell had already been down that road. The soulless look in his eyes was the same she'd seen the night he stole her father from her. Memories from that time had stayed so strong, so fresh in her mind even with the passage of time, and Reaper's brought them right back to the surface.

She'd been with her father that fated night, four years ago, when the madman known as Reaper shot him in cold blood at a gas station.

As long as she lived, Shell would never forget the horror of that night. It was late on a Saturday, and her father was driving Shell and her mother home from a family barbecue at the clubhouse. From the second row of their truck, she'd watched her dad walk out of the quiet gas station market, two coffees in hand. Seconds later, Reaper appeared from the shadows, shot her father from three feet away, then disappeared as fast as he'd materialized. She'd had as clear a view of his pale face that night as she did now.

It all happened so fast, it was over before her brain processed what her eyes had seen. But once it did, her heart broke clear in two, and she screamed so loud she couldn't speak for days.

Now, finally, more than four years later, justice would be served, MC style. And she didn't have it in her to find anything wrong with that. Maybe it was how she was raised, or maybe it was just in her blood, but she had always felt safe, loved, and protected knowing the club would do anything and everything to protect and avenge its own.

Copper had been there that night. He'd witnessed her devastation, seen her in the lowest moment of her life. In her lovestruck teenage mind, she'd hoped some of the reason for Copper's tireless search for Reaper had something to do with him wanting to ease her pain, though, in truth, he'd have done it for anyone associated with the club.

"You've been a hard man to find," Copper said as he stepped closer to his captive.

Reaper snorted. Whoever had taken him prisoner, roughed him up quite a bit. One black eye, a seeping gash on his cheek, ripped shirt, wheezy breathing. His short black hair was caked with blood, matted to his head. Not near enough punishment in Shell's eyes.

"Been easy to slip under the radar with you idiots looking for me," Reaper slurred like his tongue was swollen. He smiled, actually smiled, revealing missing teeth.

From the cover of her tree, Shell locked her knees to keep from charging forward and raining a hell of her own down on the smug bastard.

Copper chuckled. "That may be, but we got your ass now. Been waiting on this moment for a long time." As he spoke, he drew a wicked looking blade from a sheath on his belt.

Shell's eyes widened, and she covered her mouth to muffle a gasp. Maybe she hadn't been as prepared as she'd thought to watch Copper take a life.

Yet she couldn't tear her gaze away.

The rest of the men stood with spread legs, folded arms, and flat expressions as they watched Copper close the distance to Reaper. Pressing the blade against the man's throat, he said, "This is for my President, his ol' lady, and Shell." The venom in Copper's voice had Shell's eyes widening more than the act of blatant violence she was about to witness. He sounded like a different man. A lethal man completely capable of killing in cold

Copper

blood. "This is for Shell most of all because an eleven-year-old girl should never have to live with the image of her father being gunned down. Rest in hell, motherfucker."

Reaper laughed, making Shell flinch. The sound was so maniacal it could have been a psychotic movie villain's cackle. And the man dared to do it while Copper held a deadly knife to his throat.

Insanity.

"There's so much you don't know Prez," he said as though mocking Copper.

"Details don't matter. You killed my president, now you die."

Reaper might be a psychotic killer, but he was freaking brave. Not once did he cower, beg for his life, or break eye-contact with Copper. Just as Copper's arm muscles flexed with the telltale sign of impending movement, Reaper said, "Too bad I didn't notice the girl watching me that night. Might have taken her with me. She'da made a good plaything."

The growl that came from Copper sent chills skittering across all Shell's nerve endings. He didn't bother speaking, just drew the blade across Reaper's throat in one fluid motion.

Easy as slicing through butter.

Blood immediately flowed from the slash followed by a horrendous gurgling sound. This time, Shell couldn't catch the shocked gasp before it left her mouth. The moment it was out, she held her breath and prayed no one heard. Copper didn't so much as twitch. Zach watched the life drain from Reaper. Mav bounced his leg as though impatient to get the process over with.

But Rusty, Rusty met her gaze with a cold, sadistic stare. Shell gulped down the disgusting taste of bile that flooded her mouth.

As he glared at her, Rusty's lips curled into a smile that could only be described as predatory.

The hairs on Shell's arms stood straight on end. Something about that smile set her on edge because she'd swear it had nothing to do with Reaper's death and everything to do with her.

Shit. Would he rat her out to Copper? The jerk would probably take great pleasure in that. Now that she'd been busted, she could only wait and see what fate had in store for her.

CHAPTER ONE

2018

Copper downed yet another shot, then slammed the glass on the table. There weren't too many nights he let himself get this tanked anymore. Being president of a one-percenter motorcycle club came with too many responsibilities for frivolous behavior. But, hell, a man only turned forty once, and there'd been a few times in his youth Copper had been pretty damn convinced he'd never make it to forty, so celebrate he would.

Besides, the alcohol would numb some of the restless dissatisfaction he'd been battling the past few weeks. Now that he was turning forty, life seemed to be smacking him in the face, showing him everything he was missing. As each of his men dropped like flies, finding a good woman, Copper became more aware of the void in his life. An ol' lady, children, a house, maybe even a fucking dog. Two years ago, he sold the house he'd lived in since moving to Townsend, and started living at the clubhouse. He was always there, so it just seemed easier. In reality, he hated the idea of rambling around a big ol' house alone.

Fucking depressing thoughts had no business crashing his party.

"Happy birthday, old man," Zach said, slapping a hand on Copper's shoulder. "How many of those you had?"

"Don't get cocky. You ain't that far behind, brother." Copper tried to whack Zach's shoulder as well, but missed the target and knocked his enforcer on the back of the head. "Shit. Sorry. Lost count around eight or so."

He was feeling pretty relaxed at that moment. The past year had been rough on the club, but in the end, they all came out mostly whole—though a little banged up—and tighter than ever as a club. This night was as much a celebration of the end of the Gray Dragons as it was Copper's aging another year. The gang had been a burr on the Handlers' collective ass for far too long, and they'd recently been torn to shreds courtesy of Copper and his men.

The only thing threatening to kill his buzz was the fact that Lefty, leader of the Gray Dragons gang, was still out there somewhere. Sure, he was in hiding, licking his oozing wounds, and no longer running a women-trafficking gang, but the fact of the matter was, the bastard still breathed.

And that was unacceptable in Copper's eyes.

But it was also a worry for another night.

"Shell outdid herself with this party, man. You seen much of her tonight? She's looking damn good," Mav said with a fucking twinkle in his eye.

"Nah, not yet. I'm sure she's around with the girls somewhere." His men loved nothing more than busting his balls over Shell. She'd had a thing for him back in the day, and everyone was convinced he felt the same for her.

Which was insane.

She was sixteen fucking years younger than him. And his former president's daughter. Beyond off limits. Sure, she was hot as fuck, sweet as sugar, and loved by every man in the club, but none of that trumped the fact she was untouchable by him. Besides, ever since she'd returned to Townsend about a year ago, she no longer seemed interested in him in that way. She worked two jobs, raised her daughter, and kept her head down, driving him nuts with her independence and constant refusal of help.

Copper

She didn't seem to have a spare second in her life for a man. Especially not an older man with the baggage of running an MC. Not that he was interested in the spot. No, the fact that she seemed to have gotten over her schoolgirl crush on him was for the best.

Exactly how he wanted it.

Exactly how it had to be.

Jesus. "Get me another fucking shot," he growled at the laughing idiots who claimed to be his loyal brothers. Fuck that, they'd probably pick Shell over him if it came down to it.

Not that he could blame them. She was the perfect combination of sweetness and biker babe all wrapped in one sexy as sin little package.

"Here you go," LJ, one of the prospects said as he passed out another round of Patrón.

"Listen up, you fuckers!" Maverick shouted from across the room. He gave his woman, Stephanie, a sloppy kiss, then climbed up onto the bar, shot in hand.

"Don't fall, dickwad!" Zach yelled. "No one here who could cart your scrawny ass to the hospital tonight."

"S'all good," Mav slurred, wobbling on the bar.

"Careful, baby," Stephanie said with a giggle.

Shit, the whole club was a fumbling mess. But it was damn good to see everyone partying and tension-free for the first time in ages.

"Wanna make a toast to the Prez. All you fuckers get those glasses up."

Cheers and boot stomps rang out across the clubhouse. From the corner of his eye, Copper caught sight of Shell exiting the bathroom. As she made her way back into the main room, one of the prospects handed her a shot. She smiled at him, accepted it, and said something that had him kissing her on the cheek. And that made Copper's fists clench. Kid's days were numbered in the single digits.

Damn prospect needed to keep his fucking lips to himself.

He took a step in the prospect's direction only to be stopped short by the sound of his name. "Copper! Where are you, Prez?" Mav asked.

With no choice but to abandon his plight to kill the Shell-groping prospect, he stepped forward. "Right here."

The music dropped to a dull roar, and the crowd parted like the Red Sea, putting Copper in the spotlight.

"Everybody having a good night?" Mav asked.

Calls of, "Fuck yeah," ran through the blitzed crowd. All eyes were on Copper. He was used to his men looking to him for direction and leadership, but not accustomed to being the center of a celebration. Still, it was damn nice to be appreciated.

"All right, raise those glasses," Mav said, lifting his fully inked arm. "We'll keep this short and sweet so you can all get back to drinking and fucking. But we do need to take a second to honor the man we're all here to celebrate. Copper turns forty today, and I think we can all agree he is hands down the best president this club has ever seen."

Everyone shouted and cheered while Copper waved away their praise. It wasn't a job or a position to him. Love for the club flowed through his veins right alongside his blood. There's nothing else he'd rather do than lead these men.

"So let's all wish a Handlers' style happy birthday to the big man."

"Happy birthday, Copper!" everyone yelled.

Mav let out an ear-splitting whistle, and the room grew quiet again. "All right, Copper, here's to you and here's to me, and here's to all the girls that licked us where we pee."

"Maverick!" Stephanie screeched right before she doubled over with laughter. The rest of the club was split between raunchy comments, groans, and hilarity.

Copper rolled his eyes then glanced to his right. Shell's sparkling gaze met his, igniting a fire low in his gut as she did every damn time he saw her since she'd moved back. Hell, who was he kidding, from the moment she hit eighteen she'd been turning him on and turning him inside out.

She gifted him a small smile that was her unique combo of cute and sexy then lifted her shot glass toward him before knocking it back. Her delicate throat worked as the liquid slid down then she licked her glossy lips, and Copper's cock defied logic by hardening. Should never have been possible with the volume of liquor in his system, but then his body had never listened to reason when it came to Shell.

She really must have busted her already overworked ass to pull off the party, and the effort was well worth it. Now that Mav's toast was finished, the music pounded once again, and the partiers were back to doing their thing. Some sucked back liquor at the bar, many danced, and others hooked up in various corners of the clubhouse. Strippers gyrated on tables with crumpled dollar bills dangling from their G-strings. Back in the day, Copper would have been right there with his single brothers gawking and drooling over the writhing bodies, but he'd long since lost his taste for the dancers. However, had Shell not provided them, the boys might have mutinied.

She was no dummy.

Focus still on Shell, Copper found the empty table considered his by the club and plopped into a seat then crooked a finger at her. In response, Shell raised an eyebrow and placed her hands on her hips. Her curvy, leather-clad hips. The action thrust her generous rack forward, only exacerbating Copper's cock problem. Shit, why couldn't he tear his gaze away from her? His head buzzed as the latest shot joined the others in making him wasted. Maybe he'd regret it in the morning, but his booze-soaked brain seemed to think Shell was too far away. Copper curled his finger again and laughed when she rolled her eyes but started his way.

Back and forth her hips swayed with each step. How she moved was an effortless call to him that was completely unintentional. Unlike the Honeys, who calculated every glance and every touch to entice and arouse, Shell just breathed, and he wanted her.

Fuck. This was a stupid idea.

The deep purple leather dress she wore clung to her every curve like a second skin. Purple was perfect on her, highlighting the gorgeous Caribbean blue eyes she shared with her four-year-old daughter.

"Feeling good, birthday boy?" she asked with a laugh when she was close enough to touch.

She was the perfect leather-wrapped birthday present and damn if he didn't want to unwrap her slowly. What the fuck, it was his birthday, he deserved a little treat, didn't he?

"Sure am. C'mere." He snagged her hand and tugged her closer. The stilts on her feet were no match for his strength, and she toppled toward him, landing in his lap with a squeak.

Just that tiny feel of her ass against him had his cock straining behind the denim.

"Copper! What are you doing?" Shell held herself rigid, perched at the front of his lap.

That just wouldn't do. Whether it was the fact he was blitzed, the high from being the party's man of honor, or that fucking purple dress, the reasons he kept Shell at arm's length for so long evaporated.

"I said c'mere," he grumbled, banding his forearm around her small waist and yanking her flush against him. For about ten seconds, she remained still and unyielding, but then he whispered, "Relax, doll," in her ear and the tension slowly seeped from her spine. That left her soft and pliant in his arms, her back molded to his chest.

"W-what are you doing, Copper?" she whispered.

Christ, she smelled good. Sweet, like fucking birthday cake frosting just begging for a lick.

His head was just cloudy enough to think touching Shell was a good idea. If he'd been clear, he'd have realized this was the most physical contact they'd had since her father was killed and

Copper

he held her sobbing in his arms. Back then, she'd been eleven and a child, so Copper's thoughts were pure. Now, well now she'd been all woman for quite a few years, and Copper's thoughts hadn't been pure in a long time.

In fact, when it came to one Michelle Ward, his thoughts had been downright filthy.

HE'S DRUNK. HE'S drunk. He drunk.

Maybe if Shell repeated it to herself enough times, it'd sink in and tomorrow when he regretted this incident and returned to the unspoken no-touching rule he stuck to when it came to her, she wouldn't feel the crushing weight of disappointment and heartache.

"Relax, babe, I'm just saying thank you." The words were spoken directly against her ear. Soft fur from his beard tickled the outer rim of her ear making her shiver as her body went haywire. Hardened nipples, aching pussy, restless yearning, the works. All things she should be accustomed to after years of unrequited lust for the man holding her, but now that their bodies were pressed together, the need grew so much sharper.

"I-I was happy to do this for you. Forty is a big one." She shrugged. "I'd have done it for any of your brothers." And that was true, though she always put a little extra care and thought into the things she did for Copper.

She was just that pathetic.

"Know you would have, doll. In fact, I have a suspicion this was as much for all of them as it was for me." The words were spoken gruffly, and if she didn't know better, she'd almost say he sounded disgruntled by the idea that she cared for his brothers as much as him. That little lie would stay behind her lips until the day she died. As he spoke, he brushed her hair to the side, exposing her neck. Then he nuzzled his nose right under her ear, and her breath hitched. "You smell good." The rough pad of his finger scraping along her sensitive neck followed by his tickling beard had her sex clenching almost painfully.

Please end the torture.

Though she should, she'd never possess the strength to end it herself.

"W-what do you mean about this being for all of them?" She focused on her girlfriends dancing in the middle of the room. Each one of them looked smokin' hot. They all seemed to be having a fabulous time letting loose with their men.

"The club needed this. Needed to have fun, blow off some serious steam. You know I don't give a shit about strippers. That's all for them. You knew they needed this and you're amazing."

Even drunk as a skunk, the man was no fool. And his compliments were going to ruin her as fast as his touch. "Well, the club's had a hard time lately. But all that's over. The family deserves some fun." She tried to scoot forward, but the effort was fruitless. Copper's hold was unbreakable.

"That's exactly what I'm talking about. You notice what we need and make sure we have it. Like I said, you're amazing. And you look fucking gorgeous tonight." He pressed a kiss to her neck and her eyes filled with tears. Squeezing them closed, she prayed none would escape. There was one reason and one reason only for his behavior.

Alcohol.

Part of her wanted to say fuck it and soak up every ounce of his affection, but tomorrow, when things returned to normal she'd be crushed. And she'd been crushed too many times in her life to endure another smashing.

"Uh, thanks."

Again, his lips touched her neck, and this time she couldn't keep from squirming on his lap as her pussy gushed with wetness. Shit. Could he tell? Feel it? Smell it?

Something was affecting him because a hard ridge rose against her bottom. Somehow, she had to ignore it. Somehow, she had to control her breathing. Somehow, she had to resist the urge to spin on his lap and grind down on his erection until she drove him so crazy he had no choice but to shove her dress up and drive into her.

Ha. Her imagination had always been active.

"So, uh, I know a secret." Time for a distraction. Something to take his mind off her and get her mind out of the gutter.

Giving her a squeeze, he said, "Oh yeah? What is it?" His huge forearm rested directly under her breasts, with his large palm splayed out along her ribcage. God, he was so strong. She wanted him to use every ounce of that strength on her. How many times had she fantasized about his giant form hovering over her, pounding into her, dominating her, controlling her? She wanted to feel it and wear the marks as evidence of his power and claiming.

Shit, maybe she'd had too much to drink as well.

"Izzy is pregnant," she blurted out. Normally, she'd die before sharing a sister's secret, but Copper wouldn't remember it in the morning, so it was safe to break girl code this one time.

"No shit?" He threw his head back and laughed, removing his arm from her waist.

Mission accomplished.

Shell sprang off his lap so fast she would have fallen on her face if Toni hadn't wandered up. "Whoa, girl! Where's the fire?" she asked as she caught Shell by her upper arms.

With a nervous laugh, Shell said, "No fire. Just spiky heels I'm not used to walking in."

Toni's smile was full of compassion, and if Shell wasn't mistaken, maybe a bit of pity. What the hell should she expect? Every damn person associated with the club knew of her feelings for Copper. Didn't matter that she tried to hide it. Didn't matter that she denied it in front of the guys and it didn't matter that nothing would ever come of it. Even if Copper fell to his knee tomorrow and professed his love, nothing would come of it. Secrets and lies ensured that. Choices Shell had made years ago destroyed any chance she'd ever have with Copper. Yet her damn heart and her neglected body wouldn't seem to get the message.

"You okay?" Toni whispered, still clasping Shell by the arms. "Looked like you needed a rescue over here."

Shell sighed. "Yeah, thanks for that. He's just drunk and…I don't even know," she whispered back.

"I got your back, girl," she whispered, then straightened and leaned toward Copper. "Hey, El Presidente, I'm stealing your girl here. She's needed on the dance floor. Important booty shaking to attend to. Maybe you should go get yourself a cup of coffee or something. You're starting to look a little rough." Toni raised an eyebrow and smirked at Copper.

Stepping out of Toni's hold, Shell gave Copper a good look and chuckled under her breath. Glassy green eyes stared at her as though they couldn't quite see her. His much-in-need-of-a-trim hair was mussed, and there was some kind of stain on his shirt. The Handler's control-freak president was a hot mess.

"All right, get the fuck out of here," he said as he stood then stumbled.

Shell automatically shot forward to help him but was yanked back by Zach. "No way, short stuff," he said as he moved to his president. "This guy will flatten you like a pancake. I'll take care of him." He winked at Shell then kissed his woman before guiding Copper toward his office.

Shell gnawed on her lower lip, staring after them. Hopefully, Zach wouldn't let him drink much more, but knowing these guys, that was a wasted wish.

"Come on, girl," Toni said as she curled an arm around Shell's shoulders and ushered her to the dance floor. "What do you have, an hour of babysitter time left? Let's spend it shaking our moneymakers, yeah?"

Tearing her gaze away from the man she couldn't stop loving, she gave Toni a grin that probably wasn't as cheerful as she'd been going for. "Yeah, sounds perfect. Lead the way."

Copper

As she followed after her friend, Shell blew out a breath then shoved the events of the party to the back of her mind. Later that night, when she was alone in her bed, she'd indulge in the fantasy. She'd dissect every touch and every word out of Copper's mouth.

It was a method she'd employed after moving back to Townsend from Syracuse, New York the year before. Whenever Copper did something charming, something that made her fall deeper in love with him, she gave herself one hour to obsess about it at night. She'd use that hour however she liked. Dreaming about the life she wished for with him. Replaying whatever he'd done to make her swoon. Hell, even masturbating to thoughts of him owning every inch of her body.

Just one hour. When it was over, she jumped back into reality. To the world where Copper lived one life, and she lived another. Where they were friends, but could never amount to anything more.

Her choices had made damn sure of that.

CHAPTER TWO

"You and Shell were looking mighty cozy last night," Zach said with a shit-eating grin that disappeared behind his giant coffee mug. He sat across the table from Copper and next to Jig. At least five days a week some group of the Handlers ate at the diner. Copper was always among them.

It hadn't always been that way, though. Up until about a year ago, the diner was owned by the parents of Zach's ol' lady. To say they were anti-biker was the understatement of the century. None of the men in his club was allowed to set foot in the diner, let alone sit for a cup of coffee. After they passed, and Toni took ownership, she changed that rule. Shell had been working there since before Toni came along. This was her morning job. At night, she cleaned a large office building in town.

Copper swallowed his oversized bite of waffle, brow furrowed. "The fuck you talking about?" The previous night was a blur of alcohol, loud music, and laughter, but no matter how he racked his brain, he couldn't even remember speaking with Shell. He must have. She organized the party, and would have at least wished him a happy birthday. Then there was Zach's statement which led him to believe he had some interaction with her.

"Shit," Jig said. "That's right, Prez. I almost forgot about that. 'Bout time you made a move there."

Copper

Copper growled. What the fuck were these ladies running their traps about? There's no way in hell he'd ever make any kind of move on Shell. By the smirks on Mav, Jig, and Zach's faces, they knew it and were just yanking his chain. "Get the fuck outta here."

"They're right, Cop," Mav pipped in from next to Copper. "Known you both a long damn time and aside from the night her pops was killed I've never seen you do more than shake her hand. Last night you had her on your lap, nuzzling her neck and shit. Looked about ten seconds away from yanking her dress down and sucking her tits."

"Hey!" Copper slapped Mav on the back of his head, causing his brother's coffee to slosh on the table. "Have some fucking respect. That's Shell you're talking about. She's a mother for fuck's sake."

Zach snorted out a laugh. "So what? That automatically makes her unfuckable? Don't think so, Prez. Shell's hot and every man in the club knows that. Only reason they stay away is they think you've got dibs. That won't last forever, though. One day there'll be some prospect brave enough to claim her. And how do you think she became a mother? Doubt it was an immaculate fucking conception."

How Beth came to be was something Copper didn't allow himself to think about. Ever. Made him sick to his stomach to imagine some dumb kid with his hands and twiggy dick all over an eighteen-year-old Shell. Copper shot his enforcer a look that would have made a lesser man piss himself. Unfortunately, he'd known Zach about ten years, and his murder-glares weren't as effective as they'd once been.

He ran a hand down his face. Shit. How drunk had he been last night? Sure, he'd been shitfaced, that much was obvious by the throbbing head and aching eyes, but to break his one hard and fast rule and be all over Shell? Dread filled him. God, he hoped he hadn't crossed any lines. Last thing he wanted or needed was an awkward conversation explaining he didn't mean anything that had happened.

"Look, the club's had the year from hell and it was my fortieth birthday. Think I'm entitled to one night of stupidity. I don't even remember seeing Shell last night, let alone having her on my lap. But whatever happened, I know two things." He held up a finger. "First, I was drunk off my ass, which is the only reason I had my hands on her. You know I'd never have touched her if I wasn't smashed. She's a fuckin' kid."

Across the table, Jig's eyes widened, and he subtly shook his head once. Then again.

"And two," Copper said adding a second finger. "I don't want Shell, have never wanted Shell, and never will want Shell, so just leave it the fuck alone."

This time Jig cleared his throat and jerked his chin at Copper. Next to him, Zach stared down at his plate as though it was covered in naked pics of his woman.

"The fuck's wrong with you, Jig?" Copper looked over his shoulder and nearly choked on his tongue. About three feet away, Shell stood holding a full pot of coffee with a blank stare and flat mouth.

The expression lasted about three seconds before she blinked, licked her lips and plastered the phoniest smile he'd ever seen on her face.

Fuck. He'd really stepped in it. Just because he'd never admit his attraction to her out loud and never act on it sober, it didn't mean he wanted to hurt her in any way. Shell hadn't had it easy. Father murdered when she was eleven, pregnant as a teenager, single mother working two exhausting jobs. Last thing he intended was to add to her stress. Fuck, he typically went out of his way to ease her burdens. She was stubborn and independent as could be, bucking at every offer of a handout so he had to get creative in his propositions of help.

"Hey, guys," she said in a falsely chipper tone.

Zach winced.

Copper

Jig shot her an empathetic smile.

"I'm sure after last night you all need some more of this, huh?" She lifted the coffee pot that looked too heavy for her slender arms.

For a second, no one said anything, then Mav held up his mug. "Yeah, sweetie, I need an ocean's worth of the stuff. How is it you're looking so gorgeous this morning? You were out as late as the rest of us."

"I was," she said, topping him off. "But I didn't drink my weight in booze."

Jig snickered. "You have a point there. Though I think we'd have all been fine if we stopped after we drank your weight in booze."

With a sweet smile for Jig, she filled his cup as well.

"Where's Beth today?" Zach asked. Sometimes, on Sunday mornings, Shell didn't have childcare and brought Beth to the diner with her. Toni never minded. Everyone loved Beth to pieces.

"She's in the kitchen sweet talking Ernesto into putting extra chocolate chips in her pancakes." As she spoke about her daughter, her fake smile morphed into a genuine one. Nothing got a mom beaming like mention of their adorable child.

Only problem was, she hadn't so much as glanced in Copper's direction. Not once. She spoke to Mav, Zach, and Jig but wouldn't give him the time of day.

Well, he fucking deserved it. But he wasn't one to avoid conflict so he said, "Shell, can I talk to you a sec?"

Finally, she turned to him and the happiness slid right off her face. She wasn't even pretending anymore. "Sorry, Copper, this *fucking kid* has three tables waiting on food." Then she turned and for the first time in her life, dismissed him.

A sick feeling settled in the pit of his stomach, followed by anger. As president of the MC, he was used to people jumping on his command. Shell was the one person who repeatedly defied him to his face, and he always let her get away with it.

23

"Goddammit, woman," he yelled as he slipped out of the booth. Just as he was about to chase her down and drag her into Toni's office, his phone rang.

"Fuck!"

It was the prison.

"I need to take this," he said to his men who nodded.

"This is Copper," he said into his cell as he shouldered the door open and stepped into the frigid winter air.

"A prisoner from the United States Penitentiary, Tucson Arizona would like to connect with you. Please say yes or press one to continue," the pre-recorded voice said.

"Yes." There was a click then about twenty seconds of the most God-awful hold music imaginable.

"Happy fucking birthday, old man."

Copper's face split into a grin. "Thanks, Rusty. Damn, it's good to hear from you, brother. How you doing?"

Ten years Copper's junior, Rusty was serving out a fifteen-year sentence for aggravated assault in a federal prison. The entire thing was bullshit. Rusty had been defending himself and while he did nearly beat a man to death, the punishment did not fit the crime. Hell, if it'd been Copper, he'd have killed the bastard.

"Hanging in like usual. Want to hear about your birthday though. Heard the boys were going all out. Bet there was some prime pussy there. Mmm mmm mmm. Fuck, I miss pussy."

Copper's heart clenched. Rusty was missing out on a lot more than just pussy. He still had years left on his sentence. About ten to be exact. When Copper was twenty and Rusty just ten, their parents were killed by a drunk driver. After that, they left Ireland and moved to Tennessee to be near family. Copper pretty much raised Rusty from that point on. Damn near broke his heart when his little brother was sent away. He cleared his throat. Wouldn't do Rusty any good to have Copper getting all weepy. "Actually, Shell planned the whole thing. Did a good job, barely remember more than five minutes of the party."

Copper

Rusty's laugh was music to his ears. "Damn, brother, sounds like a righteous time. Please tell me at least part of your night was spent balls deep in something sweet and easy. Give me a story to fuel my imagination."

Rolling his eyes, Copper huffed out a laugh. "Sure was." Whatever Rusty needed to get him through the long, harsh days in prison, Copper would provide. Even if it was lies about his sex life. "Blond, stacked, and up for anything." An image of Shell came to mind in a killer purple dress, lifting a glass in toast to him. Shit, was that what she'd looked like last night? Now he needed more of the party to come back to him. Especially if what Mav said was true and he'd had her in his lap.

"You've always been a blond man. Not me. Love me some dark hair. Hey, Cop, I got something to tell you." Excitement laced Rusty's voice. "Think you're gonna be pretty pumped."

"What is it, brother? They change your work order?" He'd been stuck on laundry duty for the last year and bitched about it every chance he got.

"Nah, bit better than that."

"Well spit it out. You got me curious now."

"Turns out, I'm a model fucking prisoner."

Copper sucked in a breath and held it, his heart pounding. Was Rusty about to say what Copper had been hoping for every single day since the trial?"

"Two months, brother." Rusty choked up a bit, then sniffed, and said in a stronger voice, "Two fucking months and I'm coming home."

He blinked, afraid to believe the words. "You're shitting me. Tell me you're not shitting me."

"Not shitting you, Cop. Wouldn't do that to you."

Copper bent forward and rested his free hand on his thigh. The news was a sledgehammer to the gut, in the best way possible. His knees almost buckled. Holy shit, this was *fanfuckingtastic* news. The best news.

"Cop? You there?"

"Yeah, brother, I'm here. I'm just... fuck, I don't even know what I am."

Rusty chuckled. "I hear you. About passed out cold when my lawyer told me the news. I ain't supposed to be eligible for parole for another three years. But I guess I've been a good little boy. Combine that with overcrowding and boom, I'm out. Look, I only got a minute left here, but I'll be getting you more info as the date gets closer, okay?"

"Sounds good, little brother. We'll be riding out to get you. Whole club. And we'll bring your bike so you can ride home with us. Can't wait to see you," Copper said, straightening and looking through the windows into the diner. Shell was wiping down a spot at the counter with her shoulders drooping and no smile in sight. He had to fix that mess he'd made, but at least he was in a good mood now.

"Yeah, yeah," Rusty said with a laugh. "Guess I'm looking forward to seeing you too. I'm *really* looking forward to fucking my way through the Honeys. You better have some new pussy on board since I've been there."

"We do, brother. Promise you won't be disappointed. Take care of yourself in there."

"Always," Rusty said.

Copper disconnected the call then re-entered the diner and headed straight for his brothers.

"Musta been a good fucking phone call, Prez. You look like you just got blown or some shit. And we all know that didn't happen," Mav said, making the other two dipshits laugh. Mav had the kind of mouth that made people either bust a gut or want to strangle him. Wasn't hard to guess which way Copper was leaning at the moment.

Rusty's news had him flying so high, he didn't bother to go after Mav. As he folded his big body back into the small booth, he rubbed his palms together. "Just got some good news, boys. Damn good news."

Copper

"What's that?" Zach said as he stuffed a monster sized bite of bacon in his mouth.

"Rusty is getting out early on good behavior. He'll be home in two months."

"Holy shit!" Mav said with a smile. "That is good news."

"Congratulations, brother," Zach said. "Pretty spectacular birthday present right there."

"You're telling me," Copper said. He polished off the last sip of his lukewarm coffee then looked at Jig. He'd been silent since the announcement, though that wasn't entirely surprising. Jig and Rusty hadn't ever stated their dislike of one another, but they weren't close either. Though to be fair, Jig hadn't been too close to many of the guys until recently, when he got an ol' lady. Izzy was dragging the man out of his shell and turning him into someone who was actually fun to be around.

As he'd been before, Jig was looking at something over Copper's shoulder. Copper peeked, and once again encountered the shocked face of Shell. Only this time, she didn't bother with a shitty faux smile.

"Refill?" she asked in a hoarse voice.

"Please." Copper held up his cup and looked her straight in the eye. It wasn't hard to smile at her. He was flying so high off Rusty's announcement. She met his gaze but didn't return the grin. He'd be groveling later, that was for sure. Maybe he'd take Beth for a few hours after Shell got off work. The woman never had more than thirty seconds to herself in a day. Giving her some time to take a bath, drink some wine, and watch TV or whatever shit women did when they were alone ought to get him out of the dog house.

Despite being on her bad side, Copper couldn't help but feel great.

Rusty was coming home.

CHAPTER THREE

"Mommy! I'm so, so hungry!" Beth shouted from her bedroom. "My belly is yelling at me so loud."

Shell rolled her eyes as she pulled an apple out of the refrigerator. "All right, hold your horses, Bethy. I'll get you a snack."

"I don't have any horses, Mommy. Where are the horses?"

With a chuckle, she grabbed the gallon jug of milk and set it on the counter. "Never mind about the horses. Give me a few minutes, and I'll bring you something to eat."

"But I want to hold the horses." Beth's voice had the whiny, I'm-about-to-throw-a-fit quality that warned of impending loudness.

Shell glanced up at the white ceiling. *Give me strength.* "How about an apple with peanut butter?"

"Yesss!" Crisis averted. Oh, the power of distraction. Sometimes four-year-olds were so easy. And sometimes they were the fiercest opponent in the world.

Shell dug through the cabinet overflowing with kiddie cups and plates until she found one of the Elsa cups. Over the past week, Beth had refused to drink from anything other than a cup with a *Frozen* theme. Some battles weren't worth the effort, so Shell let her have that one. As she poured the milk into the cup, the doorbell rang, startling the hell out of her. She jerked so hard, the jug hit the cup and knocked it over. Milk sloshed directly onto the front of her sweatshirt.

"Fantastic," she muttered as she grabbed a wad of paper towels. "Just a minute," she called out toward the door. "I'm coming."

Blotting her pants, she walked to the door. Whoever it was probably wouldn't hang around outside the closed door until she changed, so she'd be welcoming them looking like she'd slobbered all over herself.

"Oh well." She swung the door open. "Hel—oh, Copper." The ache that had formed in her chest at his earlier words in the diner intensified, throbbing with renewed vigor. Man, those words slayed her. Sure, she'd known the truth of them all along, but without verbal confirmation, she'd always been able to imagine something happening between them one day. Now it seemed an impossible dream.

"Hey," he said, hands in his pockets.

Why, oh, why did he always have to look so damn sexy? Life's cruel little joke. A black Nirvana T-shirt stretched to capacity across his broad chest. Both tattooed arms seemed to tease her with memories of the way they held her against him the night before.

"What are you doing here?" On any other day, she'd welcome him into her home. Having him in the private space she shared with Beth was one of her favorite things. But the day had been spoiled. Now, all she wanted was to be alone, so she stood in the doorway blocking Copper's entrance. Of course, solitude was impossible with a four-year-old and only three hours before she had to be at her second job, but she'd take what she could get. Maybe fifteen minutes of peace and quiet while Beth ate her snack would be good enough.

Speak of the devil…

The surprisingly strong pounding of little feet was followed by Beth poking her curly strawberry-blond head out the door in the space next to Shell's hip. "Copper!" She flung her little body straight at him.

Vastly experienced with Beth's exuberant greetings, Copper caught her as she flew at him. He tossed her up in the air and laughed just as loudly as she did. Then he settled her on his hip like he was born for it. Shell ground her back teeth together.

"Can I come in?"

She hesitated. Was she about to refuse him for the first time in, well, ever?

"Yes, Copper. Come in! Come in! I want to show you what I drawed for you," Beth gushed.

Guess he was coming in. The smirk on his face told her he knew Beth was the only reason she'd granted him entry. She glanced at her daughter with her head now resting on Copper's broad shoulder. As usual, she beamed at him like the sun shined out his ass.

Little traitor.

Shell stepped to the side as she gestured into her tiny living room. "Sure, come on in. Can I get you anything?"

"Nah, I'm good, babe. Don't go to any trouble." He settled on her couch with Beth perched on his lap. She rested her back against his chest then lifted his large arms and locked them around her. Beth was a cuddle bug by nature, and Copper was her favorite snuggle buddy.

He whispered something in her ear that had a sweet tinkle of giggles erupting from her. Shell looked on with hot jealously coursing through her blood. Jesus, she was officially the worst mother in the universe. Jealous of her four year old for the affection she received from an adult who cared for her. Pathetic didn't even cover it. Yet, it was true. Aside from the anomaly of last night, Copper never touched her. If he so much as bumped her hand, he'd spring back like she scalded him. It was hell on a girl's ego. Yet, with her daughter, he was basically a six-and-a-half-foot teddy bear.

Copper

The truth shamed her to no end to admit, but if Beth were anyone but her daughter, Shell just might claw her eyes out. Thankfully, Copper was never seen disappearing into any rooms of the clubhouse with the Honeys. If he had been, there'd be a lot of bleeding club whores scattered in Shell's wake.

"So, what'd you need, Copper?" Shell asked, folding her arms across her chest. Acting unaffected was nearly impossible. Especially with the memory of being in Beth's position less than twenty-four hours ago so fresh in her mind.

"Hey, princess, can you give your mom and me a minute for some grown-up talk?" Copper asked.

Beth wrinkled her button nose as though the idea of grown-up talk was akin to eating spinach in her eyes.

"Why don't you run and get me the picture you made me. Actually, how about you make one for me to give to Uncle Mav, too."

"Okay!" Beth charged off to her room, little feet clomping down the hallway.

The moment she was out of sight, tension filled the space. Shell should have known this would happen after last night. Despite her feelings, she'd always been able to keep from acting awkward around Copper. Now after ten minutes of affection, their entire dynamic had shifted. She should have been stronger and resisted, but his touch had been so enticing. And felt so amazing.

"Listen, Shell, about earlier…"

If he repeated his words from the diner she just might sink into the floor, never to be seen again. "It's nothing, Copper. The guys were ribbing you. You had to set them straight. I get it. No worries."

He stared at her with narrowed eyes.

"Seriously. It's no big deal."

For a moment, it seemed as though he'd let her get away with the lie, but that wasn't Copper. He didn't let shit go. If he saw a problem, he fixed it. No matter what.

As though she hadn't spoken, he said, "I'm sorry for what I said. They were ragging me for being all over you last night. I don't remember a fucking thing, so I assume they were just shitting me. Pissed me off because they know we don't have that kind of relationship, so I barked all that shit at them."

Her heart sank a little lower with each word from his mouth. Here he was, thinking he was fixing it. Giving an apology—which is something he rarely did, and in reality, he was driving the stake even deeper into her heart. God, how she'd love to fall on the floor and wail in an epic tantrum that rivaled Beth on her worst days. But that wouldn't solve a damn thing. Instead, she forced her lips to curl into a smile. "Totally understand. And to set your mind at ease, they were definitely exaggerating about last night. You weren't all over me. I pretty much just gave you a birthday hug. That's it. You know they're just a bunch of jerkoffs looking for something to hold over you." The lie tasted bitter but she'd rather him think that than remember just how much his hands had been on her and continue with his speech about the *kind of relationship* they had.

He nodded. "Thought as much. Don't worry, I'll make 'em clean the clubhouse floor with a toothbrush or something."

Despite her mood, that had her chuckling. "Not necessary. But if you go through with it, make sure they know I had nothing to do with it. I don't want the payback."

"You got it, babe. And, Shell, I know you're not a kid. You work harder and are more responsible than anyone I've met. The guys were ragging on me." He shrugged. "That was a dick thing to say knowing how mature you are."

Hard working, responsible, mature...how sexy. Just what every woman wanted to hear from the man she lusted after. She swallowed down immense disappointment.

After clearing her throat, she said, "Thanks, but it's no big deal."

He nodded.

Guess that was that.

Copper

"Hey, can I borrow Beth for a while? I was thinking of taking her to get some ice cream then bring her back here so Mama V can take over while you're at work."

Her jaw dropped. "You want to take Beth out? Really? Why? You need me to do some heinous task for the club?"

Copper threw back his head and laughed. The action had the muscles in his shoulders bunching in a way that showed of his raw power.

Pathetic. Pathetic. Pathetic.

"Don't look at me like that. There's no catch, I promise. Just a peace offering for being a dick this morning. Thought you might like a few hours of peace and quiet."

How could he go from saying things that demolished her heart to giving her the one gift every mother longed for each day? A few hours of blessed solitude.

"Um, that would be incredible. The last time I had a few hours alone was…" Geez, it was probably before she moved back to Townsend.

He snorted. "Been too long if you can't even remember. Don't you get time to yourself at night when she's asleep?"

The assessing look he sent her way had her wanting to adjust her clothing. It was then she realized there was a huge wet spot on the front of her sweatshirt. She almost laughed. Greeting him at the door with a souring milk stain on her shirt. The night before he'd had a party full of flexible strippers with triple D boobs and twenty-four-inch waists. No wonder the man wasn't interested in her. "In theory, sure. But by the time I get home from work, it's almost nine thirty. I'm lucky if I can stay awake long enough to brush my teeth let alone get anything else done."

With a shake of his head, he clenched his fists. "You work too fucking hard, Shell. I wish you'd let the club—"

She held up her hand. "Not having this argument, Copper. You lost it a long time ago. Know that chaps your ass, but I'm not taking money from the club."

"My ass is just fine, babe."

Ain't that the truth.

He stepped forward, looming over her. That height advantage and intimidating scowl lost its effect on her ages ago. In fact, instead of scaring her, it usually turned her on. She imagined he'd have a similar look on his face as he fucked his way to orgasm. "I don't give a shit about losing the argument. I give a shit about you working yourself to exhaustion when you don't have to because you're too damn proud and stubborn to ask for help."

She straightened her spine. "I'm fine, Copper. Beth and I are *fine*. We don't need help."

He smirked, one reddish eyebrow climbing his forehead. "So, you want me to go, then? Don't want me to take Beth for ice cream?"

It was then, thirty pounds of kiddo came racing back into the living room with a white sheet of paper flapping from each hand. "Ice cream!" she screamed as though talking over music at a concert.

Copper sat back down and cocked his head, waiting. She wanted to shove that eyebrow back in place.

Fine. With a roll of her eyes, she nodded. "Not so loud, Bethy."

Squealing, Beth climbed back on Copper's lap. "Ice cream?"

"You bet, princess. Came to take you on a date. You, me and the two biggest bowls of ice cream you've ever seen."

"Yes," Beth said on a breath. Her eyes were so wide, both Copper and Shell laughed. "What about Mommy?"

"Aren't you sweet to think of your pretty mommy. I think she's going to stay here and do some mommy things while we're gone. That okay?"

Beth frowned, deep in thought. Shell bit her lower lip to keep any more laughter at bay. Beth was like her, she weighed possibilities and didn't make too many rash decisions, despite her excitement and zest for life. "'Kay. But let's get mommy ice cream so she won't be sad."

Copper

"That sounds like a good idea, princess. You know what kind your mom likes?" He was talking to Beth, but his gaze stayed on Shell.

His behavior made her head spin in so many directions. Questions popped up from every corner of her brain.

Why was he doing this?

Why did he call her pretty?

Why had he held her on his lap last night?

None of those would ever be answered, but her mind didn't seem to care. It loved to torture her with what she'd never have.

"Yep," Beth said. "Mommy loves chocolate."

"Chocolate, got it." With a wink for Shell, he scooted Beth off his lap. "Go get your shoes and your jacket."

She was off in a flash bouncing down the hallway.

"Thanks for this, Copper."

"Happy to do it, babe. You know that princess has got me wrapped."

"She's got all of you guys wrapped around her fingers."

"Truth."

They fell into silence as they waited on Beth. Copper had gotten big news today. Shell had to say something. As much as she hated Rusty and wasn't thrilled about his return to Townsend, Copper had no idea of her feelings. And Rusty was his beloved can-do-no-wrong little brother. For a time, Shell assumed his conviction for aggravated assault would knock him from the undeserved pedestal Copper kept him on, but no such luck. All five years he'd been a resident of Hotel Penitentiary, Copper had stuck to his guns, telling anyone who asked the case was bullshit. "Good news about Rusty, huh?" The words tasted sour on her tongue.

Copper lit up. Anticipation radiated from every pore in the man's body. "Fuck yeah. Thought we'd still have a few years before the chance for an early release. Best fucking news I've had since you moved home."

Her breath caught, and her heart swelled. King of mixed messages right there. Though really, was he? Everything he said could be the words of one close friend to another. Anything deeper she gleaned from it was all in her head.

"The guys must be excited."

Copper chuckled. "Most are, I think. Though not Jig. Those two never meshed." With a shrug, he scratched his beard. "I know Rusty can be a lot to take, but he's not a bad guy. Shit," he laughed at himself. "I pretty much raised him from the time he was ten. Feel more like his pops some time, you know?"

She nodded because it seemed like the thing to do.

"Tried to do right by him, but he had it rough. His childhood was violent and fucked up with our asshole of a father. Then he was orphaned at ten, I moved him away from his home, and became immersed in the MC. Fuck, it's a wonder he's doing as well as he is."

Shell couldn't keep her eyes from widening. In all the years she'd known Copper, he'd never opened up to her like this. Never given her any glimpse into the inner workings of his brain. Over the years she'd heard snippets about Copper's father being a vicious drug dealer in Ireland, but that was as far as the gossip went.

Must have been hard for Copper to take on a ten year old who'd had a violent and unstable upbringing for the better part of his life. Even harder to care enough to try and turn that life around. Part of her understood Copper's blind love and support of Rusty a little more. It had always gone beyond the bond of brotherhood. Copper felt responsible for Rusty, and probably guilty for Rusty's rough situation as a kid.

"I know you, Copper, I have no doubt you did your best by him."

Their gazes met and held for a charged second, but the moment was broken when Beth came stampeding back, shoes on the wrong feet and jacket hanging from one arm. After fixing her up, Shell sent her out the door with Copper. From the window,

Copper

she watched him lift her daughter into the car seat he kept in the back of his truck. Just for a moment, she allowed herself to plot out the fantasy of Copper being Shell's father. The two of them off for a daddy-daughter outing.

Why did she torture herself this way?

With a heavy sigh, Shell made her way into the bathroom, stripping off clothes as she walked. She turned on the water, squirted a healthy stream of bubble bath into the tub, lit a few candles, and grabbed her waterproof vibrator.

What could she say? She liked her baths.

As she sank down into the warm suds a few moments later, she sighed in pleasure. Felt like she was playing hooky from life. Her stressors were mounting, especially with the upcoming Monday being the first of a new month. And that meant parting with a considerable chunk of money courtesy of an old debt left by her father. She shoved that thought out of her head. The house was quiet, the water was warm, and she was alone. She wasn't going to waste her precious solo time with concerns beyond her control. Nothing chased away a bad mood quite like a hot bath.

And an orgasm.

On that note, Shell reached for the purple vibrator and turned it up to her preferred speed. Water rippled outward in circles as she lowered it under the foam. Closing her eyes, she allowed herself one of her favorite indulgences. Copper's face came into view, then his bare chest, arms, and of course his cock. She had no actual proof of its size, but he was a big and powerful man. He had to be packing something drool-worthy, right?

Later tonight, she could chastise herself for engaging in activities that would only make her fall deeper, but for now?

Now she'd get some much-needed pleasure from thoughts of the man always just out of reach.

CHAPTER FOUR

"All right, princess, what do you want?" Copper asked Beth.

From her spot in his arms, she grinned like they were at Disney World instead of an ice cream parlor. "That one," she said, pointing to a chocolate brownie flavor.

"You got it. Cone or dish?"

"Cone. No, dish. No, cone. No—"

Copper laughed. Being in a shit mood around Beth was pretty much an impossibility. "How 'bout this? We'll have 'em put the ice cream in a dish and shove a cone on top? Best of both worlds."

Beth clapped her hands on his cheeks, then rubbed the hair on his face. The girl was obsessed with his beard. They were gonna be in trouble when she got older and was surrounded by young bearded wannabe bikers. He'd be handing out death threats like Halloween candy. "That's the best idea ever."

A scrawny teen with braces and zits appeared behind the counter. Wide-eyed, he glanced at the patch on Copper's cut before asking, "Uh, you know w-what you want, uh, sir?"

Sir. That was rich. He appreciated the show of respect, but the last thing he wanted to be called was sir. "Yeah, that one there," he said pointing to Beth's choice. "Single scoop in a dish with a cone."

Copper

"With rainbow sprinkles!" Beth squealed. "And that one!" She pointed to cookies and cream. "And that one too" Peanut butter. "And tha—"

"Hey, princess," Copper mock growled as he tickled Beth's belly and enjoyed the sweet giggles. "You trying to get me killed? You ever seen your mom mad?"

Beth's eyes grew huge, and she nodded like he'd asked her if she knew the secrets of the universe. "Yes," she whispered in his ear. "She is scary when she's super mad."

"Exactly. And what do you think is going to happen to me if I get you five scoops of ice cream?" He rubbed his beard against her cheek eliciting another round of giggles.

"She'll be so happy!" Beth threw her little fists in the air as she continued to laugh.

"Yeah, easy for you to say. It'll be my ass she'll burn." He shifted his attention to the gawking teenage employee. Probably not every day the kid saw a huge biker making a squirt of a four year old crack up. "Single scoop, that brownie thing, dish, cone, rainbow sprinkles. Got it?"

"Y-yeah. Coming right up."

"You getting ice cream, Copper?"

The kid looked at him. "Yeah, I'll take a chocolate shake."

"Yes, sir."

Somehow, he resisted the urge to roll his eyes. After settling the bill, he led a bouncing Beth to a booth in the ice cream shop. As he was folding his body in the too small space, his phone chimed with a text. It was Jig.

Jig: Where you at?
Copper: Dotty's Ice Cream.
Jig: WTF? Whatever, be there in 5.

Interesting. What the hell could that be about?

"Good, princess?"

Beth looked up at him, a ring of chocolate around her smiling mouth. "Yummy. Want some?" She held her dripping spoon up for him. Damn, this kiddo got to him every time. Hard to maintain the image of a tough as hell MC president if he was melting over Beth faster than her ice cream.

"You bet I do." He made a big show of growling and devouring the ice cream which had Beth laughing once again.

"Copper?"

"Yeah, princess." He sucked his thick, chocolatey concoction through the insufficient straw.

"How come you aren't my daddy?"

There went the shake, straight down his windpipe. Copper coughed as the cold liquid not only cut off his air supply but caused an icy burn in the back of his throat. "Well, I, uh…" Jesus, why the fuck wouldn't she ask Shell this shit?

"Cuz, look," Beth said, grabbing one of her pigtails. "Our hair is almost the same color."

That was true. Shell's was a little more strawberry blond than true red, but it wasn't far off. What the hell was he supposed to say now? *Well, rumor has it, your mother fucked some asshole who looked like me because she was…*what? Bitter? Lonely? Desperate? Those questions had tortured Copper from the moment he'd seen Beth's red curls. "Well, what did your mom tell you about your dad?"

Huh, why hadn't he thought to ask her this before? Shell was a steel trap on the subject of Beth's' father, but she must have told the squirt something, right? And it wasn't like Beth could keep a secret to save her life.

"Mommy said there are lots of types of families. Some with a mommy and a daddy. Some with just a mommy, or just a daddy. Even some with two daddies or two mommies." She recounted it without emotion in that way children had of making everything seem simple. Even though she spoke, ninety percent of her focus was on scooping both ice cream and sprinkles onto her spoon. "But I heard her on the phone with Auntie Toni once, and she said my dad was a 'piece of shit sonofabitch.' What's that mean? It's bad words, right?"

Copper

Despite himself, Copper laughed. "Yeah, baby girl, there are a few bad words in there. Truth is, princess, I do not know much about your dad. I never met him."

Beth grunted as she shoved a giant spoonful of ice cream into her mouth. "I wif you were my dad," she said, mouth full. "Maybe you should mawwy mommy."

Whose great idea was it to hang out with Beth?

"Yeah, Prez, why don't you marry her mommy?" Jig stood at the end of their table, a snarky grin on his scarred face.

"Jig!" Beth said. "Want some ice cream?" She held her spoon up to him.

"Thanks, kiddo, I'm okay." He slipped into the booth next to Beth. She scooted until she was seated right next to him, all flush against his side. Jig tensed for a moment, then relaxed and softened his face. The guy had a daughter and a wife who had been murdered in cold blood about seven years ago. It had taken him ages to be able to stand the sight of Beth, let alone touch her. He'd come a long way, mostly with the help of his woman, Izzy. "So, Cop?"

Copper scowled at his treasurer before shifting his attention to Beth. Of course, now she wasn't focused on her ice cream, but staring at him intently. "Honey, your mom and I are not going to get married." He didn't want to hurt the kiddo's feelings, but he had to make sure she understood the finality of the situation.

Beth frowned, her little forehead scrunching in displeasure. "But don't you think she's pretty?"

Pretty? He thought she was a knockout, sexy as fuck. But he wouldn't be saying that to the woman's four-year-old daughter.

"Yeah, Cop," Jig goaded. "Don't you think she's pretty?"

"Yes, Bethy, I think your mommy is very pretty. She's beautiful."

Beth beamed. "Like Cinderella. She gets married."

With a groan, Copper said. "Beth, I'm too old for your momma. She's a lot younger than I am. So we can't get married."

The frown persisted for a moment before disappearing. "Okay," she said with a nod as she went back to her sugary treat.

Guess that was that. If only all problems were so easy to solve.

Now that Beth was occupied once again, he looked at Jig whose eyes were narrowed and mouth flat.

"You need to get the fu—heck over that sh—stuff, Cop," Jig said.

"Jigsaw." Copper made sure Jig couldn't misunderstand the warning in his tone.

"Screw that, Cop. Get over yourself. She needs a man, she needs you." Jig grabbed a napkin and handed it to Beth who wiped up a puddle she'd dripped on the table.

"What? You knocked up your woman so now you're some kinda relationship expert?"

All the teasing left Jig's eyes. He rubbed a hand over the scar on his face. "No, brother, but I am an expert in regret. What they say is true. Life's fucking short. And it can be snuffed out way too fast."

Copper grunted, shifting his gaze to the window. Every few seconds a car drove by. People going on about their lives, dealing with their own problems. Jig's words hit him hard. He'd wanted Shell for years, both in his life and in his bed. But he'd vowed to himself he'd never act on those feelings.

Sixteen years was not only a lot in number but in life experience. He'd seen and done shit that would gray Shell's hair. Not that she'd had any kind of easy, charmed life, but still…

She was twenty-four. In ten years, she'd still be in her early thirties, and he'd be fifty. Would she lose interest? These questions were a waste of time. His mind was made up.

Shell would remain a close friend, family. Nothing more.

"What the hell did you track me down for, anyway?" Copper asked.

Jig's eyes slid to Beth. "You talk to Z this afternoon? He had something to run by you."

"Nah, haven't seen him since breakfast."

Copper

With a nod, Jig said, "Okay, ears are too small around here. I'll get with you after you talk to him."

Interesting. "I'll try to catch him later."

"Yeah, Prez. That looks fu-flipping good. Think I'll grab some and go surprise my woman. Since I have one and all."

"You're so witty," Copper said, flipping Jig off when Beth was focused on her treat.

"See ya, squirt," he said to Beth.

"Bye, Jig! I love you!"

Jig ruffled her hair and headed for the counter.

The shop grew silent except for the sounds of Beth devouring her ice cream. As Copper watched Jig stroll out to his bike, he allowed his mind to wander. Even with his verbal blunder that morning, the day had been pretty fucking good. Damn, he couldn't wait to see Rusty.

He wasn't entirely sure why he spilled his guts to Shell earlier. It was true, not everyone in the club was a Rusty fan. He could be a dick at times, but couldn't they all? He'd never told anyone, but Copper felt guilty as fuck when Rusty had been arrested. He'd felt responsible. Had he screwed up raising Rusty? Did growing up in the sometimes volatile MC life screw him up? The guilt stayed with him through the five years Rusty had been incarcerated and never once had he voiced a peep about his feelings.

Until today.

And just the simple response from Shell, just her telling him she had faith he'd done his best lifted some of the weight off his shoulders. Shell's comment had been sincere. She wasn't one to blow smoke up his ass. It'd been nice to be able to unpack even a tiny bit of baggage. As much as he trusted his men, and especially those in his exec board, he didn't confide his personal shit in them. As president, he wanted to portray a confident, controlled, capable man at all times. Until he'd unloaded on Shell, he hadn't realized how lonely it could sometimes be at the top. Or how good it could feel to have a woman soothe the worries.

Shit, he was losing his fucking mind. Sounding like a total pussy.

"All done!" Beth announced, holding her empty cup for Copper to see. She still munched the cone. "What's next?"

Copper glanced at his watch. Plan was to give Shell three hours of peace and quiet. "Clubhouse?"

"Yes!" Beth shouted. "Maverick promised to draw on my arm. Like a tattoo. So I can look like him."

Copper chuckled. "Okay, but nothing crazy. Remember, I'm not trying to get in trouble with your mom."

"Okay. We'll just do a little bit of tattoos."

"Good, princess. Let's roll out." If only dealing with all women was this easy.

CHAPTER FIVE

A missed shift at work was a major concern in Shell's paycheck-to-paycheck world. Missing two shifts was one step away from catastrophic. But she was a mother first and foremost, and that meant the occasional sleepless night, sick child, and call-out from work.

And was last night ever one of those sleepless nights. Three days after Copper's birthday party, Beth had been feverish, restless, and cranky as all get out. She'd woken up fussy nearly every hour on the hour. Shell managed a grand total of two hours sleep then had to placate a sick and very grouchy child all day long. Finally, around four in the afternoon, after two rounds of vomit, three back to back viewings of Frozen, a few battles over Tylenol, and four loads of laundry, the fever broke, and Beth started to feel a little better. She'd passed out at five o'clock and was still out cold over three hours later. With any luck, she wouldn't make an appearance until morning.

Shell rubbed her eyes and sighed with exhaustion as she stared at the envelope in her hands. As usual, it was full of ten one-hundred dollar bills she needed to feed her daughter and keep a shelter over their heads. Unfortunately, this money was marked for someone else. Someone who was due to collect it any minute because they arrived precisely at eight thirty p.m. the first Monday of every month. The rest of the month would be a tough one of buying dented cans and disappointing her daughter when she couldn't afford any special activities or treats.

She glanced up from her spot, seated on the steps that led to her small house as a brown sedan pulled into her driveway. Rising, she met the driver at his car. It didn't really make any sense, but she always preferred he stay as far from her actual house as physically possible.

He exited the driver's side and stood, leaning on the open door. "Got something for me?" he asked as he did every single month. Joe wasn't a large man, in build or height, but he made up for it with the frostiest stare Shell had ever encountered. Every time she met the steely charcoal gaze, she imagined what would happen if she missed just one payment. It wasn't a stretch to picture those eyes glaring down at her as she writhed on the ground with broken kneecaps. She bet they wouldn't even show a flicker of emotion. Just cold calculation and indifference.

She extended her arm, and he snatched the envelope from her over the top of the car door. That small barrier provided a world of comfort. The dome light from Joe's vehicle illuminated the dark driveway enough for him to withdraw the money and count it out. "One thousand. You're good."

"When have I ever not been *good*?" she asked, voice thick with disgust. Maybe if her temper wasn't already hanging by a thread after dealing with a cranky four-year-old all day, she'd have thought twice about mouthing off. This entire situation was so infuriating, it took everything in her not to rake her nails down Joe's face each month. Only reason she typically kept her annoyance in check was the child sleeping inside. She'd be no good to her daughter if Joe worked her over. But tonight, she was short on patience and long on frustration.

"Never," he said with a sneer. "And that's why we've never had to have *the chat*. We could change that if you'd like. I like attitude from bitches about as much as I like missed payments."

Shell wrinkled her forehead. "The chat?"

Copper

"Yep," he said popping the *p* as he carelessly tossed the money she'd worked so hard for into his car. "The chat about that beautiful little girl you have in there."

Shell stiffened, and clenched her fists at her sides. "Are you threatening my daughter?"

Joe laughed. "Sure as fuck am, lady. That's how this shit works. I threaten, you pay. You run your mouth, I threaten some more. You keep tossing attitude my way, I make those threats a reality. Get me?" He winked as though he was having some flirty conversation instead of bullying her into biting her tongue.

"The fuck's going on here?" Copper's furious voice sliced through the quiet of the night. She jolted so hard, her heart skipped a beat then shot off like a greyhound.

Shit! What the hell was he doing here?

Her mouth opened and closed but was so dry, she couldn't get a word out.

How on earth had she missed his arrival? She was beyond screwed.

"Get in the car and fucking go," she whispered.

Joe just raised an eyebrow.

Shit, shit, shit.

Copper had parked right in front of her house, and he now climbed down from his supersized truck as though it was no bigger than her little Corolla. Then he strode his hulking form toward them looking every bit the dangerous MC president he was with his leather jacket, narrowed eyes, and deadly scowl.

Shell swallowed and wrung her hands. Her heart sped as it usually did in Copper's presence but for an entirely different reason this time. Shit was about to go south. Maybe she'd get lucky, and Joe would lie out his ass, sparing Shell the epic blowout she and Copper would have when he found out the first of her many secrets.

"Joe?" he asked as he grew close. "The fuck you doing here?"

Of course they knew each other. The club had worked with Joe's crew back in her father's days.

"Copper. Been a while," Joe replied, extending his hand across the top of his car.

Copper just folded his giant forearms across his chest. "Asked you a question."

"Nothing to get hot about, Copper. Just finishing up some business with Miss Ward, here." Joe smirked and rested his crossed arms on the roof of his car.

So much for not blabbing. For a moment, Shell had the crazy idea of swiping Joe's car keys and zooming off in his sedan just to avoid Copper's ire. It'd never work, though. The man would just be waiting for her when she returned.

"And what business would that be?" Copper's eyes narrowed more by the second, and his shoulders grew more rigid. He was working up to a serious mad, and Shell had a pretty good idea who was going to be in the direct path of hurricane Copper when it hit.

"The business of debt repayment. Only one I engage in." Joe slapped his palm on the top of his car twice then slipped into the driver's seat. "See you around, Copper. Shell," he said with a lift of his chin, "Pleasure as always. See you next month."

All she could do was nod and watch as Joe drove off leaving her with one pissed off mountain of a biker.

"Wanna tell me why the enforcer for one of the most notorious drug dealers in the east is hitting you up for money? At night? When you're home alone with your daughter? And it's dark as fuck. Christ, what the fuck are you wearing? It's fucking freezing out here."

He hadn't opened his mouth once but spoke through a jaw so tight he'd crack a tooth if he didn't ease up. God, he looked so solid, so formidable standing there, legs wide, arms crossed, muscles bulging under his leather jacket and dark-wash jeans. If only she could dive into his arms, have him wrap her up and promise it would all be okay. Absorb some of that strength so she could stop pretending she was a pillar herself. But that wasn't her reality. Her life consisted of managing the very delicate web of secrets and lies she'd been balancing for too many years. And one of those secrets was about to be blasted into the open. There was no way Copper would let this go until he knew every single detail.

That didn't mean she wouldn't at least try to escape telling him. "I'm not sure that's any of your business, Copper." She turned and trudged back up the driveway toward her door.

"Michelle Elizabeth Ward, don't you dare walk that bite-able ass one more step without answering me." His deadly voice boomed into the quiet night, so full of menace she probably would have been frightened if he were anyone else. But Copper would never hurt her. Yell at her? Piss her off? Hell yeah, he'd do those things.

But never harm her.

Slowly, she spun on her heel. "Excuse me, Aiden *Whatever* Gallagher," she said, jamming her hands on her hips. Did he even have a middle name? Didn't matter. She loved Copper's real name and often wished she could call him Aiden all the time. "Who the hell do you think you are coming to my house at night and issuing orders?"

He stalked forward until all snorting and snarling six feet five inches of him towered over her measly five-foot-two frame. Fire blazed in his eyes, but something else too. Worry. He was worried about her. And that concern is what gave her pause and made her wave her arm and say, "Follow me inside. Let's not give my neighbors any more of a show tonight, huh? At least not until we decide to sell tickets. After today, I could use the money," she mumbled under her breath.

Copper took his obligations as president of the MC very seriously. And he felt his reach extended to each and every family member of his men. It was why he and the MC had kept in such close contact with her even after her father died and she was no longer officially attached to the club. Last thing she wanted was to add to his heaping pile of responsibility, but fighting him would only make things worse. Eventually, she'd cave, and in the meantime, she'd put him through unnecessary worry and concern.

Wait...did he just call her ass bite-able?

Yeah, that's what she needed to be focusing on.

Once they were in the house and Copper had locked the deadbolt behind them, she motioned him toward her couch. "Have a seat. I'll get us a couple of beers. Unless you want coffee."

He stared at her for a second, as though assessing whether she was going to fall over, then nodded. "Beer works. Thanks, babe."

She grabbed Copper's favorite beer from her fridge—yes, she kept it on hand just for him—then took her time uncapping them. Gave her a minute to gather her thoughts and prepare for the verbal smackdown. "Time to face the music," she murmured.

When she returned to the small living room, she paused in the doorway and soaked in the sight of the man she'd loved since she was a teenager and had no business wanting.

He dwarfed her two-person loveseat as he always did. Usually, she made a quip about him breaking the thing or hogging all the space, but tonight she couldn't muster the energy for jokes.

Her options were a recliner or the itty-bitty space left on the loveseat. She started for the recliner, the safer option, but Copper shook his head and pointed to the small space next to him. Since an argument was already on the agenda, she didn't bother heaping more shit on the pile by defying him, and wedged herself in between the armrest and his solid body, sitting cross-legged and facing him. Immediately, warmth flowed from his thigh into her knees and throughout her entire body.

Why?

Why did he have to have this intoxicating effect on her? Why, even after all these years of unrequited feelings, could she not shake the all-consuming hold he had on her heart?

Copper blew out a long breath and bent his head away from her, cracking his neck. "I'm trying here, Shell. Really fucking trying to understand why that piece of shit was at your house. And I'm trying to do it without losing my shit." One hand held his beer and the other rested on the armrest, his fingers curling around the edge so hard he just might tear the worn, tan fabric.

He turned his head and met her gaze. When he eyed her like that, like he wanted to slay her dragons, banish her demons, and destroy anything that would cause her a moment of distress, she was utterly and completely lost in his spell. Of course, there was a healthy chance the meaning behind it was all in her mind. Still, it worked.

Shell sighed. "I'll tell you, Copper," she said in a small voice as shame washed over her. She was an adult. She should be able to handle her own problems without the club coming to her rescue far too often. They shouldn't even be aware of her issues.

"Fuckin' finally," he fired back. "And you can start with what the hell you were thinking parading yourself in front of that shitbird dressed like that." Gone was the concern and compassion, replaced by stormy eyes and a furious tone.

Shell glanced down, and if it were any other time, she'd have burst out laughing. Clad in a pair of tight black leggings and a fitted lavender V-neck sweater, there wasn't a damn thing inappropriate about her outfit.

Copper's anger was clearly melting his brain.

CHAPTER SIX

Copper focused on the action of swallowing his beer to keep himself from wringing Shell's neck like he really wanted to.

Sip, taste, swallow, breathe, repeat.

Dark smudges dwelt under each of her eyes, she wore mismatching socks, and he'd have sworn she swayed on her feet before going to get their drinks. The woman looked seconds away from collapsing due to exhaustion. Last thing she needed was his pissed-off ass riding her in his customary demanding manner.

Riding her ass.

Shit.

Now he had that visual in his head. Which brought him right back around that damn outfit.

Shell glanced down at her clothes before lifting her frowning face. "Dressed like this? Copper, have you lost your mind? Aside from being cold because I wasn't wearing a jacket, what is wrong with this?"

He ran his hand down his face and scratched at his beard. The beard he'd cleaned that evening before paying her a visit. Not because he knew she liked it close-trimmed. Just because it was getting unruly as he tended to let happen. "Jesus woman, those pants are too fucking tight."

Copper

She screwed up her face, looking truly confused. "What? They're black leggings. They're tight. That's what leggings are. You feeling okay?"

Yeah, sure, they were supposed to be tight, but were they supposed to hug her curvy ass in that way that made men think of one thing and one thing only? And that would be bending her over the closest flat surface, grabbing those round hips, and watching said ass jiggle as they fucked her from behind.

Shit.

"Well, your tits are showing too. And that man is the furthest thing from honorable." Michelle wasn't a twig. She'd had a kid for fuck's sake. Her body had taken on that softer quality women hated about themselves, but men loved to sink their fingers into. At least the men he knew. Michelle had always had a bangin' body, even at eighteen and nineteen when she was more skinny than curvy, but now, now she was one hundred percent woman and so fucking enticing he was hard in her presence more often than not.

Speaking of... Copper grabbed a throw pillow and placed it over his lap.

Thankfully, Shell didn't seem to notice. She was too busy staring at him with a gaping mouth. "My tits are showing?" Glancing down again, she snorted. "Copper, it's a V-neck sweater. You can see about a millimeter of my cleavage. What the hell is wrong with you? You live at the clubhouse and are practically drowning in tits every day. This is nothing."

"Yeah? Well, what about your nipples?" He sounded like a psycho. And this had nothing to do with Joe, why he was here, or what Shell was hiding from him. But the thought of Joe gawking at her body, getting hard over the sight of her, or even being near her was making him insane.

Because Joe was a sadistic enforcer for a drug kingpin. Not because Copper was jealous.

"My *nipples*?" she squeaked as her face grew bright pink. She crossed her arms over her breasts and looked at anything but him. "It's cold out," she muttered.

"Fuck," Copper practically growled. "Forget it. Just tell me why Joe was here."

Staring at the blank television screen, Shell said, "The first Monday of each month, he shows up at eight fifteen on the dot to collect one thousand dollars from me. Has since a month after I moved back home." The confession was uttered low enough he had to strain to hear it.

"You fucking kidding me? You've been back over a year!" Copper exploded forward, off the loveseat, drawing a yip of surprise from Shell.

Her slender shoulders, the ones that carried so much weight, slumped and her eyes grew glassy with unshed tears. The sight of her so close to crying is what doused the flames of Copper's anger. Sure, he still felt like a simmering volcano, but he needed to rein it in if he didn't want to cause her more upset. This problem of hers would be taken care of. Shell wouldn't pay another dime to Joe. The Handlers would make damn sure of that, as they would have right off the bat if she'd come to them in the first place.

Damn stubborn woman.

Copper returned to the loveseat, stuffing himself in the space he'd occupied before. She'd left him more than half the tiny sofa, but it was still a tight fit, and her crossed knees ended up resting on his thigh. The woman needed bigger furniture. At least the news of how much money she'd forked over killed his boner.

One thousand dollars every month. It gnawed at him like a vulture tearing flesh from his bones. No wonder she worked herself raw yet always seemed to be without. He cupped her cheek. She sucked in a breath, meeting his gaze. "Look, babe, I came here because I heard Beth was sick and I wanted to check on you. See if you needed anything. If I promise not to react like that again, will you tell me the rest?"

Copper

Shell nodded, and one tear sprung free. With a huff, she blinked fast, as though angry at herself for allowing the weakness. Weak, shit, Shell was hands down the strongest woman he knew.

Copper groaned. "Please don't cry, babe. It'll fucking kill me." He caught the runaway drop with his thumb as it trickled down her cheek.

She gave him a wobbly smile. "Apparently, right before Dad was killed, he'd received fifty thousand dollars in heroin from whoever it is Joe works for. I don't even know who runs the show."

"Really?" Copper scratched at his beard. It'd been over a decade since Sarge had been murdered, but that info didn't ring any bells. Sarge had gotten the club involved in drugs a few years after Copper prospected. They'd sold dope, heroin, cocaine, and on occasion prescription pills, but never that much at once. It'd been something he never agreed with, and that business dragged the club through a few bloody years. After Sarge's death, Copper ended the club's involvement with pushing drugs.

Shell shrugged. "So he says. It's not like I can verify it now. But he claims they never got paid for it. Joe says the drugs were given to Dad on good faith because they had a long-term relationship with him. He was supposed to make a payment the day after he was killed. They never got his money, and when they sent someone around to look for the drugs, they were never found."

"So now that you're older and back in town, they want their money."

"Exactly," Shell said with a nod. "Plus interest, of course."

Copper snorted. "Of course. Jesus, ten fucking years of interest." Hell, he ran a loan sharking business. He was no stranger to demanding repayment or forcing it when necessary. But there was one difference. Everyone who borrowed from him did so one hundred percent willingly. And if something happened, the Handlers didn't go after a single mom to collect.

"They go looking to your mother for it first?"

That had Shell laughing. "You serious? She doesn't have two pennies to rub together. And it's no secret she wants nothing to do with the club. Joe may be an asshole, but he's not stupid. He knew where to go. I'm easy prey." She shrugged. "Just threaten Beth, and I'll pretty much do anything anyone asks."

"He threatened Beth?" Copper asked. He tried to keep his voice neutral, but couldn't quite keep the lethal out of it.

"Copper," Shell said, raising an eyebrow. "You promised."

Blood simmered in his veins, just bubbling away ready to roll into a full boil. Joe had no idea the hell he'd invited into his life by going after Shell. And then to be threatening Beth? He'd be damn lucky if he lived another week. "I know, babe. This is directly related to the club." He looked at her defeated expression, something she never wore in front of him. Unable to stop himself from providing some comfort, he curled his hand around the back of her neck and gave a gentle squeeze. It was a fucking mistake, just that small touch, the feel of her soft skin against his much rougher palm had him swallowing down a mouthful of need.

"Why haven't you brought this to me, Shell?"

"Things have been rough with the club ever since I came back, Copper. First with Shark, and then Lefty." She shook her head. "I know my mom hates the MC and pretty much cut ties after Dad's death, but I've always thought of the Handlers as my family. Joe said my dad was upping the drug dealing side of business outside of the club's knowledge. Let's face it, the club was different back then. My dad was leading the club in the wrong direction. You know it, I know it. And you guys don't deserve to pay for his poor decisions."

If Shell was a man, he'd have patched her into the club right then and there. Loyal to a fault, she loved her family with every ounce of her being. But she wasn't a guy, so she couldn't patch

Copper

in, and call him a caveman, but he would never believe a woman should have to pick up any slack for the club business. He'd tried to take care of and protect Shell from the moment her father was killed, despite her protests and insistence on independence. Clearly, he'd failed miserably.

"It ends tonight, Shell. Joe doesn't get another fucking penny from you. You hear me?"

Owl-eyed, she started to speak.

"Not finished." he held up his free hand. "The club will take care of it. No, I won't give you details, you've been around long enough to know how this shit works. If you see him anywhere, if anyone approaches you, if any damn thing happens that doesn't seem right, you call me, immediately. Understand? I'll take one answer, and that's a yes."

Shell just nodded. "Okay, Copper," she said in a small voice. "Thank you."

Huh? That was way too easy. Shell didn't accept help. No matter how much he growled at her. "That's it? Just thank you? You're not going to argue with me?"

A sad smile formed on her face. "I'm too tired tonight. Maybe when I wake up tomorrow, I'll be pissed at you for managing me, but I just don't have the energy for it tonight. And, if you want the truth, giving him money each month is killing me." A blush appeared on her cheeks. "I'll be able to breathe a little easier now."

Copper closed his eyes and counted to ten. He had to assume some of her easy acquiescence was due to the fact he didn't fly off the handle over the news, but kept his cool and spoke to her rationally. So, as much as he wanted to shake her until her teeth rattled, he refrained.

"Okay. Then it's done, and as long as you don't see Joe, we don't have to speak about it again." He pushed a stray curl behind her ear. "How's Beth?"

Shell groaned. "Last night was rough. We were both up pretty much the entire night. And today she was a bear, but she fell asleep before dinner, and seems to be out for the night."

The woman should be in bed herself, not dealing with a scum sucking bottom feeder like Joe. Shell needed a man in her life. Someone to care for and protect her, from herself if necessary.

He tried to imagine a man here, filling that role in Shell's life, and he nearly ripped one of her pillows in half.

Copper rubbed his eyes as a wave of fatigue washed over him. Nothing could be done about Joe tonight, and she needed to get some sleep. "Why don't you go get ready for bed, babe. I'll lock up for you. I'm pretty fuckin' bushed myself."

"All right." They both stood. Shell placed a soft hand on his arm. "Thank you," she said, then wrapped her arms around his waist and buried her head in his chest.

The feel of her, soft and warm against him, her thin but strong arms clinging to him had his cock waking up again. He gripped her messy bun, tipping her head back. "I'd do fucking anything for you and that princess back there, you know that, right?"

Shell nodded, her chin bumping his chest. "I know," she whispered.

"Good. Now get moving." He gave her a playful swat on the ass that made her giggle as she hurried into her room.

Copper made his way through her house, ensuring the doors and windows were locked, before following her into her room. He was too beat to drive home. At least that's what he was telling himself. This wouldn't be the first time he'd crashed at Shell's. It'd happened two or three times since she'd been back in Tennessee. The other times it was because he'd been keeping an eye on her due to some threat against the club. Both times he'd stayed on that piece of shit couch, and got about fifteen minutes of sleep.

Not tonight.

When Shell emerged from the bathroom, he was lounging on her bed, eyes closed.

Copper

"Oh," she squeaked. "You, uh," she cleared her throat, "you staying here? Uh, in my bed?"

"Yeah, you mind? I'm too fucking big to sleep on that tiny-ass couch."

"No, of course I don't mind." she answered too quickly. "I'm the one who always tells you you're crazy to sleep there." Barefoot, she padded toward the door. "I'll sleep on the couch."

As she walked past the bed, he reached out and captured her wrist. God, her skin was soft. Felt like silk under his callused fingers. "Just take the other side. Trust me when I tell you that couch is no place to sleep. Actually, I think you need to stop calling it a couch. It's an insult to real couches."

"I, uh, well..." Her mouth opened and closed about three times. Combined with the wide-eyes, she looked almost comical. Seeing her so flustered was kind of funny. Normally she had a witty comeback for him. Not tonight. She must really be exhausted. He frowned and dropped the teasing.

"Look," he said. "I'm bushed and so are you. I'm not leaving you alone knowing that prick was just here. I get that you've been dealing with him for a while now, but just humor me. I'll feel better knowing you and Beth have a guard tonight, okay?"

She still stared at him like he was crazy, but seemed to be considering his words.

So he went in for the kill.

"You need a solid night sleep so you can take care of Beth tomorrow. You know you won't sleep well on the couch." He knew the moment she gave in. Her body lost its tension, and she nodded her head.

"Okay."

"Got a spare toothbrush I can borrow?" he asked as he released her wrist.

"Uh, yeah, cabinet under the sink." She scurried around to the other side of the bed.

"Thanks, babe." He climbed out of the bed just as she was slipping under the covers.

"Uh huh," she said. Her voice was high-pitched like she was nervous and Copper chuckled.

There wasn't a damn thing to be nervous about. He wasn't going to touch her. Would never touch her. Last words her dying father said was to make sure Shell was protected. Make sure she was taken care of. He'd said, "Don't let any of the fuckers in this club have her," right before he took his last breath.

Copper wasn't about to break a promise to the man that had taken him into the club and given him the life he loved.

He took a leak, brushed his teeth, then stepped back into Shell's room. There wasn't much in the way of decoration, probably due to lack of money, but the room was neat and comfortable. She was in the queen-sized bed, on her side, facing a window. And not facing him.

Copper put a hand on his belt, shook his head, then started for the bed. After two steps he said, "fuck it," and undid the belt. The past times he'd crashed there had been planned so he'd had a change of clothes but fuck if he'd get a good night sleep in jeans. He dropped the denim to the floor and stepped out, clad in his boxer briefs and T-shirt. It would have to do.

He slipped under the covers and tried to pretend his feet weren't hanging off the edge and his massive body wasn't taking up more than his fair share of the bed. Soft breath sounds came from Shell's side of the bed. Poor thing was probably out cold already.

She worked way too much for way too little, and it made him sick to his stomach to think that a good chunk of her money was being stolen by drug dealers.

Not anymore.

Copper glanced over and watched the steady rise and fall of her back for a few minutes. Then, he rolled to his right side, curled an arm around her waist, and tucked her against his body. Aside from his birthday, he never touched Shell, not hugs, not pats on the arm, not even so much as a handshake. Just didn't trust himself not to lose control and ravage her. But as he held

Copper

her soft body close, he felt more at peace than he'd felt in years. Maybe ever.

Well, most of him felt at peace. There was one part of him rapidly growing dissatisfied with the nonsexual nature of the situation. His cock hardened further with each passing second of having her body so close to his. Minutes ticked by, and he finally allowed his mind to come to terms with what he'd been fighting like hell against for years. He wanted Shell with every fiber of his being. Wanted to fuck her, wanted to romance her, wanted to sleep next to her, wanted to monopolize all her free time.

Too bad he'd never have it. Despite everything he wanted, needed from her, all he'd allow himself was one night to hold her in his arms as she slept.

Since she was already asleep, she'd never know.

Aside from having the bluest balls on earth, what was the harm?

CHAPTER SEVEN

Shell woke to a small hand patting all over her face.

"Mommy! Mommy! Mommy! I'm awake," Beth said, still smacking her hand on Shell's cheek.

Shell rolled to her back. With a groan, she grabbed Beth's hand and blew a raspberry on her palm. The giggles that ensued were music to her ears. "Sounds like someone is feeling better this morning."

"Me! I'm feeling better." Beth bounced on her knees like she'd just had a few shots of espresso instead of being laid up for the past two days with a virus. If only adults could bounce back that easily.

Shell hadn't even been sick, and she was beyond exhausted. Of course, she'd lain awake half the night with Copper's massive arm slung across her waist and the regular up and down of his breathing against her back.

Holy shit! Copper!

She shot up, eliciting another round of giggles from Beth. "Mommy you're funny," she said clapping her hands.

"Uh, yeah baby, mommy's so funny. She glanced around the room. The jeans he'd laid at the foot of the bed were no longer there, nor were the boots he'd discarded before climbing in next to her. "You hungry, Bethy?"

"Starving," Beth replied with all the drama only a four-year-old girl could display.

Copper

Shell blinked. Had she dreamed it? Had Copper even been here? Yes, he'd been here. The memory of him discovering one of her secrets was too strong to have been a figment of her imagination. But as for holding her all night long? She put her hand on her forehead. Maybe she was sick with some kind of brain disease.

"Your tummy feel good?" she asked her daughter.

Beth nodded and flopped down on the pillow Copper had used. "Mmm, this pillow smells good."

Yep. Copper had really been there.

"Go in the kitchen, Bethy. I'll make you some pancakes." She swung her legs over the side of the bed and stretched her arms up and over her head until her back cracked. "Did you go potty yet?"

"No. I don't hafta go."

Suuure, she didn't. "How about this. We'll have a race and see who can get to the kitchen first after going potty."

Beth's eyes lit up, and she sprang off the bed. "Okay. I'm gonna win!" she shouted as she darted to the Elsa-themed bathroom down the hall.

With a chuckle, Shell peeled herself off the bed and took care of her own business. As she passed by her bed on the way to her door, she paused.

Don't do it. Keep on walking, Michelle.

Of course, she didn't listen to that little voice in her head. No, she grabbed Copper's pillow off the bed, held it to her nose and inhaled. Her eyes nearly rolled back in her head. Cedarwood from the beard oil he preferred, a hint of smoke from those cigarettes he pretended not to smoke on occasion, and a zesty hint of soap.

Copper.

Like some kind of crazy stalker, Shell switched the pillow to the side of the bed she preferred to sleep on. A night with Copper's arms around her might have been a once in a lifetime experience, but tonight, she'd fall asleep surrounded by his scent, and for a few moments she could pretend he was there. She'd hoped feeling his arms around her would have gotten some of the need out of her system. Yeah, she'd been dead wrong about that. All the experience did was make her crave more of him. More time with him, more contact with him, more of anything he was willing to give her. She sighed and shook her head. Why did she have to be in love with a man who didn't want her?

Lord, she needed help.

"Mommy!"

"Coming, baby," she called back.

Shell shuffled her way into the kitchen only to find Beth standing on a chair in front of the open refrigerator as she wrestled with a mostly full gallon of milk. "Firsty, Mommy?" she asked.

Yeah, Beth was feeling better.

"Whoa there, Bethy. How about I get the milk, and you get a cup?" she asked as she relieved her daughter of the heavy jug.

"Okay!" Beth said with way more excitement than the task called for. As she scampered off to the low cabinet that held her shatterproof cups, she said, "I go to preschool today?"

"I don't know, honey. You're really feeling good?"

"Super good! Please, mommy. I want to see my friends." She did a little dance in place that reminded Shell of R2D2 rocking back and forth with anticipation.

There was a lot more healthy color in Beth's face, and her appetite seemed to have returned. She held a hand to her daughter's forehead. Definitely no fever. And being Wednesday, it was Shell's morning off from the diner. She could really use a few hours to herself to just…be alone and quietly process everything that had happened the night before.

"All right. You win. School it is."

"Yes!" Beth pumped a tiny fist in the air then held it out to Shell. "Pound it, Mom," she said, face totally serious.

Copper

"Pound it?" Shell snorted out a laugh. "Let me guess, one of your uncles showed you that one."

Small white teeth gleamed through Beth's smile. "No, it was Copper. He's not my uncle, he's my best friend."

Ugh, no one knew how to send a shot straight to the heart better than a child. Copper treated Beth like she was a princess and he was her humble servant, spoiling her every chance he got. She had that man, and most of the rough and gruff Handlers, firmly under her sparkly pink spell.

"Boom," Beth said as Shell touched her fist to her daughters. "Don't forget to explode." She made a loud blast noise and wiggled her fingers.

Shell couldn't help it, she threw her head back and laughed. Nothing put her in a good mood quite like some time with her playful daughter.

They ate an uneventful meal then Shell helped Beth get ready for school. Since Beth didn't complain of a single ache or pain the entire time, Shell assumed it was safe to send her to school. Once Beth was all ready to leave, Shell set her up watching cartoons while she got herself ready. "I'll just be fifteen minutes, honey."

"Okay, Mommy," Beth answered, already lost in the world of computer-generated characters.

When she reached her room, Shell tore off her clothes and took one of her patented four-minute showers complete with hair wash. As she stood outside her bathroom, trying to decide what to wear, a white slip of paper on top of the dresser caught her eye.

"What the…" Clad only in her favorite bra and panty set, she walked to her dresser only to find a note folded around a stack of hundred-dollar bills. Written in Copper's chicken scratch were the words:

For last night.

Shell frowned. That bastard. Was this the reason he stayed? So he could pay her back the money he knew she'd never take? She absolutely despised taking money from the club. Work was how she earned her money. Working hard, and working well. She and Beth were not a charity case, and while they didn't have excess, she was able to provide her child with everything she needed. Getting Joe to stop harassing her was one thing. Leaving cash on her dresser was quite another.

Oh my God. She pressed a hand against her stomach as breakfast threatened to make a repeat appearance. Was this the reason Copper spooned her all night? To soften her up and make her accept the money? A hot flush of humiliation stole over her.

"Who the hell does he think he is?" she said aloud into the empty room. "Well, fuck that." Slamming through the drawers on a mission, Shell shoved her legs into some black skinny jeans then reached for a T-shirt. A mischievous smile curled her lips, and she dropped the T-shirt back in the drawer then moved to the closet.

If Copper thought he could dictate her actions, he had another think coming. She reached into the back of the closet where she'd stashed a shirt Toni made her purchase a few weeks ago. Admittedly, it looked fantastic on her but showed off a little more boob than Shell was used to. Maybe back in the day before she'd had Beth, she'd have rocked something so revealing, but nowadays she leaned toward more coverage.

Not today.

Copper wanted to pay her?

She was happy to make him pay.

"I WANT TO put it to a vote," Copper said as he rested his elbows on his desk.

In a chair on the opposite side of the desk with his feet propped up, Jigsaw snorted. "You know every brother here will vote to pay her back the money, but you also know Shell won't take a damn cent if it's club money."

Shit.

Copper

Jig was right. "We'll make her fucking take it," Copper grumbled.

Now Jig was outright laughing at him. The bastard hadn't laughed for over six years, and now that he had a consistent woman in his bed every night he thought life was fucking roses and sunshine.

"Something funny?"

"Fuck yeah, it's funny imagining you trying to force Shell to take the money. Do it, Prez, but make sure I'm there to see her crush those cantaloupe-sized balls of yours under her tiny foot. Oh man, the guys are gonna love this." Jig was giving him a shit-eating smile typical of Maverick.

"Look, jerkoff, by my count, she's given this fuckwad at least eighteen thousand dollars to cover her pop's debts. Our old president, who was apparently doing some shady deals behind our backs. In what world should she be out eighteen thousand dollars when she needs to buy her girl the fucking world?"

Jig sobered in an instant. "I hear you, Cop. Loud and clear. And I agree, she deserves every dollar back, but I also know her. She's proud as fuck, stubborn as a damn mule, and does not accept handouts."

"So, you got a better idea?"

"Sure do," Jig said just as Mav and Zach showed up at the door.

"Hey, Boss. Jig," Mav said as he barged in, uninvited. "Heard what you guys were talking about. Wanted to come in and offer our help."

Copper ran a hand down his face. "This ain't a fucking locker room, boys. I ever catch you spying outside my door, you'll spend a few weeks lower than the prospects."

Zach rolled his eyes and sat on the edge of Copper's desk.

He was losing fucking control. Last night, Shell hadn't been intimidated by him, now his guys were acting as though it were lunch hour in High School. Copper ran a hand down his face and growled. This wasn't some joke. This was Shell's livelihood, her safety, her life. Maybe he was too close to his men. They didn't fear him.

"That's fucking enough," he roared, slamming his fists down on his desk. Every single object on the desk flew into the air including the full mug of coffee. "Fuck," he said as it landed on the floor, spilling hot liquid and shattering.

The three men in his office stared at him like he'd lost his mind. "Prospect," he bellowed out the open door. Then he looked at his guys. "Quit the bullshit. I want Shell out from under these assholes' thumbs, and I want her money returned. Yesterday."

"Sup, Prez?" LJ stuck his head in the door.

"Clean this shit up," he said, pointing to the mess.

"On it." LJ disappeared into the hallway.

There, that's how they should all be acting. President says jump and they don't ask how high, they just jump the fucking highest they can.

"Sorry, Cop," Zach said. "I promise we're taking this seriously."

"You know we all love Shell like family. We'll get it straight." Mav was serious for once.

"I wasn't saying Shell won't take the money back. Just that she won't take club money. So, we don't give her club money. We get it back from Joe," Jig dropped his feet to the ground and leaned forward.

"Yes!" Zach clapped once then rubbed his hands together. "Louie would be more than happy to get in on that action. Joe's a dick." As club's enforcer, Zach was the one who paid visits to clients not repaying their loans on time. His favorite form of message delivery was a baseball bat he'd nicknamed Louie.

"All right," Copper nodded. "Church Thursday at eight. We'll discuss it then."

A commotion in the hallway had them frowning at each other, then filing into the central area of the club room.

Copper

Shell stood at the bar, hands on her hips. Her hair was damp and a little wilder than usual like she'd run right out of the house after a shower. "Swear to God, LJ, if you don't tell me whether Copper's here, I'm going to shove one of those bottles up your—"

"I'm right here, babe. No need to sodomize the poor prospect."

Shell spun slowly until she faced Copper. Those gorgeous blue eyes had narrowed to slits, and he could practically see sparks flying from her head.

"Oh boy," Zach murmured. "Someone's in trouble."

"Yep," Mav said, failing to disguise his chuckle. "You piss off the fairy, Cop?"

Mav had it right; she looked like a tiny, furious fairy.

"Don't you tell me what to do, Copper." Shell stomped over to him. She held up her hand, fist full of the money he'd left on her dresser. Ahh, should have known that wouldn't sit well with her. "What the hell is this, huh?"

"Babe—"

"Don't you babe me, Copper. Was this all a little game to you? Think you can butter me up? Sleep in my bed and, what? I'm so pathetic and desperate I'll just take your handouts?" She shook her head. "I wake up to find a stack of money on the dresser like I'm some kind of whore. Well, you can take your money and shove it. I am not a charity case!" She screamed the last sentence as she tossed the crumpled money at him.

Then she spun and started to stomp toward the exit.

Oh, fuck no.

She did not come into *his* house, throw money at him, and call herself a whore. He rushed after, and with his long stride, caught her in three steps. With a hand at her waist, he whirled her around, shoved his shoulder into her stomach, and hoisted her up.

"Copper!" Shell screeched. "What the hell are you doing? Put me down, you big brute." She beat her small fists against his back, but it might as well have been stuffed animals pelting him for all he felt it.

LJ gaped from behind the bar while the other three idiots hooted like fucking loons.

"Now that's how you handle a woman, Cop," Mav said, clapping slowly.

"Shut up, Maverick. I'm telling Stephanie you said that! Bet she won't blow you for a month," Shell called out, hanging from Copper's shoulder.

"Shit," Mav said as his laughter died. "Didn't mean it, Shelly. Copper, put her down! That's no way to treat a woman! Wait… did Shell say the words 'blow you'?"

"Can one of you morons please help me?"

Zach just whistled, and as Copper passed Jig, his brother said, "Told you she wouldn't take club money."

So, she didn't want a handout from the club. Fine.

But what the fuck was she thinking traipsing into a biker den dressed like that? Christ, her tits were on full display in front of his brothers.

He stormed up the stairs toward his room, ignoring her cries for help and the guys' cheers.

Damn woman would be lucky if he didn't paddle her ass.

CHAPTER EIGHT

By the time they reached Copper's room, which was really more of a suite, Shell's head felt ready to explode from the rush of blood from the ass-up-head-down position.

Plus, there was the surge of admittedly exaggerated fury.

Copper deposited her on the floor then slammed his door shut. She'd been in his room countless times before, mostly to put Beth down for a nap in his bed, but something about this felt different. Perhaps it was the way he locked the door behind them, or maybe it was the fact she wanted to rip his face off. Whatever it was, it had electricity dancing across her nerve endings.

Copper didn't seem to notice at all. The calm indifference radiating off him only made her madder.

Well, screw him. "What the hell was that, Copper? You can't go all caveman and manhandle me in front of my friends like that." Hands fisted at her sides, she tried and failed to control her rapid breathing.

Silence was his only answer, that and the ticking of his jaw. But his eyes, they were anything but silent. They screamed with desire. His gaze focused on her very exposed cleavage and radiated with…hunger.

Mission accomplished.

Shell bit her lower lip to keep from smirking. Copper liked to think he had the upper hand at all times, but he was a man like any other. Flash some boob, and they turned to one-celled organisms.

"My eyes are about ten inches north, *Prez*." Any other day, she'd be thrilled to have snagged his attention, but today she was practically vibrating with anger that had nothing to do with his ogling.

Copper grunted and stalked forward, closing the distance between them. "Don't want me to stare at your tits, don't come into my house dressed like a fuckin' Honey."

Oh, he did not just say that.

"This isn't about my freakin' clothes, Copper. Or about where you're staring. This is about you managing my life. Ordering me not to speak to Joe, giving me vague statements about the club taking care of my problems, and leaving money I didn't want or ask for."

"Knew you agreed to that shit too easily last night," he grumbled.

She'd worked so damn hard to make a good life for her daughter. Worked herself to the bone to provide for and protect her family. That included Copper. Him leaving the money, money that was nothing to him, felt like a slap in the face. Like he was throwing all her hard work and sacrifices right back at her.

Granted, it wasn't an entirely fair assessment. The man had no idea why she made some of the choices she made, or just how far she went to protect him. She couldn't logically get mad at him for something he was blind to. But then rationality wasn't winning out over flustered anger at that moment.

"Why'd you stay over last night, Copper? Huh?" She paced in front of him, throwing her hands in the air and glaring at him as she spoke. A lot weighed on his answer. Did he play on her love for him? Had he calculated what to do, cuddling up to her all night, acting on her loneliness and fantasies just to bail in the morning and toss her some cash?

Copper

Remaining where he was, Copper folded his arms and cracked his neck. "Told you last night, woman. I didn't feel comfortable with you and Beth alone in the house after that asshole had been there. Plus, I was fucking beat. Easier to crash at your place since I was there."

Made sense. Perfect sense. Calm, rational, unemotional sense. Shell couldn't accept it. She wanted a reaction. Be it anger, sadness, agitation, whatever. She needed him to feel something toward her. She felt so much, so deep, and so agonizing. How could he stand there as though unaffected? She was sick and fucking tired of loving a man who felt nothing for her.

The tip of her nose tingled, warning her of approaching tears. This man had way too much power over her. Returning to Townsend had been a mistake. She was a fool to think she could live near him and not destroy herself, and Copper had driven that home last night.

"Then why did you hold me?" Holy crap, she'd actually asked it.

His eyes widened, but he didn't say anything.

"What? You think I was asleep or something? Well, I wasn't." She stepped forward and jammed her finger into his chest.

"So." *Poke.*
"Why." *Poke.*
"Did." *Poke.*
"You." *Poke.*
"Do." *Poke.*
"It."

He grabbed her finger, stopping it from digging into his very hard pecs one last time. "Shell," he said, voice full of warning.

"What, Copper? What are you going to do?" She rose on her tiptoes, getting in his face as much as she could given their vast height difference. Each time she breathed in, her chest rose, brushing against him.

Copper's eyes dilated until the jade green rim was almost swallowed up by the black. He leaned down. "You don't want to know, Shell. You couldn't fucking handle it."

Hunger. It was there, plain as day. Not just appreciation for her assets, but actual desire for her.

Holy shit. Over the years, she'd heard the rumors.

Copper wanted her but would never give in because she was too young.

Before his death, her father warned Copper to keep the men in the club away from her.

Copper had some notion he was her protector, and that included protecting her from himself.

All this time, she'd assumed it was bullshit. Teasing from the guys privy to her feelings. Not once, did Copper show any indication of romantic or sexual interest in her. He always treated her like a buddy's little sister or a beloved cousin. Someone he felt responsible for but wouldn't touch with a ten-foot pole.

But now?

Now everything she'd ever assumed was in question.

Did Copper want her?

"You'd be surprised what I can handle, Copper."

He snorted, nostrils flaring and his grip tightened. "Fine. You were right. I played you. Held your sexy body all night long to soften you up. Gave you what I thought you wanted so you'd take the money in the morning." The words were punishing, the tone even harsher.

Five minutes ago, she'd have bought it, but there was an unmistakable bulge resting against her stomach. He might be fighting the attraction for all he was worth, but Copper wanted her. He may have even been as starved for her as she was for him.

And Shell was done being denied.

Copper

"Bullshit." Shell spat the words as she ripped her arms from his grasp. Copper gazed at the ceiling as though praying to be teleported out of there.

No such luck, buddy.

Clearly, aliens had invaded her body because Shell whipped her shirt up and off, tossing it on the floor. She stood before him in skintight jeans and a lacy black bra that did nothing to conceal her puckered nipples.

"Jesus fucking Christ, Shell. What the fuck are you doing?"

She cocked her hip and licked her lips. Copper's molten gaze followed every movement, flowing over her bared flesh like a caress. "If you're gonna leave a stack of hundreds on my dresser like I'm some kind of whore, you should at least fuck me. Dontcha think?"

Jackpot.

Copper's entire body stilled. Well, almost his whole body. There was some movement, growth to be exact, behind his zipper. Shell's eyes widened. The man was big.

He stalked forward, and she couldn't have moved to escape if she tried. It was as though she was a little bunny caught in a trap and he was a prowling tiger circling its prey. When he reached her, he grabbed a fistful of her hair and tugged her head back. "You're playing with fire, little girl."

Two green eyes ablaze with excitement burned into hers. If only Copper would unleash all that tamped down passion on her. The red beard covering his lower face looked so soft, she longed to feel it brushing all over her naked skin. If he wasn't willing to have sex with her, maybe he'd just rub his beard all over her. On her face, her stomach, her breasts, her thighs. Hell, she'd probably get off from that alone.

But he saw her as a little girl. Once again, she dislodged from his grasp. Whatever hope she'd held died with his words and shot her anger straight to boiling once again.

"I'm not a little girl," Shell screamed. She grabbed her lace covered breasts. "I'm a woman, Copper." Still yelling, there was now a tremor to her voice. She hated that damn tremor. It betrayed her. Showed this was about much more than fucking. "I'm a twenty-four-year-old woman." The words came out softer this time. "I have two jobs. I pay my rent on time. I have a child for crying out loud." She sniffed and shrugged, palms out. If it wasn't going to happen now, it'd never happen, and she'd have to give up the dream. Because the wanting and not ever having was killing her.

"Shell, I'm sixteen years older."

It was all or nothing.

She held up a hand. "Yes. I'm younger than you are. But I haven't been a little girl in a long time, no matter how you see me. I'm an adult, Copper. A woman with needs and desires just like any other woman." A sad chuckle slipped out as she gave his deliciously large, tattooed, and muscular body a once-over. "Well, maybe my desires are a little more specific than most. But—"

In the next instant, Shell was lifted under her arms, turned and smashed against the door while all the air rushed from her lungs. "Umph." Before she had a chance to suck in, Copper's mouth was on hers and her brain cells short-circuited.

There was no hesitation, no questioning, no second guessing. If Copper wanted to kiss her, she was going to soak up every ounce of it whether it lasted one second, one minute, or one hour.

The kiss was brutal. A fierce attack of lips, tongue, and teeth. He plunged his tongue into her mouth making her knees weak and her pussy clench as she imagined his cock thrusting into her in much the same way. All it took was the first brush of his lips against hers and she was drenched in arousal.

Copper nipped her lower lip, hard, then dove back in before she even had the presence of mind to register the sharp sting. Soft bristles tickled her cheeks and chin, enhancing the sensory delight. Her mind swirled, flooded with hormones and pleasure chemicals. Her back pressed so hard into the door, there would probably be bruises all along her spine and shoulder blades tomorrow.

Worth every mark and ache.

Despite the rough assault on her senses, Copper took care of her, as he always did. He slid his massive hands up and cupped the base of her skull. Cradling her head, he prevented it from smacking against the door as he attacked her mouth.

A thick thigh nudged her legs apart then came to rest, pressed firmly against her sex. There was no doubt in her mind that within seconds, he'd be feeling exactly how much she wanted him soaking through to his skin.

All she could do was cling to his triceps, accept what he dished out, and try to give back half as good as she got.

God, he tasted terrific. Whiskey and a hint of cigar smoke. The kiss went on and on until the need grew so strong, the pressure of his mouth was no longer enough. She rocked her pelvis, grinding her jean-covered clit into his leg.

Yes. More of that was what she needed. More pressure. She canted her hips again, and again until she was basically riding his hefty thigh.

"Jesus." Copper tore his mouth from hers and stared down at her with wild green eyes, breathing like he'd just run the five miles from the clubhouse to her home. A slow smile curled his lips. Shell could have cheered.

He wasn't throwing her out. He wasn't running away.

"Helluva good first kiss, baby," he said, all growly and smug. "Hope you burned it into your memory because it's damn sure the last first kiss you're gonna have."

Surrounded by a haze of need and lust, Shell blinked. She must have heard him wrong. Whatever sex juices her brain was drowning in must be making her hallucinate. It sounded to her like Copper was claiming her.

And while being Copper's woman was the one thing Shell wished for above all, it would never happen.

It could never happen. She'd made sure of that years ago.

But sex? Sex with the man who she'd been fantasizing about long before she even knew what fantasies were? Yeah, that could happen.

And by the look on Copper's face, it would be happening.

Right now.

CHAPTER NINE

One kiss.

Sure, the lip-lock wasn't exactly run-of-the-mill. More like a soul-devouring, tornado of sensation that left Copper needing to fuck Shell more than he'd ever needed anything in his life. But it was still one kiss.

And the entire reason he'd never let his lips anywhere near her in the past. He'd known damn well a single taste would be all it took to destroy him. He was hooked, addicted, sunk, smitten, ruined. Whatever anyone wanted to call it, now that he knew the flavor of her sweet lips, he'd die before letting her get away. She was his, and he hoped to hell she could handle all that entailed.

The floodgates were open, and water was gushing in. He lifted his thigh, grinding it into her pussy, and she gasped. Well, something was gushing, that was for sure.

"Think, Shell," he said. One chance. He'd give her one chance to escape. If she didn't run, fuck it. As she said, she was an adult. She could live with the consequences. "Think hard about whether you want this. I'm a fucking one percenter president, baby, not like any college boy you may have been with in the past. I'm gonna demand a lot of you."

Something dark crossed her face for a second, but he cupped her lacy tits and brought her right back to the moment. She moaned and arched into him, offering herself. Unable to resist, he thumbed her nipples until she whimpered. "I-I know exactly who you are Copper. I've known you forever, and I've wanted you just as long."

"You may know me, Shell, but you don't know it all. Things I've done, things I'll do in the future. You should want to run from all that shit." That's what her father had meant when he warned her off men in the club.

"The Handlers are my family. I've been a part of the club my entire life. You'd be surprised what I know, Copper."

Surprised what she knew? The men made it a point to keep club business under wraps. He frowned. They'd be revisiting the cryptic comment at a later date.

"I may not be privy to all the details, but I'm well aware of what the club is. What it takes to run it and lead these men. You think I'm naïve. I'm not. Haven't been for a long time. Every man here walks outside the lines of the law on occasion. But there's a code. There's loyalty, family, protection. I trust you, Copper. Trust you as president of the MC and as a man. Ten years," she whispered. "I've wanted you for ten years. Since back when I was way too young to be looking at an old man like you."

That got a small chuckle out of him while the rest of her words slayed him. The faith, the trust she put in him made him want to beat his chest and let out a Tarzan roar. "You're still too young to be looking at an old man like me."

"I don't care about that, Copper. I've never cared about the age difference. I don't see you as an age. I just see you."

Jesus. He still remembered the first time he'd noticed her as more than his president's daughter. She'd turned eighteen a few months earlier, and showed up at a Handlers' barbecue with some friends wearing these itty-bitty denim cutoffs and a halter. Strutting around, trying to sneak beer when no one was looking. Every man there did a double take when her pert ass twitched by.

"Ten years, huh? Sounds like you got a lot of need built up."

"A whole lot." She bit her lower lip. The move was so sexy, he nearly came in his pants. Between the swollen red lips, wild mass of hair, flushed cheeks, and lacy bra, she'd have made one hell of a poster. If his brothers hadn't been downstairs, he'd have made her stand next to his bike while he snapped a few shots.

"Yeah?" he said. "Think I can help you out with that. Where you feeling it, baby? Where do you need me?"

With a sly grin, she grabbed his hand and brought it to the spot where her drenched pussy rested on his thigh. "Right here. Right where I'm getting you all wet."

This pint-sized sexpot was going to be the death of him.

More abruptly than he'd meant, he stepped back. Her feet hit the ground as she squeaked and wobbled before catching her footing.

"Bra off," Copper said as he backed toward the king-sized bed. When the mattress hit his calves, he sat then scooted back until he reclined against the headboard. "Want to see those tits. Been dreaming 'bout sucking those nipples since the moment you walked back in my clubhouse last year."

Her eyes flashed with a quick look of apprehension before she pushed it aside. Right before his eyes, she transformed into a confident siren. Licking her gloss-free lips, she took two steps forward then reached behind her back and unclasped her bra. The straps slid down the slope of her shoulders. Seconds away from fulfilling his number one visual fantasy, Copper's dick felt impossibly full. Just as the lace cups began to fall away from her luscious breasts, she caught them and held the garment in place with a teasing wink.

Copper groaned. "You trying to kill me, woman?" He slid the zipper of his fly down and sighed at the slight relief of pressure. It was either that or risk cock-strangulation, and with Shell's pussy waiting to be filled by that cock, he was going to take damn good care of it.

A sultry laugh floated from her, hypnotizing him. The entire clubhouse could be burning down around them and still, he'd be riveted to the unveiling of her body.

Slowly, as though she knew exactly how much the teasing drove him wild, she peeled the cups down and let the scrap of lace fall to the floor. Saliva pooled in his mouth. Soon he'd be all over those babies.

Shell tilted her head and walked forward, kicking off her flat shoes as she moved. Still clad in her skin-tight black jeans, she cupped her breasts, lifting and pushing the plump mounds together. "These the tits you wanted to see?" When she reached the bed, she climbed up on her knees.

Shit. Who knew she was such a sex kitten? "Fuck yes," Copper said. "Get your ass up here."

His heart galloped as she straddled his feet then knee-walked up his shins, still massaging her tits but now thumbing her nipples as well. She stopped, hovering a few inches over his knees. Fuck, he should have had her ditch the jeans first.

"Closer," the word rumbled out. "Those tits aren't in my mouth in the next thirty seconds, I'm taking over."

She threw back her head and laughed. "Let's not pretend I was ever in control here."

He narrowed his eyes. "Twenty seconds."

"Hmm," Shell inched closer. "I guess I'm feeling pretty generous where you're concerned. I can share my toys."

Close enough, he could stick his tongue out and lick her nipple. "Feed them to me."

Shell's breath hitched. "Yes," she whispered. She lifted her tits and leaned forward, brushing his lips with one nipple then the other.

Copper's stomach muscles clenched with the force it took to hold himself in check. "Didn't expect you to be so bold, gorgeous. Thought you'd be a little more shy." As he spoke, his lips grazed her distended nipples, causing her to jolt.

Copper

"I finally have what I've been dreaming about for years." She panted and trembled as he rubbed his lips on the side of her breast. "Not going to waste the opportunity being shy."

"Good fucking answer," he said then opened his mouth and latched on to the plump skin at the top of her tit.

Shell cried out and let her breasts drop. She grabbed Copper's shoulders and dug her slender fingers into the muscles. The prick of her nails sent a surge of white-hot need through his bloodstream.

A citrusy flavor hit his tongue as he trailed it through the valley between her breast. Kissing, sucking, biting, he worked the sensitive flesh until Shell was a quivering mess. She tasted so fucking good he couldn't stop the rough treatment and sampling of her skin. Tomorrow, she'd wear his marks for sure.

He couldn't fucking wait to see them.

"Please, Copper," she begged, twisting her torso and trying to get her nipples in his mouth. "Stop teasing me."

He could have spent hours driving her insane, but this first time, he wouldn't make her wait. He closed his mouth around one stiff peak, loving the way her head dropped back on a cry.

"Copper that's so good. So good. So good."

"Sure as fuck is, baby," he said, mouth full.

He sucked her until she was writhing against him, her denim-covered sex grinding and squirming all over his cock. Fuck! It felt incredible, but he wasn't fool enough to risk coming until he was deep inside her.

With lightning speed, Copper flipped them then hovered over a stunned Shell.

"For a big dude, you move fast," she said.

He winked and nudged his hard-on against her pussy. "You have no idea how big."

Shell giggled. "Looking forward to finding out."

Between her spread legs, Copper rested back on his heels. He popped the button of her jeans open then shimmied them down and off her legs. Next came the scrap of lace she called panties.

"You too," she whispered.

Gripping the hem of his shirt, he whipped it over his head and let it drop somewhere behind him.

"Jesus, Copper, you're incredible. I didn't know you had so much ink." Her gaze roamed all over him. "Pants too."

"Impatient little minx." He scooted off the bed and shucked his boots then jeans. He hadn't bothered with underwear that morning, so the reveal was quick and simple. When he rose to his full height again, his stiff cock slapped against his stomach. He noticed Shell's wide-eyed stare and couldn't help fisting himself and stroking a few times.

"Um…" Shell swallowed, making him chuckle.

"You're good for my ego, baby."

"You're gonna be good for something too," she said.

That had him laughing full-out. Funny, sexy, sweet, giving, she was the perfect woman. Copper climbed back on the bed and settled on his knees between her spread legs.

Creamy skin, full tits, round hips, she was his every fantasy come to life.

"W-what are you doing?" Shell asked when he didn't move to touch her.

"I've waited for this a long fucking time as well. Gonna take my time gawking at the most beautiful woman I've ever seen."

An adorable flush bloomed on her skin along with a shy smile. "Thank you."

He looked his fill, trying to imprint every hill and valley, every slope and curve to memory. He absolutely loved the small swell of her stomach. Proof that she'd given life. It was so feminine, so sexy, so—

Copper frowned. "What's this?" he asked tracing a horizontal pink line just a few inches above her bare mound. His heart dropped to the floor. Shell had a scar? Since when. Was she injured? Sick? Did she have surgery? Why the hell hadn't he known?

Straightening, he stared into her guilty expression.

Copper

"Shell? What the fuck happened to you?"

CHAPTER TEN

A feral animal. That's what Copper resembled, staring at her scar like he'd never seen one before. Shell grabbed his hand and squeezed. Hopefully, her touch would prevent the pressure from building to an explosion.

"Copper, it's nothing. Just a c-section scar."

His face screwed up as though in pain. "What? Beth was born by C-section? I had no idea."

She gave him a half smile. "No one here knows. Only my mother."

He tensed, running his thick finger over the raised line where her daughter had been quickly pulled out to save her life.

"I'll tell you the whole story another time."

"Were you alone?" Concern bled through his voice.

"I had friends."

This clearly bothered him. Really and truly upset him. That caring made warmth spread through her stomach. All she'd ever wanted her entire life was Copper. In her bed, in her mind, in her heart.

Him discovering that scar brought the harsh realities back into focus. It could never happen. She didn't want to talk about this now. For now, she wanted to pretend she could keep him. Imagine what it would be like if this night extended for the rest of her life.

Copper

"Were you scared?" He was so focused on the four-year-old incision she wasn't sure he'd even grasp the story if she told it.

"Please, can we talk about this later?"

He lifted his head and the depth of emotion shining back at her made her gasp. "Just answer that one question. I need to know."

Nodding, she whispered, "I was terrified."

His serious gaze bore into hers. She held her breath, afraid to shatter the connection they'd formed at that moment.

"You keep secrets," he said.

Her heart squeezed with familiar pain and fear. Keeping information from Copper was one thing. Flat out lying was another. "Yes."

He nodded. "I want them all. Someday. When you're ready. For now, I'm just so fucking glad both my girls are here and well today."

There wasn't anything in the world that Copper could ever do or say to top that moment. It would be stamped into her mind forever sure as the Handlers logo was branded on his arm. And she'd take it with her when she left. Because she had to go. And soon.

"Kiss me, Copper," she said, still whispering.

He did. Soft and slow, yet so deep she felt it in her soul. He slid his large body over hers, careful not to put too much weight on her. Dwarfed by him, surrounded by all his muscle, power, and authority, she felt safe and protected from anything the outside world could throw at her.

It was an illusion, of course, but for the time being, she'd exist in the delicious fantasy of being loved by Copper.

They kept the pace slow and languid. Hands coasted over skin, learning each other's bodies and pleasure points. When Copper left her mouth and kissed his way across her jaw and down her neck, she shivered in response. Between her legs, she was so wet, she could feel the arousal trickling down her ass. "Copper," she breathed. "I need to feel you now."

"Right here, baby," he said. "You're so fucking small. I'll try to be gentle."

"You won't hurt me, Copper. It's not possible. I was made for you." Later, when the afterglow wore off, and sense returned, she'd regret sharing such emotional intimacy. But for now, in the sheltered bubble they'd created for themselves, sharing her heart was natural.

"Fuck," he said as he reached for his nightstand. Ten seconds of rummaging produced a condom.

Shell tried not to think about how many were in there. Or rather how many used to be in there before he used them up. Most especially, she tried not to wonder how many Honeys he'd had in this very bed.

"None," he said.

"What?"

"It's written all over your face. This is *my* space, away from club bullshit. No woman has been in here beside you. And I haven't been with anyone since you moved back," he said as he ripped the packet open then rolled the condom down that very impressive length.

What? Holy shit. What did that mean? Could he possibly feel the same way she did?

Bracing on one hand, he used the other to rub his dick through her slick folds. "That set your mind at ease?"

She nodded and gripped the sheets at her sides.

"This needy pussy ready for my cock?" he asked as he nudged the tip inside her.

Her back arched off the bed. "Yes. So ready. Please fuck me, Copper."

"Fuck, that's the sexiest thing I've ever heard." He pushed in, inch by inch, swearing as more of him disappeared inside her. "You're so fucking tight."

He stretched her to just a step below the point of too much. Never before had she had such a sensation of fullness. From the inside out, he owned every cell in her being. She wanted to live like this, clasping him deep inside her, feeling him take her body to its limits.

"Shell," he said on an exhale. He dropped to elbows and rested his forehead against hers, seated in her to the hilt. "Never felt anything so fucking good in my life."

The way he said it like she was precious and he'd never let her go had her choking up. Salty tears filled the corners of her eyes.

Don't cry. Don't cry.

This was so out of her realm of experience. The intensity of the physical and emotional connection spiraled, binding down like threads of a rope. Joining together to create a force so strong, no amount of pressure could break it. But thanks to her, the center of the rope was frayed and wouldn't last long before snapping under the heavy weight it held.

She swallowed. "If you like this, why don't you try moving?" The sassy quip took every ounce of her strength.

He lifted his head and met her gaze. The man missed nothing, but he didn't question the quake in her voice. He just drew out at a maddeningly slow pace. Inch by inch, her body lost him though her inner muscles tried their hardest to cling to him. As the head of his cock dragged across the walls of her pussy, her eyes fluttered closed from the pleasure.

"Open those gorgeous baby blues for me."

She lifted her lids and encountered a straining Copper. Jaw tight, eyes fiery, muscles tense.

"Not sure how much longer I can go slow," he said, voice like ground glass.

Shell smiled. "Good," was all she said before he growled and let all that power loose.

Copper surged into her, going so deep, she had to brace her hands on the headboard to keep from shooting up the bed. Over and over, heavy thrusts pounded into her pussy, eliciting whimpers and moans each time he bottomed out.

The feeling of fullness never dissipated, even as her body softened to accommodate him further, she still felt stretched to the max.

Copper scooped an arm under one of her legs and hoisted it high, completely changing the angle of penetration.

"Aiden," she yelled as his cock stroked her G-spot at the same time his thumb strummed her clit.

"Fuck! Say it again."

She moaned. "Aiden."

"No one's called me that in a decade. Sounds so good on your lips, babe."

That's why she'd done it. Something special no one else shared with him. Though it seemed impossible, he sped up and increased the strength of his thrusts. Copper was a mountain of a man and at that moment all the dominance and force he possessed was concentrated between her legs.

A coiling pressure wound low in her stomach while her fingers and toes began to tingle. "Aiden," she said again. Her pussy clenched and released as she flew toward orgasm.

"That's it, baby," he said. His breath came in harsh pants, but it seemed nothing would throw him from his task. "All over my cock, gorgeous. Give it to me."

His words combined with the rough pad of his thumb on her clit and this thick girth inside her were no match for her body. She trembled, clinging to his shoulders and screaming his given name as a hurricane rolled through her. It left her limp, weak, satisfied and wondering when she'd have the opportunity to experience it again.

"Christ, I didn't think you could squeeze me any tighter." Copper slammed home and held himself deep inside her. With a roar everyone in the damn clubhouse must have heard, he came. Arms still around him, she felt every shudder, every flex and bunch of those impressive muscles as his body lost control to the pleasure.

Copper

Eventually, he collapsed next to her and drew her back tight against his chest. She was utterly lost inside him. Swallowed by his enormous form. And that feeling was almost as good as the orgasm he gave her.

"You good?" he said next to her ear.

"That's not the word for it."

The responding chuckle vibrated against her back. "That's fucking true. Damn woman, that was fucking out of this world. Kinda wishing I wasn't forty and could turn around and do that again in five minutes."

"Ha, I'm twenty-four, and I need a nap. You're not exactly dainty there."

That got the laugh she'd been hoping for, but it died out quickly. She was too afraid to ask what he was thinking. Actually, she knew. He was regretting it. Nothing had changed. She was still young, still his president's daughter, still like a sister to everyone in the club. Just because he hadn't been able to say no when she got naked in front of him didn't really mean he wanted her. She wasn't stupid, she knew how these men worked.

They fell silent, lost in their respective worlds as Copper traced her scar. Eventually, he broke the quiet with what she knew was coming. "Tell me what happened."

Shell sighed. Time to pay the piper. Turning in his arms, so they faced each other, she said. "Everything was fine. The pregnancy was actually a breeze as far as teenage pregnancies go. Or so I hear. I had a friend who was going to be my coach in the delivery room. I'd planned to get an epidural."

"What about your mom? I thought she went to be with you."

These memories were such a jumbled mix of fear, misery, and joy. The elation of bringing a new life, her beloved daughter, into the world combined with fear of Beth's father, rejection from her family, and concern for Beth's life. "You know things are strained between us." Shell cleared her throat. "She hates the club and, uh,"—God, this was so embarrassing—"she's convinced Beth is yours. Thinks we had some one-night stand back then. Anyway, she refused to come to the birth even though she tells everyone she was there."

"Jesus, Shell, so you had no one?"

"No, I had a friend. I told you that."

He snorted. "Some college friend? Another teenager? Was it a guy?"

Shell rolled her eyes. "No, it wasn't a guy. Do you want to hear the story?"

All she got was a grunt of affirmation.

"Anyway, two days before I was due, I started bleeding. The pain was…intense." She shuddered. Not a pleasant memory. It'd been the scariest moments of her life. Young, alone, pregnant and in very real danger of losing the baby. "My roommate called an ambulance, and I was rushed to the hospital. They took me straight to the operating room. Turns out my placenta had separated from the wall of my uterus early, which is not a good thing. I needed a few pints of blood, and spent some frightening hours worried about both my and Beth's lives, but in the end, everything worked out."

Copper's arms tightened around her. "Why keep it a secret? You know I'd have been there in a heartbeat. Anyone from this club would have. We're family, baby. What about the fucking father? I want to kill the shit who knocked you up and left you alone to experience that."

Shell gasped. Not once had anyone in Townsend spoken of Beth's father. They all seemed to understand without her informing them that the topic was painful and off limits. Leave it to Copper to push through those boundaries. She sniffed as the emotion became overwhelming. Why hadn't she told anyone? What about the father? What loaded questions. Ones that caused her to wake in the night shaking and sweaty.

"I was fine. There was no point in talking about it. I had a problem, and it was handled by the doctors. You know I'm not exactly big on sharing my burdens or asking for help."

"Yeah," he grumbled. "That shit's gonna change."

"And please don't ask me about the father. I don't want to think about it much less talk about it. Please?"

He hesitated, and she knew he didn't like the answer. He wanted to press. It wasn't in his nature to let things lie. He plowed forward, solved problems, and fixed things.

"For now," he said. "Someday, though, that won't be enough. Close your eyes. We have two hours until you need to pick up Beth. I want to hold you while you take a nap."

Nodding, Shell burrowed into the comforting warmth of his body. She rested her cheek against his heart, soothed by the constant steady beat. His words didn't send the fear through her they might have just a few weeks ago.

Someday.

It didn't matter because it didn't exist.

Someday wouldn't come for them.

Someday she'd be gone.

CHAPTER ELEVEN

"Earth to Shell."

The events of the previous day had played through Shell's head so many times in the past twenty-four hours she was almost sick of them. Despite how mind-blowing every second of her time with Copper had been.

"Hello, Shell, are you in there?"

After an hour nap, she'd woken to Copper's hand between her thighs and his mouth on her neck fifteen minutes before she had to leave to get Beth from preschool. Turned out, Copper could work some serious magic in just fifteen minutes. Two orgasms later she was sneaking out of the clubhouse to pick up her daughter. Sneaking because she'd die on the spot if any of the brothers saw her slap-happy, just-fucked glow.

"Michelle Ward, your daughter is across the room playing with knives."

In the evening, she'd gone on to her second job while Mama V watched Beth in Shell's home. The surprise of a lifetime had come when she returned home at nine fifteen to find Beth sleeping peacefully and Copper in her kitchen pouring her a glass of her favorite wine.

A girl could get used to that.

A girl could also keep her head on straight and remember the difference between reality and fantasy. Copper was her fantasy come to life, but that's all it was. A short-term departure from life. A lovely, but fictional illusion.

"And a chainsaw. Holy shit, Shell! Beth is about to cut off Copper's foot with a chainsaw. No, Beth! Don't do it!" Toni cried in a panic that rivaled the drama of a slasher film actress.

"Huh?" Shell turned to her friend. "What the hell are you talking about? Beth is at school."

"Jesus, woman, you've been drying that same juice glass and staring into space for the past six minutes. What gives?" Toni's fisted hands rested on her cocked hips. As with all her female employees, she wore a teal fitted diner T-shirt and a denim skirt. Casual was the name of the game at the diner and thank God because Shell wasn't much of one for getting dressed up. Unless it was in her favorite biker wear. She was down for that.

"So, you decided to tell me my daughter was playing with deadly weapons?" She put the glass down and glanced at the kitchen. Thankfully she hadn't missed any orders.

With a chuckle, Toni shrugged. "Hey, it wasn't my first course of action. I tried a few other things first, but you were totally zoned out." Her grin grew sly. "Although, this is better than the other thing you've been doing all morning."

Shell frowned. "What do you mean?"

"Excuse me, miss, could I get some more coffee?"

Shell glanced up at a slick businessman in a suit that probably cost more than three months' rent. "Sure thing, sir." She refilled his mug but didn't bother to hand over any extra sugar packets. If she recalled correctly, which after working at the diner since she'd moved back she always did, then he'd preferred it black.

The man winked and grabbed her free hand after she'd poured coffee into his empty mug. "Thanks, sweetheart. Had I known this town had so much natural beauty, I'd have listened to my business partner's advice and come here sooner."

Seriously? Did that kind of line actually work? If she wasn't in need of tips, the bigger, the better, she'd have told him just what he could do with his offensive pick-up line, but as she desperately wanted a whopper of a gratuity, she held back.

"Yeah, the mountains are really something," she said as she extricated her hand and flicked a glance toward Copper seated across the diner with some of his brothers.

Oh boy.

Someone was not a fan of the attention the suit was bestowing on her. Shell bit her lower lip to keep from giggling at the glower on the big biker's face.

"I'm gonna charge him if he snaps that fork in half." Toni's voice reminded Shell she was far from alone and gawking at the man she'd recently slept with. Probably drooling too. As discretely as possible, she ran her thumb along her chin.

Dry.

Phew.

"What are you talking about?"

Toni snorted. "Don't even try to play me, girl. I'm talking about what I was talking about before that poor businessman signed his own death warrant. You have been sneaking these slobbering puppy dog glances at Copper all morning."

If someone touched Shell's face at that moment, they'd come away with a third-degree burn. "What?" she said in the most unconvincing expression of shock ever. "You're crazy. They're in my section. Of course, I'm looking at their table. It's part of my job."

"Ha!" Toni shook her head and grabbed Shell's arm, towing her to a quieter spot behind the counter. "Nice try, sister. Now, usually, you look at Copper about three thousand times when he's in here—"

Shell rolled her eyes as her face grew even hotter. "I do not!"

"But today it's been about four hundred and thirty-seven thousand. And, he's stared at you just as much."

"I—" *Huh. Really?*

Copper

Toni nodded. "But his expression is different. More like a shark. All sharp teeth and hungry eyes. So…there something you wanna tell me?"

Yes. Yes, there was. She longed to tell someone she'd slept with the man she was head over heels in love with and had no clue how she was going to walk away from him. Especially since he seemed to want more from her than sex. Figures, when she was actually in a position to engage in a strictly physical relationship, the man wanted more.

"Nope. Nothing to tell."

"Bullsh—"

"I'm serious, Toni," Shell said, hardening her tone. "Just let it go, there's nothing to tell."

"Hmm," Toni said, but she relaxed her stance and released Shell's arm. "All right. You win, for now." She pointed a finger in Shell's face.

"I gotta check on my tables." Shell grabbed the coffee pot and spun around only to encounter the playful grin of the businessman. He wiggled his empty cup. Jesus, the guy sure liked his caffeine. After pouring him his third cup in twenty minutes, she dodged a few flirty comments and made the rounds of her tables.

When she reached the Handlers table, Mav said, "'Bout time, coffee wench. My blood is only one-tenth caffeine at the moment. You know I can't function unless I'm at the thirty-three percent mark. Unless we're talking about making my woman scream my name. That I can pretty much do in my sleep."

Shell rolled her eyes and poured Mav's coffee. Having known him for years, his constant barrage of inappropriate yet hilarious comments was expected. It'd only gotten worse since he'd started seriously seeing Stephanie. Now, instead of bragging about his many conquests, he boasted about having the most satisfied woman in Tennessee. Judging by the permanent smile on Steph's face, he may be right. Not that she'd ever admit it out loud. There was only so much ego she could tolerate.

"Really, Mav? Because yesterday Steph was telling me about this new vibrator she got. Said it was better than any man she'd ever been with." Shell shrugged innocently and gave the rest of her family seconds on the java.

"What?" Mav's jaw dropped to the ground. Maybe most groups of mix-company friends didn't joke about vibrators and sex all the time, but with the MC, pretty much nothing was off limits. The guys were raw, dirty, and very rough around the edges.

Just how she loved them.

"Bullshit. You're making that up." Mav dug his phone from his pocket as Copper, Jigsaw, and one of the prospects LJ cracked up. "She's not answering. Why isn't she answering?"

"Didn't she have a hair appointment this morning?" Shell asked. "At least that's what she told you. Probably spending time with her new toy."

"Fuck." Maverick scowled at her. "Sleep with one eye open, Shell."

LJ dropped his oven mitt-sized hand on Shell's shoulder and gave it a bone-crushing squeeze. Sometimes these huge men didn't recognize their immense power. "Damn, girl. That was good. He'll be tied up in knots all fucking day."

A growl came from directly across the table. All three men and Shell gaped at Copper. His gaze was glued to LJ's hand on her, and if Shell wasn't mistaken, LJ wouldn't need to bother saving for retirement. He'd be lucky to make it to the parking lot. Immediately, as though her shoulder was made of corrosive acid, his hand fell to the table.

Shell cleared her throat. "Um, anyone need anything else?" she asked, extra chipper.

Jig and Mav still stared at Copper, who hadn't stopped murdering LJ with his bullet-firing glare.

"Another pancake?" she asked weakly.

LJ squirmed like a kid sitting before a prune-faced principal. "Hey, Copper, I'm sorry, man. Meant no disrespect."

Copper

Seriously? He was apologizing for an innocent touch? The same kind of contact every single man in the MC gave her all the time. Friendly. Affectionate. Sisterly. Completely non-sexual.

Surely Copper wasn't about to make the poor twenty-one-year-old prospect pay for something so innocent.

"No worries, LJ."

"Thanks, Prez."

Phew. Bullet dodged.

"Hey, LJ," Copper went on. "Been a while since I washed my bike. Thinking when we get back to the clubhouse, you need to get on that."

"Oh, uh, yeah, Prez. For sure." LJ flicked a look at Shell then focused back on Copper.

"Thinking the guys on my exec board could use the same treatment." Copper hadn't so much as cracked a smile, but Jig and freakin' Mav were grinning like a bunch of creepy circus clowns. The assholes were loving this.

"Copper," Shell whispered. "It's forty degrees today." Usually, in their area, March was pleasantly in the sixties, but this past week had been chillier than the norm. Poor LJ's hands would freeze off if he had to wash six bikes outside.

"Ain't a thing, Shell," LJ said. "Happy to do it."

She frowned as guilt wormed its way in. Somehow, even though she hadn't done anything, this felt like her fault.

Copper turned his gaze on her and his entire expression transformed. Soft lines, no more death rays shooting from his eyes. In fact, a grin even peeked out from his bearded face. Shell swallowed as lust warmed her belly. Over the past year, she'd gotten used to hard, almost impatient looks from Copper. As though everything she did pissed him off to some extent.

None of that look remained.

"Uhh, why you staring at her like that, Prez?" Mav asked. When Copper didn't turn away but raised an eyebrow, Mav said, "You not get enough for breakfast, boss? Cuz I'm kinda getting the impression you're gonna hop up and eat our girl."

Copper just flipped him off, making Shell laugh.

"Stop it, Cop. It's freaking me out."

It was freaking her out too, but not in the way Mav meant. For the life of her, she couldn't tear her gaze away from Copper's piercing green stare. The coffee pot hung limply from her hand, in grave danger of crashing to the floor.

Seconds ticked by. Aware that she had tables waiting on food, and that Copper's men were watching them like they paid for the show, she tried to untangle herself from the web that was Copper.

Useless effort.

"Fuck it," Copper said as he sprung out of the booth. He loomed over her, grabbing the coffee put and thrusting it at Mav. "Take this."

"Uhh," Mav said, for once without a snappy quip.

With the bulky form of Copper hovering over her, Shell felt like a small animal about to be devoured. "Wha—" she started only to be silenced by the delicious slide of Copper's tongue into her mouth.

Customers? *What?*

Orders waiting in the kitchen? *Huh?*

Friends and family gawking at the display? *Uhhh...*

Her mind went berserk as he kissed her until her knees weakened and her body sparked like a live wire in a puddle of water. Hands at her lower back, he held her close and made it known to the general public, in no uncertain terms that something was going on between them.

After who the hell knew how long, he pulled back. Shell grabbed his forearms to keep from swooning like some Victorian maiden. When she turned her dazed gaze up to Copper, he was focused on something over her head, a smug, satisfied smile on his face.

The businessman. Holy shit...this had been purposeful. A public claiming.

Copper

"Holy shit, I freaking knew it!" Toni shouted from somewhere across the diner, probably still behind the counter. Shell was too stunned and slightly embarrassed to check out the reaction of the Handlers still seated at the table next to her. Turned out, she didn't have to see them to know what they thought. They started loudly cheering and yelling all sorts of Mav-style comments.

Finally, Copper turned his attention to her. Completely captivated by his gaze, she allowed herself to be caught up in him. This man had complete and utter control over her. Mind, body, and soul, he owned her in a way she'd always dreamed of. In a perfect world, she'd snatch up every ounce of what he was offering.

"Not sorry," he said, making her smile so wide her cheeks hurt. "Guess it's official now."

Toni had to be busting out of her skin behind the counter, waiting to assault Shell with a million questions.

"Damn!" Mav yelled. "'Knew I shoulda gone upstairs yesterday when you came by the clubhouse. Bet the soundtrack was pretty fucking great, huh?"

Just as she was about to bury her heated face in his wide chest the bell over the entrance jangled with the entry of a new customer.

Copper's entire body stiffened, right before he let out a tremendous whoop. "Holy fucking shit. Rusty? Jesus, guys, it's fucking Rusty!"

Starting at the tip of Shell's head, an icy wave of terror rippled down her body. She was frozen, unable to move, unable to breathe, unable to think beyond the fear. Copper grabbed her shoulders, gave her a quick hard kiss then smiled the most genuinely elated smile she'd ever seen from him right before running over to his brother.

Of course, he did. His brother was out of prison even earlier than expected. Five weeks early to be exact. Five weeks Shell was supposed to have with Copper. Thirty-five days to come up with a plan and figure out her next life move.

And now that was all gone.

She managed to get her legs to turn her in a circle in time to see Copper and Rusty collide in a giant engulfing hug. Slapping each other's backs, they spoke of how amazing it was to be in the same room.

Rusty almost had the height of Copper; he was about six-three to Copper's six-five, but maybe half of the muscle mass. Prison had bulked him up some, but he still didn't match his big brother in size. But the hair? Same red, though Rusty was close-cropped and naked-faced.

The guys vacated their booth, and all joined in the ecstatic reunion. Rooted in her spot next to the Handlers' booth, Shell watched in fascinated horror as her nightmare came to life.

A few seconds into the men back-slapping and ribbing each other, Toni joined her. "You all right, girl? Looking a little pale."

"I—" It came out as a strangled whisper. She cleared her throat. "I'm good." Better. Stronger.

Faker.

"You know this Rusty character well? I've heard some mixed things about him. Izzy told me Jig isn't a huge fan."

Huh, that was news to Shell. Most of the guys loved him as far as she knew. "Yeah, I know him. Knew him, I guess."

Copper and Rusty hugged again. With Copper's back to her, she got a full-on view of Rusty's face. His gaze, so cold and missing what she'd always thought of as the human factor locked with hers. Then he winked.

The bastard fucking winked at her.

If it wasn't for the violent lurch in her stomach, her knees would have given out. But seeing as how she needed a basin, and fast, she was able to move. Shell slapped a palm over her mouth as the cereal she'd eaten came dangerously close to spewing all over the diner. Quick as she could, she sprinted toward the restroom. Once in front of the toilet, she sank to her knees and threw up anything she'd eaten over the past week. Thankfully, Toni was anal about the cleanliness of her diner's restrooms, so that was one less thing Shell had to worry about. She had enough problems on her plate.

Her stomach heaved over and over until she expelled nothing but bile and stomach acid. Everything ached, her abdominal muscles, her head, her knees on the hard tile, but most of all her heart. It was going to break. There was no way around it. At some point in the upcoming days, her heart would shatter into pieces so small she might never be able to repair it. She only hoped the same didn't happen to Copper.

"Honey?" Toni appeared at the open stall. "You all right?"

"Um…I think so," Shell said in a trembling voice. "Just gross."

"If it were anyone else, I'd assumed you were knocked up, but seeing as how you were fine until Rusty winked one of those creepy eyes at you, I'm guessing you're not."

Pregnant. Funny. She'd been one of the lucky ones who didn't throw up once throughout her pregnancy. Now, four years later it turned out that same pregnancy was making her vomit. "Not pregnant." She flopped on her ass and rested her back against the wall of the stall, looking up at Toni's concerned face.

"He do something to you in the past?" Toni asked. She sank down onto the floor opposite Shell.

Suddenly, she had to say it. Had to get the words out. Never once had they crossed her lips, but if she didn't say it, she was going to self-destruct. Rusty's appearance was just too much.

"He—" Memories she worked every single day of her life to forget bombarded her. Rusty's hands, Rusty's mouth, Rusty's threats.

Rusty's hatred of his brother.

"He's Beth's father."

Toni's face blanched as her eyes bugged. The shock was expected, and unfortunately, so was the doubt reflected in her eyes.

Doubt over who Shell was as a person. The thoughts running through Toni's head were so loud, they were screaming in Shell's own brain.

Did you do it to punish Copper?
Do you have feelings for Rusty?
Do either Copper or Rusty know?
How could you?

The foot of physical distance separating them might as well have been an ocean. Girlfriends were so important, especially since the majority of her tribe consisted of overbearing macho bikers. Girlfriends kept her sane, balanced.

Even though she'd been anticipating suspicion from Toni, actually witnessing it was a punch to the gut.

"Please," she whispered. "I'm not ready to talk about it. I can't talk about it. But please, please believe me. It's not what you're thinking."

CHAPTER TWELVE

"Feel like I'm fucking dreaming," Copper said as he knocked back the last of his whiskey. Nowadays, he wasn't much of a day drinker. In his early years with the MC, he'd drink most of his brothers under the table, but at forty, the accompanying hangover from twelve-plus hours of drinking sucked. But for Rusty's homecoming, he'd make all the fucking exceptions in the world.

"Imagine how I fucking feel." Rusty sipped his whiskey. His eyes closed and his throat worked before he let out a sigh. "Damn, first drink in five years. Thanks for breaking out the good shit for me."

Copper snorted. "No better reason for it." Had to be a total mind fuck, being behind bars one day and free to live life the next. "You holding up okay? You look good."

After another sip, Rusty nodded. "Yeah, brother. Any day out of that hellhole is a good day. Got a lot of shit to sort out, but it's all good."

The rest of the guys had made themselves scarce, letting Copper and Rusty have some time to catch up. Seated at the bar in the clubhouse, they'd broken into the stash of Copper's favorite whiskey he kept hidden in his bottom desk drawer.

"Well, no one has used your old room since you left. We kept it ready and waiting for you, so you don't need to bother looking for a place to live."

"Thanks, brother. I was hoping you'd say that."

He hadn't been lying. Rusty did look good. Better than Copper had expected. "You work out a lot in there? Looks like you put on a shit-ton of muscle."

Rusty poured more whiskey into his glass. "Yeah. Hours every day. Not much else to do. Spending time in the yard beats hanging in the cell."

Copper grunted.

"You should talk to Zach. Bet he'd love to have you on board. I know he's looking to hire."

"Shit, Cop, been out for ten fucking minutes. Give me a few days. Last five years I've been on my best fuckin' behavior. Need to spend a few days making trouble. Work ain't on my radar today. Pussy is. Where the fuck are the Honeys?"

Copper almost pushed it, but Rusty was right. He had nothing to compare the experience to, so he couldn't pretend to understand what his brother was feeling. But if he had to guess, Rusty probably needed some time to get his head on straight. Having taken care of Rusty the majority of his life, Copper sometimes forgot his brother was an adult.

"Around. Had you told us you were coming early, we'd have planned a fuckin' blowout for tonight."

Rusty smirked. "Yeah, but your surprised face was fucking worth it."

"Definitely was the surprise of a lifetime. Party'll be Saturday night. Going all out for you, brother."

"Fuck yes!" Rusty filled his glass again.

Two p.m. and Rusty drank seventy dollars' worth of whiskey in fifteen minutes. And there Copper went acting like a father instead of a brother again. The man just spent five years behind bars. He was entitled to drink it all away.

"Ready for more?" Rusty held the bottle toward Copper.

"Nah, brother, I'm good. Gotta head over to Shell's in a bit. She was acting weird before we left the diner. Want to make sure she's not sick."

Copper

A slow smile curled Rusty's face. A predatory kind of leering grin. "You tapping that? That bitch always had one hell of a rack. She's been creaming herself over you for years too, bro."

Rolling his shoulders, Copper resisted the sudden and furious urge to wrap his fingers around Rusty's throat. Though he'd always been a little hard for some to take, Rusty hadn't spoken about women, at least the important ones in his life that way. Then again, back then he hadn't spent five years without female company, surrounded by hardened criminals.

"Ain't like that."

"No? You telling me you ain't fuckin' her? If you're not, maybe I'll take her for a spin."

Copper leveled him with a stare that typically had his men running to obey his orders.

With a laugh, Rusty lifted his hands in surrender. "My bad. I can wait. Just send her my way when you've worn through her. Though if her snatch is all used up by then, I'll probably pass."

Jesus Christ. Every ounce of strength Copper had went toward keeping his fists balled at his sides instead of smashing his brother's face. This better just be post-prison tension relief because it would be the one and only time Copper would listen to Rusty speak of Shell that way.

"She's not a fuckin' Honey, Rusty. She's family to the club and is treated as such. Don't forget that shit."

Laughter had Copper bristling. "Seriously, Cop? *She's family and should be treated as such,*" he said in a mock-Copper voice. More whiskey flowed out of the bottle and into Rusty's glass. "Good thing I'm back here to set you straight. Sounds like you grew a fuckin' pussy while I was gone."

"Didn't grow a pussy. Just got fucking old. Chasing a different set of tits every night loses its appeal, baby brother."

"So, what? You and Shell playing house or some shit? Gonna put a ring on it?"

Talking about whatever was going on between him and Shell wasn't at the top of his priority list. Didn't seem right to discuss the relationship with his brother when he didn't have a clue himself what was happening between them. Nothing should be happening, yet there he was kissing her senseless in the middle of the diner all because some slick suit made a play for her. "Don't know. Still new. She's important, though," he said, his tone making it clear it was an order, not a statement. "She and her daughter both."

The glass froze halfway to Rusty's lips. Having not had any alcohol for five years, his eyes were already glassy. "She's got a kid?"

"Oh, shit, yeah, guess you wouldn't even know about that. Got knocked up right after she left here for college. It messed up her plans, and she never finished her degree. Stayed in New York until about a year ago when she came back to be near family."

"Huh." Rusty resumed drinking but stared at the back of the bar, rubbing a hand over his chin. He may not have the beard Copper did, but the height, red hair, and chin-stroke let everyone know they were blood.

Talking about Shell had him itching to see her. Seemed like days instead of hours ago that he'd woken in her bed, curled around her softness warmed by sleep and the heat of his body. Now that he'd had her, the need for more coursed through his veins like a drug. They weren't going to be a sex once-a-week kind of couple. No fucking way.

At this point, once a day wouldn't even be enough. Might make him the worst brother in the universe, but he couldn't wait for Rusty to head on up to his room to get settled.

Copper needed his woman.

Shit.

He was off his fucking rocker, thinking of them as a couple. They couldn't be a couple. Technically speaking, he was old enough to be her father. But the seal was broken. He'd fucked her, multiple times, and wasn't willing to give that up.

Who was he kidding? It was more than sex, and he knew it.

Copper

He was fucked.

"Pass me that bottle, brother."

"HERE." IZZY SLID a juice glass filled to the brim with bourbon across the table. "Drink up, Shell."

Leave it to Izzy to come packing bourbon. "Seriously? It's three in the afternoon on a Thursday, and my child is coloring fifteen feet away. What the hell are you doing with this anyway? You're pregnant." Shell lowered her voice. Even though Toni was the only other person still in the diner, Shell didn't know if Izzy had revealed her news to anyone else yet.

"You don't need to whisper. Toni knows I'm knocked up. So does Steph. Jig hasn't told the dudes yet. And the bourbon's not for me. Toni called and asked me to grab Beth from preschool. When I asked if you were okay, she said shit from your past was blowing up. If that doesn't call for bourbon, nothing does."

"Don't start without me, bitches," Toni announced as she emerged from the kitchen with a giant basket of French fries. "Here." She tossed the basket on the table. "To soak up the booze."

Beth was happily coloring pictures for her aunties while munching on a grilled cheese sandwich Ernesto whipped up before he took off for the day. After Shell's freak out in the bathroom, Toni let her finish out her shift, but called Izzy because, as she said, "Izzy is a badass bitch who rocks in a crisis."

Not a soul knew the identity of Beth's father. Until a few hours ago. The birth certificate was blank. Hell, even her mother was clueless. Everyone assumed she fucked the first man who reminded her of Copper in some lonely and lovesick desperation. Had the truth not been far worse, she'd have been insulted by their assumptions.

But seeing as how what really happened had her in therapy for two years, she let them have their false impression.

"So, what's going on?" Izzy asked as she popped a fry in her mouth. The twenty-ounce bottle of ginger ale she was never without these past few days rested on the table in front of her. "This have anything to do with Rusty getting out of prison early? Jig called me when he left here earlier. Everyone seems psyched about it, but I gotta say, my man is not his biggest fan."

Both Toni and Izzy looked to Shell. Since she'd grown up around the club, all explanations of past goings on fell to her. But this wasn't something she really had any insider information on. She shrugged. "Not sure if something actually happened between them or if they've just always rubbed each other the wrong way. It's not like Jig is a font of information regarding his feelings on any subject."

"Hmm." Izzy played with the tail of her long braid. "I'll have to grill him about it. I have my ways of getting pretty much anything out of him," she said with a wink.

Toni laughed. "I'm sure you do, girl. But we're getting off topic. We're here to talk about Shell."

Well, damn, for a hot second, she thought maybe they'd forget about her. No such luck.

The table fell silent. Having said the words once already that day, she wasn't sure she could get them to pass her lips a second time. An invisible fist wrapped itself around Shell's windpipe making her suck air in restricted gasps. Memories of a time best forgotten bombarded her. Of a decision she made during impossible circumstances. Dropping her head to her hands, she tried to control her breathing.

"Shit!" Izzy said. "Whatever it is, Shell, we'll help you through it."

A gentle hand landed on her back, rubbing soothing circles over her spine. Within a minute, her breaths came easier and her mind cleared.

"Want me to say the words for you?" Toni whispered near her ear.

With her face still hidden, Shell nodded.

Copper

"All right." Toni's hand never stopped moving. "This afternoon, Shell told me that Rusty is Beth's father." The words were spoken low enough Beth would never overhear.

The diner grew quiet except for the repetitive swooshing of Beth's crayon over the paper. Then Izzy said, "Well, shit, give me that fucking bottle."

"Izzy!" Toni shrieked. "You're pregnant. You know you can't drink that."

"I'm not gonna drink it. I'm just gonna hold the bottle. You can't tell me news like that and not expect me to lean on my buddy bourbon. Hello, sweet baby," she said to the bottle. "One day we'll be together again."

Shell giggled into her hands. Beside her, Toni snickered as well. After a few seconds, Shell's giggle grew into a full-out belly laugh. She threw back her head and just let the hilarity happen. Izzy's comment hadn't been that funny, but something had to crack the tension and laughter was so much better than the tears threatening to burst free. The other two joined in and they hooted together until Beth looked up from her project and said, "What's so funny?"

"Nothing, baby," Shell answered wiping tears from her eyes. "You making us pretty pictures?"

But Beth was already back in the zone and didn't answer.

"Shit," Izzy said. She set down the booze. "I'm guessing this isn't something Copper is aware of."

"No. It's not. Rusty either. Actually, you two are the only people I've ever told. And if either of you tell—"

"Hey," Toni said motioning to Izzy for the bottle. "Girl code. It's in the vault."

"Thank you. I hate asking you to keep something from your men, but I just can't have them all knowing. Not yet."

"You don't have to worry about it." Izzy reached across the table and squeezed Shell's hand. "Like Toni said, girl code." Grabbing a fistful of fries, she asked, "Did you guys date?"

"No!" Her answer was immediate and so strong, both women jumped, then shared a concerned glance. "Uh, sorry, no we didn't date. Have never dated."

"So, a drunken night of fun at the clubhouse followed by a terrible mistake of a one-night stand?" Izzy asked with her mouth full of crispy potato goodness.

Shell dropped a fry midway to her mouth. She couldn't have swallowed it if her life depended on it. Showed just how bad the situation really was that she wished she'd done what Izzy predicted. "No."

"Did, um…" Toni wrung her hands. "Did he rape you?"

And there was the question that drove her to therapy even before Beth was born. For months after Rusty went to prison, Shell struggled with guilt, heartache, and shame so severe she couldn't eat, couldn't sleep, and had a difficult time making it through her basic daily tasks. Once she saw the tiny swell of her pregnant belly pop out, she knew she needed to get her head on straight. Protecting her daughter was the most important thing, and she couldn't do that if she couldn't take care of herself.

"It's more complicated than that," Shell said, tearing shreds off a napkin. "I made the choice to sleep with him, and I own that, but it wasn't because I wanted him or wanted to be with him. There were…circumstances that led me to feel I really had no choice."

The decision to sleep with Rusty was something that caused her so much anguish and guilt over the years. Because she had *chosen* to sleep with Rusty. She never fought him, never told him no, basically let him do whatever he wanted to her. But it had been a choice made under extreme duress. He'd given her two options, and the bitch of it was, she'd picked the lesser of two evils.

Suddenly her skin prickled, and she rubbed her arms, the memories of Rusty's touch like an irritating rash. The realization of what she'd just confessed crashed down around her. Oh, God, people knew her secret. The need to curl into a ball and hide her face slammed into her. "I have to go."

Toni's arm came around her shoulders. "Hold on, let's talk a little more. If Beth gets cranky, I'll just make her a milkshake."

"No, I mean leave." She shook her head. "Leave town. Move somewhere else."

Toni gasped, letting her arm fall. "No, Shell, you can't. You tried that once, and it didn't work. You were away for years and came back because this is your home. You belong here."

Shell hung her head as the weight of the world settled on her shoulders. "I came back here thinking I'd have years before Rusty was even eligible to get out. And now…it's just too risky for us to stay here." Glancing up, she took in her friend's open-mouthed stare.

"But…" Toni looked so stricken Shell wanted to hug her. "But you and Copper are just starting something. Think about Copper. You can't leave now."

The laugh that left Shell's lips wasn't one of humor. "Trust me, I am thinking of Copper. I'm always thinking of Copper. This news would destroy him. He'd kill Rusty, and then where would we be? Certainly not living happily ever after in a little ranch with a white picket fence."

"But—" Toni started.

"Okay, hold up," Izzy said, lifting her hands. "Let's all take a breath for a moment—wait, did you just say she got with Copper?"

Shell nodded, her face heating. God, she wanted to stay if for no other reason than to explore this thing with Copper. But life didn't always give you what you wanted. That was for damn sure.

"Shit, girls, I missed everything this morning. Damn job, getting in the way of my juicy gossip." Izzy waved her hand in front of her face. "I digress. Look, Shell, you don't need to give us any details. The details don't matter, and you don't owe them to us. We'll support you no matter what you decide. But you do owe them to Copper. And at some point, it's going to come out. Even if you leave. It's not as though Rusty won't find out you're a mother. And he might be a motherfucker, but I'm sure he's smart enough to add two plus two. Or one plus one in this case."

All good points. But if she and Beth were far away, Rusty couldn't blackmail her. Couldn't lord Copper over her head. Couldn't torture her as he'd done in the past. Couldn't make her...

Shit, she shuddered. Would he try to get her back into his bed? The fries she'd eaten sat in her stomach like clay brick.

"Even if you run, what's to say he won't use whatever hold he has on you to get you to come back again? Once an asshole always an asshole. If he's going to do something, you moving might not make a difference."

Well, shit. Izzy sure knew how to take a bad situation and cover it in mud. But she had a point. A valid point. Rusty wasn't above blackmailing her to return home with Beth. "Fuck," Shell whispered.

"I have an idea. Let's give it a few weeks. See how things are going to play out. For the past five years, Rusty's been in prison. I have a feeling the only thing on his mind is tearing through the Honeys and drinking himself stupid. Take that time to get your head on straight. Come up with a plan. You're going to have to tell Copper at some point." Izzy uncapped her ginger ale and took a small sip.

When Izzy said it, the idea of talking with Copper sounded so feasible. But then, Shell hadn't told her friends the entire story. Copper's devastated reaction was only one of the issues she'd be dealing with. Still, it appeared her reprieve was up, and she'd have no choice but to tell him soon.

"I think it's a good plan. Don't make any rash decisions, Shell. And when the time comes that you're ready to tell Copper, we'll have your back. I promise we'll stand with you." Toni placed a hand over Shell's.

"Absofuckinglutely," Izzy said.

Copper

A lump formed in Shell's throat. "If it comes down to it, you have to remain loyal to the club. To your men."

"You are the club, Shell." Toni put her arms around Shell's shoulders. "I refuse to believe anyone would make us choose. Besides, we're sisters as much as the guys are brothers. Never forget that."

"And," Izzy said with a shrug. "Jig already thinks Rusty is a fuckwad. He'd never side with him over you."

For the first time since the day she sat naked on her bathroom floor staring at a positive pregnancy test, the warmth of having someone in her corner eroded the icy blanket of loneliness she wore daily. She had friends, she had support, she had women who believed her and believed in her without even knowing the full story. Based solely on the power of her character.

Maybe, just maybe, there was a way to come out of this without new wounds on her heart.

But could she say the same for Copper?

CHAPTER THIRTEEN

Shell was pulling away. She'd tried a hundred flimsy excuses to get out of coming to Rusty's party. Copper had shot down every one with ease, but even after agreeing to attend, she seemed reluctant.

Shit, maybe all she'd ever wanted from him was a half dozen or so orgasms. Nothing more. For years, his brothers ragged on him, telling him she wasn't only hot for his dick, but head over heels in love with him, too.

Could they have been wrong? Was she satisfied now that he'd scratched her itch?

No. That was bullshit. She hadn't been with a man in the year she'd been back. Might make him a stalker, but he was positive no one had touched her. Shell wasn't the fuck for fucking's sake kind of woman.

She has a child, supposedly with a man she fucked to get you off her brain.

To be honest, Copper wasn't sure he believed that explanation. It was a little too pat. A little too easily wrapped up in a bow. Too out of character for the Shell he knew. Plus, it didn't explain why Beth's father was entirely out of the picture and Shell all but refused to speak of him. No, there was something else to the story. Something painful. Every time he thought of it, his gut churned, alerting him something was off. Over the years, he'd learned to trust his gut above all.

Copper

And someday, he was going to get the story out of her.

Of course, he'd have to get her to stop refusing him first. Over the past three days, she'd come up with bullshit reasons to avoid spending time alone with him. Not what he'd expected after she'd blown his mind Wednesday afternoon.

He was an idiot. Instead of complaining, he should be looking at her hesitancy as a gift from God. An easy out. Couple of hot fucks then done. Wasn't that the perfect scenario? He wouldn't have to extricate himself from the situation. He should jump on that train and get back to the way things were. He'd been tossing out reasons to stay away from her for years, yet he couldn't just walk away.

Shell had secrets. Another reason to let this fizzle out. But he just couldn't walk away. Though it didn't seem to be a problem for her. The cold shoulder was pissing him the fuck off.

Especially right then when she looked like a combination of an angel and a biker's wet dream. Rusty's welcome home party was in full swing, and unlike Copper's recent birthday event, this one was planned by the guys. That meant many, many, wasted women in barely-there clothing, brothers in various stages of fucking both behind closed doors and out in the open, and enough booze to float the entire clubhouse.

During church on Thursday, some of the single guys, Rusty included, had pleaded with him to ban ol' ladies from the party. That earned Copper some seriously pissed off glares from the men who were shackled. Back in the day, it wasn't uncommon for the club to have a party the ol' ladies weren't invited to. But back then, more of the men were unshackled. A lot had changed since Rusty'd last been around, namely the number of men in monogamous relationships.

In the end, he'd done the only fair thing and put it to a vote. But he'd be lying if he said he was relieved the result swung in favor of the ol' ladies being present. He wanted, needed to spend the time with Shell. He hadn't made any official claim on Shell, so even if the club had voted against ol' ladies attendance, Shell would still be invited, but he knew her, and she'd never show up without her girl posse.

Rusty sat at the bar, drink in one hand, a Honey's ass in the other, and his face planted in the tits of yet another Honey who stood between his legs. He certainly wasn't looking to be entertained by Copper right then. That meant Copper was free to corner Shell and put an end to her evasive behaviors.

She stood with the girls, beer in hand, laughing at something Stephanie said. As usual, she was boner-inspiring in tight black pants, knee-high black boots, and a skimpy red top that hugged her every curve and made his mouth water for her tits.

"Hey, gorgeous," he whispered in her ear as he came up behind her.

With a gasp, she started then spun around so fast, she needed to plant her hands on his chest to keep from falling.

"You trying to get close to me, babe?" he asked as her face turned an adorable shade of pink.

She cast a glance at the girls who were all gaping at him as though he had spiders crawling out of his head. "What?" he asked. While he waited for an answer, he turned Shell and snuggled her back against his stomach. She stiffened at first then melted into him. One of his large hands rested on her low belly. The strip of skin just beneath the hem of her shirt was too tempting to resist, and he strummed his fingers along her skin, eliciting a gentle shiver from her.

"You...well, you..." Stephanie pointed to him then shrugged. "I got nothin'."

Izzy, never afraid of speaking her mind, piped up. "We've never seen you like this. You're usually the gruff, slightly grumpy—no offense—MC president. Tonight, your all...cute and shit."

Copper let out a rough chuckle while Shell giggled. Hell, if Izzy's teasing made her laugh, he'd take the ribbing all day long. "Cute and shit, huh? Rusty accused me of growing a pussy."

Copper

At the mention of his brother, Izzy and Toni shared a look Copper couldn't decipher, but it certainly wasn't favorable. He made a mental note to ask Shell what the deal was later. Those girls were as tight as he and his brother. She'd know what was up.

"Gonna steal her for a bit," he said trying to keep a straight face. Shell would be frowning for sure. She wasn't much on being told what to do, especially in front of her girls. Well too fucking bad. He'd allowed her to put him off for three days.

That shit ended now.

"You bet," Stephanie said. The smile on her face was so big it almost looked fake. Jesus, was his love life really that fascinating? "Take her for as long as you want. You can even keep her if you'd like."

"Stephanie," Shell said in a harsh whisper.

"What?" The innocent look wasn't fooling anyone. That girl spent too much damn time with Maverick.

"Come on," he said, dropping an arm across Shell's shoulders. She shot him a scowl, but it only made him chuckle. Probably wouldn't do to tell her she was damn adorable when pissed.

Copper led her to a square table along the right wall of the clubhouse. Basically, it was his table. Anyone who'd been to the clubhouse knew to keep their asses out of his spot unless invited. It was also the table he'd sat at with Shell during his birthday party last week, or so he was told. Those memories never fully resurfaced. He sank onto the bench seat along the wall then pulled a slightly resistant Shell onto his lap.

"What are you doing, Copper?" She wiggled, trying to scoot off him, but it only served to grow him from half chub to full hard-on.

"Relax, babe," he said, settling her against him.

They had a tiny bit of privacy. At least there weren't' bodies jammed in around his table like they were on the dance floor.

"But everyone will see us. Even the Honeys. What if…"

Copper let out a loud laugh. "What if what? You think I give a shit what the Honeys think?"

Her head slowly moved from side to side, body still rigid in his hold. "Well no, but you're the president. You get first pick and all."

Seriously? Was she crazy? Maybe she was fishing? Probably not. Shell wasn't one to play games for compliments. "Babe, I have no interest in any of the Honeys. Haven't for years. You think I'd rather have one of them on my lap?"

"Well," she began.

"I wouldn't," he said against her ear. "The woman on my lap is loyal, hard-working, sweet, gorgeous as fuck, and an amazing mother. She loves my club almost as much as I do and understands this world far better than any of those skanks ever could. Plus, I've never felt anything as good as her pussy wringing my cock dry. So, no, babe, I don't give a fuck what the Honeys or anyone else thinks. You're right where I want you."

"Oh," she squeaked, making him chuckle.

"The guys told me I sat here for a while with you on my birthday. Said we were all cozy. That I couldn't keep my hands off you. You were on my lap, I was nuzzling your neck." As he spoke, he brushed his nose against the slope of her neck then followed it up with a nip.

The tiny moan from Shell was music to his ears. Victory. As was the way she tilted her head and allowed him greater access. Her small fingers curled around the forearm banded across her hips. Touch was the perfect weapon to knock down her walls. She might be able to turn him away when he spoke to her, resisting when his hands were on her was another story.

"You told me nothing happened that night. Said we just chatted and you gave me a birthday hug. You keeping things from me, Shell?" He caught her earlobe between his teeth and tugged before sucking it into his mouth.

Shell's blunt fingernails dug into his skin. "N-nothing did happen. We just talked."

Copper

"Sounds like I couldn't keep my hands off you." He slipped a hand under her shirt, resting his palm on the soft, warm expanse of her belly. It'd be so easy to wander down just a few inches. Dive his fingers into her panties and find out if she was as slick as he was hard. But they were far from alone. Half of these men might get off on, or at least not give a shit about getting down and dirty in public, but Copper would be damned if even one of these jokers got so much as a glimpse of Shell drowning in ecstasy.

No, he was a possessive motherfucker, and Shell's pleasure was for him and him alone. "Did you like it. My hands all over you? You get wet for me that night?"

"Yes." Her eyes were closed, head resting on his shoulder.

"You go home and touch that pretty pussy thinking of me?" The dirtier his words got, the shallower her pants grew.

"Y-yes."

Copper lifted her hand and kissed the tips of her fingers. "You shove a few of these fingers in that wet pussy imagining they were mine? Or did you use a vibrator, wishing it was just a little thicker so it'd be more like my cock?"

She whimpered. "Copper..." Tension was building. He could feel her need growing. Soon she'd be desperate for more than one hand on her stomach and his other holding hers. But he'd make her wait. If he could make it when his cock was like a pissed off bull ready to charge, she could hold out as well.

"Tell me."

"I did...b-both."

He groaned at the mental image of her fingering herself then fucking her own pussy with a buzzing vibrator.

"You need to do something, Copper. Touch me. I can't stand it."

"This isn't the time or the place," he rasped. "And I'm not going to fuck you again until we set shit straight between us and there's no way I won't be fucking you tonight. So we're talking."

An adorable feminine growl left her. "Now?"

"Now. Turn around so I can see those baby blues."

After a second's hesitation, Shell wiggled around until she straddled his lap. He rested his hands on her ass and gave her his full attention. The rest of the crowd disappeared. The guys knew to give him and his woman space, even in the midst of a party. No one would interrupt them unless there was an emergency.

"What did you want to talk about?"

Like she didn't know. That was all right. They could play it her way. He wasn't going to beat around any fucking bushes so she'd know exactly what he had on his mind in about two point two seconds. "Want to know why you've been avoiding me since we fucked each other's brains out."

"What are—" Her eyes widened. Had she not realized he was on to her?

"Don't play dumb, babe. Not with me. I can read you like a book. You made up bullshit excuses not to see me the last two nights. I wanna know what gives."

She turned away for a moment, gazing at a few of his younger guys talking to a cluster of women he'd never seen. Tourists probably. Not uncommonly, groups of women visiting the Smokies for the weekend partied at the clubhouse. They'd be away on a girls' trip and looking to get a little wild. His brothers made sure they fulfilled that wish and more.

"I'm not sure what you want from me," she said still focused on the room. "You went from never touching me, not even a hug, to…Wednesday. It's a lot to take in."

Fair enough. He sighed then took her chin between his thumb and forefinger. With a gentle nudge, she was no more than a breath away. He kissed her. Soft at first, but their out-of-control chemistry didn't allow for softness, and the kiss soon grew wild and hungry. When he pulled back, Shell's eyes were glassy and her breaths stunted.

"I've wanted to do that since you were eighteen fucking years old. You wanna know how much time I spend around you hard and aching? Not sure I could even count as high as the number of times I've whacked off imagining you on your knees before me. Or dreaming of the taste of your pussy. Or the feel of you squeezing me as you came. Fucking years, Shell. Even when you lived in New York, I wasn't safe. One of the guys would tell me they spoke to you and *bam* I'd be fucking hard for days. Yeah, I never touched you, babe, but it wasn't because I didn't fucking want to."

Owl-eyed, Shell blinked. "So...what? Why did you stay away?"

"Stayed away because you're sixteen fucking years younger, baby. Stayed away because your pops made me fucking promise you wouldn't become an ol' lady. Stayed away because the shit I've done could catch up to me at any time. I'm the king of this castle, Shell. I'm the one any number of enemies would come for."

Gorgeous blue pools of emotion held his attention. Shell might be confused but those eyes didn't lie. She felt something for him, and it ran deep in her veins.

"And now?" she whispered.

With a chuckle, he slid his hand up her back until her curls were fisted in his hand. He held her head immobile then whispered against her lips. "I'm only a man, baby. You walked in my room, stripped off your clothes and taunted me with the sexiest body I've ever seen. You broke my resolve, and now you have to live with the consequences. And that's me, taking you, every chance I get."

Worry wormed its way into her gaze. There were still secrets buried in the ocean blue depths. Something causing her to hold back. As much as demanding answers and expecting his mandate followed was his style, it wouldn't work with his stubborn Shell. She'd close down. Waiting it out was the only option. Showing her she could trust in him, trust in what he offered her enough to one day open up.

Hopefully, before it destroyed whatever they were building. Because now that he'd had a taste of her, he wasn't sure he could survive without more.

"So you want a relationship with me?" Uncertainty tinged the words.

Moment of truth. Did he? Part of him was fully on board with that idea, but another part still screamed it was a mistake. The years between them. The club's enemies. So many reasons to walk away. But goddammit, he couldn't make his feet move.

"I want you, Shell. You and that beautiful daughter of yours. There's only one thing missing from my kingdom. One thing I need to make it complete."

"What?"

"A queen."

Happiness should have been radiating from her. In his mind, she'd thrown herself in his arms, and they'd attacked each other with the force of their need. In reality, she gazed at him with the kind of sadness that fed off a person's soul. Despair that ate away at a person until nothing remained but a rotting carcass. Whatever had a hold on Shell caused her severe anguish.

There it was, an itch at the back of his neck telling him to pull the plug. To be smart and think with his head instead of his dick.

Or fuck, his heart.

But all he wanted was to fix whatever had her eyes dimming. No matter what or how long it took. He'd fucking fix it.

"I'm not sure I can be that for you. Not sure I can give you what you want. There are things…" She curled her lips in and shook her head. Not able to give him the words yet.

"Shh." He cradled her face between his palms. "Just give me you for tonight. Then tomorrow, when you wake up, give me you again, for one more day. Then, the next day, we'll do it again. One day at a time until you realize you own me, and I will do anything to keep you safe, even battle your own secrets."

Copper

The blue of her eyes darkened as the tip of her pink tongue peeked out and swiped across her bottom lip. She pressed a hand to his chest, right over his hammering heart.

He had to taste her. Had to have her flavor burst through his system. Leaning in, he licked right under the angle of her jaw. There was a spot on her neck he'd discovered on Wednesday, right at the base where it gently dropped off to shoulder that turned her to putty in his hands. He kissed, then sucked on that spot. Instantly, her body went lax in his arms, and a mix between a hum and a moan crossed her glossy lips.

"Copper," she said, breathy and wanton. "I'd give you pretty much anything with you doing that to me."

He gave her the most wicked grin he could manage. "Fuckin' know it, gorgeous. Think I'm not above playing dirty? I'll do damn near anything to get between those silky thighs again. Take me home with you tonight." He inhaled as he ran his nose along her neck. Goddamn, the woman smelled heavenly. Something fruity tonight. Peach, maybe? Whatever it was, it only ramped up his desire to take a big juicy bite.

She groaned and tilted her head to the side, giving him better access. "Yes."

"What time do you have to pick up Beth?" He caught a tendon between his teeth making Shell cry out. She slapped a palm over her mouth.

Copper chuckled. "What time?"

"Uh, my mom is keeping her for the night. I'm picking her up after my diner shift tomorrow." She blinked as though trying to focus her thoughts.

Damn, for a second, he forgot she worked Sunday mornings. It'd be nice to spend half the day lounging around in bed. In time, he'd work toward convincing her to cut back her hours. Fuck, she wouldn't need to work at all, but that wasn't his Shell. His woman was independent, hardworking, and driven. "How'd you get her to agree to keep her so you could come here?"

There was no love lost between Shell's mom and the club. After her husband died, she cut all ties with the MC and tried to get Shell to do the same. Most of the time, she refused to help Shell with Beth if Shell was doing anything Handlers related.

Shell gave him a mischievous grin. "She doesn't know I'm here. She'd wanted Beth for the night, and we'd scheduled this weeks ago. Well before the party was planned."

"So, you're all mine for the night? And I can make you scream as loud as possible since there won't be a four-year-old in the next room?"

"Scream, huh? That's a pretty tall order. Sure you're up for the task, old man?"

He shifted his hips giving her a hard demonstration of just how much he needed her. "Yeah, babe, I'm *up* for it."

"Well then, what are we waiting for?"

He patted her ass. "Give me thirty minutes. Then we'll head out. Gotta speak to a few of the guys first."

Her eyes narrowed. "What? Thirty minutes? But...you're..." She sputtered and waved toward his crotch. "And now you've got me all hot and bothered." Her voice lowered to a notch above a whisper.

Copper threw back his head and laughed. "Anticipation, baby." After scooting Shell off his lap, he kissed her, then headed off to find Zach.

When he was about ten feet away, he turned to see Shell watching him, a hungry and mildly pissed off look on her face.

Damn, Zach had better talk fucking fast.

CHAPTER FOURTEEN

Well, what the hell am I supposed to do now?

Shell took in the atmosphere of the clubhouse. Tonight's party was electric. Bodies—had to be close to two hundred—packed the open space in front of the bar. Some danced, some drank, and quite a few were breaking in their nightly hook-up. She shifted as uncomfortable dampness between her legs made its presence known. Damn Copper for getting her all worked up. Now she was stuck in what could amount to a low budget porn movie with soaked panties and no outlet for her tension. At least not for another thirty minutes.

With a sigh, she wormed her way through the writhing couples with the bar as an end goal. Might as well drink the next half hour away.

"What can I get ya, darlin'?" one of the new prospects asked. Thunder was his name, and since he was brand-spankin' new, he got stuck with bartending the shittiest shifts. Explained why the poor guy was slinging drinks during the wildest party in ages.

"I'll take a gin and tonic, please, Thunder," she said. "And thanks." She always tried to be extra sweet to the prospects. Poor guys took so much shit from the patched members, she felt obligated to bring a little sunshine to their rainy days.

"Sure thang, sweets."

Shell studied him as he poured her drink. The guy was southern as they came. At least his accent was. Word among the ladies was Thunder was a stage nickname, and this guy had a day—or night—job as a stripper. She wasn't sure she believed the bit of gossip. What kind of stripper had Saturday night off to attend a biker party? Unless he was a shitty stripper working with the day shift. Though, if the sexy way he unconsciously moved his hips to the music while working the bar was any indication, he didn't suck. Sandy hair, matching beard, a body that filled out the upper portion of his T-shirt before fading into flat as hell abs...yeah, the man would have dollar bills hanging from every inch of his g-string. Or speedo. Banana hammock? What exactly did male strippers wear?

"Here ya go, darlin'."

"Thanks, Thunder." She sipped the drink and nodded her approval. After a quick wink, he was off taking care of someone else.

"Not sure big brother would like you ogling the baby birds like that."

Her spine shot straight. Shit. Five years of freedom from that voice blasted away in an instant. Everything rushed back in the blink of an eye. The fear, helplessness, anxiety, guilt, shame. Every negative emotion her sixteen-year-old self had been forced to deal with while wholly unprepared. Her first instinct was to curl into a tight ball, making herself as invisible as possible. But she couldn't cower, couldn't show fear, couldn't run. Facing Rusty was the only option. The frightened sixteen-year-old girl she'd been didn't exist anymore. Shell was an adult. A mother with a daughter to protect above all else. Rusty had no power over her.

Lie.

One threat and she'd be right back where she was. Only this time, it was even worse. He now had two aces to play. Two people Shell would move heaven and earth to protect.

Copper and Beth.

Rusty wedged himself in next to her at the bar. She faced him, digging deep to gather her courage. "Welcome home, Rusty."

Copper

"Well thanks, doll. You miss me?" Same green eyes as Copper. Same red hair and beard. Similar height. Clearly cut from the same physical cloth, the similarities stopped there. Whereas Copper was rough, raw, and fierce with a massive heart that bled for each and every man under his command, Rusty was nothing more than a narcissistic sociopath bent on satisfying his own desires at every turn.

And one of those wanted to be everything Copper was and then some.

To say Shell didn't trust his motives would be the understatement of the year.

"Excuse me," she said. "Copper will be looking for me in a minute. Might as well get a jump on tracking him down." She set her drink down and took a step only to have a strong hand clamp down on her upper arm with punishing strength.

"Don't think so, doll. We've got some unfinished business." Hot, stale air wafted across her ear. She wrinkled her nose as the strong stench of stale booze and weed hit her nostril. Swaying on his feet, Rusty jerked her closer.

He was bombed. Which only made him more unpredictable. She would know.

"There's nothing we have to talk about." Shell tried to wrench her arm away, but the grip only intensified. Fear slithered through her, not so much of Rusty, there were too many men at the party that would never let a thing happen to her. But if Copper caught a glimpse of his brother's hands on her? Shit would hit the fan in the messiest way.

"Sure we do, doll," he slurred.

God, how she loathed the nickname. He'd called her doll all those years ago. It's exactly what'd she'd been to him. A doll he could pull off the shelf and play with whenever he wanted. A toy that would take whatever was dished out and not fight back. Hearing the nickname again had her stomach rolling, and recollections she'd hoped were long buried rising to the surface.

"Been away from women a long time. Gotta lot of need stored up if you catch my drift." Shell trembled. Her tongue thickened in her mouth, unable to form words. This was why she needed to leave. Rusty wouldn't stop. And once he found out he'd fathered her child, he'd own her.

She *had* to leave. Opening her eyes, she saw Izzy making her way through the crowd toward her. Relief washed over her. Izzy was tough, so much stronger than Shell, and holy crap did she look like she was out for blood.

Narrowed eyes, flaring nostrils, clenched fists, she had it all going on. Jig called it her *oh-hell-no* look and warned them to run if she cast it in their direction. Right now, that look was precisely what Shell needed to bolster her confidence.

"Let go, Rusty," Shell said with bite, ripping her arm out of his grasp. She refused to rub the sore skin. Wouldn't give him the satisfaction of knowing he'd hurt the tender flesh of her inner arm.

"Hey, girl," Izzy said, drawing Shell close for a hug. Her way of removing Shell from Rusty's reach.

"Well, well, well," he said. "Who do we have here?"

"Izzy." She held out a hand. "You must be Rusty."

"In the flesh." He slithered next to her and slung an arm around her shoulders. "Damn, woman, that is one bangin' body. Say bye to your friend. You and I got a date in my room."

Izzy snorted. "Don't think so, buddy. I sure as fuck ain't a Honey, and you sure as fuck don't get to demand anything from me."

Lips curling, Rusty snarled. "Look, bitch, your ass is in my house right now. You want to stay and play, you gotta pay."

The rolling in Shell's stomach morphed into full-on acrobatics. Shit. This could turn ugly fast. Izzy was the type to show Rusty the error of his ways with a knee to the balls and a wicked right hook to the jaw. Shell had seen her lay a large man out flat in the ring. But Izzy was also pregnant. A brawl would not only have

Jig's head exploding, it'd put Izzy at risk. Shell prayed her friend remembered to keep her cool.

"Rusty," Shell said. "She's—"

"Shut up," he barked as his arm fell off Izzy's shoulders. Inches from her face, he said, "If you're not in my room and on your knees in the next sixty seconds, I'll make sure you never show your face here again. Got it, bitch?"

To Izzy's credit, she remained calm despite the sparks shooting out her eyes. Being unable to pummel Rusty's misogynistic ass had to be killing her. Instead of murdering him, she crossed her arms and snorted. "Pretty sure my ol' man would have something to say about that."

"Who the fuck's your ol' man?" Rusty wrapped his hand around Izzy's arm much as he did to Shell a few moments ago.

"Jigsaw."

Throwing back his head, Rusty laughed long and loud. Shell clenched her back teeth as well as her fists. Izzy looked to be doing much of the same.

"Jig. That's priceless. You gonna tattle to that pussy? Think he's gonna protect you? Pretty sure he let his first wife get murdered. Trust me, you're better off with a real man."

Shell sucked in a sharp breath. Jig's wife and daughter had been killed around seven years ago in a tragic act of violence that nearly destroyed him. Only recently, with the addition of Izzy to his life, had he begun to heal and learn to live again. Rusty's words were the lowest of blows.

Izzy grew deathly quiet. The two stared each other down, and Shell knew her friend was employing every restraint technique she knew to keep from wrapping her manicured fingers around Rusty's throat.

A few of the partiers nearby had taken notice of the interaction and started forming a circle around Izzy, Rusty, and herself. Glancing over her shoulder, Shell searched for someone to intervene. Someone who wouldn't fly off the handle and cause an even bigger scene.

Just as she was about to call out for help from Mav who was the closest, Jig and Copper emerged from Copper's office. As though drawn by some mystical connection, Jig's gaze zeroed in directly on Izzy. His face turned thunderous, and he immediately started shoving through the crowd, Copper hot on his heels.

"Rusty," Shell said in a calm, even voice. "Jig is on his way over here. You might want to let Izzy go. He'll flip his shit if your hands are on his woman when he gets here."

Rusty turned to her, distracted for a moment, which allowed Izzy to extricate her arm without a struggle. What Shell saw in Rusty's eyes had her shivering. Nothingness stared back at her. No anger, fear, hatred, just a blank stare, cold as ice and just as hard. "You think I give a shit? Am I supposed to be scared? I back down for no man, doll."

"There better be a good reason you've got your fucking hands on my fucking woman. I'm thinking nothing short of her bleeding out and you trying to save her life is gonna be fucking acceptable right now."

Whoa.

Never before had she heard Jig speak with such lethal intent. Rusty was a dead man if he didn't choose his words carefully.

"Babe—" Izzy said. When Jig cut her a look she raised her hands by her head and took a step back. "Okay, do your macho thing."

Rusty did a slow turn, a smirk on his face and not an ounce of remorse for miles.

"My bad, brother. Thought she was a Honey. Trust me when I say she was asking for it. Practically begging for it."

"No, I fucking wasn—" Izzy started.

Jig lunged forward but stopped when Copper snagged his shoulder. "Let's settle the fuck down here. Rust, Izzy is Jig's ol' lady. She gets all the fucking respect that goes with the title. Jig, Rusty has been gone a long time. Doesn't know everyone anymore. Sure it was just a stupid ass mistake. Right, Rust?"

Copper

Rusty snorted and rolled his eyes. "Sure, big brother. Whatever you say. You're always fucking right."

Copper frowned, and Shell's heart squeezed. Copper's blind spot was far too big where Rusty was concerned. He'd be crushed when it all became crystal clear as it one day would. Too much poison flowed through Rusty's veins for him not to ruin Copper's image of who his baby brother was.

"Fucking animal should still be in his cage," Jig muttered under his breath.

Quick as a striking cobra, Rusty tossed the liquid in his glass right in Jig's face. Alcohol splashed all over both Jig and Copper. The sound of shattering glass drowned out Jig's shocked grunt. Not even a full second later, Rusty's fist plowed into Jig's jaw. Jig staggered back two steps before flying forward with a punch of his own.

"Motherfucker," Izzy yelled as she took a step forward.

Shell grabbed her arm and yanked her backward, giving her a hard stare. "Don't even think about it, *mama*," she said.

Izzy's hand fell to her stomach. "Shit." She stared helplessly at the men pounding each other.

"Rusty, what the fuck?" Copper cried as he wrapped a thick arm around his brother's chest.

Rocket appeared behind Jig, capturing him under his arms and pulling him back. At first, Jig struggled, nostrils flaring like a pissed off bull. But Rocket whispered something in his ear that had Jig looking at Izzy and calming. She nodded at him but didn't step closer.

Rusty still screamed obscenities and lewd comments toward Jig and Izzy. Finally, Copper roared. "That's enough!" as he shoved the center of Rusty's chest. Blinking, Rusty staggered into Zach, who was holding his trusty bat, Louie, and looking ready to bust heads.

"Rust, get the fuck in my office. Izzy, take your ol' man home and calm him the fuck down. Want him here at noon tomorrow." After looking around at the crowd of onlookers, Copper shouted. "Shows over. Get back to drinking and fucking. Thunder, get this glass cleaned up."

Rusty stormed off toward Copper's office with Zach trailing behind.

The tension of the past fifteen minutes began to seep out of Shell as Izzy hugged her and whispered, "Thanks, girl." They made quick plans to take Beth to the playground after Shell's Sunday diner shift, then Izzy slipped under her man's arm, and together they headed toward the exit.

Shell raised a trembling hand to her hair, shoving it behind her ear. Even though she was used to these guys, and that meant the occasional drunken brawl, that had been more intense than usual and rattled her core. She glanced up and found Copper staring down at her.

"You okay?" He asked as he picked up her hand and tugged her close.

"Yeah. Think so. That was just a little unexpected." She gave him a small smile.

"Fuck, yeah it was." Copper scratched at his beard.

With a genuine smile this time, Shell reached up and stroked the soft hair. A low rumble reverberated in Copper's chest. "You start petting me now, babe, and you'll be bent over that bar before you can blink." The man had one hell of a dirty mouth. Beneath her lacy bra and tight top, her nipples tightened. Not Copper's most effective threat. He leaned down and gave her a quick, hard kiss. "Give me ten minutes to deal with Rusty then we'll get out of here. I need my hands on you."

Warmth pooled in her belly. Yes, his hands on her sounded like the perfect plan. She wrinkled her nose. But first... "You might want to take a shower. You smell like a distillery."

"Will you join me?"

Warm water, steam, and a soapy Copper? Count her in. "Yes. Now go. And hurry."

After another kiss, a little longer this time, Copper squeezed her ass and was on his way to his office.

Copper

Shell kept her attention on his retreating back—okay maybe on the tight flex of his retreating ass. There was no doubt in her mind, Rusty would worm his way out of Copper's ill will. It was just their dynamic. Rusty fucked up, and Copper cleaned the mess, making excuses for his brother.

She sighed.

A wicked storm was on the horizon and Shell feared there was no way for her to find shelter before it made land.

CHAPTER FIFTEEN

Copper expected a period of adjustment for Rusty after he returned from prison, but disrespecting an ol' lady and sucker punching another brother? That he hadn't anticipated.

"The fuck, Rusty?" Copper asked as he closed the door behind him, drowning out at least some of the chaos.

For a moment, defiance flashed in Rusty's eyes before he shrugged. "That fucker rubs me the wrong way. Always has." With a snort, he plopped into Copper's leather chair.

Okay, it looked like he was standing in his own office. He'd be damned if he sat across the desk from Rusty in the number two chair. Crossing his arms, he propped himself against the closed door. "Can't go around hitting on ol' ladies."

Rusty opened a drawer and pulled out the whiskey Copper shared with him a few days ago. For some reason, it rubbed him the wrong way. Back in the day, Rust had at least respected Copper's role as president. Now, it seemed he felt he was entitled to do whatever the fuck he wanted.

He's your fucking brother, and he just got out of fucking prison.

"Didn't know she was an ol' lady." He unscrewed the cap and sucked back a long swallow directly from the bottle. "And fuck that shit. Since when have ol' ladies trumped brothers around here?"

"Brothers still come first, but an ol' lady has always been a position of respect. They're a vital part of the family. You ask any one of those guys, and they'd die for their woman same as they'd die for the club."

Rusty scoffed and took another drink. He needed to faceplant in his bed and sleep it off for the next twelve hours. Alone.

He stood, bottle in hand. "We done here? Gonna go find some more accommodating pussy." Coming around the desk, he stopped about two feet from Copper. "You gonna block my way, big brother?"

"Look, Rust, I can't pretend to know how much it sucks to be in prison. And I have no idea how you feel being dropped back in here after five years have passed. Shit's changed, and that can't be easy. But you gotta take it down a notch. Can't have you starting shit. You hear?"

They stared each other down for a moment. Something flashed in Rusty's gaze. A cold and rebellious glint Copper had never witnessed before. Something close to hatred. For one hot second, Copper thought Rusty might take a swing at him with that bottle. But then he blinked and it was gone. His lips curled. "Shit, Cop, I know I gotta get my head on straight. Spent five years hardening myself and proving I don't take shit off no one." He shrugged. "Habit by now." He strode forward and held his free hand out. "Won't happen again."

Copper gripped his brother's hand and tugged him forward. They hugged and slapped each other's backs. "Fucking glad you're here," Copper said.

"You ain't gonna cry and snot all over my shirt, are you?"

With a laugh, Copper shoved Rusty back. "No, asshole. Your ugly ass ain't worth crying over."

All the tension from moments ago evaporated. "Fuck you! Now get outta here and go give your woman some dick," Rusty said.

That was a damn good idea. "Lock up behind you when you go, okay? Don't want anyone rummaging through my shit when they're too drunk to find the can."

"You got it, big bro."

After one last hug, Copper went off in search of Shell. He found her sitting at the bar, laughing at something the new kid said. Thunder seemed promising, but Copper wasn't sure about his career choice. It wasn't the stripping he minded, fuck if the guy could make money shaking his junk in women's faces, more power to him, but the schedule wasn't exactly conducive to club business. It remained to be seen how available and loyal he'd be to the club. So far, he'd been a model prospect.

Though his staring at Shell's tits like they were a treat meant for him was something that was going to end in the next thirty seconds.

Copper snuck up behind Shell, resting his hands on her rib cage right under her tits. In a tiny gesture, no one would notice, he brushed his thumbs over the sides of the mounds that had been on his mind constantly the past few days. He hadn't spent nearly enough time tasting them, sucking them, squeezing them.

Something he planned to remedy in the very near future.

"Ready to head out, gorgeous?" he asked while making eye contact with Thunder.

The prospect nodded once then lifted his hands in surrender. "Have fun kids." He moved on down the bar. Good. The kid got it. He knew he'd never patch if he so much as bumped into Shell in the future.

Shell gazed up at him, concern in her baby blues. "Everything okay with Rusty?"

Last thing Copper would let Shell do was stress over club shit. She had an overflowing plate as it was. She didn't need details of his club business weighing on her mind as well as everything else she dealt with. "All good, baby. Let's roll."

Fifteen minutes later, Copper's cock was so hard he wasn't sure there was enough blood left for his brain to remember the way to Shell's house. The moment she'd climbed on his bike, she dove her hands under his shirt with a muttered, "It's freezing," and had been softly stroking his skin ever since.

Copper

Riding a motorcycle with a rigid cock wasn't an easy feat. Especially with a passenger who seemed to know her effect and use it to her full advantage. Her short nails scraped over his lower abs just as he turned into her driveway. After he killed the engine, he said. "Gonna pay for that ride, baby."

Giggles floated over his shoulder. Shell didn't often get the chance to be uninhibited without responsibilities. Made the occasions she could really let loose and have fun extra sweet.

"You had it coming,' she whispered. "Teasing me like that in the clubhouse. Then I had to ride with both you and that giant vibrating machine between my legs for six miles. I'm so turned on, I could probably come just from watching you strip at this point."

Copper groaned. Damn minx. "Climb off, Shell. Then walk into the house. Don't want to fuck you out here in the cold, but I don't trust myself to touch you without taking you."

A shiver ripped through her, shaking her body against his back, but it had nothing to do with the cold. He bet if he reached in whatever scrap of panties she was wearing, she'd be dripping.

Shell did as he asked, gripping his shoulders for leverage as she swung her leg over the bike. Her ass swayed back and forth in a hypnotizing pattern as she strode toward the house. When she reached the two steps leading to her stoop, she peered over her shoulder, one eyebrow arched. "Coming?" she asked.

"After you do at least twice." He dismounted the bike and stalked after her.

Those gorgeous blue irises deepened in color, resembling the ocean right before a turbulent storm. He took the keys from her hands and unlocked the door. Holding it open, he gestured inside. Once she was safely through the door, he did a quick visual sweep of her yard. Call him paranoid, but he worried about her safety constantly.

"You wanted to shower, right?" Shell bit her lower lip and rocked back on her heels, seeming suddenly unsure of herself. "I can throw your clothes in the wash while you're in there. You want a drink or something?"

The rambling was cute but unnecessary. What the fuck did she have to be nervous about? The woman pretty much had him by the balls. "Yeah," he said. "I need to shower, but there's no way I'm going in there without you. Fuck the clothes. We can wash them later. There won't be anything between us tonight, so the clothes don't matter."

"Oh," she said, eyes wide and mouth forming an adorable O.

"Come on." He had yet to touch her, mostly because he meant what he'd said outside. The moment he got his hands on her, he was going to fuck her. And he didn't want to do that smelling like the cheap whiskey Rusty had dumped on his clothes.

Shell led the way to her small but neat bathroom. She'd decorated the ensuite space with a rustic theme. The entire tiny house was decorated the same way. She'd never said, but the way she'd set up her place led him to believe she longed to live in a country cabin out in the woods. The house was warm, inviting, cozy, and never failed to draw him into a state of comfort he failed to find in his own space.

Though perhaps it was the woman more than the atmosphere.

When she stepped into the bathroom, she immediately flicked on the shower, testing the water. "Give it a few minutes. Takes a while to warm up."

The shower definitely wasn't big, but it would be more than adequate if they were willing to get a little close. Which Copper was. The closer the better.

Copper crossed his arms at the hem of his shirt and stripped it over his head. Shell's focus stayed riveted to him as he moved his hands to the button of his jeans. Licking her lips, she reached toward his zipper.

"Don't," he barked, sharper than he meant. If she touched him, all bets were off, and he had a fantasy he wanted to fulfill tonight.

Copper

She jumped and snatched her hand back. Finishing the job, Copper worked his jeans down his legs. He'd forgone underwear. What was the point? It would only strangle the hard-on he'd known he was going to be rocking all night.

Shell stared at his cock as it emerged from his jeans, thwacking against his stomach. "Strip," he said. "Then get in the shower."

She met his gaze before bending forward and lowering the long zipper that ran the length of her boot. Once she'd removed what could be used as a deadly weapon, she did the same to the other. Next came the sinfully tight black pants. Copper grabbed the base of his dick as she shimmied the clingy material over her hips. When they were gone, she straightened. A tiny red thong matching her red top clung to the damp folds of her pussy.

"All of it," he managed to say.

She'd gotten distracted and stopped removing her clothing, staring instead at him stroking himself.

"Shell. Get fucking naked."

With a chuckle, she crossed her arms and peeled the form-fitting top off one inch at a time. Copper groaned at the sight of her ample tits encased in red silk. They rose and fell in a rapid clip, echoing the force of her breaths.

"Copper," she whispered. "You're just staring at me, and I feel like I could come."

He worked his hand up and down his length at a leisurely pace. "I'm right there with you."

She smiled then, extra confidence in her expression. Women liked to know they had power over men with their bodies. Reaching behind her back, she unclasped the bra with feminine ease and let it tumble to the ground, cast aside.

"Fuck me," Copper whispered. "Swear to Christ they're even sexier than they were on Wednesday." Plump and high, with tight, pointed nipples, those tits were screaming for his mouth. But he didn't move toward her yet. "Panties."

Her grin grew wicked. Thumbs in the silky string wrapping around her hips, she eased the panties down her shapely legs and off her body. He'd hoped she'd toss them in his direction so he could inhale her arousal, but no such luck.

Although what she did might have been even better.

"These sure are wet," she said in a husky tone that betrayed her desire.

Copper just smirked. "Step under the spray."

"In a minute." She fisted the damp panties then lifted them and ran them across her breasts. With a moan, she paused and paid special attention to her nipples, scraping the fabric over the sensitive peaks.

Copper's entire body jerked with the sharp rush of arousal. He squeezed the base of his dick to keep from shooting his load across the bathroom. His head spun as more blood surged south. "Shell," he growled.

Her head fell back on another moan as she continued to torture her nipples with the soaked material, imprinting the scent of her arousal on her skin. "Feels good." Her free hand came up and tweaked the other nipple, pinching and rolling it between her fingers. "Though nothing feels as good as your mouth."

He was going to lose his shit in about three seconds. "Get in the fucking shower," he said.

Shell giggled. "So stern," she said then tossed the red silk at his feet. Two backward steps later, she was in the shower and under the spray. Water saturated her hair, weighing down her curls and lengthening them until they no longer existed. Rivulets of water ran down her body, creating trails Copper wanted to capture with his tongue.

"Spread your legs."

This time, she obeyed immediately, stepping her feet wider than her shoulders.

"Sit."

Copper

A narrow bench extended along the back wall of the shower. Large enough for her to perch her ass on, but it wouldn't be the most comfortable.

Once again, she complied and kept her legs spread wide. So trusting, so giving, so his.

Now he had a full-frontal view of her glistening pussy to go with her slippery tits. Perfection...almost.

"Touch yourself."

He'd thought she might hesitate but was quickly finding out when it came to sex, Shell was not at all what he expected. She was open, curious, creamed when he talked dirty to her, and most important of all seemed to revel in following his direction. She looked to him, allowed him to lead, took his instruction.

Case in point, without hesitation, she slid her palm over the small swell of her stomach and straight down to her mound. Bypassing her clit, she parted her folds with her thumb and middle finger then inserted her forefinger straight into the slick channel. He was dying to see the expression of bliss on her face, but couldn't tear his gaze away from where her pussy devoured her finger.

Working the digit in and out, she picked up the pace then added a gentle hip thrust, riding her own fingers.

He wished the water wasn't running so he could hear the squelching of her wetness as she fucked herself. But she'd freeze if he cut the hot shower now that she was drenched.

Copper stroked his engorged cock, giving an extra squeeze each time Shell whimpered. His dick was so full and tight the skin felt stretched to capacity. "Another finger."

A groan left her lips. Her head fell back against the wall as she inserted a second finger then continued going at herself.

"Pinch your nipple." Deep mauve and puckered, those puckered buds needed attention.

"Copper," she said, gasping for air. "I'm not going to last long. I'm gonna come. You got me too worked up at the clubhouse."

"Good," he said stroking faster. His stomach muscles clenched when she plucked at her left nipple. "Fuck, I want those babies in my mouth. You want that? You like when I suck your tits?"

"I love it," she said, arching her hips off the bench. She was fingering herself with fury now. Hand ramming into her pussy again and again.

"Make yourself come."

"I want...ahh...I want..."

"What, baby? What do you want? You want my cock in that hungry pussy?"

She shook her head, rolling it against the tile wall. The entire time, her gaze had been fixed on his hand tugging his cock.

"You don't want this?" he asked, slowing his strokes. He didn't believe that for a second.

"I want you in my mouth," she said, as she raised her gaze to meet his.

He froze for a second, mind blanking. Holy shit, he'd officially died and gone to heaven. "You want me to fuck that pretty mouth?"

"Yes, Copper." She moaned again.

"Okay, baby. Get yourself off for me. Let me see that beautiful face get lost in pleasure, and I'll feed you my cock as a reward."

"Yes," she said. She added her thumb to the mix, rubbing over her clit with short fast strokes. Clearly, Shell had this down to a science. Twisting her nipple with more force than he'd expected, she fingered herself and thumbed her clit all at the same time.

Copper couldn't do anything but gawk at the live show before him. It was so much more than he'd fantasized, but what got to him the most was Shell's trust in him. And sure, there'd been men before him, she was a mother for Christ's sake, but there had always been an air of inexperience around her. To know she trusted him enough to bare her body in this way was humbling.

"I'm gonna come," she said, voice high-pitched and strained.

"Fuck yes," he answered. He'd stopped jerking himself in favor of watching her tip over the edge. Her fingers sped up and

Copper

in the next second, her back arched, coming off the wall as her face contorted with pleasure. Her hand fell from her breast and gripped the edge of the slippery bench as she cried out in release. Copper could have watched it again and again. That moment when her mind gave way and her body surged in ecstasy. Lucky for him, he had the entire night to do just that.

Her eyes fluttered closed, and she sagged against the tile as she floated down from the highest of highs.

He prowled forward, stepping into the small booth and under the heavy spray. Too tall to stand directly under the shower head, the water beat against his side instead.

With one step, he was in position, cock directly in front of her slack lips. Copper cupped her cheek. "Open those eyes for me, Shell."

Her eyes opened, and he got to witness the moment she discovered his erection so close to her mouth. Her breath hitched, and she licked her lips, giving them a glossy coat. Even though she was still inches away from his dick, he swore he felt her tongue as it peeked out and swiped across her lips.

"Hungry for me?" he asked.

"Starved," she croaked.

"You trust me?" He peered down at her waiting for that beautiful gaze to lift to his. When it did, she nodded.

"Completely."

That in itself was an aphrodisiac. "Then open up, baby. And keep those hands on the bench."

Her eyes flared, and she sucked in a breath. For her first time sucking him off, he asked a lot. Asked her to trust him enough to have control of how deep, how fast, and how long his cock journeyed down her throat. Not so much as a flicker of doubt crossed her face as she curled ten fingers over the edge of the bench and dropped her lower jaw.

Goddamn, that was a sight. Shell seated before him, mouth open, lusty eyes staring up at him. He took a mental picture that would last him a lifetime of lonely nights should she ever leave him.

Not that he'd accept that decision.

Slowly, he inserted his cock into her mouth. She kept her lips wide but swirled her tongue around the head as it crossed the threshold into the warmth. He didn't want to shock her or scare her off, so he stopped moving before he hit the back of her throat. Her lips closed around him and immediately hot, hard suction engulfed his cock.

Copper was an MC president, and he'd had his share of blow jobs. Never had one second of oral nearly brought him to his knees and made him howl at the moon simultaneously.

"Fuck, Shell," he ground out as his hands hit the wall above her head. Without it to ground himself, he feared he'd melt right into the water spiraling down the drain. Her mouth was that damn hot. "That mouth is fucking lethal."

He hadn't moved again, so she took matters into her own hands, drawing back and sucking him deep once again, only this time, his dick butted up against the back of her throat. She gagged slightly, the pressure of her spasming throat squeezing his cock head.

"Jesus." There was no way in hell he was going to last more than two minutes. His head bowed, and he became completely captivated by the picture she made. Lips spread wide to accommodate his bulk, eyes closed, lips stretched around his girth, fingertips white with the force it took to maintain her grasp on the bench.

She let up on the pressure, allowing him to slip almost fully from her lips then kept her mouth open as he gently thrust back in. This time, when he bumped her throat, she was prepared and swallowed. Nothing had ever felt so good. Time to kick it into gear before he shot down her throat too early.

"Ready for more?"

Eyes on his, she nodded and hummed around a mouthful of cock. The vibrations traveled up his dick and seemed to settle in

Copper

his balls making his hips snap forward involuntarily. After that, it was game on. Over and over, he thrust deep into her mouth. For a second, he worried it was too much, but the pleasure was so sharp, so overwhelming he couldn't stop if a gun was at his temple. Shell had no complaints, she took every rough drive into her throat and sucked him like she was trying to remove his skin.

Couldn't have been more than a minute later when his balls grew tight and heavy. The muscles in his stomach seemed to clench into a tight coil of tension. His hands dropped from the wall to her head, and he shoved deep one last time, pouring everything he had down her throat.

She swallowed convulsively as she tried to keep up with his release.

When he was spent and his cock no longer twitched, he realized he was still clenching her heavy wet hair. Shell softened her jaw and let his wilted cock slide from her mouth. He gasped and jerked as the hypersensitive tip passed her lips.

Copper stared down at her for a second, then hauled her up under her arms. Her feet left the ground as he kissed her lips, hard. Then her jaw, her neck, across the top of her breasts. "Let's get clean then I'll return the favor," he said as he let her slide down his body then reached for a coral bottle of body wash.

"Actually," Shell said, her face turning an adorable shade of pink. How could she be embarrassed now, after she sucked him like a porn star? "I was wondering if you'd do something for me when we get out."

"Ohh," he wagged his eyebrows. "Sounds promising."

With a chuckle, she shook her head and averted her eyes. "Will you just hold me for a while?"

The vulnerability in her voice killed him. As a two-job working single mother solely responsible for the safety and happiness of a child, she had to be exhausted. Hell, he knew she was. He'd do anything in the world to give her a little relief and comfort.

Gripping her chin, he tilted her head up then kissed her lips. "I'll hold you for as long as you need me, Shell. Forever if that's what you want."

She tensed, just for a fleeting second. Had he not been so in tune with her body, he would have missed it, but it was there. Was it his use of the word forever?

With a small smile, Shell turned away, squeezing a giant dollop of body wash onto a poufy purple thing.

He'd seen it though. A quick flicker of sadness in her eyes. For whatever reason, Shell didn't believe this would last long term.

Was it him? Did she doubt him? Or was it some ghost lurking in her past that kept her from going all in?

All good questions, but the biggest of all bounced around in his head like a ping pong ball. When the fuck had he started thinking in terms of forever?

CHAPTER SIXTEEN

Shell woke before the sun even thought about lighting the sky, unused to an enormous naked man heating her bed to the boiling point.

Both literally and figuratively.

Careful not to jostle Copper, she nudged the comforter down, allowing some much-needed cool air to wash over her nude body. Of course, fifteen seconds later, she was shivering and pulling the blankets back up to her chin once again.

She rolled to her side and closed her eyes. Might as well snag a few more hours of sleep. Her Sunday morning diner shift didn't begin until eight which meant she had about another two hours to sleep before she needed to get ready.

Like that was going to happen. With a sigh, she opened her eyes and stared at Copper's sleeping form. It wasn't often, or ever really, she had the opportunity to study him so closely without his knowledge. His body was just so…big. It was a tiny word, but nothing else described him more accurately. Big hands, big feet, big in stature, big muscles, big…other things. She'd fallen asleep surrounded by him. The feeling of safety and security that came with slumbering next to a powerful man wasn't something that could be matched. No alarm system, pistol in a nightstand, or barking dog compared to the knowledge that another human had her and would do whatever it took to keep her safe.

Shell wanted to hold on to that feeling, permanently. She was so tired of always being in charge, always making important decisions, always bearing the burdens. That wasn't to say she didn't value being an independent woman. Knowing she was capable, able to handle the challenges of life on her own was imperative. She'd proven to the world—and especially her mother—that she was self-sufficient, responsible, and trustworthy. She didn't *need* anyone. Especially not a man. She was surviving on her own, raising a happy and healthy daughter.

And she hated every second of it. Feminists everywhere would probably cringe, but it was what it was. She was sick and tired of doing it alone. She didn't *need* a man, but she wanted one. Not to remove her independence or take over her established roles, but to share life. Complement each other, comfort each other, support each other, and to kill the soul-crushing loneliness of going to bed solo each night.

And she didn't just want any man. Only the one lying six inches away, his chest rising and falling with the gentle rhythm of sleep. Copper was strong. Tough enough to swing at whatever curveballs life threw his way and smash them out of the park.

She sighed. How had what started out as her gawking at his sexy tattooed body turned into such a maudlin reflection on her existence?

Well, lying there for the next few hours was pointless. Might as well get up and make a hearty breakfast for her and Copper to share before she had to run off to work. Without a sound, she slid out of bed, shivering as her toes hit the cold wooden floor. She shoved her feet in the slippers that lived next to her bed then went in search of her clothes. At least, that was the plan until she spotted Copper's T-shirt dangling from the edge of her bed. Wearing the oversized cotton tee that had been absorbing Copper's essence all night seemed like a much better option.

She slipped it over her head then padded into the kitchen, flicking on lights as she passed. Copper was a fan of waffles in the morning, and she had a fantastic buttermilk waffle recipe handed down from her grandmother. One of the few things she actually received from her mom.

And she had a waffle iron…somewhere. Shell stood in the center of the kitchen, scratching her head. During her last attack of organization, she'd stowed the thing in a perfectly logical spot so the next time she needed it, it'd be accessible… right?

That showed just how often she whipped up breakfast. Working at a diner kinda squashed the desire to cook in the morning. She spun on one heel. Was it in the pantry? The low cabinet with the pots and pans? Maybe up high…

It hit her then…she'd stashed it pretty much in the highest spot in the kitchen. Of course. Being five-two on a good day, she couldn't reach the fourth shelf of her cabinets if her life depended on it. Luckily, she had a lifetime of practice scaling countertops.

With a small grunt, she hefted herself up onto the counter. If only she could recall which cabinet she'd stuck the damn thing in. Starting closest to her sink, she pulled the door open and rose onto her tiptoes. Even with the extra few inches, she had a hard time seeing onto the top shelf, so she reached her hand in. A serving bowl…a table cloth…oh that vanilla cupcake candle she'd been looking for. But no waffle iron.

"Come on, where the hell are you hiding?" she murmured as she closed the cabinet and moved on to the next. "Are you in here?" She ran her hand along the top shelf, smacking into a small appliance. "Ah ha! Victory."

"Now that is a damn pretty sight to see first thing in the morning."

Shell shrieked and wrenched her neck looking over her shoulder. Still stretching to reach the top cabinet, her jaw dropped. Holy shit, Copper stood in the doorway, arms folded across his inked chest and shoulder resting against the door frame. Besides the ink, he only wore a beard and a sexy smirk. Lordy, that was one impressive naked man.

"Hi," she squeaked as she started to lower her heels.

One eyebrow slowly crept up his forehead as the gleam in his eye grew predatory. He unfolded his arms and prowled forward.

She started to lower her arm.

"Nu-uh," he said with a shake of his head. "Stay just like that. You have any idea how fucking edible this ass looks peeking out the bottom of my shirt?"

It was then she realized standing on her toes with an extended arm had caused the borrowed shirt to ride high on her ass. Copper had an up close and personal view of her uncovered butt. Which, if the expression on his face was any indication, he quite enjoyed.

"Come down off your toes, but leave your arms up. Face the cabinet," he said from right behind her.

She lowered to completely flat feet raised her second hand to the shelf, gripping it for support. He had something up his non-existent sleeve, and it would no doubt involve an orgasm or two for her. Hopefully, she wouldn't rip the damn cabinet right off the wall.

"Wh-what are you going do to?" A tremor of excitement raced down her spine. Not being able to see him or feel him sent the thrill of anticipation through the roof.

"Whatever the fuck I want. Got any objections?" His tone was harsh, the words practically growled.

"N-no, no objections." Who did that breathy, sultry voice belong to?

The next thing she knew, two huge hands cupped her ass. Shell groaned and let her head fall forward. His hands were warm, and her ass filled them to capacity. He squeezed, kneading the soft flesh until wetness began to ease from her core.

"You have any idea just how smokin' hot you are, do you, babe?" Hot breath wafted across her cheeks leaving a million goosebumps in its wake.

She giggled. Hearing those words from him was a dream come true.

Copper

"Ain't playing. I mean it, Shell."

"I know you do." And she did. He meant every word he said. Always. Copper didn't feed anyone a line of bullshit.

He slid his hands around her hips then down to grip the front of her thighs. Next, his lips landed on her ass. She gasped and tried to pull away, but he anchored her firmly in place. He kissed and licked over the globes, occasionally placing a sharp nip here and there. She gripped the shelf hard and locked her knees to keep from buckling. This treatment kept up until Shell's arms ached and wetness trickled down her thighs. Who knew her ass was so sensitive and a little attention to it could work her into such a frenzy?

"Aiden," she whispered just as he trailed a finger between her cheeks. That was an area that had never been explored before. She'd never been interested, apprehensive if she was honest, but at that moment she could have begged Copper to go further.

"Last night that sexy mouth sucked me off so good I nearly passed out. Now my name falls from those same lips. Fuckin' heaven, baby. I'm in fucking heaven."

"Think I'm the one in heaven here, Aiden."

He let out a rough chuckle. "Not yet, but you will be." He continued to slide his finger forward until it encountered the arousal coating her lower lips and upper thighs.

"Jesus," he whispered. "All this cream for me, Shell?"

"Uh huh." She couldn't even speak with his blunt fingertip rimming her entrance.

Teeth scraped across her ass cheek once again. "You like this, don't you? Me playing with this plump little ass?"

The finger moved back again, toward that untested spot she'd never been more aware of than she was in that moment. When he pushed his finger against the tight hole, she tensed for a second then relaxed as pleasure moved through her. Shit, he hadn't inserted so much as a fingertip and the sensation was already more intense than she could have imagined. How would she survive it if he wanted his cock in there?

Another chuckle. "Yeah, you fuckin love it. But you're not ready for more yet. We'll get there." Then he groaned. "Though your pussy is so tight I barely survive it squeezing the fuck outta my dick. Might kill me once I get that fucker in this ass."

It was her turn to chuckle, but it turned into a frustrated groan when all of a sudden, his touch disappeared.

"Wha—"

"Turn around," he barked. "I'm fucking hungry."

Disappointment lanced through her. She'd been seconds away from demanding he fuck her and he wanted to eat? Maybe she'd built his attraction to her up in her head, making it more than it was.

If so…that was embarrassing.

"Oh," she said as she lowered her arms then rolled her stiff shoulders. She slowly turned and gazed down at him. Deep, dark green eyes stared back at her. He sure gawked at her like he wanted her. "That's why I'm up here. I was looking for the waffle mak—"

His hands landed on her inner thighs, shoving them wide. "Not what I'm fucking hungry for."

Shell squeaked as her legs were forced apart so hard, she almost lost her footing. "Then wha—oh, my God."

He took a long lick up her thigh, gathering all the wetness that had spilled from her. He cleaned her thoroughly, driving her crazy as his tongue traveled closer and closer to her sex without actually touching her. Then he kissed up and down one thigh. Really kissed it, like he kissed her neck or even her mouth. Deep, harsh, sucking kisses that were sure to leave marks all over her. More wetness poured out of her, eliciting a deep growl from him.

"Copper," she said. "Please…" Her head fell back, thunking against a shelf behind her.

"Please what?" he asked against her skin.

"Please touch me. You're making me crazy."

"Hmm. Think I like you crazy."

Copper

"Copper…" She said it as a warning, in much the same tone she used to scold Beth.

He just laughed then said, "This better?" as he took a long swipe up her pussy and straight to her clit.

"Yes, yes, yes," she said, panting. "Much better."

"How about this?" He circled her clit a few times with his tongue, then before she had time to process the change, he sucked her lower lips into his mouth.

She cried out, hands landing on his head. Her hips jerked against his face before she had the sense to try and still them. Last thing she wanted was for him to stop because he thought she was too forward and ramming his face against her pussy.

He released her, hands moving to her ass and giving a hard squeeze. "Go ahead," he said.

"Huh?"

"Don't hold back. You let me fuck your mouth last night. What makes you think I'm going to deny you fucking my face? Go ahead, gorgeous, let loose and rub that sexy pussy all over me."

If she survived this, letting him go would kill her. So she might as well enjoy it. Have some memories to take with her when her life exploded.

She tightened her grip on his hair and moved her hips, testing her options. Copper growled and went back to work, alternating light and hard licks with soft and firm pressure suction on her clit, labia, and even thighs.

He was a freaking oral master. All sides of his tongue were used to turn her into a quivering mess. He flattened it, then extended it, using every trick in the book. When he finally shoved his tongue deep into her pussy, she screamed and lost all sense of self-preservation. Shell ground herself wildly against his face, completely lost in the insanity of Copper's mouth on her sex.

She could barely think, barely breathe, but she could damn well chase that orgasm. His mouth was wide as he fucked her with his tongue and each time she thrust forward, his upper lip —or maybe it was his nose, who the hell knew—bumped her clit. Whatever it was, it was working for her. Shell's legs began to tremble. Within seconds, they were full on shaking. The only thing holding her up was the strength of Copper's hands on her ass.

"Please, please," she said on a moan as the room grew fuzzy. "I'm going to come. Oh God, everything's tingling." Her grip on his hair loosened as the pins and needle sensation in her fingers grew too strong to control the digits. Then, before her arms dropped to her sides, her muscles seized. Her hands fisted yanking hard on the red strands.

Copper grunted and fucked her even harder with his tongue.

The orgasm crashed into her like a five-car pileup. She cried out with a few profanities she usually avoided and ground herself against Copper's face. The entire room spun for a good few minutes as her body rode the high and took its sweet time settling.

Eventually, the world calmed, and she blinked her eyes open to find Copper watching with an expression no less hungry than he'd had before he blew her mind. His beard glistened with the evidence of his recent activity. Never would Shell have guessed she'd find it hot, but knowing he was so into eating her out that he was covered in her juices, made her pussy clench with need all over again.

Hands still on her ass, he drew her forward and into his embrace. With a gasp, she wrapped her legs around his waist and arms around his shoulders.

He spun, took three steps, then squeezed her ass. "Legs down," he said, and she obeyed at once. After making sure she was steady on her legs—or at least stable enough not to land in a heap at his feet—he roughly spun her.

"Bend over," he said at her ear. "Tits on the table."

Shit. She'd just come harder than she ever had before and one gruffly spoken order from Copper had her body craving him as though she hadn't had him in years. She stared at her round table just as his heavy hand pushed the center of her back.

"Tits on the fucking table. Need in that pussy. You have no idea how jealous my dick is of my tongue right now."

She laughed right before a sharp slap on her ass had her jolting into action. Palms flat on the table, she bent over until her breasts rested against the wood surface. As her nipples hit the cold surface, she hissed out a breath.

Copper stepped in behind her, wasting no time. His hips butted against her and he ran his dick through her juices. "Fuuuck," he said. "Pill?" Seemed the man wasn't capable of a complete sentence anymore.

"Yes."

"I'm clean."

"Me too," she said.

"Haven't been with anyone since you moved back."

"I believe you, Copper." No one? Holy shit. Over a year and no women. That was big, wasn't it?

"Good. Hope you're fucking ready for me, Shell, because this is going to be fast and fucking hard." He was already breathing like he just hopped off a treadmill.

"I'm always ready for you, Aiden." She smiled at the deep rumble her words elicited from him, but the grin quickly turned into a yelp as he slammed in her to the hilt with one mighty thrust.

There was no waiting. No giving her time to adjust to his healthy girth as he'd done the other time. The was just straight, hard, fucking.

He powered in and out, grunting each time he bottomed out. Shell was helpless to do anything but receive what he chose to give. And that was a lot. His hands completely controlled her hips, slamming forward and back on his dick so many times she couldn't keep track. Every time he moved her, her nipples dragged against the firm surface of the table. The sensation was just shy of painful, an intense pinching sensation that shot to her pussy each time. Her hip bones banged into the table with every thrust. Tomorrow they'd be sore as hell, but for now, she felt nothing but the buildup to another orgasm rushing toward her at a hundred miles per hour.

High pitched whimpers and cries mixed with the low grunts and groans of Copper. She came hard, harder than she had moments ago, and before she was prepared for it.

"Aiden," she screamed as molten pleasure coursed through every cell in her body. One more thrust had her lower body jammed against the table, then a loud roar above her signaled Copper's orgasm.

He held her pinned for a long moment as they both took their time weathering the storm.

"Shit, Shell," he said as he stepped back and slipped out of her body. She almost cried from the loss of connection even as her sore body thanked her for the reprieve.

Gently, in complete contrast to the rough sex, Copper helped her upright and spun her to face him. He dropped to his knees and ran his fingers over the red splotches on her hip bones.

"I'm so sorry, baby. You're going to be bruised as hell tomorrow. I was so hot for you, I completely lost control. I was like a fucking animal." He pressed his lips to the tender spot, and she jumped. "Fuck. Is it that sore?"

Smiling down at him, she ran a hand through his hair. "No, Copper, it's not bad at all. You just tickled me. I'm fine, trust me. If I had enough energy, I'd bend back over and beg you to do it again."

His beard still bore hints of how much she'd wanted him. "So you like it rough, huh?"

Her face heated. "Apparently so."

He stood and drew her into his arms. "That's good, babe because I have a feeling I'm going to lose control around you for the next forty years or so."

Tears flooded her eyes. What a lovely picture he painted. Him still craving her well into their golden years. The sweetness of the image blurred into a wave of guilt and shame. Shell had a choice on the horizon. Tell him her secrets or leave Townsend. Either decision would kill any affection he might feel for her.

She tightened her arms around him as despair threatened to ruin the moment. It couldn't happen. These magical moments would be gone soon enough. The bleak future couldn't be allowed to ruin her present perfection.

CHAPTER SEVENTEEN

Copper fished a Cuban cigar out of its hiding spot in the lower drawer of his desk. Running it under his nose, he inhaled the pungent aroma and immediately experienced the calming effect he always achieved when he smoked. Shell wasn't a fan of the cigarettes, and now that he was more addicted to her mouth than the nicotine, he figured he'd better kick the habit. But, she'd admitted last week when they were relaxing on the tiny patio in her backyard during an unusually warm afternoon, she didn't mind the lingering scent of cigar smoke on him. In fact, her words had been something like *sexy* and *manly*.

That was a green light as far as he was concerned, and hopefully, the occasional cigar would make the transition to no cigarettes more bearable. Just as he was about to light the sucker, a heavy fist pounded on his closed office door.

Fuck.

He stowed the cigar. For some reason, he preferred it to be a solo activity. Always had. Probably because it allowed himself a rare few moments to be still and process. Though he had to admit he enjoyed his stogie just as much when Shell was on his lap relaxing with him as they'd done last week.

"Come on in," he said.

The door opened and Zach's blond head popped through the crack. "Got a minute, Prez?"

He waved Zach in. "Yeah, brother. Have a seat."

Copper

"Thanks." Zach strode in dressed in workout clothes and his cut, probably fresh off his job as owner of a local gym. One of the MC's more profitable businesses, Copper never regretted fronting club money to start Zach's dream up about seven years ago.

Zach planted himself in one of the two empty chairs opposite Copper. Sniffing he asked, "You sneaking cigars in here without me?"

Busted. Zach appreciated a good cigar just as much as Copper did. What the hell. He could share with his enforcer. Copper laughed. "Just about to before your bumbling fist knocked on my door."

There wasn't an ounce of apology in Zach's smirk. "Wasn't it you giving Beth a lecture a few days ago about sharing her toys?"

With a roll of his eyes, Copper snorted then dug out two cigars. "Yeah, yeah. Shut the fuck up." He rolled one across the desk to Zach who snatched it up and immediately smelled the stogie.

"Damn, Cop. That's nice shit."

Copper raised an eyebrow. "Now you know why I don't like to share."

The laugh that left Zach was infectious. "See your point. And I'll consider myself loved."

They wasted a few moments lighting the cigars and puffing in silence before Copper ended the quiet. "How's Rusty working out?"

Zach flipped his cigar, staring at the tip for a second before he lowered the smoldering stick. He leveled Copper with a look that had his stomach twisting.

"Shit. That bad?" There went the tension-reducing effects of one of his favorite activities. "What? He not showing up for shifts or something?" Copper inclined forward, resting his forearms on the desk.

Zach shook his head and leaned back, propping an ankle on his knee. His mouth formed an *O* right before a perfect ring of smoke floated into the room. Clearly, Zach wasn't stressed by Rusty's behavior. "Nah, it's not that bad. Well, he missed one shift and was two hours late for another, so that shit's not ideal." He cocked his head. "It's more an attitude thing, to be honest. He's short-tempered as fuck. Aggressive with my customers. To be honest, Cop, and I say this with all due respect, he's just been a dick since he's been out."

Well, fuck. That wasn't what Copper wanted to hear. He needed to check in more with Rusty. Spend some quality time with his brother and help ease the transition back to real life. Since the night of the welcome home party over a week ago, Copper had spent nearly all his spare time with Shell and Beth. It was fucking fantastic, but didn't do his blood brother any favors.

"I'll have a chat with him." Soon as he was done with Zach, he'd give Rust a call. Shell had the night off from her second job and had scheduled dinner at her mom's for her and Beth weeks ago. Since she wasn't masochistic enough to bring Copper along, he'd planned to catch up on some club shit, but now he could devote the night to hanging with Rusty.

"Appreciate it, Prez." Zach's demeanor grew serious. "Not why I busted in on you, though."

"What's going on?" Copper asked as he puffed on his cigar, watching the tufts of smoke rise from the tip. At Zach's heavy sigh, he shifted his focus to his enforcer. "Shit. Don't like the sound of that."

"And you shouldn't." Zach dropped his foot and sat straight in his chair. "We got a problem. Least I think we do. Beginning of a problem, maybe."

"Spit it the fuck out, Zach."

With a grunt, Zach pulled something out of his pocket and tossed it onto Copper's desk. The small baggie slid across the desk, coming to a stop directly under Copper's gaze. "Fuck."

"Yep."

Copper

Lifting the clear bag, Copper inspected the product that looked exactly like its namesake. Small white crystals. "Meth," he said more to himself than to Zach.

"Some Walter fucking White shit right there."

"The fuck you get it?"

Zach snubbed out the last of his cigar in a skull ashtray on the desk. "Screw copped it off some shitheel who owed him. Guy couldn't pay his debt so he offered that shit to Screw instead."

"And Screw accepted it as payment?" He'd strip that fucker's shiny new patch in a heartbeat.

Zach laughed. "What the fuck kinda operation you think I'm running, Prez? Fuck no, he didn't accept it. He pocketed the meth, busted a kneecap, and told the guy he'd be back in a week for payment in full."

Huh. Not bad. Screw was one of the newer young patches, being groomed to function as Zach's second in command. At first, Copper had been skeptical when Zach wanted to take Screw under his wing. He wasn't nicknamed Screwball for nothing, but he'd taken the job seriously and was stepping up to the plate in ways Copper hadn't expected.

He'd be sure to mention it to the kid later.

"Ragnar?" Copper asked.

Zach ran a hand through his always perfect hair. "That'd be my guess. Guy Screw lifted his from said there's been a huge surge in meth dealers over the last month. That shit is getting easier to buy than fucking ice cream."

Leaning back in his chair, Copper stroked his chin. Yeah, he knew he did it whenever he was deep in thought. Just a fucking reflex that made him a shit poker player. By the time he realized what he was doing, every damn player was on to the fact he had a shit hand and was deciding to bail or not. Only good thing to come of his men learning his tell was that they gave him a wide berth and allowed him to string his thoughts together when they noticed it.

And Zach remained silent, permitting just that.

Ragnar was Joe's boss. As in Joe, the motherfucker knocking on Shell's door each month. Thing of it was, they weren't based out of Tennessee. Which meant they'd need someone local running the operation. So who the fuck was it?

Copper's hand stilled, and he looked Zach in the eye.

As though reading his mind, Zach nodded. "Yeah, Cop. I'm tracking the same way."

"Lefty."

"Gotta be. No one else stupid enough to push meth through our town."

"Christ, this guy's been nothing but a fucking thorn in my ass for too damn long."

Zach's eyes narrowed. He might look like a pretty boy gym rat, but he was fucking lethal when necessary. "Shoulda known when he went into hiding after we dismantled his trafficking operation that it wasn't the end of him. Guy's got a serious death wish if he's fucking around on our turf again."

Copper jammed his cigar into the ashtray. Just when the waters were finally calm and the clouds were white and puffy. "We need—"

"Cop?" Jigsaw called out as he rapped on the door.

"Jesus, what the fuck now?" Copper mumbled as Zach snickered. "Come on in, Jig."

The door flung open, and a grim-faced Jigsaw stormed into the office. "We got a big fucking problem, Prez." It was then he turned and noticed Zach. "Glad you're here, Z, this concerns you too."

Great. This day was shaping up to be a toilet full of shit. And he couldn't even end it by sinking into Shell's slick heat. No, he'd be capping the day off sipping beers with his fucked-up brother.

Perfect.

"Sit your ass down, Jig. What's going on?"

Jig tossed an envelope on the desk. As club's treasurer, he handled all the money collected from client's debts. Most of the men took a turn doing a run to collect cash. If someone couldn't pay Screw or Zach were called in, but most of the time that wasn't necessary. The money was turned over to Jig who counted and logged it then stored it in a safe in Copper's office.

Copper picked up the yellow package. "What is this? Looks like a regular deposit to me."

Shaking his head, Jig said. "It's fucking short. Second week in a row. Thought last week was an anomaly so I let it slide. Two though?" He lifted his hands. "Now it's a pattern."

Goddamn, could this day get any more fucked? "How much?"

"Five G's both weeks."

"Jesus," Zach burst out. "You saying someone took it from your office?"

Jig's expression grew thoughtful. "Not sure, to be honest. The guys drop their money right into the envelope. Got a clipboard with the amount to be collected and by whom. When they hand over the money, they write how much was collected. If money is owed, they star it, and I pass it along to you, Z." Jig had been wearing his beard thicker over the past month, and it almost completely disguised the puzzle-piece shaped scar that covered most of his right cheek. "One of two things is happening. Either one of our guys is lying about the amount they're dropping off, or someone went into my office and helped themselves to some cash."

Who the fuck would be so stupid as to steal from the MC? The betrayal was grounds for having one's patch stripped, which was a big fucking deal. "You talk to all the guys who did the pick-ups the last two weeks?"

Head nodding up and down, Jig said, "Yep, each swears they were accurate in their count and would die before stealing from the club. Not sure what to believe, Cop. This has me fucking baffled."

Copper looked from Jig to Zach. "Either of you hear any chatter 'bout anyone in trouble? Short on cash? Fuckin' ex-wife looking for more? Anyone using?"

Both men shook their heads in tandem. "No," Jig said at the same time Zach said, "Not a goddamn peep."

"All right," Copper said. Fuck, he did not need this right now. "Jig, next week have the guys hand money to you directly. Count it in their presence and keep the cash on you or in the safe at all times. Get with Mav and have him install a camera in your office. Keep it fuckin' quiet though. Don't want to tip the traitor off."

"I'm fucking sorry about this, Cop," Jig said, averting his eyes. "We don't figure this out soon, you can take it outta my cut."

Copper waved his hand. "Fuck that, brother. Ain't your fault. Never needed to police this shit before. Always been on the honor system. For years." He rested his head back on the top of his chair and stared at the cracked ceiling. Killed him that someone, one of his own, would steal from the club he'd die for. "So we've got a thief in our house and meth in our town." As he spoke the words aloud, anger began to creep up his spine. His family had been fending off attack after attack for the past year. Now, to know the threat came from inside their ranks?

That was a fucking betrayal like no other.

"What?" Jigsaw said. "Meth?"

Copper didn't bother to move. "Zach will fill you in. Get the fuck out, you two. Need some time to think about this shit. Spread the word, next fucker who knocks on my door leaves without his teeth."

Both men stood. "I'm here all afternoon, Prez. Shout if you need me," Jig said.

"Thanks. Keep this shit about the meth quiet for now but let the guys know we got church tonight at eight." So much for his night of hanging with Rusty. Maybe they could grab a few cold ones after the meeting.

Copper

"You got it, Prez." Zach knocked his knuckles against the desk then the two men disappeared leaving Copper to his thoughts.

Sometimes, the heavy weight of running the club grew burdensome. For Copper, falling into the position of president after Sarge's murder was natural. He'd always been a leader. Always in control, running the show, giving the orders. But that also meant bearing the responsibility of his and his men's actions.

Some of the guys might not agree with him, but he felt everything the club did was ultimately his responsibility. He felt the elation of each triumph and the stabbing pain of each failure. And this year, there'd been one too many failures.

The biggest being letting the scum of the earth, Lefty, survive. Just a few short months ago, Copper had sat across the table from Lefty in an attempt at a truce. He hadn't wanted to drag his club through a messy war that would potentially cost lives.

His greatest regret was letting Lefty live that day. How easy would it have been to plug the asshole between the eyes? Too easy. And now, the club was still paying for that poor decision.

Teenage girls had been kidnapped and raped. Another young woman had been raped and beaten severely. Stephanie was almost kidnapped. Izzy was attacked. And now meth was circulating his fucking town. All things that could have been avoided had he lodged some lead in Lefty's cranium.

It stops today.

Every resource at the club's disposal would go toward finding and eliminating Lefty.

Right after he cut the head off the snake in his own house.

CHAPTER EIGHTEEN

"Mom? We're here." Shell held her wriggling daughter on one hip while pushing the door open.

"Put me down," Beth whined as she practically dove from Shell's arms.

"Whoa, girl, careful. Don't want to drop you. You are seriously heavy."

Beth giggled and shot off toward her grandmother as Cindy's small frame appeared in the short hallway leading to the master bedroom. "Gramma!" Sometimes Shell was amazed at how young her mother still looked, but then she recalled her mom was actually young. She'd had Shell at nineteen so she was only in her early forties. Shell's pops had been a decade older.

"Hey, Mom," Shell said as she set down her suitcase-sized purse. "Brought some dessert."

"How's my Bethy-girl?" Cindy said, scooping Beth up and peppering her little face with kisses.

Beth squealed in delight and returned the affection.

As she waited to be acknowledged, Shell pulled the box of donuts she'd purchased from a local bakery out of her purse. After another thirty seconds of being ignored, she rolled her eyes and said, "Want these in the kitchen?"

Once again, not even so much as a glance from her mother. Shell was used to it. Cindy hated the MC with a fiery passion. Blamed them for her husband's death. What she'd never come to realize, or never been willing to admit, was that her husband's own actions were the reason for his death. He'd been coloring too far outside the lines and without the knowledge or backing of the club. Not that his death was justified or deserved in any way shape or form, but it wasn't the fault of the club. Even if it had been, her mother had known what she was signing on for when she married Sarge. Hell, her mom grew up in an MC in California. One that was much bloodier and grittier than the Handlers.

But after Sarge was killed, her mom cut off all ties with the MC. Refused any financial help, got pissy and huffy anytime they were mentioned and rode Shell hard for continuing her association with them. Especially after Beth was born. Her mom was convinced Beth was Copper's daughter. The product of some drunken night of passion Shell wouldn't 'fess up to. Made her hate the MC even more.

If she only knew…

Thing of it was, even if Shell hadn't been in love with the club's president since she was a kid, she'd still want to be involved with the club. They were her family. The only family she knew, and not only did she want them in her life, she needed them. The whole rough, tough, gruff gang of 'em. That had become obvious when she'd lived out of state and was miserable for five years.

Shell frowned as her mom turned and walked into the kitchen with Beth in her arms. Usually, she wasn't *this* standoffish. Sure, she and Shell were far from besties, but she wasn't completely ignored in her mother's house. "Mom?" Shell asked following them. "Everything all right?"

Her mother turned and set Beth down. After pulling a cookie from a sheet cooling on the stove, she said to Beth, "Here, sweetie. Why don't you go in Grandma's room and eat that cookie?" She winked. "There might be a surprise for you on my bed."

Beth's eyes lit like little Christmas trees. "Yay!" she shouted, pumping her cookie-filled fist in the air as she ran through the matchbook-sized apartment to her grandmother's bedroom.

Once Beth was out of earshot, Cindy turned to Shell. They shared the same curly blonde hair, but Cindy kept hers waist length. Any trace of playfulness or sweetness she'd bestowed on Beth was absent in her gaze now.

"Are you out of your freaking mind, Michelle?" she asked.

"Well, I'm a single mother of a sassy four-year-old, so probably," Shell shot back as she deposited the box of fresh-baked donuts on the small kitchen table. "But I have a feeling you're referring to something specific, so I'm going to need a bit more information."

"Don't you run that smart mouth at me. You may have all but cut me from your life, but I'm still your mother."

Resisting the urge to roll her eyes was something Shell had perfected over the years. Her mother was nothing if not a drama queen. Always had been. She lived to play the victim, and anything less than positive that occurred in her life was a personal and purposeful attack against her. "Look, Mom, I had a crazy shift at the diner today and I'm exhausted. Can you just skip the games, and tell me what has you upset?"

Cindy let out a nasty chuckle before grabbing a tall glass and taking a healthy sip. One ice cube floated at the top; the rest was probably sixteen ounces of vodka. "Surprised you're still working now that *he's* got his claws in you."

Ahh, someone told her mom about Copper. "So this is about my being with Copper?"

"Don't you say his name in this house!" Cindy's free hand flew about wildly. "That man and those damn bikers are responsible for your father's death. How can you betray me like this?"

"Betray you? My relationship with Copper has nothing to do with you. And those damn bikers are the ones who took care of you for months after daddy's death. He was their president, for crying out loud. Mom, they are our family. Bad things happen in every family, but you don't just write off your family members."

Cindy spat at Shell's feet. "Fuck them. The moment I came to my senses I walked away from them. What happened? Copper finally decide to claim Beth as his own and you hopped right back on his dick? Maybe you should just go be with that deadbeat who knocked you up, and Beth and I will have dinner alone. I'm not sure I want you here when you're trying to ruin my life like this."

Shell breathed through her nose, trying to quell the blue flame of anger surging inside her. "I'll say it one more time because it seems the other thousand times weren't enough. Copper isn't Shell's father. I can't tell you how much I wish he was, but he's not. And there is no way I'm leaving Beth here alone with you when you're acting like a lunatic." Shell absolutely despised parents who used their children as bargaining chips in relationship feuds, but her granddaughter was the only thing Cindy seemed to care about these days. "Now, Beth has been excited to see you all week, and we're here, so if you can keep your tongue civil in front of my daughter, *we* will stay for dinner. But I will not continue to bring her here if you are going spew vile nonsense about my ol' man."

Jesus, ol' man. It was the first time she'd put any kind of claim on Copper, and the words felt heavenly rolling off her tongue. Of course, they also squeezed her heart in the most painful of ways. Because things were unraveling and soon she'd be unable to pretend all was right in her world. In fact, she planned to speak with Copper about Rusty over the upcoming weekend, just two days away.

Made her sick to her stomach thinking about it.

Cindy shot daggers at Shell with her eyes. Two seconds later, Beth flew into the room, a swipe of chocolate smeared across one cheek. Cindy's eyes softened as she took in her disheveled granddaughter. Exactly the way she used to look at Shell, with love and affection. Been a long time since Shell received anything other than cold indifference or disgust.

"What's for dinner, Gramma?" Beth asked, inching closer to the cookie sheet.

Cindy snatched it up milliseconds before little hands pilfered another sweet treat. "Spaghetti," she said with a wide grin.

"Yes! My favorite," Beth sing-songed. "Me and mommy brought donuts for dessert. Can we eat those first?"

With a chuckle, Cindy bopped Beth on the nose. "No, silly Beth, you cannot. In fact, if you want a donut, you have to eat all your spaghetti and three broccoli trees."

Beth's face fell into such a pitiful look of disgust, Shell had to cover her mouth to hide the burst of laughter. Broccoli was Beth's mortal enemy.

Dinner was uneventful though a little stilted. Beth remained blissfully unaware of any tension between Cindy and Shell. She rattled on throughout the entire meal regaling them with stories of the "trouble-boy" in school. The one who not only kissed her on the mouth, but dropped his drawers and gave Beth a glimpse of his "hanging thing" the other day. Her incessant chatter allowed Shell to remain quiet and avoid questions from her mother.

By the time she'd helped clean up, dessert was eaten, and Beth watched Frozen with her grandmother, it was nearly nine at night, a solid hour past bedtime. Thankfully Shell had anticipated the late hour and brought Beth's pajamas and the stuffed unicorn Copper gave her for her birthday. She refused—loudly—to sleep without the stupid thing. To top it all off, she'd named the animal Horny on account of its sparkly pink horn. Didn't matter how many other names Shell offered up, Beth was sticking with Horny.

"Thanks for dinner, Mom," Shell said, giving her mother a stiff hug.

"I'm going to be away at the end of the month, for about ten days," Cindy said, standing in the doorway of the house.

Copper

Shell adjusted the drowsy Beth on her hip. Her mom couldn't have brought this up before she was holding thirty-five pounds of sleeping child? "Where you going?"

"On a cruise." A grin broke out across Cindy's unwrinkled face. "A singles cruise."

And how on earth was she affording that? Knowing Cindy was spending money on vacation while Shell had been forking hers over to Joe had her grinding her back teeth. "How nice for you."

"I deserve this, Shell. I've been alone for a long time. Some girlfriends and I are going to have some fun."

"Great. Enjoy yourself." With a nod, Shell turned and hefted her daughter down to the car. There was no point in getting upset over her mother's actions. Cindy was going to do what Cindy wanted to do. Always had, always would.

"Want to see my granddaughter another time before I leave," Cindy called from the open front door.

"It is what it is," Shell whispered to herself, a mantra that had gotten her through many a tough time. Suck it up, accept reality, and deal. "Sure, Mom. Text me when you're free," she called out.

"Don't you dare bring that man around me, you hear?"

"Wouldn't dream of it," Shell yelled, rolling her eyes.

After securing the many buckles on the car seat and making sure Horny was snuggled into her daughter's arms, she slipped into the driver's seat.

Another evening survived.

It said something about her enjoyment of the dinner that she'd have preferred to be cleaning offices that night.

Just as she was about to turn the ignition, her phone alerted her to an incoming text message.

Maverick: *Any chance you can swing by the clubhouse for a few hours? Steph would be happy to watch Beth for you.*

Shell glanced in the rearview mirror. Beth was already out cold.

Shell: *She's passed out in the car. I can put her to sleep in a spare room. Everything okay?*

A horde of elephant-sized butterflies flitted through her stomach while she waited for the response. Had something happened today?

Oh, God...

An icy wave of fear washed over her.

Did Rusty say something to Copper...

Maverick: *Your man had a shit day. Club business fucking with his head. Could use something soft and sweet tonight.*

Air she hadn't realized she'd been holding rushed from her lungs.

Okay, club business. Chances were, Rusty hadn't spilled his guts about Beth. Thank God. Once the grip of fear left her, concern for Copper took its place. He'd never ask her to come himself, always ready to shoulder the club's loads on his own. Hopefully, he wouldn't turn her away. If she could offer even an ounce of support and peace, it would be time well spent.

Shell: *On my way.*

A string of eggplant and kissy-face emojis was his response.

Glad for the levity, Shell pulled onto the road and tried not to let her laughter wake Beth.

Twenty minutes later she'd been admitted through the gates of the clubhouse and parked her car near the door. Not two seconds after she'd killed the engine, Beth's door opened, and Mav appeared.

"Hey, sweet stuff, I'll carry this monkey in for you."

"Thanks, Mav. You're the best. The monkey is getting heavier every day."

Mav expertly unbuckled her sleeping daughter and gathered her into his arms without so much as making her peep. All the men were so good with Beth and willing to help Shell at a moment's notice. She was beyond grateful for her family, unconventional as they may be.

Copper

"Where you want her, Shelly-belly?" he asked as they strode toward the clubhouse.

"You can put her in that room across from Copper's if no one crashed there already."

"Nah, it's free."

"Thanks, Mav. I really appreciate this. Especially you looking out for Copper."

He came to a halt in front of the door. "Got some shit going on with the club, sweetie. You know I can't tell you more, but it's got your man in a bear of a mood. Know he's too damn hardheaded to call you himself. If he's a bit of a dick, try to let it roll off, okay?"

Her lips curled up. Every man here was always looking out for her. Surrogate big brothers. That's what they were. "Got it, Mav. I can handle a growly Copper."

Inked arms full of her passed out daughter, Maverick speared her with a stern look he didn't often sport. "If he's too much of a dick, you come find me or Z, and we'll set him straight."

"Like I said, Mav, you're the best." Shell landed a peck on his cheek just as the door opened, revealing Stephanie.

"Hey, Shell," she said with a smile.

It'd taken a bit of time for Shell to feel comfortable around Stephanie. She'd been an undercover FBI agent when she met Mav, and the betrayal hit hard. But as time passed, she'd proven her love for Mav and loyalty to the MC over and over. Now they were close as sisters and part of the sacred club of women devoted to the Handlers.

"Hey, Steph."

"Look, babe," Mav said, glee oozing out his pours. "Shell just kissed me. Pretty sure you know what that means?" He bobbed his eyebrows then winked at his ol' lady.

"What?" Shell said. "It was a peck on the cheek."

With a roll of her eyes, Steph waved a dismissive hand at Mav. "Just ignore him. Come on in, it's freezing."

As Steph stepped to the side, Shell slipped into the clubhouse.

"Threesome, babe. Means I've finally found the woman who is just dying to join us."

Shell burst out laughing while Steph gave Maverick an exaggerated nod and patted his cheek. Throughout the entire exchange, Beth didn't stir.

"Sure, honey," Steph said as though placating a child. "How about this. We'll get naked and wait for you right here while you go put Beth to bed then tell Copper that you're going to have a threesome with his woman."

Mav's smile faded so fast both women cracked up. "Why you always gotta ruin my fun, woman?" he grumbled as he made his way to the stairs. "All I want is a little threesome with one of your friends. But nooo, first I gotta tell Copper and risk getting my balls shoved down my throat."

Three steps up, he turned and speared Steph with a smoldering look. "I'll remember this."

"I'm counting on it," she fired back with a wink.

"Shit, woman, I'm holding a child. Don't get me all riled up."

Laughing, Shell hugged a giggling Steph then trailed Mav up the steps. Mav's antics were legendary around the club. Nothing that fell out from his lips surprised anyone. They'd all come to expect the outrageous every time he opened his mouth.

"Thank you one more time, Mav," Shell said after he'd tucked her daughter into the queen-sized bed across the hall from Copper's suite. "She'll be dead to the world until morning."

"That's good," he said with a wink. "Though I have a feeling what's about to come will be loud enough to wake the dead."

Heat rushed to Shell's face. The sexual side of her relationship with Copper was still so fresh, she wasn't accustomed to being teased about it. She better get used to it fast with friends like Mav.

"We'll try not to offend your delicate ears," she said, face burning.

Mav barked out a laugh. "Sassy," he said. "I like it, babe." He gently nudged her toward Copper's door. "Give it to him good,

Copper

girl. The man was dished up a whole plateful of shit today." With a smacking kiss to her cheek and one last wink, he jogged down the stairs, leaving her nodding at his retreating back.

Shell tapped her knuckles on the door. In the five seconds it took Copper to yank it open, her mind had run through every possible issue the club could be encountering. The sound of Copper's gruff, "What?" grated over her exposed nerve endings.

"I, uh...hey," she bumbled over the words and shot him what she hoped was a sweet smile. His large frame took up the entire expanse of the open door. The fierce look on his face softened a fraction as he stared down at her, but not enough to have her anxiety subsiding. She'd dealt with Copper's temper many times in the past, but tonight she felt the added pressure of needing to be the one to soothe the beast.

"The fuck you doing here?" he practically shouted at her. A half-full bottle of whiskey dangled from the hand resting on the top of the door frame. Shirtless, he wore only a pair of charcoal sweat pants. The damn things hung low enough to expose a healthy portion of the V she had dreams about licking. That was one dream she needed to turn into a reality. Tonight.

"I..." Jesus, it was like she swallowed her tongue at the sexy sight of him.

He huffed out a laugh. "Asked you a question, Shell."

She forced her gaze to leave his mouth-watering body and met his none-too-welcoming stare. "Maverick texted me. Said you might be up for some company."

He took a swig from the bottle. "Meddling motherfucker."

"Huh?" What had he said? She was too distracted by the flex and play of his throat as he swallowed. "Uh," she cleared her throat. "You gonna let me in?"

"I'm shit company tonight, Shell. Just go on home, and I'll call you tomorrow."

With a snort, she slipped under his arm and into his room. "I don't think so."

Copper spun, bottle in hand and stalked toward her. She stepped back until she hit the wall opposite the door. His forearms landed above her head, boxing her in. The damn man loved to hover over her. Sometimes she wished she could grow a foot just so she could be on even footing with him when he was pissed at her. Being a full thirteen inches smaller was such a disadvantage. Not that she ever felt threatened by him, but it would be nice to eliminate his ability to loom.

"What exactly is it that you think you're going to do for me?"

Heat poured off his naked torso. Shell had to clench her fists to keep from stripping and rubbing her breasts all over that hard chest of his. "Whatever it is you need from me." She let her gaze roam his body once again. "Mav mentioned something about soft and sweet."

Copper set the bottle on a nightstand within reach. With his now empty hand, he traced the curved collar of her T-shirt then circled her slender neck. The fingers squeezed, not hard, just exerting enough pressure to remind her he had the upper hand. Like she could ever forget who and what he was. It was why she loved him.

"And if soft and sweet is the last thing I need tonight?" Copper asked.

She swallowed, feeling the muscles of her throat ripple under his unyielding grip. "Then take what you do need. I'll do anything for you, Copper. Everything for you." Even pretend for a time that this relationship had long-term potential. Pretend there wasn't a ticking time bomb counting rapidly down to a destructive blast.

"And if I want to take you so hard your legs give out and your pussy aches for a week?" He breathed the words against her ear sending shivers through her.

The pussy in reference clenched at the promise of what was to come. Maybe he needed more than her words. Perhaps he needed to see how willing she was to submit to anything he asked of her.

Copper

She took a step back, and he immediately released her neck, probably assuming she was pulling the plug. Instead, she slid her fingers into her panties. His emerald gaze followed the movement like a hawk tracking a rabbit. When she drew her hand back out, her fingers glistened, coated in her arousal. "What do you think?" she asked, holding her hand up.

He grabbed her wrist, nostrils flaring as he inhaled her scent. Then he licked the seam between her second and third fingers, cleaning them of her juices.

Holy shit, that was some powerfully sexy stuff right there.

"Strip," he ordered as his own hands went to the waistband of his sweats.

She was about to work on her jeans when he lowered his pants. Having gone commando yet again, his cock bobbed out, hard as a lead pipe.

Her mouth and pussy watered at the same time.

Damn, that thing felt so good inside her and knowing she'd have it soon nearly made her jump for joy.

"Shell!"

Oh right.

His bark had her whipping into action and scrambling to shed her clothes. Once they were both fully nude, Copper strode toward her again. His large hands landed on her waist and the next thing she knew, she was moving through the air only to have her ass land on Copper's dresser.

Mouth grim and eyes smoldering, he worked the rubber band out of her hair, releasing the messy bun that was part of her mom uniform. Once the strands were unbound, he sank his fingers into her hair and gripped a healthy handful. With full control over her head, he tipped her chin back until her entire neck was exposed to him.

"Like fucking silk," he said against her ear. "And if I want to fuck you over and over? Fill you with so much cum, it leaks out of you all night long?"

Breathless, Shell said, "Maybe you need to grab a dictionary and look up the definition of anything. Stop asking me and just take it."

"Careful what you wish for," he whispered before capturing her earlobe between his teeth. He tugged then moved onto her neck, sucking at the taut skin until she squirmed in his hold. He made love to her neck with his mouth until her hands landed on his waist, curling her short nails into his skin. The prick of pain only spurred him on more as the pressure of his suction increased.

Shell moaned. Body on fire, her breasts felt heavy and full, nipples longing for Copper's attention. Between her spread legs, her pussy ached to be filled by him. But his attention stayed at her neck and jaw, too far above the collarbone for her needs.

"Copper," she pleaded, aware and unashamed of the whine.

He chuckled, then one large hand drifted down her spine, leaving a trail of tingling goosebumps in its wake. Continuing lower, he dipped his fingers between the globes of her ass to the place only he'd explored.

"Anything?" he asked.

"Copper," she said trying to convey with her eyes that four-letter word she refused to admit because it would only end in heartbreak, "I am here, in this room, to give you anything you need from me. Let me be what you need. Let me be your woman."

At least until her truth came out, and he couldn't bear to look her in the eye any longer. The pain of that would be beyond excruciating, but at least she'd have these moments of perfection to look back on. Hopefully, they'd carry her through the dark and lonely days to come.

CHAPTER NINETEEN

Let me be your woman.

Those words, that plea reached deep inside Copper and stroked his soul, dousing enough of the day's anger for him to take a mental step back and appreciate what he had spread out before him.

One hand gripped her sleek thigh while the other hovered millimeters from her untried asshole. Legs spread impossibly wide to accommodate his bulk, Shell stared at him without a single wall around her delicate heart. Those gorgeous blue eyes reflected every thought, every emotion she was experiencing. Trust, desire, and maybe even love shone back at him.

Love? Was he headed there? He'd never so much as given it a thought. Love wasn't something he'd witnessed, let alone experienced much in his life. Only in recent times, since the men in his club started dropping like flies, had he even contemplated the idea. And he wasn't yet sure it was a comfortable fit.

They weren't there yet. Weren't ready to speak those words. Shell might trust him with her body, but there were events in Shell's past she still didn't trust to voice. Namely the circumstance surrounding her pregnancy. Until she was able to release those secrets to him, he couldn't call it love.

But it was damn close.

Let me be your woman.

And she could be, if he gave himself over to her. This tiny woman had the internal might of a hundred warriors. She was just what a man needed to balance the often-harsh role of motorcycle club president with the rest of life. When he laid his head on the pillow and whispered into the quiet night, Shell would be there to lend her strength and soothe him. She wouldn't judge the acts he'd done and would continue to do to keep his club and men safe. And when he put a voice to his fears and doubts, she'd bolster him with her love.

"My queen," he whispered.

"What?"

"I'll let you be my queen." Gently, he ran a fingertip through her saturated folds. "Anyone with one of these is a woman. Takes a helluva lot more to be a queen. You've always been exactly what I needed, baby. You're my queen."

Shell's breath hitched, and she reached up, grabbing the bottom of his beard. One firm tug, and her mouth met his. Hungry, demanding, full of fire and passion.

He kissed her until they were both breathless; until the room spun and his need for oxygen almost outweighed his need for his woman...his queen.

Shell's tits smashed into his chest as her arms wound around his neck, pulling him closer. The hardened tips of her nipples prodded his heated skin. Her soft belly cushioned his hard-as-hell cock. She didn't seem to notice or care precum was leaking from the tip and dripping down her stomach. Hell, knowing Shell, maybe she did notice and fucking loved it. He wanted to be everywhere at once, her mouth, her tits, her pussy, even her ass, but at some point, he had to choose where to concentrate his efforts.

He slid one hand from her ass to her lower back, then brought the other one between her legs, coating his fingers in the slippery arousal. Shell moaned. When he took the pleasure and his hand away, she cried, "What? No!".

Copper

"Shh. I'll be back, baby. I won't ever leave you wanting." He winked. "We're just doing this on my timetable."

The little snarl of frustration that came from Shell had him laughing. She may be accommodating most of the time, but in the bedroom, she wasn't willing to be denied.

He was tempted to lift his fingers to his mouth and grab another sample of her essence, but instead, he snuck them around to her ass once again as he continued to devour her mouth. Inching inward, he brushed one finger against the tight hole causing her to jolt and reflexively sink her teeth into his lower lip. The sharp bite had him groaning against her lips and slipping the tip of his finger inside her.

Shell's head fell back. Mouth open, she breathed in short, rapid pants and her hands clutched his back as he worked the digit deeper inside her.

"More?" he asked. "Good?" Full sentences were impossible. Blood continued to rush away from his brain and toward his throbbing cock. The urge to ram inside her and pound away until they were both screaming ravaged him, but somehow, he found the strength to ignore it. He wanted her totally mindless with lust before he drove home.

She nodded, gasping as he pulled out then sank his finger deep into her ass. "Intense," she whispered.

He thrust his finger in and out, picking up the pace. With his other hand, he strummed her clit. Shell whimpered and held him so tight he'd be bruised in the morning.

Fuckin' A.

Her head rolled across her shoulders. That exposed curve of her neck beckoned him, and he zeroed in on her pulse point, sucking hard. He wouldn't be the only one wearing evidence of their lovemaking in the days to follow.

After leaving a calling card, he kissed his way down her chest and over the plump mounds of her breasts. He rubbed his beard over her nipple and chuckled when she jolted. Saliva pooled in his mouth at the thought of having that puckered bud in his mouth, so he pulled it between his lips.

Why deny himself?

Layer upon layer, he built the erotic sensations until her body quivered in his hold. Finger buried in her ass, another torturing her little clit, and firm suction on her nipple. She writhed and made the sexiest sounds of need. Soon, in a matter of seconds, she'd be right where he wanted her...out of her mind with the need to be satisfied by him.

And only him.

"Copper." Desperation tinged her voice.

Fuck yes.

"Tell me, baby?"

"I need you."

"Know it, beautiful. Tell me more."

A tiny groan of frustration erupted from her, and she wiggled her hips trying to get closer. He knew she needed his cock, but wouldn't give it to her until she said the words. Until she begged for it.

"I need to be fucked. I need you inside me. Please, Copper, you know what I want."

With his finger still in her ass but not moving, he gripped his cock and ran it across her soaked sex, pausing right at her opening. Her pussy sucked at the tip, making pleasure shoot through him. His eyes crossed as he gritted his teeth to keep from tunneling straight to heaven too early. He kissed her lips quickly. "Tell me what you're feeling. Want to hear what I'm doing to you."

Her eyes were closed, lips were swollen and parted in a way that had him imaging them sliding up and down his cock. Next time. He'd never make it more than a second. "I—I'm empty. My pussy aches. It keeps clenching, but there's nothing there. You're not there. And I need you to be. When you're inside me, I'm so full, and it feels unbelievable. Like there's nothing in the world

Copper

that can hurt me. Nothing that can ever end the pleasure. Then when you move, I—ahhh."

Fuck it. He thrust forward with a powerful snap of his hips, driving as deep as her body would allow him. Shell came instantly, her pussy rippling around him in agonizing waves of ecstasy that nearly made him unload right then and there. Only the fierce desire to tip her over the edge one more time before he came kept him from blowing.

Shell was so wet, her juices had run down her thighs and onto his dresser, creating a slippery surface. Perfect for sliding her back and forth along his cock. He did just that, gripping her by the ass as he pounded into her each time he jerked her hard against his body. She held on for dear life, crying out with each plunge of his dick.

"Jesus, Copper," she said as he showed no mercy. His finger was still buried in her, but he was too far gone to remember to work it as he fucked her. The pressure of it filling her seemed to be more than enough to compound her pleasure. Her ass squeezed his finger each time her pussy clamped down on him.

Their mouths met and he swore she was trying to inhale him with the intensity of her kiss. He had no idea how long it went on for, fucking into her over and over, reveling in every cry of passion and every demand for more. Could have been minutes, hours, hell a whole day could have gone by before Shell ripped her mouth away and yelled, "Fuck, Copper, I'm coming again."

Her small body went rigid in his arms as her pussy nearly crushed his cock. "Fuck, fuck, fuck," she chanted, banging her head against his chest. He never let up, pummeling her with his cock through her orgasm. When her shaking finally subsided, she shifted her head and captured his nipple between her teeth. A shock of electricity zinged straight to his cock. The most mind-altering orgasm he'd ever experienced blasted through him, catching him off guard with its intensity. His back arched and he shouted, shooting his firehose-strength release into Shell's warm, willing body.

Just as he was coming down off the high, an aftershock moved through Shell. Her core squeezed his overly sensitive cock, making him jolt. With his hands still full of her ass, she jerked forward as he lurched back. And damn that slippery dresser. Shell slid straight off the bureau and crashed into Copper. Since he was already on a backward trajectory, he couldn't catch his balance. As they careened toward the ground, Shell's surprised shriek filled the air along with the sound of shattering glass. He'd had an empty rock's glass on top of the dresser. Not anymore.

The wooden floor broke their fall, a thin rug doing nothing to cushion his tailbone. Shell landed on him with another shrill cry. Thankfully his dick slipped out of her or he might have been maimed. An ER trip due to broken dick wasn't how he envisioned the rest of the evening playing out.

"Holy crap, are you okay?" Shell asked at the same time a "What the fuck?" sounded in the hallway.

Thankfully, the moment Copper heard someone yell in the hall, his brain kicked into gear. He reached for his bed, and yanked a blanket off, tossing it at Shell.

Chaos ensued, a million things happening at once. The blanket floated down over Shell's head, ghost-style. A short pound on his door was immediately followed by the damn thing flying open revealing a panicked Maverick, Zach, and Rocket. "Fuck boss, you okay? We heard a crash and some fucking glass shattering," Zach said before the door was fully wide.

"Copper!" Shell said in an exasperated tone as she started to sift her way out from under the blanket. "What the hell?"

"Don't move that blanket. We're not alone, babe," he said which made her squeak under the blanket.

"Who's here?"

Mav was the first to lose his shit. The asshat doubled over, laughing so hard it turned into a strangled choke. Zach and Rocket followed closely behind until all three dipshits were practically pissing themselves with hilarity.

Copper

"Fuck you all." Copper said. "Can you get the fuck out of my room?"

"N-No," Mav said between bouts of laughter. "No I don't think we can do that. At least not before this." He whipped his phone out of thin air and snapped a picture. "Priceless."

"Oh man," Zach said, wiping his eyes. "The fuck kinda kinky shit you two get up to?"

"Copper, what the hell is going on?"

He looked up at his woman, straddled over his naked body, a blanket fully covering her body, head included, and he couldn't help but join his brothers in their amusement. "Nothing, babe, these assholes just think they're funny."

"Well get them out of here! And did I hear someone take a picture? Was that you Maverick? If you don't delete it, I'll tell Stephanie to stay away from your itty-bitty penis for a month!"

The men started laughing all over again at the waif of a woman sitting astride a huge naked man with a blanket over her head. All but Maverick. He snorted and said, "Please, like that woman could make it two days without my cock."

"Maverick!" Shell screeched.

"Yeah?"

"Get the hell out of here!"

"All right, fuckers, show's over," Copper said. "Get the hell out of here. Send Thunder up in ten minutes to clean the fucking glass."

The men filed out, still laughing. When the coast was clear, Copper tugged the blanket off Shell's head. Hair a mess, cheeks flushed from the heat of being covered with a blanket and a bit of anger, and hands on her hips, she looked sexy as fuck. His mouth curled into a huge smile. He'd laughed more in the past five minutes than in the last year combined. Shell did that. She softened him in some ways, brought levity and joy into his life. On the surface, it seemed to be nothing but positive, but would it change him too much? Would she dull his sharp edges to the point he'd lose his advantage as a leader?

And what if she never let him fully into her heart, never shared her secrets? Would he survive the loss of her in this new role of lover?

"That was so *not* funny," she said, but her lips quirked totally killing the serious effect. "Your brothers are idiots."

"Can't argue with you there." He let his head fall back against the floor. "You good? I was a bit of a prick when you came in."

Resting her palms on his chest, Shell smiled down at him. "I'm better than good. Think you made up for any grumpiness tenfold."

He arched an eyebrow. "Did I?"

"Yep. And you can continue making it up to me right now."

Damn, his woman was insatiable. "What'd you have in mind, gorgeous?" He crunched to a sitting position, gave each of her nipples a brief suck then kissed her upturned lips.

"Food," she said with a mischievous smile as she hopped off him and searched for her jeans.

With a groan, Copper forced himself to stand. "Well played. Watch out for the glass."

Two hours later they'd raided the kitchen and engaged in another round of sweaty play. Now, Shell sat with her back against Copper's headboard happily munching on some pita chips. She'd loved those damn things for as long as he could remember, so he made sure to always have them stocked in the clubhouse kitchen. He reclined against his pillow one arm tucked behind his head, the other hand idly drawing circles on Shell's smooth thigh. They'd been silent for the past ten minutes, but it was a contemplative and comfortable silence.

"Thanks, baby," he said, ending the lull.

Chip midway to her mouth, Shell paused. "What for?"

"I needed you tonight. Didn't even realize how much, but you did. So you came." He winked. "In more ways than one."

Her beautiful face flushed as she threw her half-eaten chip at him. When he caught it in his mouth mid-flight, she rolled her eyes but then grew serious. "Copper, while I'm with you I will walk across hot coals to give you what you need."

While I'm with you. What the fuck did that mean? Did she have an ending in sight? "You planning on going somewhere?"

"What? No, I mean, uh, maybe, I mean, we never know where life is going to take us. Maybe you'll get sick of me and kick me to the curb. I just meant while we're together." She shoved a chip in her mouth and crunched effectively ending that conversation. He'd give it to her for now. She was skittish.

Fine.

With time she'd come to realize he wasn't going fucking anywhere.

And when had he made that life decision? Despite the fact that Shell made him laugh, calmed his demons, and the sex was off the charts, she was still sixteen years his junior. For her sake, he should walk away.

Too bad he was so selfish.

Shell dropped the bag of chips over the side of the bed, brushed her hands together, then laid back, resting her head on his chest. Her soft weight lifted and fell as he breathed. Club business wasn't generally shared with the ol' ladies, but it wasn't necessarily a hard and fast rule. In times of crisis, when the women needed to be alert and wary, they'd be given enough information to keep themselves safe, but generally speaking, club business was for club ears only.

"Someone's stealing from the club," he said in a quiet voice, breaking his own rule. But it didn't feel wrong. Didn't even feel risky. Right then, in that bed, in that moment, Shell was his woman. Seemed she was just naturally an extension of him. She was also the most loyal person he'd met. Nothing he confessed would leave the sacred vault of his bedroom. In fact, he was pretty damn sure Shell would die before betraying him or the club.

Perfect ol' lady material.

She breathed out, then lifted her head and gave him her full attention. "You sure?"

"Yeah. Ten Gs so far. To add insult to injury, we've got an increase in meth sales in our county. Club's worried Lefty may be running the drugs from whatever hole he's been hiding in."

"Shit, Copper, no wonder you're stressed. What can I do for you?"

He stroked his hand up and down the silky skin of her back. "Just this, babe. This is more than enough."

She rested her head back down and gave him a squeeze. "Remember what I said, Copper. Anything."

And he'd give her anything in return. As soon as the club shit was sorted, he'd be sorting Shell's shit. Because whatever ghost from her past making her hesitate, needed to be destroyed.

CHAPTER TWENTY

"You heading out now, Prez?" Zach asked as Copper exited his office.

"Yeah, brother. Feel up for a ride?" A two-hour ride into questionably friendly territory without his enforcer was just plain stupid.

"Fuck yeah," Zach answered. "Always. Been hoping you'd ask." Zach deposited a full crate of liquor on the bar and made his way toward Copper.

"Anything you gotta take care of before we roll?" Copper asked.

"Nah, I'm good. Told Toni I'd probably be riding out with you today. She won't expect me till later. Let's handle this," Zach said as he held his closed fist out.

Copper bumped his fist against Zach's. A president couldn't ask for a better enforcer. Zach anticipated what was required of him before Copper even floated an idea. A sit-down with Joe was set for midafternoon. Ragnar would have been preferred as he was at the top of the food chain, but the fucker wouldn't come down off his kingpin throne in Maryland to make a trip to Tennessee. Joe was Ragnar's eyes and ears in the area and apparently his mouth as well. Unfortunately, the agreed upon location was a good few hours outside of town. Since the Handlers requested the meet, Joe wouldn't go out of his way and drive to Townsend.

Copper was no fool. Joe couldn't be trusted and wasn't an ally. He'd be remiss not to take backup along, but he didn't want to appear as though he was rolling up with the whole MC in tow. There was a difference between protection and an outright show of force. Joe needed to understand Copper took this shit seriously and wouldn't be fucked with, but he wasn't interested in sparking a war with Ragnar either. The man's reach was too far and too wide.

"Thanks, Z. Rusty is riding too. I just talked to him. He should pull in any minute."

Zach opened his mouth then shook his head and sat at a table to wait.

"Something on your mind, brother?" Copper asked.

Waving a hand, Zach said, "Ain't a thing. Forget it."

"Don't give me that shit." Since when did he hold back? "You leave your balls in Toni's purse? Speak your mind."

Zach cocked his head then shrugged. "Just surprised you're bringing Rusty is all."

Copper frowned. "Why are you surprised?"

"Look, Prez, he's your family, so sometimes the guys don't wanna say shit about him, but he ain't exactly snuggling back into the fold if you know what I mean."

"You're all my fucking family." Seriously? Zach was going to play word games with him. "No, I don't fucking know what you mean. Man the fuck up and give it to me straight."

Zach ran a hand through his hair as he grumbled, "Fine, Prez, but remember I'm just the damn messenger." Of course, when he was done abusing the blond strands, they fell back into place exactly as they'd been.

"Z," Copper growled.

Raising his hands by his ears, Zach said, "He's pissed off just about every brother he's run across since getting free. He's mouthing off, hitting on women who aren't available to him, and he's overly aggressive."

Copper

Fuck. Copper had suspected the transition wasn't going well. Sucked to have his doubts confirmed. Half his head had been on the clusterfuck of missing money and meth running through his town. The other half was consumed by Shell. Meant he wasn't giving enough brain power to his brother who was obviously struggling. "Aggressive?"

Zach nodded. "Drove away a few of my members at the gym. Lost his shit over nonsense. Screaming at them, getting up in their face, tossing them off equipment. He doesn't quite understand the *customer's always right* mantra. Hell, he doesn't think the customer is ever right." He scratched at his cheek where an unusual amount of stubble had been allowed to sprout. Zach was usually the cleanest shaven of the MC.

"Gets worse. Last week, LJ took him on a debt collection. Good customer. Borrows a shit-ton from the club, never once late on a repayment. Fucking ideal situation. That morning, the dude's wife was in a minor car wreck. It made him late getting his hands on the cash. He asked LJ to come back in two hours. Rusty went apeshit. Pulled a fucking gun on the guy. Took LJ all afternoon to get my guy to agree to keep borrowing from us."

"Goddammit," Copper spat. This was shit he didn't need. Between the stolen money and increased meth in town, he had enough garbage on his plate. Last thing he needed was to start babysitting his grown-ass brother. "All right. I'll get on his ass. Anything else?"

Zach looked uncomfortable. "Sucker punched Maverick a few nights ago."

"The fuck? That's how Mav got that black eye? The jerkoff told me it was some kinda acrobatic sex injury."

They stared at each other and for a moment then the tension dissolved as they chuckled. Leave it to Mav to turn his injury into some kind of kinky sexcapade.

"Nah, nothing so glamorous, Prez. You know a bunch of the guys went to see Jig's fight three nights ago. Well, Steph tagged along cuz she loves that shit. And I think she and Mav have some kinda thing going where they try to fuck at each of the fights." He swiped his hand as though dismissing his own statement. "Anyway, Rust drank enough to float a fucking barge and got a little handsy with Steph. Grabbed her ass and tried to shove his tongue down her throat. She gave him a good knee-to-nuts shot, but Mav got up in his face anyway. Nothing major, just warning him to back the fuck off his ol' lady. Rust clocked him."

"Jesus. I'll talk to him. Maybe he's just gotten too used to the way shit's done in prison."

"Fuck that." Zach's face grew stormy. "We've both known plenty of men, brothers even who came back from the joint. They didn't act like fucking douche bags at every turn."

Zach had a point. "I know he's always been a little tough to take, but when it comes down to it, he's as committed to the club as any of us." Tough to take was a nice way of saying Rusty could be a shit. He'd been that way since he was a child. Copper had bailed his ass out of trouble more times than he could count. But he was blood and had been handed a shit deal most of his life. Guy deserved to be cut a little slack. "Let's see how this shit goes today, then I'll find out where his head's at."

Just as Zach began to agree, the clubhouse door burst open, and Rusty made his entrance. He swaggered over to the bar and grabbed a bottle of whiskey. After a long swallow, he made his way to Copper and Zach. "Morning, ladies," he said.

Copper frowned. "We got a two-hour ride, brother."

"Know it, *Dad*." Rusty sucked back another swig of whiskey then let out a resounding belch. "Just a little hair of the dog."

"Shit, man, ever think about brushing your teeth?" Zach said, waving his hand in front of his nose. "You look like fucking roadkill. Smell worse."

He did. Yesterday's gray Henley was rumpled, his eyes were bloodshot, and a scraggly beard covered the once smooth skin of his face. Rusty looked like he'd been living on the streets rather than staying at the clubhouse the past few weeks.

Copper

"Had me an epic night, boys. Just rolled outta some chick's bed about," he looked at his watch, "'bout ten minutes ago." He winked. "She had two roommates. Mmm, mmm, mmm," he said kissing his fingertips like an Italian grandmother appreciating her slow-simmered sauce. "Good fucking night. Not that you boys would understand seeing as how you're fucking the same old stale pussy—when you can actually talk your ol' ladies into spreading their hairy legs."

Neither Copper nor Zach laughed, but Rusty didn't notice or didn't care that his crass humor at their ol' ladies expense wasn't appreciated.

"Although," he said, whacking Zach on the back. "I hear your ol' lady used to get up to some pretty freaky shit back in the day. Way to go, brother. You bagged a wild one. You ever need a hand with her—"

"All right," Copper broke in before Zach had a chance to commit homicide. He slung his arm across Rusty's shoulders. What the fuck was his brother thinking with that below-the-belt-comment? Zach's fists curled as his mouth flattened with displeasure. The club's enforcer knew how to control himself, but taunts about Toni's past were the one thing that could send him off the rails. Years ago, she'd been involved with a motherfucker who took advantage of her and messed her head up. The banger ended up being an enemy of the club and nearly killed Toni not even a year ago.

In Rusty's defense, he hadn't been around to see the devastation Toni went through with Shark. But Zach's memories were too fresh for Rusty's taunts. If Copper hadn't stepped in, shit would have gotten ugly real fast. "Hey, Z, we'll meet you outside in five."

After nodding, Zach trudged outside without so much as a glance in Rusty's direction.

"Something I said?" asked Rusty on a laugh.

Staring at the ceiling, Copper rubbed his beard. "Listen, Rust, you gotta put a lid on that shit. Hear me?"

"Oh, come on, that fucking pussy can't take a joke?" He lifted the bottle, but Copper grabbed it before he could drink again. He was seriously considering making Rusty stay behind. They did not need the cops on their asses because his bike was swerving all over the goddamn highway.

"I'm serious, Rust. Hear you been pissing a lot of the guys off. You gotta tone it down. Shit's different than it was before you left. Lotta guys got ol' ladies now. They're protective as fuck and won't tolerate your hands-on ways or insults to their women."

Rusty's eyes narrowed, and he seemed to grow a few inches as his stance stiffened.

Jesus, was he gearing up for a fight?

"Giving me orders, Cop? This little lecture coming from my brother or my President?"

An ache formed behind Copper's eyes. He didn't have time for this shit. Getting Shell out from under Joe's thumb was the problem of the day. Rusty's behavior would have to wait. "Does it matter? Just want you happy and back with your family. Come on, let's table this for now. We gotta move out if we're gonna get there in time, and I'm sure as hell not walking in late."

The ride took a little under two hours. Thankfully Rusty managed to keep his bike pointed in the right direction the entire trip. They made sure Rusty rode between him and Zach just to be sure.

Copper had no problem meeting on Joe's turf mainly because he didn't want the asshole in Townsend or anywhere he'd risk running into Shell.

The initial plan had been to put pressure on Joe. Get him to return the money collected from Shell. After some debate, a new idea came to light. Ragnar wouldn't let the debt slide and wouldn't return Shell's money without a fight. A fight the Handlers didn't need. Not with Lefty crawling out from whatever rock he'd been hiding under and getting back in business. The club could use Joe's help. Pissing him off wouldn't get that help. So, they'd have to give the man what he wanted to get what they needed. The enemy of my enemy is my friend and such shit.

Last night, the club voted almost unanimously to cover the debt Shell's father incurred and reimburse the money she'd already forfeited to Joe. Rusty had been the only one to shoot down the vote. Said they shouldn't be cleaning up bitches' messes. Even after reminding him the debt wasn't actually Shell's, but the club's prior president's, he stuck to his guns.

Whatever the fuck was going on with him, it was bleeding into club business and had the potential to fuck with Copper's personal life as well. Not that he'd let it. Blood brother or not, Shell would be protected at all costs. And getting her to accept money from the club was a battle for another day. He smiled to himself. There were plenty of ways to get her to take the money. Very pleasurable ways.

After dropping their kickstands, they strode through the dimly lit bar to a back-corner booth as directed by a meathead bouncer. Zach slipped into the booth followed by Copper, while Rusty stood guard near the bar, arms folded across his chest. Normally Zach's role, but he didn't trust Rust to keep his yap shut. Fucking up this meet was not an option.

Even though they were ten minutes early, Joe was already seated and had his own muscle lingering much in the same stance as Rusty. "Copper," he said with a grin. The smaller man had grown a goatee since he'd last been in Townsend. Darker than the graying hair on his head, it looked dyed, fake. "Can't say I was surprised to hear from you after running into you at our girl's house."

Our girl.

Fuck that.

Copper's fists curled, but he managed to avoid busting Joe's teeth. The goal here was to get the fucker off Shell's back. Not leave with a target on his own. While going home with some of Joe's pearly whites littering the floor of the bar might feel satisfying, it wouldn't accomplish the goal.

"Here." He tossed a thick envelope on the table in front of Joe.

One of the man's eyebrows rose into a triangular point. "What's this?"

"Payment. In full. Every cent Shell owes you plus interest as though you continued to collect from her monthly."

The other eyebrow met its counterpart. "Bitch must have a mouth like a Hoover for you to go to all this trouble."

Across the room, Rusty laughed. Funny how Copper could let Joe's taunt roll off his back, but when Rusty laughed, he wanted to rip his brother's throat out. Zach's foot landed on his. A subtle *don't fucking do it*. Copper rolled his shoulders. "We square?"

With a shrug, Joe said, "Looks like it." A sly smile curved his lips. "Hell, had I known you'd fork over the cash this easily I'd have come to the club in the first place."

That was a pile of bullshit if he'd ever heard one. Joe was far from stupid. Had he darkened the Handlers' door, he'd have been sent packing with a few motorcycle boots up his ass. He'd played the game well. Gone after what he considered a weak link. Probably figured it was only a matter of time before Shell went crying to the club for help. Then they'd be forced to pay. The end result was the same, but Joe underestimated Shell. Had Copper not discovered her secret, she'd have surrendered every penny from her meager paycheck to clear the debt on her own.

"Got some other business," Zach said, speaking up for the first time.

"Oh yeah? What's that?" Joe clutched the envelope as though afraid Copper or Zach would snatch it back and make a run for it.

"Seem to have an uptick in meth sales on our turf over the last few weeks. Got any idea what that's about?" Zach practically snarled the words.

"Nope. Can't say that I do. Ain't us, boys." Joe smirked.

Zach's snort filled the booth. "Right."

Copper held up a hand. "Let's cut the shit. We ain't looking to start shit with you guys. You got a guy on payroll called Lefty."

Copper

When Joe opened his mouth, Copper slapped his palm on the table. "Don't fucking deny it. He's selling in my town. Now, I want two things. I want your shit out of my territory, and I want Lefty."

The silence that followed was thick with tension. "Fuck it," Joe muttered. "Look, I know there ain't much love between us, but Ragnar has no desire to get on the Handlers' shit list. We ain't selling in your town. I make sure of that."

"Fuck this," Zach said. His hands hit the table, and he rose, looming over Joe. "Waste of our time, Cop."

"Calm your dog down, Copper. I ain't finished." Funny he cared because Joe filled the exact same roll Zach did. Enforcer. The muscle. The beat-down guy.

"Cool it, Z," Copper said. Beside him, Zach sat, but his body still held the rigidly of anger.

"Lefty is one of ours. But he's under strict orders to stay out of your territory. Like I said, we ain't looking to start shit with your club. Anything he's doing is on his own. You got my word, I'll get him to back off."

"Your *word*," Zach spat as though the concept was hilarious.

Copper put a hand on Zach's shoulder, silencing his enforcer. This was why he was president. This was why his men trusted him to lead them. He didn't lose his temper. He kept a calm head and thought through his actions and words. Not like many of his guys who flew off the handle all too easily.

"Not good enough," Copper said. "I want Lefty. Has nothing to do with you or your boss. But I need Lefty delivered to me."

Joe tilted his head, an evil grin curling his mouth. "I can get him off your turf free of charge, but anything else is gonna cost ya."

With a nod, Copper said, "We're prepared to work with that."

Laughter was Joe's reply. "You prepared to unload a shipment of meth for us?"

Copper didn't find the exchange nearly as amusing as Joe did. "Hoping it won't come to that. Hoping we can be of service in another way."

"Fucking Boy Scouts," Joe mumbled. Growing quiet, he tossed back the rest of his drink and waved to the bartender for another. "Got a few low-level dealers in your area." He held up his hand when Zach scoffed. "Not in your town. I fucking told you, that's Lefty stepping outside his box. These jokers are behind on getting me my cut of what they sold. Was planning on heading down there and busting some heads next week. You boys save my knuckles a few cracks—"

"We'll do it," Zach said before Copper even had a chance to run the potential outcomes through his head. He'd be speaking with his enforcer about that later. He got it, though. Every man in the club wanted Lefty, and most were willing to do whatever the fuck it took to get him. Even push a haul of meth. Copper didn't plan to let it get that far.

"How many we talking 'bout?"

"Five guys," Joe said. "Each owes upwards of twenty."

Zach whistled. "Not chump change."

"Exactly," Joe replied. "You get me my cash, I'll have Lefty delivered to you alive and kicking."

Zach faced Copper, his eyes imploring. For a second, Copper let the thrill of having Lefty in his custody wash over him. The motherfucker deserved everything that'd be coming to him, and a lot of pain was headed his way. "Deal," he said then turned to Zach. "Give him your number, Z." Then to Joe, "You can send Zach the information he needs to collect your money."

Pulling out his phone, Joe lifted his chin then entered the digits as Zach rattled them off. "You'll have what you need by tomorrow."

Copper stood and nodded at Joe. Immediately, Zach followed suit and Rusty pushed away from the bar. There'd be no handshakes, no fist bumps, no slaps, no pounding on each other's back. No one here liked each other. Just held a grudging respect for the fact that they ran successful operations in the same crooked underworld and wanted no trouble. Honor among thieves kind of thing.

Once they were outside, Copper took his first full breath. The sun still warmed the air but would be dwindling by the time they returned home. The temperature was warmer than it had been over the past few weeks and was slated to continue that way which was why they'd rode their bikes. Driving in a cage sucked, and they only did it when the alternative was hypothermia.

"So how we gonna play this?" Rusty asked when they reached their bikes.

"What do you mean?" Zach asked.

"Well, we ain't fucking doing this asshole's dirty work. We just paid him a shit ton of money, above what Shell actually owed. Now we're gonna do him favors? Do his job for him? Don't fucking think so, right, Cop?"

With a roll of his eyes, Zach zipped up his leather Handlers' jacket. "Seems to me like you forgot the fucking meaning of brotherhood while you were locked up." As he spoke, he threw his thick leg over his bike.

"Fuck you," Rusty said, starting for Zach. This wouldn't be like Mav or even Jig. Zach wouldn't suffer an underserved punch. He'd fight back, and both men would end up damaged. Which would make the ride home suck.

Copper slammed a hand against Rusty's chest, stopping his forward progression. "Shut the fuck up, both of you." Standing between the two snorting bulls with one hand on Rusty's chest and the other extended toward Zach, Copper turned toward his brother. "Rust, we ain't doing anyone any favors. This is price of doing business. I need something from him. Never expected him to hand over Lefty for free. Just be glad he ain't asking us to sell his fucking meth."

Rusty threw his hands up. "Jesus, bro, you think you got the better option? You know how much fucking money we could make selling his shit? Wasted fucking opportunity if you ask me."

Copper narrowed his eyes and worked not to crack a molar. "Club makes plenty of fucking money. We walked away from that shit for a reason, Rusty. Way before you went away. You remember what it was like back then. A bloody fucking mess. Club's not going down that road again. You hear me?"

"Loud and clear, *Prez*," Rusty said, the title dripping with sarcasm. He stalked toward his bike, mounted, then rode off in a thick cloud of dust before Copper even made a move toward his bike.

"Fuck," Copper bit out.

"Pretty much sums it up," Zach said.

CHAPTER TWENTY-ONE

"Look, Mommy, I'm doing it. I'm doing it!" Beth screamed with extra loud glee. Typically, Shell would have her take it down a notch, but her excitement was so genuine and uninhibited, she figured a few shrill yells wouldn't hurt.

Her little legs pumped in and out as she worked the swing back and forth, her smile so wide it took up her entire small face. A pang hit Shell's heart. Silly, really, but each time Beth learned a new skill, she needed her mother a little less, and that was a hard pill for Shell to swallow. She'd been Beth's everything since day one, and it wouldn't be long before she wasn't needed at all.

"Jesus," she muttered as she watched her daughter swing higher and higher, still shrieking with happiness. Here Beth was just swinging solo for the first time, and Shell had her moving out of the house in her mind. "Dramatic much?" she asked the wind.

"What Mommy?"

"Just said you're doing a great job, baby!" she called to her playground-loving kiddo. The air had finally warmed, so Shell decided a day of much-needed outdoor play was just what the doctor ordered. Copper had out of town business to take care of, but he'd checked in about a half hour ago. He was on his way and planned to meet them when he rolled into town.

Beth swung so high, the chain slackened for a second. "Whoa!" she yelled. "Mommy, I think I'm too good at bumping my legs! I almost flipped over the top!"

"It's pumping, Bethy," Shell said with a laugh. There was nothing like the pure and innocent joy of an excited child to make the world look rosy again. It was a reminder Shell needed as she'd been noticing a black cloud hovering overhead.

"I said that, Mommy. I said bumping. Weee," she called as she swung up high once again.

Shell clapped for her daughter. All of a sudden, the hair on the back of her neck stood straight on end. Something was off. She immediately closed the distance to Beth, standing next to her daughter as she swung. Scanning the area, Shell looked for something that could be responsible for her unease.

"What's wrong, Mommy?" Beth relaxed her legs, and the swing lost much of its height.

Shell forced a smile even as she remained alert and on the lookout for danger. "Nothing's wrong. Just wanted to be closer to you." There was no point in alarming Beth unless absolutely necessary, though Shell was ready to rip her daughter from the swing and run if it came to that.

As she glanced around at the vacant park, heart racing and nerves skittering up her spine, she frowned. Had she fabricated this entire concern? Not usually one to overreact or search for monsters lurking in the closet, Shell had always trusted her instincts. Wasn't like them to serve her wrong.

Just as she was about to shake off the paranoia, she caught sight of a man walking across the opposite side of the park. Shell tensed, gazed fixed on the man as he met up with another, smaller guy. The shorter one wore baggie jeans, hanging to his knees. A black hoodie shielded his face. They shook hands. Too far to hear, Shell squinted her eyes and took an automatic step forward for a better look.

"Mommy?"

Copper

"Shh," she said, attention only partly on Beth. "How about we play the quiet game, Beth. You keep swinging, and let's see who can stay quietest for longest. Okay?"

"Okay. That sounds fun. I'm gonna beat you."

One of the men fished what looked like a meth pipe from his pocket and heated it up. Not totally surprising since Copper told her there'd been an uptick in meth sales in the area. "Okay, honey. Be quiet starting now."

Beth fell silent, only the occasional squeak coming from the swing.

Confident her daughter was taken care of for the moment, Shell paced a few more steps away from the swing set. Was the taller man wearing...

Oh shit.

He was wearing a Handlers cut. Oh, my God. Shell's stomach rolled, and her knees nearly buckled. As the identity of the larger man became clear.

Rusty.

She didn't dare breathe, as though that would somehow keep her from being discovered. Rooted in place, Shell gaped at the scene before her. The men passed the pipe back and forth then the smaller man pulled a brown paper package out of his backpack. Rusty inspected it, nodded, then handed over an envelope before stowing the package in a bag on his own back. The men spoke for a minute before the smaller one counted the money.

Holy shit, that was a tall stack of bills. Any chance they were singles? Probably not. Where the hell did Rusty get that kind of cash?

Her stomach clenched.

Oh no. No, no, no. He wouldn't dare...She almost laughed at her own naive thoughts. He sure as hell would. Rusty was exactly the type of man who'd steal from his own club and use it to buy drugs. Although with that size package, he was probably selling as well as using.

She should not be witnessing this exchange.

"Come on, Beth," Shell whispered, turning toward her daughter. "We gotta go now."

"What?" Beth whined, face crumbling. "Copper isn't here yet. I don't wanna go!" Her voice rose with the hysteria children got as they teetered on the edge of a full-on tantrum. Any other day, Shell wouldn't give in to that kind of behavior. But now? Priority number one was sneaking away unnoticed. "Yes, we have to go. If you leave with me now, we'll go get ice cream." She'd bribe her daughter with the Hope diamond if it got her off that damn swing.

"Okay!" Beth yelled making Shell flinch.

Shell risked a glance over. Rusty was stalking straight toward them about half the distance he'd been, his long stride eating up the inches.

Shit! Her hands shook as she reached for the chain to stop the swing, then thought better of it. They'd never make it to her car before Rusty caught up to them and she didn't want him within spitting distance of her daughter. "You know what, honey?" Shell said as she worked to keep her voice from shaking. "Changed my mind. Keep swinging." She wiped her sweaty palms on her jeans then gave Beth a push to get her going again. "Whatever you do, Beth, do not get off this swing. Do you hear me?"

"Yes, Mommy."

"Say it to me, Beth."

"Stay on the swing."

"Good girl. I'll be right over there where I can see you." Shell pointed toward Rusty right before she took off at a jog on legs that felt like rubber bands, meeting him as far from her daughter as she could manage.

"You spying on me, doll?" Rusty said, grinning as though he hadn't just been caught red-handed.

Like she didn't have a million better things to do with her time than follow him around?

Copper

"No Rusty. What the hell do you want?" Shell glanced around and let out a breath of relief. Whoever he'd been meeting with was long gone. But that meant there was not another soul in sight. No one around to hear her scream. For the next few moments at least. "Copper is meeting us here any second. You need to leave now."

He smirked, and her stomach dropped. Each and every time he'd come to her in the past, that smug king-of-the-world smirk taunted her. In the five years he'd been behind bars, that smirk hadn't changed one bit. Memories, all unpleasant and unwanted, assaulted her.

Clothes off, blondie, got something for you.

What, Rusty? Now?

Right fucking now. Get naked and get on the bed. Spread your legs.

Rusty, we can't do this now. Copper is going to be here any second to fix the leaky faucet in the bathroom. We had to schedule it while my mom was out so she wouldn't freak.

Guess you better hurry then, huh? Stop running your trap and get ready to be fucked.

Rusty! We can't now.

Need I remind you why we can and will do it now?

And then the smirk would appear. No, he'd never needed to remind her. For the three years he'd owned her body, he never once needed to remind her. Though he did, often and cruelly.

"Hey!" He snapped his fingers in front of her face. "Where the fuck did you go?"

Shell jumped then glanced toward the swings. Thankfully, Beth played, blissfully unaware of the monster nearby.

"Nowhere. What do you want?" she snapped.

He stroked the beard that needed some serious TLC. Instead of sexy, like his big brother's facial hair, Rusty's looked about three weeks past the need for a trim. For whatever reason, it wasn't growing in evenly, and some tufts were longer than others. After an inhale, she wrinkled her nose. He also smelled... like—

"Pussy," he said with a wink.

"Excuse me?"

"Had a pretty wild fucking night last night. Didn't have time for a shower. Probably smell like pussy. A few of them."

Her wrinkled nose turned into a full-on grimace of disgust. "You're a pig, Rusty. I'll ask you one more time before I leave to be with my daughter. What the fuck do you want?" She jammed her trembling hands on her hips and tried to make her whopping five-foot-two inches look bigger and at least somewhat menacing.

"Whose daughter?" he asked, the smirk-from-hell growing even more arrogant.

I hate him. I hate him.

"What. Do. You. Want."

He threw back his head and laughed. God, how she'd love to hit him. But first off, her daughter was present, and she needed someone in her life who didn't condone violence since she sure as hell wasn't going to get that lesson from her many uncles and definitely not her Aunt Izzy. Sometimes, Shell wished for Izzy's courage. Izzy would rip Rusty's nuts off and force him to eat them. Shell just didn't have that in her.

"Well, doll, I want to know what you think you just saw."

"What?" She faked it harder than she'd ever faked anything in her life. "I'm just here playing with my daughter, Rusty. Told you I wasn't spying on you."

The narrowed eyes and continued smirk told her he wasn't buying it. And that meant she'd been right. He'd stolen from the club and was using that money to buy meth. And probably sell it for quite a hefty profit.

She had to tell Copper.

And Rusty knew it.

He leaned close, the familiar scent of him rolling through her system like food poisoning. Shell bit her lower lip. Hard. Hopefully, the sting from her teeth would override the urge to vomit. "Still have that video, doll. You remember the one?"

Copper

I'm going to fuck you, Shell. Club pussy is great, but sometimes I want something a little less...broken in. Before you say no, let me show you a video.

Those were the words that turned her entire life upside down years ago. And she'd be damned if she'd allow him to control her again.

She forced a huff, working to sound incredulous instead of hysterical. "I'm not a kid anymore, Rusty. You don't scare me like you used to." She had resources now and an adults way of thinking and seeking help.

He shrugged like the words held no meaning. "I'm pretty sure I can get you to come around to my way of thinking." The smirk disappeared, replaced by an ugly sneer. The man looked like he needed a shower with an iron scrub brush. "Thinking a girl needs her daddy in her life, know what I mean?" One red eyebrow arched.

Rusty had so many commonalities with Copper. Same green eyes, same red hair, similar height, and many mannerisms that mirrored each other. How could the brothers be so far apart in personality and morals?

Shell swallowed a rise of bile. This was all too familiar. The threats, the fear, the helplessness.

"What do you want?"

"Well, I'd love a repeat of our time together, wouldn't you? But with you fucking my big bad brother, that might be a little harder this time around." He winked. "I might be able to figure out a workaround though. You remember how it was back then?"

Quiet, doll. You know what the club'll do to me if we're caught, don't you? And you know what that means for your precious Copper?

She shuddered. She remembered all right. Remembered countless nights crying herself to sleep. Remembered the shame, the guilt, the hatred, the feeling of being dirty no matter how many showers she took. Remembered the panic when the little stick had showed a plus sign. Remembered the all-consuming fear she wouldn't be able to stomach holding her own child. Remembered the hours of therapy just to be able to look at herself in the mirror.

Yeah, she remembered it all.

"Go to hell, Rusty."

He folded his arms across his chest and scoffed. "Been there, blondie. Ain't going back. But Copper, now he could very well end up where I was, couldn't he? Except for much longer. For the rest of his life."

The very same dread that threat caused eight years ago rose in her and her vision tunneled. In all her life, nothing else had brought on the intense, visceral reaction Rusty's threat invoked.

Copper in jail for murder.

For the rest of his life. So much for her not giving into the fear.

She was shaking now, unable to control her body's reaction to his words.

"You saw nothing today. You hear me, bitch? Not a goddamn thing. And you don't say a goddamn word about me to my brother. Not unless you want your man in a cell and your daughter splitting time with me."

The world grew hazy and her chest constricted to the point she couldn't drag in air. Over her dead body would Rusty spend ten seconds alone with her daughter. She was so fucked. Loyalty to the club was the most important thing in the men's lives. Rusty's betrayal, his thievery from the club, was an offense that would never be overlooked. If she kept it a secret, she was just as guilty as he was.

But the alternative? Jailtime for Copper and possible custody for Rusty?. That was a fate worse than anything the MC could dish out.

"Mommy! Mommy, look! Copper is here!" Beth dragged her feet through the dirt under the swing, slowing to a stop. She then took off at a dead run and threw herself into Copper's waiting arms. He may have caught her daughter and now held her close

Copper

to his chest, but his eyes were glued to where she and Rusty were talking.

And, yikes, he wasn't pleased. Those huge booted feet gobbled up the distance across the park.

"Mouth shut," Rusty said. "We'll talk soon." Then he threw a cheerful wave toward his brother, turned, and hightailed it out of there.

For all his bravado, the man was nothing more than a chicken.

Shell sucked in two shaky breaths and plastered a smile on her face before she went to meet her daughter and the man she wished with all her heart was that little girl's father. Dangerous thinking, right there. Reality was so very different.

As she moved to be near the two people she loved above all else, she felt disconnected from the world. Her body advanced at a slow pace, but her mind raced with a thousand worries and doubts.

"What was he doing here?" Copper said without so much as a hello. His narrowed gaze tracked Rusty's retreating form.

"Oh, uh, nothing. Just passing through, I guess. He said hi then took off." Shit, did her voice crack? Was anything believable about her wooden smile and stiff posture? Try as she might, calm, cool, and collected wasn't happening.

His assessing gaze downshifted. "He's on a few of the brothers' shit lists. I got into it with him earlier, and he rode off ahead of Zach and I. He giving you any shit?"

Shell swallowed. For the first time in her life, she was about to tell an outright lie to the man she loved. In the past, she always managed to avoid direct untruths with clever wording and omissions. Not this time. "N-nope, no trouble. He did seem a little off, but that's all."

"Hmm." Copper still stared down at her, and she had the distinct impression he didn't believe her, but thankfully, Beth took that moment to interrupt.

"Your face feels like Bobby's dog," Beth said, rubbing her hands across Copper's cheeks. That girl was definitely a facial hair loving girl. Every time one of the bearded bikers held her, her hands assaulted their face.

"Oh yeah? Who's Bobby? He a friend from preschool?" Copper asked in his best dad voice.

Beth giggled. "No, silly, he's my boyfriend. And he has a puddle."

Copper's forehead wrinkled as he looked to Shell.

"Poodle," she said around a chuckle. Beth comparing Copper's beard to a poodle was pure gold.

"Boyfriend, huh? Well, I think I need to meet this dude. Make sure he's treating my princess right. What do you say?"

"Yeah. He can come over with his puddle. You can meet them both." As she spoke, she continued to pet Copper's cheeks.

"Great. Set it up, Mommy," Copper said as he tickled Beth's tummy. She broke out in a fit of giggles. "You like my fur?" He rubbed his cheek against Beth's, eliciting even more sweet little-girl giggles.

"Uh huh," she said around her laughter.

Emotion clogged Shell's throat and had her blinking back tears. This moment was everything she'd fantasized about her entire life. Happiness, love, and laughter with Copper and the little family they made up. It was perfection.

The dream.

And it was fake. A lie doomed to end in a pulverized heart and crushed future. Instead of filling her up, the moment nearly choked her with thoughts of the man threatening to take away everything.

She couldn't let that happen. Somehow, she'd find a way to get them out from under Rusty's thumb. With a forced grin, she shook off the desperation. Copper would pick up on her anxiety if she acted out of character.

"Your mommy likes it too." Copper winked and her face heated. Yeah, she liked it. Only she preferred it between her legs rather than against her own face. Maybe she could get a reminder of exactly what that felt like in a few hours.

Copper

"Mommy loves it," Shell responded, shooting for normal.

Bobbing his eyebrows at her, Copper said, "All right, kiddo. Where to first?"

"The slide!" Beth squealed. She launched herself from Copper's arms and darted toward the spiral slide.

"Hey, gorgeous." Copper's arms circled her. Two large hands fisted her ass and hauled her against him. The second her breasts molded to his hard chest, her pussy clenched and flooded. Just like that she was turned on and wishing they were alone.

"Hi," she whispered back, placing her hands over the flat planes of his pecs.

He bent his head down, hovering millimeters from her lips.

"Missed you today. God, I fucking missed you. Haven't tasted these lips in over ten hours."

"Uh huh." Her head spun as the faint smell of cigars, motor oil, and whatever soap Copper used tickled her nostrils.

"I see I've rendered you speechless." Those were the last words spoken before his mouth crashed against hers, and he not only rendered her speechless, but brainless as well. She loved her daughter above all else, but man, if Beth wasn't around, Shell would have dropped to her knees right there and made him howl at the wind.

She moaned, and he chuckled against her lips. "Hold that thought, darlin'. Just for a few hours." Then he winked and took off after her daughter. "Here I come, princess."

Beth squealed in delight when Copper bounded up the ladder and sat behind her on the spiral slide.

Covering her mouth with her palm, Shell giggled. That slide practically groaned under the weight of her colossal man. The thing probably wasn't designed for two hundred and fifty pounds of muscled biker. "Here we go! You ready, Mommy?"

"Hold on! Let me get a video of this."

"Mo-om," Beth whined. As she dug out her phone, Shell caught her daughter peering up at Copper. "Mommy always wants to take videos of me."

"Well you're pretty special," Copper said. "And Mommy wants to be able to watch all the special things over and over again."

Hello, pang to the heart.

They sounded like such a real family. And from the outside, they probably appeared that way. Playing at the playground with Copper referring to her as Mommy. Then they'd head to her house where they'd eat the casserole she prepared. Copper would read to Beth because she now refused to be read a story by anyone but him. Then after her daughter drifted off to dreamland, she and Copper would finally get the chance to give in to the desire that grew throughout the day. They'd fall into bed exploring each other for hours then sleep wrapped so tight they were almost one body.

Domestic. Perfect to any outsider gazing in. Too bad it was all a fragile web of deceit. She paused, phone at her hip. If she played her cards wrong, this man could end up in prison for the rest of his life. Rusty would do it. Despite Copper's love for his brother, Rusty hated him. Maybe hate was too strong a word, but he was so green he'd do anything to have what Copper did. And that was a dangerous thing.

Could she do it? Would she do it? Keep vital information from the club? While she'd go to any lengths to keep Copper out of jail, and had in the past, she wasn't sure she could continue to lie to him. She'd break. And where would that leave her daughter?

Rusty's daughter?

Shell shuddered at the thought of that man having a relationship with her daughter.

"Mommy, what's taking so long?" Beth asked.

"Yeah, Mommy, what's taking so long?" Copper exaggerated Beth's whine, making Shell laugh despite her mood.

"Sorry, I'm coming." She hurried forward until she was at the optimal angle to capture her two loves coming down the slide. "Okay, let 'er rip!"

Copper

Beth let out a whoop of excitement as Copper pushed off. They careened through the first loop of the slide then came to a dead stop. "Hey!" Beth said. "What happened?"

Copper wiggled his hips, then frowned. "I'm stuck." He took his arms from around Beth's waist. Without him holding her, she coasted the rest of the way down the slide with a "weee." Hands going to the sides of the slide, Copper tried to push himself forward.

"Damnit, I'm really wedged the fuck in here," he grumbled.

"Mommy! Copper said fuck!" Beth called as she ran from the bottom of the slide over to Shell. "Mommy, did you hear him?"

But Shell couldn't drag in enough breath to reply. She was laughing so hard her stomach hurt, and she bent forward.

"What's wrong with Mommy?" Beth asked. "Her face is all red."

"I-I'm o-kay," she said, finally able to suck in a breath. Oh my God, she'd never seen anything so funny in her entire life as the giant badass MC president wedged into a child's spiral slide.

"You fucking laughing at me, woman?" Copper growled as he shimmied an inch at a time further down the slide.

"N-no. N-never at y-you." Shell hiccupped and wrapped an arm around her own stomach. Oh, the cramp. The muscles constricted and spasmed as she continued to laugh like she'd never laughed before.

"We'll see how fucking funny you think it is when I get my ass out of here," Copper said.

"Mommy! He said it again. Two times."

Shell sank to her knees, unable to remain upright. "I got it a-all on v-video," she said as another round of hilarity began.

"Can you please control yourself long enough to help me out here?" Copper asked, twisting to glare at her over his shoulder.

"S-sure." Shell inhaled a deep breath then blew it out through pursed lips. She turned off the recording then struggled to her feet. On wobbly legs, she walked to the bottom of the slide. "I'll pull your feet."

As best she could, she wrapped her hands around Copper's ankles and pulled with all her might. That combined with Copper's upper body strength finally dislodged the man. "Oh shit!" Shell flapped her arms as she tried to combat the backward momentum, but it was useless. She sailed back, landing on her ass in the dirt. Seconds later a heavy-as-hell biker flew off the edge of the slide and landed face down on her.

Shell burst out laughing all over again. Bracing on his hands so as to avoid squishing her, Copper scowled. "You're going to be deleting that video the second we get up."

She shook her head back and forth. "No way, buddy. I'm sure I'll need something to hold over your head at some point."

A growl rumbled in his chest as his fingers slid under her shirt. He tickled along her sides making her squirm and shout. "Ready to delete it?"

"No," she said between gasps. "Never!"

The tickling stopped. "Hmm." One of his copper-colored eyebrows rose. "I'm sure I'll think of a way to get what I want."

He dropped his mouth to hers, his fingers switching from tickling to pleasuring as they stroked the skin of her stomach.

"Yay!" Beth yelled. "Wrestle time." Then she took a flying leap, landing on Copper's back which made his arms buckle and his big body land on Shell's.

"Ooof," she gasped as the air left her lungs.

"Do you smeeelll what the Rock is cooking?" Beth screamed as she bounced on Copper's back.

Slapping a palm over her mouth, Shell suppressed the laughter that wouldn't seem to stop. Copper rolled his eyes then reached around his back, snagging a giggling Beth. "Who's been watching old school WWE with you, princess?"

It was one of the happiest ten-minute chunks of time in Shell's entire life.

She would do anything to keep this magic alive. But it might not be possible.

Copper

There might be only one way to keep Copper out of jail and her daughter away from Rusty, and that would be to leave town.

And end things with Copper.

CHAPTER TWENTY-TWO

The moment Copper's eyes opened, the same goofy grin he'd been sporting for days appeared. Shell still slept, her smooth-as-silk bare back to him. Good thing he spent most nights at her house. If his men caught him looking so blissed out first thing each morning, he'd never hear the fucking end of it.

Shifting, he winced. There were a few downsides to crashing at Shell's. Mainly, the queen-sized bed. Nothing more substantial would fit in her tiny room. It wasn't that he objected to sleeping all cuddled up to Shell—that would happen even if the bed was swimming-pool sized. But his big ol' body straight up didn't fit. Both feet hung off the edge which drove him nuts, making him curl in a tight ball on his side. Each morning he woke stiff and achy. For more reasons than one.

Reaching down, he adjusted his hard cock which was half morning wood and half the naked woman next to him.

Shell let out a soft sigh and burrowed deeper into her pillow. As she wiggled, her sweet ass brushed Copper's hip.

Okay, now the boner was one hundred percent sexy woman.

Maybe it was time to think about moving out of the clubhouse. Get a place with a yard Beth could run in, a kitchen large enough to house a table for more than two people, and a monster-sized bed he didn't wake in feeling like a craggy eighty-year-old. He closed his eyes, visualizing himself coming home to Shell and Beth at the end of a long day. Beth would be on the floor, building a tower with those pink and purple blocks she'd become obsessed with. He'd stop for a few minutes, tickle her until she squealed, then continue on to the kitchen. Shell would be at the stove, hair high on her head in a sexy pile, denim cutoffs cupping her ass and drawing his gaze. She'd be barefoot, those adorable pink-tipped toes tapping to her favorite country song, unaware of his presence.

After stealthily admiring her for a few seconds, he'd move in behind her, resting his hardness against her. With a sweet smile, she'd automatically tip her head up to accept his kiss. And he'd kiss her all right. He'd kiss the hell out of her.

Copper sighed. Yeah, it'd be nice to come home to their house each night.

Wait. His eyes flew open.

Their house?

Shell barefoot in the kitchen?

When the fuck had he become interested in domestic bliss? He glanced at his sleeping woman. Did the when matter? It was time for his mind to accept what his body already had. Shell belonged with him. All the reasons he'd fought being with her still existed. But he was ready to say fuck it. Fuck whoever thought he was robbing the cradle. If Shell grew bored with her ol' man, fuck that too. He'd do what he needed to keep her interested and tied to him. Hell, it wasn't a problem now, but he'd take out fucking stock in Viagra when the time came if that's what he had to do to keep his woman satisfied.

And the other reasons? His role as president of the MC? His promise to Sarge? The club ran through Shell's blood. There was no separating her from her family. He could ensure her safety and happiness far better with her than apart from her.

Yeah, it was time to officially claim her as his ol' lady.

Shell's pert ass settled against him making his dick twitch. He could continue his planning later.

Right now, he had other business to attend to.

Rolling to his side, he brushed his lips back and forth across Shell's spine, directly between her shoulder blades. Her skin was warm and satiny-smooth against his lips. She didn't react, so he kissed her again, right above the first one. Then another, and another until he sucked at the little ridge of her spine right at the base of her neck. A soft whimper and gentle shiver was her response.

His woman was awake, playing possum. He slipped one hand around and cupped a soft, warm breast in his hand. When he thumbed her stiff nipple, Shell moaned. "You holding out on me? Pretending to be asleep?" he whispered against her ear.

"No," she said shaking her head against the pillow. He squeezed the sensitive tip of her nipple, and her ass arched into his cock. "Just enjoying the way you're touching me. Didn't want you to stop, so I stayed quiet."

"I'll never stop touching you, baby. Anytime you need these hands on you, just say the word, and they're yours."

She rolled over until they were facing each other and traced a finger across his lips. Catching the tip between his teeth, he sucked it into his mouth. Her eyes flared with heat. "And your mouth?" she said, a little sass in her tone. "Do I get that whenever I want?"

"Yes ma'am," he said as he released her finger then took her tempting mouth. She bowed into him, boldly slipping her tongue into his mouth and rubbing her tits all over his chest. Each time they had sex, Shell grew bolder, more willing to take what she needed.

"And this?" Her small hand circled his cock. She grasped what she could of his girth saying, "Can I have this whenever I want?"

"Fuck, yes," he breathed as he hardened to the point of agony. Each time she touched him, he had the almost uncontrollable urge to pound her into the nearest flat surface. "You thinking you might want it now?"

Copper

Her smile turned sly. "Hmm," she said, stroking his length. He squeezed her ass in response. "I suppose I could be persuaded…"

Christ, she wasn't even working to get him off, just idly gliding her fist up and down his length. His body wasn't getting the message that it wasn't quite time to unload. His balls heavy and full, drew close to his body as fire burned low in his gut.

A teasing glint glittered in Shell's eyes. Damn woman knew exactly what she was doing to him. And she fucking loved it. While nothing was better than seeing her happy and carefree, he wasn't about to shoot his wad all over her stomach before he even had a chance to hear her cry out in pleasure. Best sound in the world.

He swatted her hands away and ignored her giggles then lifted her top leg over his hip. Grasping the base of his cock, he squeezed, hard, and counted down from a thousand by eights.

992, 984…

Wasn't working. Well, it worked enough that he wasn't going to embarrass himself on thrust one. Guiding his head to her dripping pussy, he was about to sink in when the blaring of his phone had them both starting.

"Ignore it," he said with a growl, sliding the weeping tip of his cock into her.

She groaned, fingers curling into his chest. "Copper, it's five forty-five on a Tuesday morning. If someone's calling, something is probably wrong. You should at least check it."

"Fuck." Shell had a point. Who the fuck would be calling at this hour?

One of his men, but only if they had a serious problem. Rolling to his back, his dick slipped out of her, making Shell whimper with the loss. Not exactly the sound he'd been after.

He snatched his phone off the turquoise nightstand and frowned at the screen. "It's Jig. Shit. What's up, brother?" he answered.

"Sorry to call so early, Cop, but this couldn't wait."

Copper rubbed his eyes and stared at the wet tip of his wilting cock. Shell remained on her side facing him, with one hand resting on his stomach. "Don't worry about it. I was up."

Was being the key word.

"We got another five-grand missing."

It took a second longer than it should have for Jig's words to register. Probably because of the early hour combined with the fact most of his blood was still concentrated in the dick area. But the moment he comprehended Jig's words, he flew to a sitting position.

"What the fuck do you mean? I put the money in the safe myself last night after we counted it together. It was fucking dead on."

Copper could practically see Jig's stony expression through the phone. This shit had his treasurer fucking pissed.

"Know it, Cop. Guessing someone got in the safe."

"What the fuck!" He started to throw his legs over the side of the bed as violent anger heated his blood, but Shell swung her slender leg across his lap and straddled him, pushing him back down to the pillow. Sitting astride him, she rubbed his chest, and he found himself able to rein in the fury caused by Jig's shocking revelation. "You and I are the only ones who know the combination to that safe."

"So we thought."

"You saying someone knows it and just opened the fucker right up?"

"That's what I'm saying, Cop. There's no damage to the safe. We put cameras in my office but not yours which was a mistake I'll have Maverick remedy today. We need to catch this motherfucker."

Shell's soft hands soothed circles on his abdomen, the only thing keeping him grounded and able to control the rage bubbling close to the surface. Without her, he'd have lost his legendary control for sure. It didn't happen often, but when it did, most scattered far and wide. Not Shell. She always stuck

Copper

around and helped calm him. Since long before he'd given in to his desire for her. "Church at eight this morning. I don't care if you have to personally yank every fucking member of the club out of their beds. No one misses this fucking meeting. You hear me?"

"Yeah, Cop. I'll get the word out. See you in a few hours."

"I'll be in soon." He disconnected the call and stared at the ceiling. Three times. Three separate times one of the men he considered family, one of the men he'd have given his life for, stole from him.

He didn't even have an inkling of who it could be. If someone asked him two weeks ago, he'd have said there was no fucking way one of the Handlers would steal from the club. Clearly, his judgment wasn't as sound as he thought.

"Hey," a soft voice said from above. "I know I'm not supposed to listen, but I'm pretty nosey." Shell's sheepish smile made him chuckle. "So, I'll probably eavesdrop a lot."

He placed his hands on her hips letting the feel of her flow through him. "It's all right baby. If you weren't here, I'd have lost my shit."

"Look," she said as her face pinked. "I've known you a long time, and I've been smitten with you for almost as long as I've known you."

Hmm…he liked where this conversation was going.

"So, I think I know you pretty well. You're questioning your judgment? Feeling unfit as a leader, am I right?"

Shit, she did know him. He nodded, fingers kneading the fleshy skin just above her hips.

"Stop that bullshit," she said in a harsh tone that had him barking out a laugh.

Probably her goal.

With her own small laugh, she played with the smattering of hair on his chest. "I just mean that this doesn't have a damn thing to do with you. You've got a rotten apple in your bunch, and you'll deal with it. Not your fault. The rest of your men are solid to the core, and any one of them would willingly follow you into hell. Focus on them."

A fierce lioness, that's what Shell reminded him of. Loving and protecting her chosen family until her last breath. Which made perfect sense. Lions were king of the jungle; the lioness their queen.

And he'd make Shell his queen if it was the last damn thing he did. The moment the club's shit was sorted, he'd be demanding answers. It was time to move forward with Shell, and it wouldn't happen until he knew the details of whatever held her back.

"You heading in?" she asked.

"Yeah."

She sucked her lower lip between her teeth. "You got time for something first?"

"Sure, got a few minutes. What'd you have in mind?" His cock had filled to capacity once again. With Shell astride him, wet pussy dripping all over his stomach, plump tits staring at him, who could blame him?

"For you to fuck me until I'm screaming," she said as she rose up, gripped his thick cock, and slid down until he was buried to the root. "Shit." She echoed his thoughts. Her eyes fluttered closed. "I'm not sure I'll ever get used to how huge you are. You fill me so damn good."

He was one lucky fucking bastard.

After taking a moment to adjust to his penetration, Shell's eyes popped open. "Ready, big boy?" she asked, wagging her eyebrows.

"Bring it, baby."

And she did, riding him until they both collapsed in a tangle of sweaty limbs and heaving breath.

Two hours later, Copper sat at the head of the table staring at the grim faces of his men. Any of the pressure relief a good romp with his woman provided had vanished the moment he entered the clubhouse. It did help to see Rusty at the table. Sure, things had been a bit rocky as far as his integration back into the club, but having his blood brother at the table meant a lot. Meant he had Copper and the club's back. They'd get past whatever was eating at Rusty with time. One of the men, however, was missing.

"Where the fuck's Rocket?" Copper turned to Jig.

With a shrug, Jig said, "Couldn't get him, Prez. Called about ten times. Texted double that. Went by his house and anywhere else I could think of. His ass is in the wind."

No. Fuck no. No way in fucking hell Rocket was stealing from the club.

Was he?

Goddammit. He hated uncertainty. The inability to trust men he'd counted on to watch his ass a number of times.

"All right. Anyone sees him later, I wanna chat with him. I'm gonna get straight fucking to it. Fifteen thousand dollars has been stolen from debts we've collected." He held his hand up when murmurs rounded the table. "Shut your fucking mouths. It ends today. I want to know who it is. You're done with the club. Now, you nut up and come to me on your own, I'll think about letting you walk out with your bones intact. I find out another way, and I fucking will find out, you might need to be carried out instead. Not that a single man here would so much as toss a cup of water on you if you were burning. Not anymore."

Tension shot to a palpable level. Copper stood and rested his palms on the table. The men knew he was pissed and they knew one of them was to blame. Mistrust was rampant. They eyed each other across the table trying to determine who was the thief among them. This kind of thing was hell on club morale. He gave them a minute, letting his message sink in.

"That's all I'm going to say about that for now. I'm too fucking pissed to talk about it further. We got a possible lead on Lefty. Someone who might be able to deliver him to our door. But we gotta do them a favor. Collect a few debts for him. Should be a cakewalk since we do this shit all the time. Zach will get with you if he needs you in on it."

The men perked up slightly. Lefty being handed over on a silver platter was just about better than sex...just about. Too bad it was tainted by a traitor betraying the club. Hopefully, when all was said and done, getting a little revenge on Lefty would boost club morale after losing a member. Because a member would be lost. Didn't matter if the money was stolen to fund one of his men's mother's cancer treatment. Stealing from the club was a hard and fast fucking no.

"That's it for now." He did a slow perusal of the men sitting at the table, pausing to make eye contact with each and every one of them. Well, all but one. Rusty played on his phone, looking bored as hell. So much for having his back and being invested in the club. "My door is open if you got something to tell me. Rust, want to talk to you for a few."

Rusty rolled his eyes and Copper had the distinct feeling he was raising an attitude-laden teenager. He'd pretty much already done that being the one to raise Rusty after they moved from Ireland. At the time, he'd tolerated it, maybe more than he should have, but who could really blame him. Rusty had just lost his only parent, been ripped from his home, and thrust into an entirely new country. Some pushback was to be expected. Granted, Copper had been so busy with the club at the time, he probably didn't parent Rusty as much as he should have, but for a twenty-year-old suddenly responsible for a ten-year-old, he thought he did all right.

Copper sat behind the desk. Rusty strode in two seconds later. "Sup, Cop."

"Just checking in after yesterday. You were pretty steamed when you took off."

Rusty shrugged. "Wasn't nothing. I'm over it." He moved into the room and took an empty seat. "But I still think you're missing an opportunity for some big fucking paydays."

"Selling meth?"

Copper

"Meth, heroin, Molly, whatever the fuck the people want." Rusty propped his boots on the edge of the desk.

"Club's been down that road already brother. Nearly destroys us. Destroys most clubs or gangs in the end."

With a laugh, Rusty said, "So? You earn enough, and it don't matter. Don't you ever get fucking sick of managing these assholes?"

"No." Voice hard, Copper stared at his brother. "You want out, Rust? That what your shit attitude is about? Done with MC life? If that's it, grow some fuckin' balls and tell me. Until then, shut the fuck up and start acting like you wanna be here. Got it?"

Rusty stood and tossed his smoldering cigarette into Copper's ashtray. "Fuck this shit," he said. "Need some fucking pussy." He tromped out of the office. "Becky!" he shouted. "Five minutes, in my room, on your knees."

That went well. Copper pinched the bridge of his nose where an ache seemed to start and shoot out across his forehead. The day would have been much better if he could have stayed in bed with his woman.

CHAPTER TWENTY-THREE

The perfect opportunity had been presented to Shell, and she'd chickened out.

Big time.

The entire time she'd been in bed with Copper listening to his phone call about the stolen money, her mind had been screaming at her to confess what she'd seen. To share her information about Rusty. But the words wouldn't leave her mouth. Part of it was fear due to Rusty's very real threats. Part of it was her desire to comfort an agitated Copper at that moment instead of adding to his heavy burdens by ruining his relationship with his brother. And a third part was the paralyzing fear that once she opened her mouth, she'd never stop talking and would vomit out her entire horrifying past which would effectively put an end to her relationship with Copper.

Could she be more selfish?

While she'd been riding them both to an explosive release, Shell had convinced herself she'd made the right decision. Her man had needed her to ground him. He'd needed her to take the edge off so he could meet his club having a clear head and calm emotions. But now, a few hours later, she saw her actions for what they really were—cowardice and selfishness.

What the hell was she supposed to do now?

"Girl," Izzy said, sidling up beside the treadmill Shell was currently running on. "What's going on with you this morning?

Copper

You barely said two words in the car, and now you're running like the devil himself is chasing down your ass."

She was right. Shell panted as she pumped her legs faster than she ever had before to keep up with the speed of the revolving belt. Screw it. The run wasn't helping to escape her thoughts or settle her anxiety. She jammed her forefinger on the minus button until she slowed to a swift walk. Legs aching with exhaustion, she wanted nothing more than to lie down and take a nap.

"Izzy, how are you ten weeks pregnant and still have this much energy?" Shell asked as she slowed the treadmill further. "You're supposed to be sick to your stomach and falling asleep all over the place." She hit the stop button, hopped off the machine, then flopped onto a mat directly behind the row of cardio equipment.

Her friend didn't seem to mind that Shell had ignored her question. "That how you were?" Izzy hovered over Shell's head, hands on her hips, peering down.

"Not the sick part, but I was constantly tired for the first few months. Didn't matter if I slept twelve straight hours, I could barely keep my eyes open throughout the day."

"Huh," Izzy said, extending a hand toward Shell. "At night I'm more tired than usual, but I feel pretty good during the day."

"How nice for you." Shell allowed a snickering Izzy to tug her to her feet. The OB had informed her friend she was strictly forbidden to fight in the ring, even sparring was off limits, but she could stick to her regular exercise routine as long as she was feeling well. About a month ago, Izzy coerced Shell into joining her at the gym, and now they tried to work out together whenever Shell found the time to get there. Which was the reason her muscles were screaming at her at nine a.m. on a Wednesday. Beth was at school, the men at the clubhouse, and she wasn't scheduled at the diner.

Perfect time to put herself through some pain in the form of cardiovascular exertion.

Zach came strolling out from the back rooms of the gym. The employee parking lot was behind the building with an entrance there as well. He lifted his chin in their direction before making his way to the check-in desk.

"Looks like church is out. You know what's going on?" Izzy asked as she uncapped her water bottle.

Shell shrugged and reached for her own drink. She'd never betray Copper's confidence, even for her girlfriends.

"I'm pretty sure you do, and I won't mention specifics, but I know a little as well. I was with Jig last night when he discovered the...discrepancy. This shit's gotta be fucking with Copper's head."

After swallowing a cooling gulp of water, Shell said, "You have no idea."

"This the reason you seem off today?"

"Part of it."

"You know," Izzy said, reaching out and grabbing Shell's hand. "I may be a snarky bitch most of the time, but I can listen. You seem like your struggling today. Need an ear?"

She needed more than an ear. She needed someone to tell her whether or not to let Copper know what she saw and how to deal with the blowback. Could she talk to Izzy about it? Her friend already knew about Beth's paternity. Maybe she could help Shell sort her thoughts and come up with a plan.

Izzy was a ballbuster, a real take-no-shit woman. Had she been the sixteen-year-old Rusty tried to blackmail, she'd probably have kicked his ass, stolen the video, ripped off his dick, and delivered it all to Copper in a nicely wrapped package with a big red bow. Shell couldn't imagine Izzy ever being as afraid as she'd been back then.

And was right then.

She looked Izzy in the eye. As always, Izzy had her hair back in a flawless Dutch braid. The bottom layer was shaved which only accentuated her badass vibe. Even ten weeks pregnant, Izzy could model the workout clothes she wore. She was the epitome

Copper

of sleek strength. "Actually, I could use some advice if you have the time."

"For you? Always. What's up?"

Shell bit her lower lip. "Not in here."

Eyes narrowing, Izzy nodded. "So it's that kind of conversation. Okay, ready to call it quits in here? I told Jig I'd find him at the clubhouse when church let out. We can talk in the car."

"Yeah, that works. I don't have to pick Beth up for a few hours, so I planned to go to the clubhouse after this anyway."

Izzy waved the hand holding her giant water bottle. "Let's go see your man."

Shell smiled. Everyone had been calling Copper *her man* for the past few weeks. The phrase still sent a thrill through her each and every time she heard it. Would it always be like that? Or would the novelty eventually wane?

She almost snorted. It would certainly wane. Probably down to absolutely nothing when Copper found out he was her daughter's uncle.

After a quick hug and hello for Zach, they left through the front entrance and stared around the parking lot. "Where the fuck's my car?" Izzy asked. "Holy shit! Did someone steal my car? I swear this fucking parking lot is cursed." A few months back, Izzy was attacked leaving Zach's gym.

Shell burst out laughing. "We parked around back. How could you forget? Oh my God, you freaked right out. That was hilarious."

Shooting her a sideways death glare, Izzy said, "I have baby brain, what's your excuse? You came in with me, and you didn't remember where the car was either."

Rather than walk back inside then out again through the back door, they headed around the outside of the building. "Yeah, but I didn't start screaming about being carjacked."

"I was not screaming, biatch," Izzy said as she led the way to her car. Once they were inside with the doors closed, she immediately turned to Shell. "Okay, spill your guts, girl. I can see something is eating you. Are you stressing about being with Copper?"

With a harsh chuckle, Shell rested her head back on the seat. "No. Well, yes, but that's not what this is about." She turned, giving Izzy her full attention. "I have to say it fast or I'll lose it, so just let me get it all out."

"All right." Izzy furrowed her brow.

"Yesterday I was at the playground with Beth. I saw two men smoking a pipe—I think it had meth—across the park. One was Rusty. I should have grabbed Beth and run, but I was so shocked, I couldn't move. Anyway, Rusty handed a huge wad of cash to the guy and was given a large parcel of what I assume was meth in return."

The fighter in Izzy came out full force as she clenched her fists and tensed behind the wheel. "Holy shit. He motherfucking stole from the club and is using that to buy and sell meth."

Looked like great minds did think alike. "My thoughts exactly, which were confirmed when Rusty spotted me and threatened me if I breathed a word of it to Copper."

A long breath left Izzy. "And now you're stuck between one big rock and a very hard place."

"Pretty much," Shell whispered. "I have no idea what to do, Iz. Copper raised Rusty. He feels paternal toward him. This will kill him." She threw her hands in the air. "If he even believes me. But how can I not tell him? I may not be a patched member, but my loyalty has always been to the club." Tears filled her eyes. Despite the challenges life threw at her, it wasn't often Shell cried. At one time, she'd wondered if she'd used up her allotment of tears as a teen. "He threatened to try and get custody of my baby," she whispered.

A hard mask fell over Izzy's features. "Well, that won't fucking happen. I'll kill him myself before he gets near her." Reaching across the center console, Izzy hugged Shell. "You already know the answer, Shell. But I get that you need to have someone say it to you, so I will. You need to tell Copper. All of it, back from the beginning when you were a kid and Rusty took advantage of you. It may get ugly for a time, but your man is solid. He'll listen, and he'll take it in, and he'll believe you. Even if it's not the moment the words are spoken. He will also protect you and that sweet kid of yours with his life. And if he fucks this up? If he doesn't believe you? Every other man in the club will, and they'll beat some fucking sense into him."

Shell huffed an exhausted laugh. God, it felt good for someone to have her back. Someone to validate her fears and help guide her in the right direction. Izzy was right. Shell knew what she had to do but needed someone to push her off the ledge. Now that she was dangling by her fingertips, there was nothing left to do but drop.

"You're the best, Izzy."

"You got that right, girl. And I'm about to get even better. I'm coming with you."

"What?" Shell pulled back and stared at her friend.

Wrapping the tail of her very long braid around her fist, Izzy nodded again. "I'm coming with you. Moral support, back-up, strength in numbers, girl power, whatever you want to call it. We'll do it together."

Resigned to the horrible task, Shell sighed. "Thank you. Let's get it over with.

With each mile that passed, Shell's stomach coiled tighter, and her insides shook harder. By the time they pulled into the clubhouse, her heart was lodged in her throat, pounding so hard she felt each pulse in her neck.

Like a prisoner being led to death row, Shell walked unseeing through the clubhouse straight to Copper's door. Nothing registered. She had no idea who was hanging around, what time it was, or if anyone noticed how off she was. Standing in front of Copper's door, trembling, she lifted her hand to knock on the door.

Her arm froze.

Almost a full minute later, Izzy knocked. Shell hadn't been able to do it. Her fist had refused to curl and track to the door.

"'S open," Copper called out.

"We got this, girl." Izzy gave her a thumbs up.

Shell wasn't so sure. Her stomach churned like the ocean after a hurricane. There was a very high chance she'd be making use of Copper's trash can. Her brain told her legs to move, but the damn things just wouldn't obey.

"Said it's fucking open," Copper yelled.

"Go." Izzy nudged her forward, and Shell opened the door.

"H-hey, hon," she said popping her head in the office. Strong. She had to be strong enough to get the words out and stand by Copper when they wrecked him.

Copper's face lit up at the sight of her, which only made her feel worse. "Hey, gorgeous! Didn't know you were coming by, but damn am I glad to see you. Sorry I snapped. Thought you were Rocket coming to bother me with bullshit. I've been expecting him since he walked in late a while ago." He sprang up—as much as a giant man could spring—and had her in his arms, stealing her breath through her mouth before she even pushed the door all the way open.

A throat cleared behind them making Copper lift his head. "Oh, hey, Iz. Sorry, didn't see you there." No shame in being caught devouring Shell. He shifted his gaze between the two women. "You ladies are looking pretty glum. You're not just here to make out with me, are you, babe?"

"No. We—I need to talk to you about something important." The words felt like they were dragged out of her desert-dry throat by someone else.

"This a door closed kind of conversation?"

She swallowed, trying to speak again when Izzy said. "Please."

"Shit. Okay, come on in. Have a seat, Izzy." Copper shut the door, keeping one hand curled around Shell's. Then he drew her to his giant leather desk chair and guided her down to his lap.

Copper

She remained stiff as a board, unable to relax into him knowing she was about to topple his world.

"What's going on?"

"I think—" Shell cleared her throat. "I mean, I saw—" Closing her eyes, Shell shook her head. She couldn't bear to look at him. "Just a minute."

"Want me to say it, Shell?" Izzy asked, her voice unusually compassionate.

Copper's arms tightened around her waist. "She can get it out," he said. "Give her a minute."

Oh, his faith in her. That undeserved faith that made her love him even more than she thought possible.

Part of her was tempted to spit the words out with her eyes closed, but despite her past secrets and fears, she wasn't a coward. So, she opened her eyes, gave Copper her gaze, and said, "Yesterday, when you saw me talking to Rusty at the park? I spotted him handing over a very large stack of money to a man I didn't recognize. On the shorter side, baggy clothes, hoodie covering his face. They were smoking. Meth, I think. And after Rusty handed him the money, he gave Rusty a big package of drugs. Rusty spotted me and pretty much confirmed my thinking that he stole from the club and was selling drugs when he came over and threatened me. That was right before you arrived." The words rushed out in one long breath as though a quick Band-Aid rip would make some kind of difference.

Behind her, Copper stiffened and just stared at her.

Heart pounding, she remained silent waiting for his response. Izzy didn't speak but nodded along with her words, her face grim.

"You sure you didn't misun—"

The office door flew open. "Got a question for you, bro," Rusty said as he barged straight in the office.

Shell hopped off Copper's lap and stared like a deer caught in high beams. She'd been wrong when she thought her heart was racing a few seconds ago. Now, it beat so fast she grew lightheaded.

Rusty laughed. He was disheveled, eyes darting all around, sweat dotted across his brow. "Looks like I broke up a little pow-wow, huh? Or maybe a threesome? Care to bump it up to a quad?"

"Cut the shit, Rusty," Izzy said. The woman spoke her mind at all times and didn't know how to back down from a challenge.

"What's the matter, Izzy? You pissed at me for showing that pussy you're fucking that he ain't shit around here?"

"Rusty," Copper said, warning in his tone.

"Sorry, Cop. I know Jig is the club's treasurer and all, but really? How can you trust a man like him? A man who can't even keep his own wife alive?"

"Jesus, Rusty, can it," Copper said on a growl.

Izzy seethed. "Copper knows what you've done," she said, with an evil smile.

Shell's eyes widened. She wanted to warn Izzy to shut it, but her tongue felt too big for her mouth.

Rusty looked at Copper. "What the fuck is this bitch talking about?" The man couldn't stay still, fidgeting like his drawers were full of fire ants.

Izzy stood as well. "Shell. Told. Him." She poked a finger into Rusty's chest. What was she thinking? Was she crazy? "You. Stealing from the club. Selling drugs. She saw it all."

Rusty threw back his head and let out a loud, slightly crazed laugh. "You two bitches fucking kidding me? You don't believe this shit, do you, Copper? Anyone else happen to *see* me?" He never gave his brother a chance to answer before he focused on Shell. "Really, doll? That's how you're gonna do me? After all we've had together?"

Panic clawed at Shell's throat stealing her ability to respond. She risked a peek at Copper whose forehead was wrinkled with confusion.

Copper

"What's the problem?" Rusty continued. "You having so much fun playing house with big brother you're afraid of what's going to happen when he finds out the truth?"

Oh my God. Now? He was going to say it now?

Shell's started shaking, and for the life of her she couldn't quell it. "N-no. Rusty, d-don't. P-please," she said, finally finding her voice, pathetic though it was. The weakness in her trembling tone was mortifying, but couldn't be helped.

Copper's head ping-ponged between the two of them. "One of you two better tell me what the fuck is going on."

"Oh, you know, Copper. Shell's just worried you'll find out you're Beth's uncle."

Shell gasped, her legs quaking so hard, there'd be bruises where her knees knocked together.

"Rusty," Izzy barked. "That's enough."

As though in a trance, Copper stood, backing as far away from her as he could manage in the small office. "Her uncle? That's not possible."

Rusty smirked. "Sure is. Amount of fucking Shell and I did back then? Shit, I couldn't even guess the number of times I had your girl. We fucked for years. Bitch never told me I got a daughter out of the deal, though. Just let me rot away in prison for five years without a word. Cold-hearted, that one."

"Jesus Christ," Copper said, his tone incredulous. "Years?" Now he sounded angry. "Who the fuck are you?" He stared at her as though it was his first time laying eyes on her.

Her heart dissolved into a trillion pieces so tiny, it'd be impossible to ever repair. "N-no. It wasn't—It's not—No." Fat tears flowed in rivers down Shell's cheeks. Her brain couldn't process what was happening. She could barely breathe, barely stand. Reaching out, she grabbed the edge of the table to keep from crumbling to the ground. A sob caught in her throat then burst forward like a dam breaking. Years of fear, shame, agony, and guilt poured out of her eyes and her mouth as she wept.

"Just tell me it's not true, Shell. Tell me Rusty is not Beth's father. That's the only thing I want to hear out of your lying mouth right now." Never had he looked at her with such flat eyes or spoken to her with such a cold, loathing tone. If hatred had a sound, Copper's voice at that moment would be it.

She continued to stand there, trembling and shaking her head.

"Copper..." Izzy started.

"Tell me it's not fucking true," he screamed, as he turned and punched the wall. His fist went straight through, leaving a huge hole. When he pulled out, blood trickled from his knuckles. How crazy was it that in the midst of all the chaos, Shell's first instinct was to run to him and help stem the bleeding?

Like he'd ever accept her touch again.

Through it all, Rusty's smirk gleamed like a neon *fuck you* sign. He was destroying her life once again, and reveling in every second of it.

"I c-can't," Shell said so low the words were barely audible.

"What? Can't hear you. Is it fucking true?"

"It's true," she said, head hanging. The damn thing weighed about a hundred pounds. "But—"

"Say it louder," Copper yelled. "Fucking say it, Shell. I want to hear the words out of your mouth. Not that I can trust anything you say anymore."

Her breath hitched. She stared at the man she loved, a man she barely recognized right now and her insides twisted. She'd done this to him. Broken him. Made him hate her with her choices.

"Fucking say it!" he screamed.

"Rusty is Beth's father," she whispered. All she could see was that fucking smirk gracing Rusty's mug. The moment the words were out of her mouth, she spun and lost her breakfast in Copper's trash can.

"Get out." Ice had returned to Copper's tone.

"Copper, back the fuck off," Izzy said, rubbing a hand over Shell's back. "She's—"

Copper

"I said get the fuck out of here!" Copper roared.

On her knees, her stomach still spasming, Shell jolted as though his words had been the harsh crack of a whip, spurring her into motion. Rising on unsteady legs, she started for the door only to be met with Izzy's hand against her chest.

"And I said that's fucking enough," Izzy screamed. "Get the fuck out of here, Rusty." With her free hand, she shoved Rusty out of the office then yelled, "Jig, get your tight ass in here. I need help."

Shell had no idea what Copper was doing. She couldn't see him through the torrent of tears and hysteria, but he appeared to be standing stock still in the corner of the office.

"You," Izzy barked pointing to him. "You stay the fuck there. Don't you dare say another damn word to her."

Jig appeared literally three seconds later. "Babe, you okay? The baby okay? Holy fuck, what's going on?"

"I'm good. I need you to take Shell to our place then call Toni and have her pick Beth up from pre-school. Ask if she can keep her for a few hours."

"Babe—" Jig began.

"Nuh-uh," Izzy said to her ol' man. "Don't look at him. I don't care if this is his clubhouse and he's president or king-shit or whatever. He's a fucking dipshit right now. I'm your ol' lady, and I'm the one asking you to help Shell out of here."

"All right, babe," Jig said tossing another wary look Copper's way. He kissed his woman then came over to Shell. "Come on, sweetie, let's get you home."

Shell tried to follow, but her knees buckled, and she almost hit the ground. Her limbs didn't want to work. Her body was trying to curl in on itself and ride out the pain. Jig scooped her up and held her against his chest. "Good luck, Cop," he called as he carried her out of the office. "Izzy's fucking pissed. Next time I see you, you'll be shitting through two assholes."

RUSTY IS BETH'S *father.*

Rusty is Beth's father.
Rusty is Beth's father.

The words played through Copper's head like a broken record. He'd been through some serious shit in his life. Dead parents, moving from Ireland with his kid brother, raising his brother, death of MC brothers, killing, yet nothing came close to the hurt and betrayal of knowing the woman he loved had fucked his brother and bore his brother's child.

All behind his back.

Jesus Christ, how could he not have known?

Now that it had slapped him in the face, the resemblance was painfully obvious. Beth with her mother's crystal blue eyes but her father's red hair. Lighter than Rusty's and with Shell's curls, it had always been obvious Beth's father was a redhead.

But his own fucking brother?

Why did she do it? Because she wanted him and couldn't have him? Or was it more sinister? A big fuck you to the man too old for her at the time?

And years? Rusty said they fucked for years.

When did it start?

How fucking young had she been?

Why did it start?

How long did it last?

Did he love her?

Did *she* love him?

She'd never seemed to care for Rusty much. Never wanted to be around him back then. Had it all been a ploy to hide their relationship? He could barely breathe let alone wrap his mind around the giant bomb dropped in his office.

"Hey!" Izzy said, snapping her fingers in front of his face. She was tall but still had to extend her arm to reach his eyes.

Copper blinked. They were alone in his office. Where had Shell gone? He vaguely remembered screaming at her to leave. And what happened to Rusty? Jesus, not only did his brother just get out of prison, but he found out about a daughter he was denied knowledge of. No wonder the guy had been off lately.

He glared at Izzy as the room fully returned to focus. "Get your hand out of my face."

"Oh no." Izzy dropped her hand to her hip. "Don't you take that tone with me, asshole."

He raised an eyebrow. Were she one of his men, she'd be sporting a black eye right about now. As it was, she was his brother's ol' lady and a pregnant one at that. Probably why she felt safe to get up in his face.

Oh, who was he kidding, Izzy would confront anyone or anything if she felt it necessary. "Watch yourself, Iz. Don't forget who you're talking to."

"No," she said getting on her toes and right up in his personal space. "You need to watch yourself. You also need to remember why Shell and I came in here to talk to you in the first place."

Right. Spewing some bullshit about Rusty stealing the money and dealing meth. Like he could believe a word out of Shell's mouth now. She didn't want her little secret exposed which gave her every reason to get rid of Rusty.

"Stop it." Izzy pointed a finger in his face.

He counted to ten. *Don't snap her finger off.*

"Whatever fucked up shit is going through your head, stop it. And remember who your woman is. Remember *who* she is. She is the woman who has been head over heels for you her entire life. She is the woman who would lay down her life for you in a heartbeat."

"She's the woman who fucked my brother and had his kid. Then kept it a secret for years."

"Fuck you," Izzy spat.

Copper swore to God she was testing his patience like no other. How did Jig deal with this woman day in and day out?

"You don't deserve her. I do not know all the details, but I know what happened between her and Rusty was not what you're thinking." She lowered her voice. "And I'm pretty sure it wasn't entirely consensual."

He reared back as Izzy's words hit him like a slap. "What?"

"You heard me, big guy. So while you're sitting in this office chewing on your self-pity, think about two things. Remember who your woman is. And remember who your brother is."

"The fuck is that supposed to mean?"

"It means your woman is one of the best I've ever met. She loves you and this club with every fiber of her being. And your brother is a piece of shit who'd steal from his own club, sell drugs behind your back, sucker punch his brothers, and spend years in jail for nearly beating a man to death. Sounds just like the kind of man who'd force a woman." With that, she stormed out of his office.

Copper dropped into his chair, a marching band suddenly traipsing through his head. He rubbed at the left side of his chest where another, more intense ache formed.

With a sigh, he pulled the bottle of whiskey out of his drawer and sucked back a long drink. Then he gripped the half-full bottle by the neck and flung it across the room with a roar of "Goddammit."

The bottle exploded in a sharp spray of glass and whiskey.

Very fitting considering his heart had just suffered the same fate.

CHAPTER TWENTY-FOUR

Five days after finding out he was in love with the mother of his niece, Copper sat outside behind the clubhouse polishing off yet another bottle of whiskey. He'd had more to drink in the past five days than the past five years.

He was fucking struggling. Dealing with shit he'd never imagined he'd have to handle and doing a shitty-assed job at it.

All signs were pointing to Shell's information being accurate. His brother had stolen a total of fifteen thousand dollars from the club and turned it around to purchase crystal meth which he was both using and selling. Icing on the cake was the fact that he was buying the meth from Lefty's guys.

That discovery went down like fucking ground glass. Lefty must be laughing his ass off knowing Copper's own brother was betraying the club and getting into bed with him.

And speaking of getting into bed, Copper had been doing that particular activity alone for the past five nights. He just couldn't drum up the courage to talk to Shell. The longer he thought about it—and with all the sitting around whiskey-consuming that he'd done, he'd thought about it a fuckton—he realized Izzy was probably dead on.

Something about the entire situation reeked. And while he longed for Shell, ached to see her, touch her, speak with her, he was terrified of the truth. Because one of two options were accurate, and both choices made his skin crawl. Either his woman was a liar or his brother was a piece of shit who took advantage of a young girl.

So, after forty years, he'd come to the realization he was a fucking coward. It was a hard pill to swallow.

The back door to the clubhouse swung open, and someone ventured out. Copper didn't bother to turn. Whichever of his brothers dared to come nag him over being a grouchy asshole would get to their point soon enough.

As he took another drink, the footsteps drew closer. Softer than the heavy clomp of motorcycle boots, it must have been one of the ol' ladies. Sure enough, Toni appeared by his side holding a fold-up chair.

She opened it then plopped down rubbing her sweatshirt-covered arms. "Damn you, Copper. It's freezing tonight."

The sun was minutes from dipping below the trees, and the temperature reflected that fact. Shell would be starting her shift, cleaning the large office building on the opposite side of town.

"By all means," he said. "Head on back inside."

With a scowl for him, Toni yanked the bottle out of his hand and took a long swing of his expensive whiskey. When she grimaced and shuddered, he couldn't help but chuckle. "You think that shit would taste better for how much it costs," she said, wiping her mouth with the back of her hand.

"Not a whiskey girl, huh?"

"Nope."

They fell into silence for a few moments just watching the sun lower. Toni was a sunset fan. It was her thing. She and Zach often disappeared around this time of day, checking out a new location to view the phenomena.

Copper's stomach wouldn't settle. Had nothing to do with the quiet between them; it was the fucking voices in his own head. Taunting him with what ifs, whys, and images of his brother fucking his woman.

Eventually, Toni sighed "Here's what I know," she said.

He turned to her. Toni knew something?

Copper

"I wanted to talk to you earlier, but Zach made me promise to give you some time. He said you haven't been the friendliest of men lately."

"That's one way of putting it." Copper let out a rough laugh. "Bet my life that's not what he said, though."

She gave him the side-eye then said, "You're right, he actually said you were up to your asshole in self-pity, and acting like a constipated hyena."

"Ouch."

"Yeah," she said with a shrug as she snuggled herself. "So here it is. The day Rusty showed up at the diner to surprise you, remember?"

Of course he remembered. It'd only been a few weeks ago, and he'd been over the fucking moon. "Yeah."

"The second Shell saw him, she darted into the bathroom and threw up. I got worried when she was in there for a long time so I went to check on her, and in a weak moment, she told me about Rusty. She was so freaked out, pleading with me to believe it wasn't what I'd initially think. And you know what?"

She'd gotten physically ill at the sight of Rusty? That had Copper frowning. "What?"

"I believed her. Because I love her and know what kind of person she is."

"Toni, it's not that simple. I'm being asked to choose sides between my brother and my woman."

"Yeah," Toni said with a nod. "You are. And I think you know, somewhere deep in that thick skull of yours that there is not only a good choice but a right choice."

What the fuck was with all the ol' ladies talking to him like he was dog shit the past few days? Though he had to admit their loyalty to Shell was admirable.

"Rusty is an asshole," Toni continued. "And you know it. You just don't like it, so you've ignored it your entire life. I get it somewhat. You feel partly responsible for his shitty childhood. But guess what, Copper? Lot of us had shitty upbringings. We don't all turn into backstabbing, thieving psychopaths. You've buried your head in the sand because of guilt or love or whatever. Now, you can't ignore it anymore."

Christ, did every one of his men blab club business to their ol' ladies? The information about Rusty stealing the money was supposed to be need to know only.

"Anyway," Toni said, holding her hand out for the bottle. He handed it over. This time she downed the whiskey with ease. "Not as bad now that I know what to expect. Anyway, Iz and I sat down with her and straight-up asked her if they dated or had a one night stand she'd regretted. She denied both those things."

Oh, God was it…

His horror must have been written across his face because Toni said, "We asked her that too."

"What did she say?"

She handed him the bottle and met his gaze with her serious one. "She said it was complicated and that she agreed to sleep with him but didn't feel like she had a choice."

"What the fuck does that mean?" There was always a choice. Maybe a shitty one, but still a choice. His stomach turned. Shit… is that what happened? Did Shell feel sleeping with Rusty was the better of two lousy options? Jesus, what the fuck could be awful enough to make her sleep with him?

"I don't know. She wasn't willing to give us details without you knowing them first. Might be about time for you to get over yourself and go talk to your woman."

Copper grunted his response and stared at the trees blanketed by a now dark sky.

Toni stood, hands in her sweatshirt pouch. "I know one other thing."

Raising an eyebrow, he looked up at her.

"I know she loves you and would die before willingly hurting you. Have a good evening, Copper."

Toni made her way back to the building, the soft snick of the door indicating her departure. Copper stayed where he was, unmoving for hours. Until his fingers were frozen and his ass ached from the shitty fold up chair.

At nine, he forced his stiff legs to uncurl and walked around the building to his bike. He hadn't had a sip of whiskey since Toni left, and was sober as a judge.

Mounting his bike, he inhaled the fresh mountain air. Toni was right. It was time to go to his woman. Pulling out his phone, he placed a quick call then rode out into the night.

SHELL DRAGGED HER weary ass up her stoop. If she were any more tired, she'd have to use her hands to help heft her legs up the steps. Each and every muscle ached with the complete and total exhaustion of someone who hadn't gotten a full night's sleep in days. Five, to be exact. But it was nothing compared to the pain in her heart.

The scene from Copper's office had replayed in her mind so many times, she'd analyzed it from every possible angle. All led to the same heartbreaking conclusion. Copper hadn't been able to stand the sight of her. Her worst nightmare and there was no waking from it. The past five days were full of second-guessing, guilt, and a renewed sense of the shame she'd spent so many hours in therapy combating.

Would his reaction have been different had she confessed the truth herself?

Should she have kept her mouth shut about seeing Rusty at the park?

Hell, her doubt went back five years to wondering if she never should have left Townsend when she found out she was pregnant.

She'd slogged through the past work week, put on a happy face for Beth, and did her damnedest to ignore the half-concerned, half-pitying looks from her girlfriends and the men of the MC. Then at night, once again lonely in her bed, she'd cried until her eyes blurred and her heart felt like a wet sponge wrung out until it was bone dry.

With a sigh, Shell shoved her key in the door. She was sick of living in her own head, but couldn't manage to turn off the obsessive thoughts. Her door swung open, and she trudged inside only to come up short with a gasp at the large man dwarfing her sofa.

"Copper," she said, hand flying to her drumming heart. "W-what are you doing here?" Suddenly, shock turned to worry, and she started down the hall. "Is Beth okay?"

He rose and followed. "She's fine, Shell. Having a sleepover with Toni and Zach tonight."

Her shoulders fell. Shit. This conversation was going to be so awful, he'd felt the need to send her daughter elsewhere.

Slowly, Shell turned and forced herself to glance up at the man whose mere presence was breaking her heart. God, she'd missed him every second of the past five days. Even though he looked as wrecked as she felt with his messy hair, bloodshot eyes, and—was his shirt on backward—he was still irresistible to her. And she wanted nothing more than to fling herself in his arms and feel those strong limbs surround and protect her. It was one of the biggest regrets of the past few days. Had she known the way this would all end, she'd have been sure to hold him one last time before it all imploded.

"I'd like to talk to you if you're willing," he said, making her eyes widen. No malice, no accusation in his tone, just resignation. He sounded broken, beaten down. Something she'd never heard from him. Being the cause of it made her ill.

"Um, sure, we can talk." Least of what she owed him, though she dreaded saying the words. "Do you, uh, want to sit?"

With a curt nod, he returned to her small couch.

"I'm going to stand if that's okay," Shell said. There was too much nervous energy zinging through her bloodstream to be still. The fatigue of moments ago replaced by a rush of adrenalin at the sight of Copper. She needed to prowl. Plus, if she touched him, she'd lose it, and there was no way that small couch would allow distance.

Copper

"All right," Copper said as he settled.

"What do you want to know? Or where should I start?" She sighed. "I guess you want to know about Beth."

"Yes, among other things."

The fact his voice was so calm helped to keep her from coming undone. Throughout the years she'd rehearsed how she'd one day tell him, and now all that planning flew out the window, and she could barely think. Shell paced back and forth in front of the couch, wringing her hands. "Bear with me," she said. "I've only told this story one time before. There's only one person who knows the whole truth aside from me." She risked a glance at him and saw his raised eyebrows.

"Your mom?"

The snort that left her had him frowning. "No. Not my mother. My mother knows none of this." Heat filled her cheeks. "My therapist."

"Therapist?" His frown deepened.

How mortifying was this entire conversation? "I was a little messed up for a while after…everything, so I saw a therapist for a few years."

"Shit." Copper scrubbed a hand over his face and sighed. "So aside from some stranger you paid to help, you've dealt with this all alone?" It wasn't an accusation, more a plea. She got the impression he was dying for her to contradict that statement. To tell him she'd had support and help through the most challenging years of her life.

She stopped and stared at him. "When you hear the story, you'll understand why I kept it to myself." She started pacing again. His gaze on her felt like a physical touch, staying with her each time she turned and traipsed across the room. "Oh God, this is hard," she whispered, pressing her fists over her suddenly stinging eyes.

"Shell," he said. "I'm not going to react like I did the other day. I promise." His eyes relayed nothing but sincerity and openness.

She laughed but didn't find his words remotely funny. "You haven't heard what I have to say yet. Okay, I'm just going to do it." After a deep breath, she began. "When I was sixteen years old, I snuck out of the house one night and rode my bike to the clubhouse. Then I followed you, Zach, Maverick, and Rusty into the woods."

She could practically see Copper's wheels turning as he rubbed his chin and tried to figure out times and dates.

"It was the night you killed Reaper."

"Jesus," he bit out. "You were there? Saw what happened?"

Shell swallowed and shuddered at the memory of the night that set the course of her life in motion. "Sort of. I hid behind a tree and peeked out a few times. Saw Reaper on his knees. Your back was to me, but I could see everyone else's face." Lost in the story now, she stopped pacing and let the words flow. "After you killed him, I glanced around the tree again and made eye contact with Rusty. He'd spotted me. Knew I was there. For months I avoided him and was waiting for him to rat me out. But when he never did, I eventually relaxed and just went about my life."

"But…" Copper said.

"But when I was almost seventeen, Rusty showed up at my house one day. My mom was at work." She remembered that day like it was yesterday. The unease at being alone with Rusty which morphed into fear, then horror at his demands. "He hates you, Copper. Always has. Maybe hate isn't the right word, but he's so jealous of who you are and what you've built for yourself that he wants to destroy you. He came on to me that day. Strong. Wasn't the first time he made inappropriate comments, but he'd never touched me before. When I turned him down and threatened to tell you, he just smirked at me." She shuddered. "I still see that smirk in my nightmares. He always smirked. Every time he…" Shaking her head, she stared at a spot on the wall above Copper's head.

"What did he do?"

Copper

Her gaze shifted to him. His fists were clenched on his knees, shoulders bunched, and jaw tight. Though still bloodshot, his eyes were focused, determined. Anger was igniting. Before long, it'd be a raging inferno. "He showed me a video on his phone. It was you, killing Reaper. And it showed everything so clearly. I'd been there, so I knew it wasn't doctored. You were the only one it showed. Clear as day. Your voice, your face, you killing him." A note of hysteria snuck into her voice.

"Shell," Copper said, rising from the loveseat. He came around the small coffee table and gripped her upper arms. "What did he say to you?"

She struggled against his hold. He had to stop touching her if there was any chance of holding it together. "I was too young to handle that kind of choice," she said, then laughed. "Though I'd choose the same today, sick as that is. I never really saw it as a choice at all." Shit, now she was rambling, still unable to give life to the words.

"Michelle." Copper never used her full name. No one did. It sounded nice coming from him. Would have been much better if it happened in the quiet of night because he loved her instead of during the most painfully revealing conversation of her life. "Tell me what he said to you."

Fat tears leaked from the corners of her eyes. Memories of the pain and fear were so intense she wanted to wail and scream as though she was living it all over again. "He told me he'd turn the video over to the police if I didn't sleep with him whenever he came around. He lorded the threat over me for two years. Until he went to prison."

Copper released a strangled choking sound, and his hands dropped to his sides. The three feet he put between them felt like miles.

"Two years?" he whispered.

With a nod, Shell whispered, "A few times a month, when he got bored with the club girls, he'd show up at my door. He did two things every single time. Showed me the video and smirked like it was all some big joke."

God, how she hated that fucking smirk. To this day it appeared in her nightmares, a reminder of a time she'd worked so hard to put behind her. Just once, she'd love the chance to punch Rusty right in the mouth while that smirk was present. Though she had a feeling once her story was told, Rusty would take a punch from her any day over what fate would be awaiting him.

CHAPTER TWENTY-FIVE

Copper caught every word falling from her lips, but it was as though he was watching a movie. Present, observing, but slightly detached from the reality of it. Until she said Rusty threatened to have him sent to prison for murder if she didn't fuck him. Then the harsh truth of what Shell had actually gone through slammed into his gut.

And it hurt.

Physically hurt.

His stomach cramped, chest ached, and a throb built behind his eyes. "So you did it," he croaked.

One slow nod. "I did it," she whispered. "I had to, Copper. The thought of you rotting away in jail for executing the man who murdered my father was unfathomable. As awful as the consequence of my decision was, the alternative was so much worse."

Christ. Sixteen. *Sixfuckingteen* years old and she'd given up her body to protect him. She'd taken on burdens even an adult would struggle with and bore them for years. Planned to bear them for the rest of her life.

Alone. Scared. Ashamed.

He had so many questions. So much more he needed to know. *Needed* to know. He'd never survive without knowing exactly what his brother put her through.

"Did he hurt you, physically? Was he rough with you?" His eye twitched and horrible mental images of Shell being violated danced before his eyes. That was why he needed to know. His own imagination would run rampant if he didn't get the specifics.

A heavy sigh left Shell. "Do you really want the details, Copper? They don't change the outcome. You don't need the facts torturing you for the rest of your life."

He walked to her again. Somehow, some way, he would convince her none of the past mattered when it came to his love for her. Actually, that was a lie. It mattered a great deal. The tremendous sacrifice she made to protect him demonstrated the strength of her feelings for him more than any words could ever convey. Even if it took the rest of his life, he'd show Shell she was worthy of every ounce of his love. She was precious. She was remarkable.

She was his queen.

"I need to hear it, Shell. Every single detail."

"Why?" She blinked up at him.

"Because when I'm killing Rusty in the most painful way I can drum up, I want to know exactly what I'm killing him for." If she were anyone else, he'd never utter those words, but Shell would live with the security of the knowledge that the man who hurt her no longer breathed. He'd never come for their daughter, never touch her again.

With a gasp, Shell shook her head. "No, Copper. You can't kill him. He's your brother. Your blood."

"And he took you against your will. For years," he replied as the grip on her shoulders tightened. "I'd have killed him for one time alone. But to know he did it for years? Fuck, Shell."

"That's the other reason I never told anyone. I can't live with that on my conscience."

"His death?" Copper frowned.

She gripped his T-shirt. "No, not his death, but knowing you felt like you had to kill your own brother because of me. How are we supposed to have a life together when every time you look at me you think of how you killed your brother over me?"

Unfortunately, Shell had a small point. Not that he would ever blame her for Rusty's death, that motherfucker sealed his own fate, but could he actually pull the trigger? Could he actually end the life of his own flesh and blood? Could he kill a man he'd loved and looked after his entire life?

One look at Shell's tear-stained face and the anguish in her eyes and the answer was so clear it was practically transparent.

Fuck yes, he could end Rusty. He'd killed before and never once lost an ounce of sleep. Never wasted a moment on regret because the world was a better place for each life he'd taken.

"You're wrong, Shell. After I end his miserable life, I won't think of him ever again. I won't waste one second of the time I have with you and Beth thinking about that piece of shit."

"Copper...he's still your brother."

"No. He's fucking not. If it helps, his fate was sealed for more reasons than what he did to you. He stole from the club. He partnered with Lefty." Fuck, how could he have been so blind? Along with obsessing over Shell, he'd spent the last five days second guessing his ability to lead the MC. How would he hold the men's trust if he couldn't see his own brother was a sociopathic traitor? "Now tell me if he hurt you physically."

Shell groaned and banged her forehead against his chest. "No. Not the way you mean. Sometimes it was...uncomfortable because I never wanted it, was never in the mood, if you know what I mean. I can't believe I'm telling you all this," she mumbled into his shirt.

That fucking piece of shit. He knew exactly what she meant. Rusty wanted to fuck and didn't give a shit if Shell was wet or dry as the desert. Even the Honeys were treated better than that.

Copper wrapped one arm around her back and grabbed her hair with the other hand. A gentle tug had her looking up at him. Red blazed across her cheeks while her gaze refused to meet his. "There is nothing to be embarrassed about, Shell. There will be no secrets between us any longer. I will know you inside and out just as you will know me. Nothing that has happened to you makes me think any less of you. Amazing isn't a strong enough word to describe you, baby, but it's all I've got because I'm completely amazed by you. By your beauty." He kissed her once, soft and sweet. "By your strength." Another kiss. "By your loyalty." Kiss. "By the way you raise your daughter." Kiss. "And by your heart."

"Copper…" Tears fell from her eyes. Eyes that shone with so much love for him. He was the luckiest fucker in the world. Completely undeserving of her devotion but selfish enough to snatch up every ounce of it and keep her all to himself.

"Tell me, baby."

"All right. You win. I'll tell you. Later, when you wish you didn't know, remember I warned you." She gave him the first small smile of the night.

"Start talking."

Now she rolled her eyes and relief hit him. That was his Shell. "Always so bossy."

"You're stalling." He tugged on her hair.

Shell bit her lower lip and emitted a small growl before she began. "Ninety percent of the time, Rusty would show up at my house while my mom was out. He'd have that smirk on his face, tell me to take my clothes off, and he'd do his thing. It was usually over in fifteen minutes tops, thank God. Then he'd leave, and I'd take the hottest shower possible and cry myself to sleep."

Copper swallowed and steeled his features. Showing the fury burning his gut wouldn't help Shell. She'd just feel worse. He was coming to realize she was right, he didn't want these details, but he still fucking needed them so he'd nut up and internalize every single word. The rage would come in handy later.

"But there were times, usually whenever something good happened to you, that he was different. It'd be your birthday or a club celebration where you were getting credit for whatever happened, or you'd come down on him for something, and he'd show up all full of hatred for you. He'd rant and rave for a while then turn his attention to me. Those days, he'd whisper in my ear that he owned me. That you would never touch me because he'd been there first. And he'd touch me. Different than his norm. Like he was a man on a mission, trying to make me," she cleared her throat, "trying to make me c-come." The last part was said so low he almost missed it. "I faked it after the first time because he slapped me when nothing happened. So, I guess he did hurt me the one time.

"Anyway, afterward, he'd talk about how much I loved what he was doing to me. And he'd tell me that one day he would let you know how much I wanted him and how hard I came for him." There was a hitch in her voice, and the tears increased. "I fought it in my mind, but there were two times he was particularly persistent. Doing things to try and get me off. And… and it happened."

Her knees buckled, and he tightened his hold as her tears morphed into full body-wracking sobs. Never in his life had a feeling of helplessness quite like he experienced at that moment overtaken him. Combined with gut-wrenching guilt and disdain for his own brother, and his head was fucked.

"Baby," he said, the words sounding like they came from a dying animal.

"I'm so sorry," Shell said around the most heart-breaking sobs he'd ever heard.

"Jesus Christ, baby, you don't have a fucking thing to be sorry for. Not one fucking thing." He loved her with every fiber of his being and had no clue how to take this pain from her. So he held her plastered against his chest with a grip so tight she probably couldn't breathe. But he couldn't let her go. All he wanted was for some of his warmth and love to bleed into her and heal her battered soul.

Slowly the sobs abated and turned to hitching breaths. "That's why I saw a therapist. I couldn't live with the shame and guilt of it all. I couldn't wrap my mind around how that could happen during an act I hated. She gave me studies to read, told me it was not uncommon for a woman's body to have a physical reaction even when being raped. Learning that helped some, but I was messed up for a long time, Copper. The day Rusty was arrested for assault was the same day I found out I was pregnant. As soon as he was convicted, I packed my bags and took off. For a while, I had some negative feelings about the pregnancy that make me want to throw up when I think about them today. Eventually, my roommate convinced me to seek help. She didn't know anything about what had happened, but she could see I was in a dark, dangerous place."

Every word drove the dagger deeper into his heart. "Did it help, baby?"

"Yes. After a while. I saw the therapist for almost two years. Every single session she would tell me it wasn't my fault. Wasn't my shame to bear. That I couldn't blame my body for reacting in a way it was programmed to respond. Then she'd make me say it. Over and over. Until I started to believe it.

"The first time she called what happened rape, I got pissed and left the session early. I hadn't thought of it as rape because I allowed it to happen and never fought him. The next time, she told me if I didn't want to view myself as a rape survivor I didn't have to, but when it came down to it, I was coerced into sexual acts I didn't want. So it technically was a sexual assault. Anyway, Beth was born, and I fell in love with her. But as time went on, I missed home until I could barely breathe. With Rusty in prison, I thought it was safe to come back for a few years. Until Beth was older and raising her wasn't so all-consuming."

Rubbing a hand over her slender back, he said, "So you never planned to stay here?"

"Not long term. But I'd never imagined Rusty getting out on good behavior."

"I should have seen who he was and what he was. Fuck! I should have protected you." The guilt was almost unbearable. How could she stand to look at him let alone be so giving with her body and heart? She should hate him for what she endured on his behalf.

"No, Copper. Please don't say that. Don't make me regret telling you. You said you needed to know, so I told you, but I'll never forgive myself if you look at me with guilt in your eyes from now on." Her pleading voice and the desperate way she clutched fistfuls of his shirt nearly did him in. Never again would this woman know an ounce of suffering at another's hands. He'd make sure of it with his fucking life.

"I'll try," he said. It was as far as he could promise at that moment. How the fuck was he supposed to keep himself from feeling guilty? Killing Rusty would go a long way toward solving that problem, but some element of guilt would always lie with him. A step toward paying back the deep debt he owed her was necessary. But he'd keep that tidbit to himself because his sweet and wonderful Shell would never see it that way.

"What now?" she asked in a small, uncertain voice.

"If you think for one second that we are over, you better reset your mind. Cuz there's no fucking way I'm letting you walk ten feet out of my life." He'd chase her to the ends of the earth if need be. She wasn't getting away from him. Not now, not ever. He loved her, and her place was by his side. Always.

Finally, a genuine smile graced her perfect lips. "That's good because I need you so much." She swallowed and gazed up at him. "And I love you. I've loved you most of my life. I think I was born to love you, Copper. Please don't feel guilty about my past. I'd make the same choices again if I had to because they gave me Beth, kept you out of jail, and led us to each other."

She loved him.

His knees buckled. He didn't deserve her. There wasn't a man in his club who'd disagree because no man on earth was good enough for her. But he'd work toward deserving the coveted spot in her life.

And he'd make damn sure his queen never had to choose to protect him over her own wellbeing again.

CHAPTER TWENTY-SIX

The moment the admission of love tumbled from her, a tormented groan left Copper. He dropped to his knees at her feet. Immediately, his fingers went to work on the button of her jeans. After he'd popped it open, down went the zipper.

"Copper!" Shell swatted his busy hands. "Wait, what are you...we have more to talk about—"

Her efforts were useless. Those callused hands worked the denim over her hips, shoved her shirt above her breasts, then landed on her ass.

"Copper, hold on a minute." Man, that felt good. His palms were hot and so big, they spanned her entire ass with an eye-crossing squeeze. Why was she protesting this again?

Oh yeah, she'd just admitted her most traumatizing experience to him. Not to mention revealing she loved him. And his psycho of a brother was MIA. A few things were needing to be worked out before they got naked.

In the next instant, Copper's lips pressed to her C-section scar, soft and adoring. Starting at one end, he kissed a reverent path across the thin pink line that saved her daughter's life. Wide-eyed, Shell swallowed a lump of emotion. She froze, staring down at him with her arms hovering in midair. For a million dollars, she couldn't have shifted from that spot.

After he loved on her scar, Copper rested his forehead against her bare stomach. He circled his arms around her lower back, locking them in a tight embrace. Shell dropped her hands to his hair, running her fingers through the soft strands as he held her. After a few seconds, her forehead wrinkled.

What was—

A drop of moisture trickled down her stomach soaking into the band of her lowcut bikini panties. Her breath came to a complete standstill.

Oh my God. Copper is crying.

Never in her life had she imagined anything taking the pillar of a man down. He seemed impervious to the elements, was almost always in control, and made every obstacle he encountered look like an ant hill instead of a mountain. But there he was at her feet, weeping for her. For what she'd endured. The need to comfort him swamped her. Such a powerful man should never have to experience something that would take him to his knees.

Knowing what toppled him was what happened to her? That he felt so deeply for her? It was a moment she'd never forget. A moment imprinted on her heart and her mind in a combination of love and dismay.

"Baby," she whispered. Wrapping her arms around his neck, she held him tight and rocked them back and forth. "I'm okay, Aiden. I have a beautiful daughter I love more than life, and I have you. Yes, it took time, and I needed help, but I survived and moved on from what happened. I meant what I said, no guilt. No more sadness. It's over. We both need to let the past stay where it belongs now."

Maybe it was easier for her to say at this point because she'd had years to learn to live with her past while the information was brand new to Copper. Facing Rusty and making him suffer for what he did would be Copper's therapy. A man of action, he'd need to physically do something to come to grips with her experience. She couldn't condone it, should try to stop him, but she wouldn't. He needed to handle things his way, the MC way.

Shell both trusted and loved him enough to recognize who he was and let him do what he needed to keep them safe.

Copper lifted his head and stared up at her. The dampness on his cheeks hurt her heart. As tall as he was, when he rose to a high kneel, his head reached her chin. The hands she loved on her body grasped her head, and he whispered, "Michelle Ward, I love you so fucking much. I was an asshole in my office the other day. The way I reacted haunts me. Please forgive me. If you allow me in your life, I will spend every day proving to you how much I love you and your beautiful daughter."

Best declaration of love ever.

Her heart filled to capacity. Although she'd been in love with him for as long as she could remember, she never expected anything to come of it. The first time Rusty touched her, her dream died. The memory of that horrifying moment would never fully fade away. Not what he did to her physically, that she couldn't recall at all because she'd been so lost in her head, despairing over the fact that the one thing she'd wanted her whole life would never occur. The certainty that Copper wouldn't be able to stand the sight of her once he'd found out she'd been with Rusty. Yet, here they were, years later, declaring their love for one another. Every wish she'd ever cast into the universe was for this very moment to transpire.

"You don't need to apologize for anything, Copper. I don't blame you for your reaction. Not only were you blindsided, but you were blindsided by something you'd never considered a possibility. I'm just so grateful you gave me this chance to explain what happened and that you believe me. Of course, I want you in my life," she said, stroking the soft hair on his face. "You're the only man I'll ever want in my life," she said.

He kissed her then, sensual and so deep it felt like he was trying to merge them into one. The room spun, and Shell's body responded with a sudden, overwhelming need. It'd been an emotional night for the record books. She needed the pleasure of the mind and body connection she'd found with Copper.

Copper

He stood, scooping her up as though she weighed no more than a bag of feathers. Immediately, she locked her legs around his bulk, clinging to him as they continued to devour each other. Copper walked them down the hallway toward her bedroom, pausing halfway and pressing her against the wall. He ground his erection into her, leisurely, torturously. Every move was unhurried, deliberate. Not a frantic race to come, but a gradual simmering build of heat. Shell just knew he was going to drag this out all night long.

And she planned to make the most of every single second.

With a maddeningly slow roll of his hips, he thrust his cock against her pussy. The silky panties were soaked through. They needed to go. As did his jeans and whatever he had on beneath. Copper took his sweet time exploring her mouth with sensual sweeps of his tongue. Each time he rubbed his cock between her legs, he squeezed her ass, and she shivered. Part of her wanted to groan in frustration and demand he fuck her while another part of her relished the unhurried pace.

"So fucking perfect," he whispered, before diving into another core-shaking kiss.

After what had to be a solid few minutes, Copper pulled her from the wall and completed the short trek to her room. Down she went, onto the bed as he cradled her like she was made of fragile glass.

Finally ending the mind-melting kiss, he held himself over her. Heavy-lidded eyes met her gaze. She wiggled beneath him, grabbing the hem of her shirt, and shimmying it up and over her head. Then, with her gaze still on him, she arched up, unclasping her bra. Seconds later, it joined her top somewhere on the floor.

Copper's heated stare traced her body down to where his tented jeans rested against her core, then back up to her face. Everywhere his gaze stroked burned for real touch. Her nipples were so tight they almost hurt. "I need your skin," she said as she tugged on the bottom of his T-shirt. "I want to feel you all over me as well as inside me."

"Fuck, you kill me." He sat back on his heels and gave her a sexy grin through the fur of his beard. Gone was the tension, guilt, and remorse of the past hour. All that remained was a hungry outlaw about to pillage. He reached behind his head and pulled off the T-shirt, revealing hard pecs, hills and valleys of six-pack abs, and to-die-for shoulders. "This what you wanted to see, baby?"

Shell sucked her lower lip between her teeth and nodded. "Yes. But the best part is still hiding from me." As she spoke, she reached out and ran her hand over Copper's tight stomach.

"Oh yeah? I think I know what you're looking for." He scooted off the bed.

Shell's gaze stayed locked on his pelvis as he lost the denim. His cock sprang forward, long, thick, and deliciously hard. The lack of underwear didn't surprise her.

"Better?"

Oh yeah. "Much, much better." She gave him a sly grin. "Now bring that bad boy over here."

With a chuckle, Copper crawled between her spread legs and fisted his cock. "You want this cock, baby?"

"Yes, Copper."

"Bad?"

"So bad."

"You wet for it? That pussy ready to be filled by your man?"

She groaned. Why the hell was he chatting when he could be fucking? "Copper I'm soaked, and I need you inside me. I'm dying here."

"Hmmm," he said. "I'm not so sure that's what you need just yet."

What? She was going to combust if he didn't get moving soon.

Still holding his cock, he reached between her legs and pulled her panties to the side. "Oh yeah," he said. "That pussy's nice and fucking wet, isn't it, baby?"

"I told you it was."

Copper

He tsked. "Don't get snarky. You'll get what you need, you just might have to wait a little bit."

Two thick fingers slid deep inside her, stroking along the front wall of her sex. "Oh God," she whispered. Three times, he rubbed over her G-spot making her cry out and rock into his palm. Then he disappeared. "No!" she cried. She was going to combust.

Copper's grin was full of mischief. God, she loved him like this. Almost playful. It was a side of him reserved for her alone and made tolerating this torture worth it. As did the promise of a monster orgasm. His fingers glistened with the evidence of her arousal. Transfixed, she gawked as he brought those fingers back to his dick and covered himself in her juices. Then he moved his knees to the outside of her body.

"W-what are you doing to do?" Her body hummed with anticipation. Whatever he had planned, it'd be hot for sure.

"Something I've fantasized about for fucking years," he said as he knee-walked up her body. When his dick hovered above her breasts, he came to a stop. "Have I told you how much I fucking love these tits?"

"Once or twice." She was so breathless, she sounded like she'd just hopped off the treadmill. Only this was a hundred times more fun.

He gripped them both, pushing them together as he thumbed her puckered nipples. A hot punch of electricity shot straight to her clit making her cry out. "Like that, baby?"

"Uh huh," she said as she fisted the comforter.

"How about this?" He lowered, sandwiching his cock between her breasts. "Fuuuck." He stroked back and forth, moving easily due to the slickness created by her cream. "Damn that's even hotter than I'd imagined."

It was. Having him fuck her tits wasn't something she'd ever contemplated but he was right. It was hotter than hot watching him loom over her in obvious pleasure. His thumbs still strummed her nipples as he fucked between her breasts giving her as much pleasure as he seemed to be in. Each time he pushed forward, the tip of his dick came within reach of her mouth. At first, his eyes had been open and on her, but the lids had dropped a few seconds ago.

Hmm...this could be good...

She curled her head up and opened her mouth. This time, as his cockhead came toward her, she closed her lips around it and gave a quick, hard suck.

"Holy fuck!" he cried, eyes flying open.

Now it was her turn for the impish grin.

"You little shit," he said on a gasp.

Shell laughed. "Want me to stop?"

"Fuck no. That's fucking incredible." He pumped his dick through her tits again and again. Each time he glided forward, she sucked or licked. It wasn't long before he was grunting and his grip on her breasts had increased to just shy of too much.

"Jesus," he said, finally slipping free. "I'll come on you next time. Tonight, I need to be so deep inside you, you feel me in your heart."

"I already feel you there, Copper. Every single day."

He paused. "Good. I'm here to stay, baby." With a touch that was more tender than a man of his size should be capable of, he smoothed his hands over her entire body. Starting at her wrists, he stroked up to her shoulders then down to her chest, pausing at her breasts where he licked up every drop the arousal he'd spread around. Neither of her nipples were neglected either. Once she was a squirming, panting mess, he continued his ministrations, kissing and caressing every inch of her stomach. Her pussy felt so empty. Every few seconds, it clenched and squeezed as though he were actually inside her. But there wasn't anything to grasp, and all the involuntary muscle spasms did was make her needier.

"Copper, please. I'm dying."

He chuckled and scraped his teeth over her nipple.

Shell held her breath when he reached the top of her panties.

Copper

"Lift this beautiful ass for me," he spoke against her skin.

Shell obeyed, and he peeled the damp fabric away. He pressed one long kiss just above the hood of her clit. A sigh slipped from her lips, but it quickly turned into a gasp when his tongue slid through her folds.

He ate at her like he had nothing but time, licking in leisurely flat-tongued strokes over her clit. Shell tried to control her breathing, but the pleasure was too intense. Three times, she made the slow journey to the peak only to have him abandon her pussy and latch on to her thigh just as she started to tremble with the first signs of orgasm.

"Copper," she said with a growl as he backed off yet again.

His laugh vibrated through her pussy, ripping a gasp from her. "I was wondering when you'd hit your limit."

"Consider it hit, Copper, please." She grabbed his hair and tried to guide him back to her pussy, but the damn man was too strong and too happy licking circles on her inner thighs. "I need to come."

Those words drew a rumble from him, and he moved back to her center. Shell kept her hands in his hair, holding him against her as he licked circles around her clit. As she moaned, she bent her knees and lifted her hips into his face. He seemed to like it when she demanded more from him. Copper wrapped his lips around her clit and sucked while sliding two fingers inside.

"Oh, Aiden!" she yelled, legs trembling. The telltale tingling sensation started in the very tips of her fingers and toes. It traveled through her limbs and coiled in a ball, low in her stomach. Her hands tightened in his hair.

He pumped his fingers deep into her then hummed his approval, vibrating his lips around her clit. The ball of tension in her exploded outward in a violent burst of pleasure. "Holy shit," Shell screamed. The intensity of the release shocked her. The only other times she'd come that hard, they'd been going at it with much more fury.

Copper stayed with her, giving gentle licks through her whole release until she shoved at his head. "Too much. Oh, my God, it's too sensitive. Back away from the pussy."

After one last soft kiss to her clit, Copper crawled up her body. He took her mouth, and she moaned as she tasted herself.

"Love you," he whispered against her lips.

"Love you more."

"Not fucking possible, babe."

CHAPTER TWENTY-SEVEN

Watching Shell come hard then melt into the mattress like her bones had liquified was hands down Copper's favorite pastime. It was so good, he was able to push aside the fierce need to track Rusty down and carve his heart out. There'd be time for that later. Now was the time for loving on his woman. His dick was so hard it actually hurt, but he'd delay getting it wet even longer if it meant witnessing Shell react to the pleasure his fingers and mouth brought her.

She, however, had other ideas.

Not that he was fucking complaining.

Shell shoved his chest. When he didn't budge, she gave him an adorable frown. "You're too damn big," she said.

With a laugh, he nudged his cock against her pussy. "You sure you want to complain about that, babe?"

Her eyes sparkled as she pushed again. "Okay, maybe you're the perfect size, but I can't push you around to save my life."

Flopping onto his back, he asked, "You got something specific in mind here?"

A flush stole across her cheeks, and that pouty lower lip disappeared between her teeth as she sat up.

"If you haven't figured it out by now, Shell, I want you morning, noon, and night. I want you in every way and every place possible. And I will have you in every way and every place." He cupped a heavy breast, running his thumb across the puckered nipple. "There won't be an inch of this sexy body I don't claim. And this?" He gestured down the length of his body. "You fuckin' own this shit. You want something from me, you ask for it, cuz you'll get it. Every damn time."

His woman ran a fingertip through the center dip in his abs. "Sit up," she said. "Back against the headboard."

"Yes, ma'am." He moved into position. "You gonna climb in my lap, baby?"

Shell nodded.

Worked for him. "Facing me, or away?"

She straddled his legs and shimmied as close as she could get. Two slender but surprisingly strong arms came around his neck. "Facing you. I told you earlier, I want to feel you everywhere."

Yeah, this was a pretty damn good position to meet that goal. Their fronts flush, he could easily reach her mouth or neck while the hardened tips of her breasts seared two points into his chest. Her pussy dripped onto his cock, and her silky thighs hugged the outside of his hips. Then there was the smooth expanse of her back which he ran his hands over, pausing to squeeze her ass every now and again. "Perfect."

"Yeah," she said, all breathy and needy.

"Put me in." Sure, he could do it himself, but there was something about having Shell's hand circle his cock and guide it into her that drove him nuts. Just as she was doing right then.

Fuck that feels good.

Hot and slick from her recent orgasm, Shell's body accepted him with ease. She glided down, engulfing the entirety of his cock. The instant her pelvis met his, their mingled sigh and grunt filled the room.

"Nothing better than this, Shell." Their gazes locked. With his fingers splayed across her back, he could feel the shallow rise and fall of her breathing.

"Uh huh," she said.

Speechless. What could he say, his woman's pussy loved his cock. He winked and gave her his hungriest grin. Her lips curled as well, right before she squeezed her inner muscles with strangling force around his cock.

He jolted, driving even deeper inside her.

Okay, maybe his cock was the one who loved her pussy.

"Do it again," he ground out.

And she did, squeezing him over and over while she rocked her pelvis against him.

The pace wasn't rushed or even hurried, no frantic thrusts or heavy pounding. Just a connection, deep, intense, and so powerful each ripple of her pussy flowed through his entire body.

This wasn't fucking, wasn't even sex, it was a full-on union of body, mind, and soul. The kind of shit that made a man hand over his balls. And he fucking couldn't get enough of it.

Couldn't get enough of her.

"Good?" he whispered as she whimpered.

"You have no idea."

"So, tell me, baby."

Her hair was a disaster, curls frizzing out in every direction. A few strands clung to her damp forehead. The face he loved was makeup-free except for a smudge of mascara under one eye. Swollen lips and fuck-drunk eyes.

Fucking beautiful.

He must have said that out loud because her face lit up. Still grinding on his dick, she said, "I think you're deeper than you've ever been. And I'm so full I could burst. Your chest hair is tickling my nipples making my pussy squeeze you. And every time I roll forward, my clit rubs against you." She beamed her pearly whites at him. "And you told me you love me. So, yeah, it's good. Really fucking good."

Damn this woman blew his mind.

He leaned forward and slid his tongue between her parted lips. All the things he would tell her if he was a man who could come up with poetic words flowed from him. He had no idea how much time passed; it didn't matter if it was five minutes or five hours.

Clench. Kiss. Rock. Grind. Moan.
Clench. Kiss. Rock. Grind. Moan.
Over and over.

A subtle tremor rolled through Shell. Two seconds later, she gasped into his mouth as her pussy fisted him with a crushing grip. Her head fell back. She went still in his arms except for the rhythmic pulsing around his cock. His own orgasm crept up, starting at the base of his spine and undulating through his body. He locked her against him as he shuddered out his release.

Never would he have thought something so powerful could have come from sex that wasn't rattling the windows. But fuck if he'd been wrong.

Earth-shattering was the best way to describe it.

"Jesus," Shell whispered.

"Nah, just me, baby. Though I can understand if you thought you saw the face of God. Pretty damn sure I did too."

"Nah," she said with a chuckle, tugging on his beard. "Just me, baby."

Copper laughed with her, completely at ease for the first time since she was last in his bed. There was a peace here he only ever found with Shell. The woman soothed something inside him. It was only in here he was fully capable of letting his guard down. Nothing he revealed to her would ever be used against him or lorded over him.

Sure, he trusted his brothers with his life. Fuck, he trusted them with Shell's life. But Shell was the one and only person he trusted with his heart.

He didn't have a single doubt she'd protect it as ruthlessly as he'd protect her and Beth.

"Tired, baby?" he asked as he stroked her damp back.

"Exhausted. More emotionally than physically." Her face pinked. "I've kinda been a wreck this week."

Copper

Copper snorted. "Pretty sure I was gonna be impeached if I snapped at one more person this week. Izzy threatened to chop off my balls and send them to you with a pink bow."

Shell slapped a palm over her mouth.

Too late. He heard the giggle. "Not fucking funny," he grumbled. Any other time, Copper would have run out and put a balls-to-the-wall search for Rusty in motion the moment he heard the full story. But this time with Shell was too important to delay. She needed this time to connect physically and emotionally with him. He wanted her to know without a doubt he believed her, believed in her, and loved her. Surprisingly, he needed these tender moments just as much. Maybe even more.

With another giggle, she rested her cheek against his chest. "It's a little funny." Her sated body went completely lax as she snuggled into him.

He grunted. After a moment, he scooted down until he was reclined against the pillows, Shell draped all over him.

"Want me to move?" Her sleepy voice cut through the quiet.

"Fuck no."

A hummed sigh was her response.

"Got something I wanna ask ya."

"Shoot." She didn't bother lifting her head. A soft hand ran up and down his side, lulling him further into a state of relaxation. Wouldn't be long before he succumbed to sleep and there was something else he needed to know.

"You ever sleep with anyone else. You know…after?" Jesus, fucking smooth.

She tensed but quickly slackened under his roaming hands. "Once," she said in a small voice. "My therapist was strongly encouraging me to branch out, try dating. Said it was the only way I'd fully move on from the experience and from my feelings for you."

It was his turn to tense. Shell must have noticed because her soft lips pressed a comforting kiss on his chest. Fuck, the thought of another man touching her made him murderous.

Why the fuck had he asked?

Because he had an insatiable need to know every damn thing about her.

"Anyway. I'm pretty sure she just meant for me to go out on dates, but I had to know if I could do it or if my head was too screwed up." She shrugged against him. "So I did it. Beth was around one at the time."

"And?" He held his breath.

"And I didn't try again until you."

Should he be pleased by that? Or was there another motherfucker he'd have to hunt and kill? "Why? Did he hurt you?"

"Nah." Her voice was soft, almost embarrassed. "He just wasn't you. None of them were you."

Well, fuck me.

If that wasn't enough to make his hard heart melt, not a damn thing could.

No more words were spoken. What else needed to be said?

Within seconds, Shell's breathing evened, and she stopped exploring him.

Sleep didn't come as quickly for Copper. Once she was out, and the room was quiet, there was nothing left to distract him from thoughts of his brother.

Of his fucking psychopathic rapist of a brother.

After hours of sifting through past memories, trying to find a clue he'd missed, a hint he should have picked up on, anything he could use to punish himself for allowing Shell to be used by Rusty, he gave up. Eventually, he fell into a fitful sleep even Shell's soft weight and trust in him couldn't calm.

The following morning, after waking to Shell's hot mouth on his cock then watching her come twice before leaving the bed, he drove her to pick up Beth then to work. With Rusty in the wind, he wasn't thrilled about the idea of Shell running around town by herself. Of course, he'd allowed it all week, something else to kick himself over.

Copper

Surprisingly, she didn't put up a fight. Just kissed him and climbed into the passenger seat of her old beater.

Now that she was officially his woman, he'd be getting her a better car. She couldn't call it charity anymore. Now it was just a gift for his woman.

Fuck, he'd wasted so much damn time.

After he dropped her off, he drove her car back to her house to pick up his bike. Halfway to the clubhouse, his phone rang through the Bluetooth in his helmet.

"What?" he barked after answering.

"It's me."

Rusty.

Copper slowed then rolled to a stop in the shoulder of the quiet country road. Shit, he had to play this just right. "Where you been, brother? Whole club's been out looking for you."

"You worried about me, Cop?" Rusty's voice was heavy with disbelief.

"Of course. You lit outta there last week like your ass was on fucking fire. The fuck you been?"

"Yeah, well, wanted to give you space. Wasn't sure where your head would be at. What'd your ol' lady say about me?"

And here's where Copper had to be ultra-cautious. With a snort, he said, "Not a fucking thing. You think I wanna talk to that lying bitch?" The bullshit words turned his stomach.

"You ain't with her no more?" A note of hope rang out in Rusty's voice.

"Fuck no. You think I wanna keep fucking a woman who had my brother's fucking kid? Didn't call her a lying bitch for nothing." As he spoke, Copper stared at the sky. Hopefully, the universe recognized it was all horseshit. "Why don't you come on back to the clubhouse. Have a drink. We'll sort shit out."

Rusty was silent for a few moments. "What about the garbage she and Izzy were spewing in your office?"

"That shit about you stealing the money? Come on, Rust. I ain't a fucking fool, okay. Sure, she might have played me for one, but it usually takes more than a pretty face and a wet pussy to fool me. You came back, she was feeling the fucking heat. It was a good story. I'm ashamed to say it mighta worked if you hadn't exposed her lies. But I don't believe a fucking word of it. Just sorry she kept news of your daughter from you."

Rusty barked out a laugh. "Like I want to be a daddy to a fucking rug rat. We just gotta find a way to keep her from coming after me for cash. I ain't paying a dime to that slut. Shit, Cop, she was all over me back in the day. Couldn't get enough of my dick. Now the greedy bitch goes after you? I'm at that overlook we used to drink at when we first moved here. Got a bottle of jack. Meet me?"

He was gonna have to put a call into his dentist because he was pretty sure he cracked a damn tooth working to keep the hatred in his mouth. God damned piece of shit trying to play it off as Shell's fault. Now that his eyes were finally open, he didn't believe a word outta Rusty's two-faced, thieving mouth.

Would he have believed it three days ago, before he talked to Shell? Didn't really matter now. But the shame of the way he shunned Shell after hearing Rusty's news would hang from his neck forever.

"Yeah, I'm ten minutes from you."

"See ya, bro," Rusty said sounding much more upbeat than he'd been moments ago. He could almost be called fucking giddy.

The ten-minute drive only took him eight. Copper dismounted after cutting his engine in the clearing used by tourists as a scenic overlook. He had to admit the view was breathtaking. Sometimes, living surrounded by such gorgeous sights, it became easy to take it for granted. He paused and breathed in the fresh mountain air.

Maybe he'd bring Shell and Beth here for a picnic after the dust settled.

Copper

"Rust?" he called, looking around. His brother's truck was there, but no sign of the man himself. "Where the fuck are you, brother?"

He gave one last look at the mountain view then turned around before calling, "Rusty!" again.

"Right here." The sound came from directly behind him. Before he had the chance to turn, a bone-crushing pain cracked across his right shin.

His knees buckled, and he hit the ground like a stone. "Fuck," he cried as instinct kicked in and he curled around the throbbing shin. Glancing up, he squinted against the blinding sun. "What the fuck?" Rusty stood over him, a baseball bat slung over his shoulder like a lumberjack with an ax.

Each time his heart beat, pulsing blood through the arteries in his legs, the injured shin throbbed with a ferocious pain. Fuck, if that leg wasn't broken, he'd eat that fucking bat.

"Hey, *brother*," Rusty said with a grin that had the hair on Copper's neck standing on end.

"Why?" It was the only word he could think to say at that moment.

"You think you're so untouchable. Leader of the pack. Always acting like you're better than me. Lording your authority over me. Acting like you're my fucking father. Who's got the power now, asshole?"

Jesus. He'd heard from Shell how much hatred Rusty had for him, and he'd believed her words, but experiencing the vehemence firsthand was shocking. All his life, he'd tried his damnedest to do right by Rusty. His failure was monumental.

"I only wanted what was best for you, Rusty."

"Bullshit. All you wanted was to be better than me." He spat on the ground next to Copper's head. "Not better now, are you?"

Never once, in his entire life had Copper considered himself above Rusty. Sadness swamped him. Would Rusty have turned out another way if Copper had raised him differently? Was this just who Rusty was, a narcissistic sociopath? Or had Copper made him? His gut told him Rusty was who he was. Like Toni said, not everyone with a difficult upbringing turned into a monster. In fact, most didn't. "So this is how it's gonna be, Rust?" Copper asked. He rolled to his back and propped on his elbows. No chance in hell of standing on that leg.

His blood brother shrugged. "Nah. *This* is how it's gonna be."

Before Copper had a chance to react that cryptic statement, a size twelve biker boot careened toward his face. Rusty's boot made contact against the side of Copper's head with an audible crack. Seconds before his skull collided with the rocky ground, Copper had one thought. *Shell was going to lose her shit when he didn't show at the diner.*

The pain in his head made it impossible to fight the inevitable. The sound of Rusty's laughter penetrated the looming fog of unconsciousness.

Copper was fucked. He hadn't told a damn soul where he was going. His brothers were smart fuckers though.

Someone would find him.

As long as Rusty left something to find.

CHAPTER TWENTY-EIGHT

"Egg white omelet?" Shell asked Izzy. At least three days a week Izzy ate at the diner, and always had an egg white omelet with spinach, tomatoes, and a side of fresh fruit.

Boooring.

But it could explain why Izzy looked like some kind of goddess whereas Shell still hadn't returned to her pre-baby weight over four years later.

Such is life.

"Nah, not today. I'm going to have the cinnamon roll waffles with bacon. No…sausage. No…bacon. Actually, I'll take the bacon, but can I have an extra side of sausage?"

Shell blinked, and across the booth from Izzy, Stephanie snorted out a laugh. The death-glare Izzy shot her had Shell laughing as well. After picking up her butter knife, Izzy pointed it at Steph. "You, shut it." Then she swung the blunt weapon in Shell's direction. "And you! You've had a child, you should empathize with me. Buncha bitches," Izzy muttered.

Shell rolled her lips inward and did her best to squash her laughter. After she had herself under control, she patted Izzy's back. "I'm sorry, honey. You're very right, I should be more understanding. I remember how insatiable I was all the time."

Izzy bobbed her eyebrows, snit long gone. "I'm insatiable in other ways too."

Stephanie's hands flew into the air. "And that's all we need to hear about that, folks. Shell, I'll have her egg white omelet."

"Hey!" The knife was back and pointing at Steph again. "I had to see your man's scrawny ass last week and don't tell me it wasn't plowing his dick into you. Granted I didn't see you because my eyeballs melted out of my face as soon as I realized what was going on."

Steph gave them a sheepish smile as her face turned pink.

"Where were they?" Shell asked. Those two crazy exhibitionists.

"Hood of Steph's car. Saw them when Jig and I were leaving the clubhouse three days ago." She shuddered. "Trust me, Mav's pasty ass is not a sight you want to see."

Steph rolled her eyes and Shell wanted to laugh. Their friend was unapologetic about the fact that she and her ol' man liked to get it on out in the wide-open world. "His ass is not pasty…it's inked."

The three of them dissolved into giggles.

"Now wait a second," Steph said waving a hand in Shell's direction. "What's going on with you? You're looking kinda floaty."

Shell cocked her hip and set the heavy coffee pot down on the table. "Floaty? How does one look floaty?" Thankfully the diner wasn't busy so she could shoot the shit with her friends for a few moments.

"You know," Steph said, waving her hands about. "Like you're floating around the room."

"Yeah," Izzy added. "Because you got a got a big dick in ya, and your feet can't reach the ground."

Both women stared at Izzy. "What?"

Steph cracked up. "That doesn't even make sense."

Izzy shrugged. "Sure it does. Shell knows."

"You're ridiculous," Shell said, but she was pretty sure her face was the color of the tomato going in Steph's omelet.

Copper

"Take it you patched things up with Copper?" Izzy asked. She sipped her decaf coffee then scowled at the mug.

"Yeah. He came over last night. I spilled my guts. He believed me, and—"

"Of course he believed you," Steph cut in. "I think what happened the other day was just shock. Couldn't have been easy for him to have a bomb like that dropped on him. He reacted like an ass, but we all know Copper doesn't usually flip his shit."

"Yeah." Shell dropped into the booth beside Izzy. Might as well enjoy a hot minute off her aching feet. "It'll take us both some time to get used to living with the knowledge of my past, but we're going to give it a serious go."

"You feel comfortable sharing what happened with your sisters?" Steph asked. Nothing but sincerity and concern radiated from here. This wasn't some gossipy interest in the past, this was her family truly wanting to support her and know her.

"Yeah, but I don't want to say it too many times. The story isn't exactly a fairy tale. Girl's night next weekend? My house."

"You're on," Izzy said.

"'Kay, great." She rose from the booth. "Let me get your orders in before mommy badass starts gnawing on your arm, Steph."

"Funny." Izzy hooked a finger in the handle of Stephanie's coffee mug and started to slowly drag it to her side of the booth. "See if I name my baby girl Michelle."

With a scowl, Steph slapped Izzy's hand away. "Unhand my caffeine."

"Oh my God," Shell said, bouncing on the balls of her feet. "You found out it's a girl? Wait…it's way too early to know it's a girl."

"*Oh*, it's a girl," Izzy said. "I refuse to birth a penis."

Shell was still chuckling minutes later when she moved on to her other tables. The women were the heart of the MC. And quite possibly the backbone. Each strong and kickass in their own right, Shell couldn't ask for better sisters. And that's what they were. Maybe not by blood, but sisters just the same.

Four hours later, Shell sat on a bench outside the diner frowning at her phone. It was ten to three, and all the other employees were long gone. Toni hadn't even been in, taking a rare personal day to hang with her man. Apparently, Louie had gone missing, and Zach had been a raving lunatic for the past few days. Toni was hoping to sex him into a better mood before she took him to buy a new baseball bat. Though Zach swore he didn't need one. He was convinced Louie would turn up somewhere. Toni's theory was someone from the gym swiped it from Zach's office.

Wouldn't want to be that poor schmuck once Zach caught wind of them.

Shell's shift ended at two, though Copper promised to swing by around one thirty. Over an hour late was definitely not like him. Especially without so much as a text message. He wasn't answering her calls either. Shell was officially worried. Time to call in reinforcements.

She pulled out her phone and gave Zach a ring.

"Hey, sweetie, what's up?" he asked after the first ring.

"Hi, Zach, I'm really sorry to bother you, but have you seen Copper? He was supposed to meet me around one thirty, and he never showed. Not answering his phone either. I'm guessing he just forgot, but you know I'm a worrier."

"Sweetie, he's not here. Hasn't been here all morning."

"What?" Her stomach sank. "He dropped me at work and was going to swing back by my house to get his bike then go straight to the clubhouse. I think he even had a meeting with Jig."

"Fuck, yeah he did. Never showed for the meeting. Jig assumed you guys were spending the morning fu—uh making up."

Oh, my God, he hadn't made it to the clubhouse. Visions of Copper lying bloody in a ditch on the side of the road danced through her mind. "Well, shit, Z, where is he?" A note of hysteria tinged her voice. "I'm going to drive around and look for him."

"No!" Zach yelled through the phone. "Don't leave the diner." Then there was some muffled mumbling. "Screw and I are on our way there. Mav and LJ are gonna head out and drive the route to your house. Gonna call Rocket too. See if he can get some of his crazy contacts to track Cop's phone. You do not move that ass one step away from the diner, you hear me?"

Being idle while someone she loved was potentially in danger went against every fiber of her being, but she understood Zach's concern. "I-I hear you. I'll be here when you get here. Just please hurry." She ended the call without waiting for more.

There was no point in driving around aimlessly. They needed a plan and would come up with a good one together. And that was what she was telling herself to keep from full-on freaking out.

Zach and Screw, who it seemed was being groomed to be assistant enforcer, made record time. Thunder was with them, driving her car.

Heart pounding, Shell rushed to their idling bikes. "Anything? What did Rocket say? Can he trace the phone? What about Mav? Did they find Copper? Is he okay?"

"Shhh, sweetie come here." Zach snagged her around the shoulders and drew her in for a hug. "No news yet. I can't get a hold of Rocket, but we'll find your man. I promise you. Then Copper will have Rocket's ass. This is the second time he's been out of reach lately."

With a nod, Shell swallowed her fear and said, "What can I do to help?"

After giving her a quick squeeze, Zach released her. "Head on back to the clubhouse. The rest of the ladies are making their way in. Toni will grab Beth for you and meet you there."

"Oh no." She shook her head. "No way am I sitting this out."

"Shell..." Zach's tone took on the hard edge all the bikers seemed to master. Especially when ordering their women around.

"No, Zach. That's my ol' man out there. Give me something to do besides sit on my ass and wait for the big strong men to find him."

"I'll ride with her." Screw piped in for the first time. "We can run my route together."

Zach leveled her with a look that had a chill racing down her spine.

Yikes.

In all the years she'd known the Handler's enforcer, she hadn't actually experienced him in the role. And she kinda hoped to never see it again. Because the man with the perfectly styled hair and pretty face was downright scary when in business mode. No wonder he held the title.

"Listen to me and listen good, Shell. I'll let you tag along with Screw on one condition. You do every damn thing he tells you. No lip, no sass, no questions, no fucking thinking on your own. Just yes sir, no matter what. You hear me?"

Shell swallowed and nodded. Probably a good time to ignore the fact that she took offense to him saying he was *letting* her tag along. "I hear you."

"Swear to fucking Christ, Shell, Screw tells me you're giving him trouble and I'll hogtie you and dump you at the clubhouse. Then I'll make sure Copper blisters your ass after we find him."

"I get it, Zach."

He folded his arms and continued glaring at her in a way that made her want to cower in the corner. Poor Toni. How could she ever win an argument against this version of Zach?

"You got any idea what Copper will do to me if something happens to you on my watch?"

"Z!" she shouted. "I get it. Now let's stop wasting time and find my man."

Copper

A toothy smile overtook Zach's face. "Damn, sounds good to hear you calling the prez your man."

Shell rolled her eye and threw her hands up in the air as she stomped toward her car. "You coming?" she called over her shoulder to Screw.

"Yeah, babe." He jogged after her. "And don't think for a fucking second you're driving. Thunder take my bike back to the clubhosue. You ding it, you buy it. Get me?" Screw tossed his keys toward the slightly green-faced prospect.

"Uh, yeah sure, Screw."

Twenty-four hours later, Shell paced the floor of the clubhouse with a knot the size of a soccer ball in her stomach.

Nothing. The entire club had been out searching for Copper for a full day and not a damn clue as to what happened to him. Something was very wrong. Shell could feel it deep in the pit of her soul. Copper was hurt, and there wasn't a damn thing she could do. She'd been wracking her brain for hours and couldn't think of a single place they hadn't explored. Sleep had been impossible. She couldn't even tolerate the idea of lying down and attempting a nap. Every ounce of thought and energy needed to be geared toward finding Copper.

"Hey, honey, why don't you sit for a bit. Have a drink or something to eat." Toni slung an arm across Shell's shoulders and tried to guide her to the bar.

After casting a glance at her daughter coloring at a table, blissfully unaware of the seriousness of the situation she shook her head. "No. I can't sit. My body stops moving, and my mind starts running wild. At least if I'm walking, I'm not going completely crazy in my own head."

Toni nodded. She understood. She'd lived through fear not that long ago. "All right, hon. Just want to make sure you're taking care of yourself."

The door to the clubhouse started to swing open, and Shell swore her heart came to a complete halt. "Copper?" she yelled, charging toward the entrance. She ripped the door the rest of the way open and groaned when she encountered a startled Rocket.

"Where the fuck have you been?" Zach roared, just steps behind Shell. He reached over her head, grabbed Rocket by the shirt and slammed him against the wall. "Our fucking president had been MIA over twenty-four hours and where the fuck were you? I've been calling your phone all fucking day."

"Zach." Toni came up behind him, laying her hands on his back. His bulky shoulders visibly relaxed.

"Fuck," Rocket said. "I got held up with some personal business. Fuck! I'm here now. What do you need from me."

"You got anyone who can trace his phone?" Zach asked as he released his hold on Rocket's shirt.

Rocket shifted his gaze to Shell. She'd been taking the whole thing in, standing stock-still just a few feet from Zach. "You okay, babe?"

"Freaking out," she said.

A single nod was Rocket's response. "Let you know as soon as I have something."

A rush of air left Shell's lungs in an audible whoosh. It might not be much, but it seemed like progress. Zach turned and wrapped his arms around Toni. She whispered something in his ear that had him closing his eyes and nodding.

Shell closed her eyes, unable to witness their closeness just then. Her own arms ached to hold Copper and be safe in his embrace once again.

"Get your asses over here," Viper, the club's VP, called out, waving everyone toward the bar. Shell moved with the crowd. Once everyone was gathered around, Viper scratched his long gray beard and said, "Let's put our fucking heads together. Who are the major players here? Who'd have a reason to want Cop out of the picture?"

"Lefty," Screw called out.

Copper

Shell bit her lip. Lefty was the most likely and also worst-case scenario. God, she hoped he didn't have Copper holed up somewhere.

"Could it be Joe?" Mav said.

"Could be," Zach spoke up. "But I'm not feeling it. Joe specifically said they didn't want to fuck with us."

Izzy caught Shell's eye. She pointed to Beth then at the stairs. Thank God for this amazing family. Shell nodded to her friend. The things they were talking about weren't for Beth's ears, and she appreciated her friend getting Beth away from the chatter.

"I'm with Z on that one," Viper said. "But we ain't ruling him out completely."

"Can't rule out Rusty either," Mav said. "That fucker's been in the wind for a week."

Shell's money was on Rusty. Just a gut feeling, but she'd learned to trust them over the years. If only she could think of somewhere Rusty would stash Copper. Was there a place he'd loved when they were younger? Anywhere Copper loved that Rusty might want to poison for him?

A hazy memory started to make its way to the forefront of her mind. Rusty hovering over her naked body, whispering something in her ear. Normally she squashed those memories like the cockroaches they were, but this time she allowed them to come. She'd been eighteen at the time and had been at a club party earlier that night. Copper's eyes had tracked her from the moment she walked in the door to the second she left. And it hadn't escaped Rusty's notice.

One day, I'm going to be fucking you like this, pounding you in this bed, and he's gonna walk in and see me with my dick in you. Or hell, maybe he'll find me with my cock buried down your throat. Yeah, that'd be fucking sweet. Can you imagine the look on his face? It would destroy him. That's my fucking dream Shell. To destroy him. To have him look at this bed and know I'm the one who fucked you in it. I got here first. I ruined his perfect little MC princess.

Shell shoved whoever was standing in front of her aside and moved into the circle around Viper. "What's today's date?" she asked, tone panicked.

"March twenty-second, babe, why?" Viper asked.

Her mother was out of town. On a ten-day cruise.

"Holy shit! I know where he is," she said, then spun and sprinted for the exit.

"Goddammit, Shell, fucking wait!" Zach's voice chased her, but she didn't slow.

She had to get to Copper. There was no time to explain.

They could follow.

CHAPTER TWENTY-NINE

Copper was no stranger to pain. He'd had his ass beat more than a time or two back in his younger days when he was far more hot-headed and hadn't learned to lock down his temper. Back in Ireland, his pop was in an outlaw MC. The old guy had been involved in some shady shit. Drugs, weapons trafficking, prostitution, even some murder-for-hire, and he hadn't been afraid to drag his sons into whatever was going on. Copper'd been stabbed by the time he was fifteen. Drug deal gone bad. That was part of the reason he'd pulled the Handlers out of that shit when he took control. He had first-hand knowledge of the havoc that lifestyle could wreak.

The pain of the past day, however, was unlike anything he'd yet to experience. He woke to a burning hot sensation combined with tearing agony. Goddamn, he hoped it was the worst he'd ever feel because it fucking *hurt*.

"Welcome back, brother," Rusty said as he dragged the tip of a knife up Copper's exposed thigh, way too fucking close to his balls. A thin stream of blood immediately flowed everywhere the knife sliced.

Copper hissed out a breath, nostrils flaring and teeth clenched to keep the growl of white-hot pain at bay. "The fuck am I?" Clad in nothing but his boxer-briefs, he was on a bed with his arms extended and cuffed to the posts. He gave his one functioning leg a wiggle.

Ankles were bound, too.

This was pretty much how the past day went. Copper would wake to some kind of agony, demanded to know where he was, endured more pain, then drifted off to a fitful sleep without any answers. Although he had a sickening suspicion he knew where he was being held.

"We're in one of my favorite places."

Guess Rusty was finally willing to chat. Probably feeling pretty damn good about himself, having kidnapped and beaten his brother. The first few times he'd woken, it'd been to the whack of a baseball bat on various parts of his body. A baseball bat that looked suspiciously like Louie.

Zach was gonna flip his shit.

Hell, his enforcer would probably be happier to find Louie than his own president.

After Rusty removed the knife from Copper's skin, he flicked a Zippo open, then stuck the tip of the steak knife in the flame. As he rotated the blade in the flame, Rusty stared at the glowing point.

Fuck.

No wonder that shit hurt. A searing hot knife slicing the fuck out of his skin. Glancing down, he noticed two jagged lines identical in size running from his knee to his groin. Shallow cuts, thank fuck because they were right along an artery that could take him out in minutes. He must have been dead to the world to remain unconscious through the first slash.

"Man, the memories I made in this bed. Shell was a damn wildcat back then. She still like that?" Rust removed the knife and tested the burning tip against his finger. "Shit." He shook out his hand with a gleeful smirk then flipped the lighter open again. This time, he picked up a glass pipe from the bed and held the bowl over his flame. Copper watched the smoke swirl up the tube. The smell of burning plastic filled the air. After a few seconds, Rusty lifted the pipe to his lips and inhaled the

Copper

smoke deep into his lungs. His eyes closed for one second then popped back open, smirk present once again.

That smirk. Must have been the one Shell spoke of. Evil, cheerful, and excited all rolled into one shit-eating leer. If there was even a cracked window of an opportunity, Copper'd rip that knife from his brother's hands and cut the damn grin right off his face.

It'd be just the beginning of what Rusty had in store for him. The start of evening the score.

"Not gonna kiss and tell?" Rusty's pinpoint pupils rolled skyward. His red beard was a scraggly mess, as was the hair on top of his head. Looked like the man hadn't so much as run a brush through it since he was released from prison. Hell, he smelled like he hadn't fucking showered in as long. A combination of piss, stale pussy, meth, and booze. The hand stabilizing the knife shook slightly as he said, "So fucking noble, my big brother. S'alright, I don't mind sharing the details. Musta fucked your girl a hundred times, right in this very bed. Ate her pussy. Choked her on my cock. Made her come again and again. That bitch couldn't get enough." He thrust his hips forward and back.

Lies. Fucking lies.

"Damn, I miss those days. Wasn't sure I'd still want her when I got out, but I gotta say, I'm thinking of starting back up with her again. We got a kid after all. Should be a happy little family, ya know?" He lit the lighter, and the knife went right back in the flame.

Breathing through his clenched teeth, Copper fought to keep himself in check. He stared at the flicker, feeling his own spark ignite deep in his belly. Images of Rusty's hands and mouth on his woman had him crazed with the need to slaughter. But it was a reality he was going to have to accept. It had happened, so he had to learn to live with it. It'd been Shell's reality for years. All Copper had to do was listen to the stories. She actually had to live with the sensory memories of the experience.

"Big man, huh, Rusty? Forcing yourself on a teenage girl. Couldn't find a grown woman to fuck you? None of the club whores willing to spread for your toothpick dick?"

The cords of Rusty's neck strained as his eyes flashed and a vein popped out across his forehead.

That's right, fucker.

"Fuck you!" He dragged the flame across the entire length of the blade. Back and forth at least ten times.

Copper steeled himself for the impending pain.

Suddenly, Rusty tossed the lighter on the bed as he shot forward. The Zippo landed directly on Copper's mangled shin at the exact same time Rusty pressed the length of the smoldering knife against Copper's abdomen.

"Aggg," he ground between gritted teeth.

There was an audible sizzle as his flesh melted under the heated metal. Copper breathed through his nose, nostrils flaring and head spinning. Nausea hit, sharp and swift.

"You're not in charge anymore. Not in here. For fucking once, I've got all the control," Rusty said against his ear. As quickly as he'd spring forward, he jerked back, ripping the knife away and taking a charred chunk of skin with it.

Blackness rimmed Copper's vision, but he fought the oblivion. "That's what this is fucking about? Your panties in a wad because you're not top dog?"

Rusty prowled the small room like a rabid, caged dog. It gave Copper his first chance to check out his surroundings. The bed he was tied to wasn't large, a double maybe, and the walls were decorated simply with a pale-yellow paint. Across the room, a white dresser held a few picture frames.

Shell with her mother. Shell with Beth. Shell with Sarge as a young kid. Jesus Christ, he was in Shell's childhood room. Where the fuck was Cindy?

"All my fucking life you've ordered me around, taken shit from me, thought you were better than me. You even dragged me to a different country. Didn't give a fucking shit if I wanted to go."

"You pissed we left Ireland? Fucking twenty years ago? The men who killed Pop would have come after us. We had a shit life there. You'd have been dead before you turned sixteen. Cry about something else."

"Shut the fuck up." Rusty charged forward, ramming his fist into Copper's face.

Copper spit blood onto the comforter.

"Fucking MC president! Acting like you still have control over me," he screamed, so red-faced Copper wouldn't be surprised if he keeled over from a heart attack.

I should be so lucky.

Then like a switch flipped, the anger was gone and the smirk returned. "Shell was just your type. Little blonde, curly hair, big tits, sweet as pie. All American girl. Kind you loved to fuck."

Christ, his brother was crazy. "She was a fucking kid, Rusty. I didn't so much as glance at her back then. Not in the way you mean."

"Oh, I know. The great and honorable Copper would never do a goddamn thing wrong. But that girl was fucking obsessed with you. Knew she'd turn eighteen someday. And come on, all that sweetness turned your way?" He snorted. "You'd have hit that eventually. Remember, I've tasted those tits too. Guarantee they're part of the reason you did hit that."

Copper swallowed the metallic taste filling his mouth. Didn't help his nausea. "You're a sick fuck, Rusty."

His brother threw back his head and laughed long and hard. "I'm good with that, brother. I go to bed each night remembering the feel of your woman on my tongue. And I sleep like a fucking baby knowing how much it's eating at your fucking soul. You may never admit it, but I know it kills you that I was there first."

It was the damn truth. It ate at his fucking soul like a starved piranha. But it wouldn't for long. Because soon Rusty would die a painful death and that would be like a magical balm. He just had to stay alive long enough for the club to find him.

"Hey! I'm fucking talking to you!" Rusty screamed, hitting Copper's face again. Then he sunk the knife deep in Copper's thigh. Straightening, he left the blade buried to the hilt, lifted his boot, and stomped it against Copper's ribs. His chest caved inward with a sickening crunch. Clenching his fists, he breathed as best he could without being able to inflate his chest.

Something had to give. He wasn't sure how much longer he'd last with the way he was now bleeding.

"The fuck's your plan here, Rusty?" Copper asked as he glanced at his thigh. Blood pulsed around the knife, running down his thigh and soaking the bed beneath him. The artery had been hit for sure. If Rusty decided to remove the knife, Copper would be in serious fucking jeopardy. "You gonna let me bleed out all over Cindy's sheets? Then you're gonna haul my two hundred sixty-pound dead ass outta here and clean the place before someone realizes what the fuck is going on? Good fucking luck. How the fuck you get me in here anyway?"

"Wasn't fucking easy." Rusty paced the room again, gripping his hair with both hands. He was losing his shit. Whether that was a good or bad thing remained to be determined.

"You forget, Rusty, the entire fucking club's gonna be searching for me. No way in hell you cart me outta here unnoticed. Just take the fuck off. Get outta town."

He lifted panic-filled eyes to meet Copper's gaze. "You gonna call off the hounds if I leave?"

Not a fucking chance in hell. "Sure. You disappear, and we'll let it the fuck go." He inhaled wincing at the pain and whistling that came from his lungs. It ended in a fit of wet coughs. Shit, were his lungs filling with blood?

"You think I'm stupid?" Rusty screamed. "Maybe I just slit your fucking throat and leave you here. Cindy won't be back for a week. You'll be nice and ripe by then, and I'll be long gone."

Copper

Copper snorted, the action sending a shooting pain from the bridge of his smashed nose straight through his head. "Won't matter where you fucking hide. Club'll find your murdering ass. Then they'll skin you alive. My one regret will be not participating." He shrugged as best he could with his shoulders aching. "But it'll happen."

Anger blazed in Rusty's eyes. How long had Copper been here? He glanced out the window.

Twilight. The sun was nearly gone. I'd been early in the day when he rode off to meet Rusty. He vaguely remembered coming to when the sky was dark once before. Had a full day really passed?

The smirk was back, curling Rusty's lips. He stalked forward at a slow pace. "Actually, think I got my plan." When he was within striking distance, he wrapped his fingers around the handle of the knife, giving it a twist.

Shit. Copper tensed, pulling on the cuffs in a useless effort to break free as the pain shot to near blackout levels.

"How 'bout I yank this sucker out, then go visit your ol' lady. Maybe remind her which brother had her first. Thinking I'll fuck her till she can't walk anymore. Then maybe my daughter and I take a little trip. How 'bout that for a plan."

Fuck. Fuck! Copper pulled with every ounce of strength he had left. It wasn't much, but enough to hear a loud crack as wood on one of the bedposts split. "You lay one hand on either one of them, and I'll use that knife to peel your skin off one inch at a time."

"Huh." Rusty grinned. "Don't think so, brother. You'll be fucking dead," he said then pulled the knife out with a harsh jerk.

Copper growled through the pain. Blood spurted from the wound in pulses like a faucet with air in the line.

Wouldn't take long for him to bleed out at this rate. Damn, he wished he had even thirty seconds to kiss his woman goodbye.

Rusty straightened and smiled. "It's been fun, Cop," he said, tossing the knife on the bed. "Can't say I'll miss ya, though."

Copper opened his mouth then snapped it shut again. He strained his ears. Was that…fuck yes, it was. The low rumble of a motorcycle. He'd know that fucking sound anywhere.

"Game over, Rusty," he said, mustering a smirk as evil as his brother's.

Chrome cavalry had arrived.

CHAPTER THIRTY

Shell jammed on the brakes and winced as the car screeched to a stop in front of her childhood home. Hopefully, the element of surprise wasn't crucial because she'd just killed that.

Hands shaking, she shoved the door open and darted out of the car without bothering to close the door.

"What the fuck do you think you're doing?" Zach called out as his bike coasted to a stop. Another five motorcycles and one monster-sized black pick-up pulled in behind him.

Shell blew by him, charging for the front door. Three days ago, her mother left for her cruise. She wasn't due back for another ten days. If Rusty needed a private location to do God knows what to Copper, this was the place.

"No fucking way, Shell," Zach said as he tossed his helmet in the grass.

A large hand wrapped around her upper arm, yanking her back when she was halfway to the door. She spun, prepared to fight and claw her way to her man, but stopped cold when she saw Zach's expression. Second time in as many days she encountered Zach The Enforcer.

Scary as shit.

"You're not going in there, Shell," he growled down at her.

"Zach, let me go. We're wasting time. Copper could be hurt. Please, I need to get to him."

The others climbed off their bikes eyeing her and Zach. Mav seemed to be running the show behind her as he ordered the men to circle the perimeter and report back.

"Sweetie," Zach said, tone much calmer. "We don't know what we're going to find in there. What kind of condition your man will be in, who is with him, or if he's even fucking in there. We need to play this smart."

A whimper escaped. Part of her appreciated Zach for giving it to her straight, but the thought of Copper suffering was killing her. "I'm not staying out here." Chest heaving, she clenched her fists at her sides. "I'm *not* staying out here. Not while he's in there. You'll have to tie me to your bike. Even then I'll find a way out."

Zach stared at the sky then blew out a breath. "Fuck! Okay, you stay behind me the entire time. You hear me?"

"Yes, I promise. Behind you."

"Copper's gonna shred my fuckin' patch for this," he grumbled then turned as Mav called his name.

"Think they're in the back room, right side of the house. Seems to be the only light that's on," Mav said. Energy crackled from each of the men. They were ready for action.

Ready for blood.

"My old room," Shell said. "Rusty used to tell me he fantasized about Copper walking in on us...you know. That he'd love to see the look on his brother's face when he caught us." God, how embarrassing. She stared at the grass unable to meet the brothers' eyes. "It's what made me think to come here."

Mav reached for her hand, entwining it with his inked one. After a reassuring squeeze, he said, "Hey, no shame, sweetie. I don't know how it all went down, but I know you don't have to be ashamed of a damn thing. Now, let's go get your man so he can kick all our asses for letting you in the house."

Their support meant everything to her. This time, admitting to some of her past didn't seem as traumatizing. She nodded and fell in step behind Zach as he barked orders at men to stand

Copper

guard and others to join them. Looked like he wasn't going for subtle because he booted the door open and ignored the flying splinters of wood that pelted his face. With a gigantic black gun hovering at eye level, he resembled some kind of badass mercenary.

If Rusty was in the house, he had to be aware they were there. None of them were quiet. Was he just waiting with his hostage? Was he actively hurting Copper? She refused to even entertain the idea that Copper wasn't alive.

Zach at her front and Rocket behind her, they stormed down the hallway. Both men appeared focused and lethal, one hundred percent at ease with rifles in their arms. She'd known these men for years, yet apparently still had a lot to learn about them.

Zach lifted a hand and came to a dead stop. "Game fucking over, Rusty. You know how many guys we got here? You don't stand a fucking chance."

Laughter sounded behind the closed door. The kind of laugh that had Shell's blood running cold. High-pitched, insane, out of control. "Please tell me you have Shell with you," Rusty said. "There's someone here who'd love to see her."

Her eyes widened. Zach turned and met her gaze with his narrowed one. She shook her head. No. She wasn't walking out. Even if it gave Rusty a sense of satisfaction to see the horror on her face when she laid eyes on Copper. She wasn't leaving. Zach was right, Rusty didn't stand a chance here tonight. So even if the smug devil-smirk was present, it wouldn't last long.

Zach shook his head. He turned back to the door, repositioned the rifle, then held up three fingers, then two, then one. As that last finger disappeared, he slammed his boot into the door. As the front door had done, this one splintered around the knob then shot open.

Shell couldn't see a damn thing around Zach's bulk.

"What do you think of your president now, Zach?" Rusty asked.

"Rocket, get her the fuck outta here," Zach yelled.

"You fucking brought her?"

Jesus, was that weak, thready voice Copper's?

A thick arm banded across her waist and yanked her back against a hard chest. "No!" she cried out.

"You don't want to see this, Shell," Rocket whispered in her ear. "Promise we'll get your man out of there. Just wait by the bikes."

Rusty's laughter could be heard over Zach's voice. That sound, that high pitched, crazed sound had a shiver racing down her spine. Her feet left the ground as Rocket started to drag her down the hallway. "No! Please." She writhed and kicked with all her might. One of her heels connected with something that had Rocket jolting and cursing. His arm loosened for a fraction of a second, but it was enough for her to slip from his grasp.

"Fuck!" he shouted. "Z, incoming."

Shell ignored the men, focused on getting to Copper. By now, Zach had stepped into the room and braced, feet wide with the rifle snuggled against his shoulder. Ready for action.

Shell slipped into the room and stuttered to a stop to the left of Zach. "Oh, my God." Her hand flew to her mouth. "Copper," she whispered.

"Goddamn it, woman," he said, but the words held no bite. Blood was everywhere. The dark red substance ran down his stomach, dripped from his split lip and swollen nose, and spurted at an alarming rate from his inner thigh. One leg was purple and bent at an unnatural angle below the knee. But the most horrifying sight was Rusty on his knees behind Copper. He'd propped Copper into a sitting position, mostly hidden behind Copper's bulk. His arms hung at his sides, cuffs dangling off each wrist. Deep gouges ringed each wrist, beginning to split the skin. He wasn't bound to the bed at the moment, but the evidence clearly showed he'd been restrained

Where could Zach even shoot?

Copper

"Shell, go outside. Get her the fuck out of here, Zach," Copper said, then coughed a horrible wet cough. Where the hell had that come from? He wasn't sick yesterday morning. Now he sounded like someone dying of pneumonia.

"No!" she cried as Rocket joined them, flanking her other side. "I'm not leaving you." Weaponless and without the physical strength of any of the men in the room, she wasn't able to fight, but she could still help. She could distract, maybe give Zach or Rocket a chance to maim the bastard.

Rusty threw back his head and laughed. "This is fucking priceless. The bitch stays." His crazy-eyed gaze shifted to her, but the knife never moved. It remained lodged against Copper's exposed throat. "Good times in this room, huh, Shell?"

Her insides trembled like a gale force wind was ripping through. She swallowed, locked her knees, and dug one fingernail into her palm to keep from showing fear on the outside. Whatever was going to happen in his room, it wouldn't be with her cowering and begging for Rusty's mercy. No matter how the horrifying memories affected her.

She didn't beg back then, and she wouldn't do it now.

"Not sure I'd call being blackmailed into sleeping with you good times, but to each his own."

"Shit, Rusty," Zach said. "That the only way you get a woman to take your dick? You gotta force it? Fucking pitiful man. See you got Louie there. Thanks for bringing him. I look forward to cracking him over your skull."

She could practically smell the smoke rising from Rusty's ears. His ego would be his downfall for sure.

"Fuck you, bitch. You loved every second of my cock in you." He jerked his arm. The knife nicked Copper's skin, causing yet another trail of blood.

Shell snorted. She forced her gaze away from the blood. If she looked at Copper, she'd lose her shit, and it'd be game over.

Play on his weaknesses.

"You call that thing between your legs a cock? Always thought of it more as a cocktail weenie. Now, your brother," she said, letting her lips curl into a satisfied smile. One she usually reserved for Copper. "Now there's a man with a cock. Knows how to use it, too. Maybe he can give you some pointers." Her cheeks flamed. Under normal circumstances, the guys would never let her hear the end of a comment like that.

Nothing about this was normal.

"Thanks, baby." Copper chuckled weakly. It quickly turned into another round of hacking coughs.

"You know you'll never be what he is, right, Rusty? Not in bed or in life," Shell said. "You'll always be second best."

On her left, Rocket remained silent. His intense focus and control were almost creepy. But the silence served its purpose. As they goaded Rusty, Shell almost forgot he was there, waiting, watching.

"Shut the fuck up, bitch," Rusty said. He dug the knife a little deeper.

Shell swore her heart stopped. Was this a huge mistake? Was she provoking Rusty into killing Copper?

"He ain't even second best," Zach piped in.

Shell shuddered out a breath. He was on board with her plan.

She prayed they weren't making the ultimate mistake. "You're right, Z. Every man in the club looks up to Copper. Respects him. Hell, you guys would follow him straight into hell and back again. Wouldn't you?"

Zach grunted.

"Bet you wouldn't follow Rusty into the kitchen."

Beside her, Rocket shifted so subtly, she almost missed it. Something was going to happen. Rocket could sense it.

"I said shut the fuck up, bitch!" Rusty screamed. Eyes shooting sparks, he rose higher on his knees, jerking Copper's abused body.

Copper grunted.

A loud pop sounded to her left.

Copper

Her left ear rang.
Blood sprayed.
Shell was shoved to the right.
Rusty screamed.
The knife fell.

Rocket and Zach charged forward. Zach dragged Rusty from behind Copper as though the man was Beth's size instead of a six-foot man.

It all happened so fast, Shell could do nothing but stand there, trembling as the blood pounded in her head.

"Shell...Shell, baby, look at me." Copper's faint voice had her jerking her gaze from the man lying on the floor to her man lying on the bed.

"Copper," she said on a gasp. Her legs kicked into gear and she rushed to his side. Shit, he looked awful, full of bruises and blood. "I don't want to touch you."

"All right, brother, this is gonna fucking hurt," Rocket said as he worked his black canvas belt from his pants.

Shell glared at him. "What are you doing to him?"

"Saving his fucking life."

Copper took her hand in a weak grip. "It's okay."

She stared, slack-jawed as Rocket worked the fabric under Copper's thick thigh. Right at the top, pretty much in his groin. "Ready, Prez?"

Copper gave a small nod. "Just fuckin' do it," he replied. "Give me those eyes, gorgeous."

Shell looked away from the mess of Copper's leg and into his pain-filled eyes. She held his gaze as he clenched his teeth and growled a wounded-animal sound. His grip tightened beyond the point of discomfort, but it had to be nothing compared to what he was enduring.

"Done. Let's get you the fuck outta here," Rocket said.

"Thanks, brother."

Shell risked a glance at Copper's leg. Rocket had secured the belt so tightly around Copper's upper thigh, the blood slowed to an ooze.

Her breath came a little easier.

She moved off to the side as a few more of the club members entered the room. It took five of them, but they managed to lift Copper and carry him out. A sharp hiss was the only indication he was in pain, but the jostling had to be agony.

It was then Shell realized Rusty was no longer in the room. She looked at Screw who'd come from outside. His white T-shirt was speckled with dots of blood. Rusty's?

"What will happen to him?"

Screw stared at her, as though trying to decide how much to tell her. Then he sighed, running a hand through his hair. When he'd first prospected, he'd been a constant jokester, a real screwball. With the passage of time and increased responsibility, he was turning into a different man. One packed with new muscles and a new respect for his obligations. "We'll hold him in the box until Prez is released from the hospital." He shrugged. "Up to the boss man after that."

Jigsaw stuck his head in the room. "Hey, Shell, we're getting ready to cart the big guy's ass to the hospital. He's refusing to go unless you're with him."

Oh, yes, she wanted, needed to be with him. "Thanks, Jig. What are we going to tell them at the hospital?"

"We'll take care of it. You're going to just play dumb. You know nothing. We picked you up on the way to the hospital because Copper asked for you. All you know is he was injured. Play up the club not telling you shit, huh?"

She nodded and speed-walked across the lawn to keep up with Jig's long stride. "Okay. That's easy enough." Thank God. She wasn't sure she had the mental capacity to recall a complicated story after all she'd been through the past twenty-four hours.

"Yeah, we wanted to keep you out of it as much as possible."

Copper

"Where is he?" She looked around but didn't see Copper anywhere. Panic had her grabbing Jig's arm. "Did they take him already?"

"Nah." Jig pointed to the massive black pick-up. "They got him lying in the bed of the truck. You can ride back there with him. Stay low. We got some blankets back there so you shouldn't be too cold."

"Thanks, Jig." Shell took off toward the truck. Zach helped her climb into the back. Copper was lying on a thick stack of folded blankets with another covering his body.

Shell lowered to her knees and crawled over to him. As carefully as possible, she laid down next to him. Comfortable wouldn't exactly be the word she'd use to describe the set-up, but she'd lie on broken glass to be next to Copper.

"Closer," he mumbled, eyes closed.

"I don't want to hurt you."

"Need to feel you." His slurred words had worry skittering across Shell's nerve endings. Copper was a steel pillar, and those should never crumble. Seeing him in such a weakened state was unnerving, to say the least.

She inched her way closer until her body was pressed along his side. Gently, she rested her arm across his chest. "Better?"

He grunted.

"We're done, Shell, you hear me?"

Her heart stopped. Literally died. "W-what?" He was breaking up with her? Tears spilled down her cheeks.

Now?

"Done with this bullshit. Soon as I'm on my feet, we're getting fucking married."

Shell couldn't help it, she laughed. "Copper, you've lost a lot of blood. I think you're delirious."

"Not fucking delirious," he muttered. "Say yes."

"You didn't ask me a question."

"Goddammit, woman."

Shell bit her lip to keep from laughing again. God, she loved this man. Some of the intense anxiety she'd been experiencing since he went missing abated. He was going to be just fine if he could still *goddammit* her.

Might as well agree. It wasn't like he was going to remember it come morning. "Yes, Copper."

He just grunted.

The rest of the trip was made in silence, but with a smile on her face.

It was over. Whatever the club decided to do with Rusty, Shell had no doubt it was over. He'd never bother her again. She no longer had to hand over half her salary to Joe each month. Copper knew her secrets and still loved her.

Once he was healed, everything would be perfect.

CHAPTER THIRTY-ONE

"Babe, what's it gonna take to get you to go home and catch a few hours' sleep?"

Shell glanced up from her phone where she'd been reading about tibial fractures. She blinked at Copper. "Huh? I told you. I'm not leaving until you do." She bounced her knee and went back to her reading. Turned out there were a few ways to repair a tibial fracture depending on where the actual break was. And the type of surgery determined the restrictions and rehab course.

Huh, she'd have to remember to question the orthopedic surgeon next time he came around. Since they dragged Copper back to surgery, she'd been doing everything she could to learn about his injuries, how best to care for him, and what to expect recovery-wise. Drumming her fingers on the armrest of the most uncomfortable chair she'd ever sat in, she scrunched her forehead.

No weight on his leg for a few months? That wasn't going to go over well.

As she concentrated, she kept up the knee bouncing. The moment the trauma doctors dragged Copper behind the thick operating room doors, anxiety shot through her, and it hadn't left, even now, hours after surgery. It felt like she'd been zapped with a live wire, aftershocks zinging every few minutes.

"Babe, put down the phone and lie next to me," Copper said.

Was he crazy? She looked up at his bruised face. "What? No, I'll hurt you." There were way too many injuries for her to be crawling into bed with him. The tibia and fibula were broken on his right leg. The femoral artery on his left leg had required surgical repair as well as the broken bones, but he'd be allowed to stand on that leg, thankfully. Then there were a host of stitches in his thigh as well as cracked ribs, a broken nose, and countless deep bruises. Oh, and the nasty blade-shaped third-degree burn on his abdomen. Couldn't forget that one.

Copper reached out and snatched the phone from her clutches. He tossed it on the two-drawer nightstand on the opposite side of his bed.

"Hey!" Shell yelped. "I was reading that."

"No," he growled. How the man could be two hours out of major surgery and still so commanding was beyond her.

It was kind of a turn on.

"Look at me, Michelle."

Yeah, the tone was definitely sexy. As was the use of her full name. She met his solemn gaze.

"I'm all right, baby. The doctors fixed me all up. All of my injuries will heal. Might have a few gnarly scars, but I'm pretty sure you can handle those."

Her throat constricted and her eyes burned. It'd been so close. If they'd been just a few minutes later...

"I'm all right," he said again, tugging her hand. "Baby, please relax. It's killing me seeing you so worked up like this. If you want me to sleep and heal, you're gonna have to take care of yourself. I can't be calm until you are." When she resisted his pull, he only tugged harder.

How could he still be so strong with all the blood loss?

After a thirty second stand-off, Shell relented. As gently as possible, she stretched out beside him on the bed. "Please tell me if I hurt you."

"Not possible, babe," he said. "I feel ten times better already just having you next to me."

Copper

A small smile tilted her lips. His warmth seeped into her, proving he was in fact very much alive. "It was terrifying," she whispered. "Seeing you like that. I can't even tell you how scared I was."

His large hand stroked over her hair and down her back. "Fuck, I wish you hadn't been there."

She knew he did. He would be pissed over her presence for a while. She actually felt bad for Zach, who'd already gotten an earful and would undoubtedly get a lot more once Copper was back on his feet. Horrifying as it was, she'd been where she was supposed to be. No way could she have stayed back at the clubhouse waiting around for news. She'd needed to participate in Copper's rescue. "You're really feeling okay?"

He chuckled. "Well, no, I feel like dogshit. But I *am* okay. Promise, baby."

She sighed. Guess that was the best she could expect. "All right."

"I really need you to get some rest. One of the guys will take you home for a few hours so you can sleep."

She fell silent, playing with the hospital gown that didn't quite fit her over-sized man. The thought of leaving had her near panic. "Can I please stay? I know you're okay, but I need to be near you right now. I just need to be where you are."

He didn't like it, she could tell, but after a moment he said, "Fine, but no more researching my injuries. The docs will tell us everything we need to know." Scooping his arm beneath her, he positioned her head on his chest.

"Okay. I love you, Copper." The steady beat of his heart under her ear helped to calm her anxiety.

"Jesus, babe, I love you so fucking much."

They were gifted about ten minutes of peace before the door to his room swung open. Zach, Screw, and LJ burst in. "We got a problem, Prez," Zach said. "Oh shit. Sorry, didn't know you were still here, Shell."

"No worries," she said, frowning. Did Copper really need to deal with club business right now? So soon after being injured? One peek up at his determined expression told her all she needed to know. Her man was ready for action. His head was already back in the game. If it ever left. With a sigh, she slipped off the bed. "I'll give you guys some time to chat." Squeezing Copper's hand, she turned to leave but didn't make it more than one step before she was yanked back toward the bed.

"Don't fucking think you're getting out of here without giving me those lips," he growled.

Shell leaned down to give him a quick kiss, but he had other ideas. His mammoth hand gripped the back of her head, holding her against him while he ravaged her mouth. Within seconds she was flushed, lightheaded, and wishing they were anywhere else.

When she righted herself, Zach whistled. "That's some hot shit right there, guys. We better talk quick, I'm gonna need to find my woman, asap."

Face burning, Shell giggled.

"Love you," Copper said.

She took a stumbling step toward the door making all the men laugh. "Love you too."

Jig stood in the hall, arms folded across his chest. Shell went right to him. "I need you to promise me something, Jig."

One of his dark eyebrows crept upward. "What's that?"

"Please don't let Copper be the one to kill Rusty," she whispered.

"Shell—"

"No." She held up a hand. "I'm serious Jig. It will mess his head up. That's his brother who, until a week ago, he believed was a good man. Up until last week, he loved Rusty and felt responsible for him. Promise me."

Jig banged his head against the wall and groaned. "I can't make that promise, Shell. You know that."

Her heart fell. Of all the men, she'd have thought Jig would understand. He knew what it was to lose someone he loved.

Copper

"I can't promise you, but I agree with you, and I'll do whatever I can to keep him from killing Rusty. Okay?"

She nodded and ran a hand through her hair and exhaustion washed over her. She was going on about forty hours without a wink of sleep. Wouldn't be long before her body took over and crashed her, hard. "Thanks. You know what they're talking about in there?"

With a shake of his head, Jig said, "Nah. Zach got a call, freaked, and asked me to guard the door. All I know."

The important thing now was for Copper to rest and heal. Hopefully whatever news his brothers brought to his literal door wouldn't impede his recovery.

"GO WITH HER, LJ," Copper ordered before Zach could start talking. "Make her sit that fine ass down and eat something. I don't care if you have to tie her to a chair. I want her fed and off her feet for a while. Hear me?" He wasn't above using force to get Shell to take care of herself.

"You got it, prez," LJ said with a nod. He was almost as big as Copper, but with the way he worked out, would probably be even bigger in no time. "What happened?" he asked once the prospect was out of the room. LJ was a fantastic prospect, nearing his patch-in date, but he was still a prospect and wouldn't be the first to hear any significant club news.

Zach ran a hand through his hair, messing the typically perfect style. Dark circles rimmed both his and Screw's eyes, speaking to the long days they'd had searching for him. The men appeared almost as wiped as Shell. He cleared his throat.

Shit, this wasn't going to be good.

"Rusty's dead," Zach said.

Copper blinked. He swore his heart missed a few beats.

Fuck.

Fuuuck.

"How?"

"Thunder and Mav were transporting him to The Box. We were gonna let him simmer there until you got released or gave other orders. Halfway to the clubhouse, they were run off the road. SUV fucking flipped twice. Mav was disoriented, but conscious though he couldn't get out of his seat. Thunder was out cold. Next thing Mav knew, there was a pop and Rusty had a bullet to the brain."

"Jesus fuck." Anger had him curling his fists. To the right above his head, the monitor started beeping.

"Take a fucking breath, prez," Screw said. "Your heartrates jumping up. The nurse will be in if you can't calm your shit."

Fucking thief. That was *his* kill. Rusty was his. He'd been fantasizing about the end of Rusty's life for days. Countless scenarios and plans, not one involving someone else pulling the trigger. "They okay?"

"Mav's good. Banged up and pissed off, but that's the worst of it. Thunder broke a wrist, busted his nose, and has a concussion. Lucky as shit, all being said."

"Who?"

"Mav was pretty sure it was Lefty. Thank fuck a couple of our guys were close behind. They startled him into fleeing. If they'd been alone, Mav and Thunder might have bullets in their skulls, too."

Lefty. Copper ran a hand down his face, wincing when it bumped his nose. "Get Joe on the line for me." The club had held up their end of the bargain, collecting Joe's money, and delivering it to him four days ago. Lefty should have been on Copper's fucking doorstep by now, not running around killing his men.

Zach nodded and turned away, phone to his ear.

Goddammit, this was fucking with his head. Not the fact that Rusty was dead. That was the only way this fairy tale would end, but Copper had wanted, no *needed* to be the one to pull the trigger. Only one who deserved the kill more than him was Shell and he'd set fire to his bike before letting her live with the burden of taking a life. Copper needed the closure. And to have Lefty be the one who took it from him...the universe's sick joke. He was fucking done with this bullshit. If Lefty wasn't trussed up and waiting for him by the time he got out of the hospital, there'd be hell coming Joe's way.

"Here, boss," Zach said, tossing the phone his way.

Copper caught it easily. Before he even had it to his ear, Joe was rushing to explain. The man hadn't been shitting him when he said his crew didn't want trouble with the Handlers. "We fucking had him, Copper, but we underestimated him. Guy looks like a cheesy Rambo wannabe, but he's smarter than we'd anticipated." The growl of frustration had Copper believing Joe's words.

"What happened?"

There was a loud crash on Joes's side like he'd thrown something across the room. Copper understood the sentiment. "We snatched him up easy. Set up a meet to deliver some product, and grabbed his unsuspecting ass, no problem. But the guy killed two of my men and escaped."

Well shit. Would Joe be gunning for Lefty just as hard as Copper now? Were they gonna battle over rights to Lefty's death?

"Heard he killed your brother. Sorry about that, man," Joe said, sincerity in his voice.

Copper cleared his throat. He wouldn't waste a second of time mourning Rusty, but Joe didn't need to know that. That was club business, personal business for the eyes and ears of his men only. "Thanks," he managed to choke out. "You can understand why we want to get our hands on him.

"Look, my guys are chomping at the bit to find him. We got a lot of manpower on this. But I gave you my word I'd deliver him to you, so when we find him, he's yours. We're gonna fuck him up first though, you hear?"

Copper didn't respond.

"Promise we'll leave enough of him for you guys to get your pound of flesh and for you to finish the job. But I need to give my men something. The two he killed were good fucking men."

Looked like that was as good as he was going to get unless the Handler's found Lefty first. And with Joe's guys working with him recently, they had a better chance of sniffing him out. He got it, though. Had he been in Joe's place he'd want some sweet revenge just as bad.

"Just as long as he's conscious enough to enjoy his time with us."

"He will be. You have my word. I'll be in touch, Copper," Joe said before disconnecting.

Copper handed the phone back to Zach.

"We're gonna take off so you can rest, Prez," Screw said. Neither he nor Zach asked for the details of his phone call. Most likely they'd gotten the gist from his side. "We've also got guys searching Rusty's laptop and phone. We'll destroy any evidence he had against you."

Shit. In all the drama of being sent to the hospital, he'd forgotten Rusty supposedly had a recording of him committing murder.

"Want us to send Shell back in?" Zach asked.

Fuck yes, he wanted his woman with him. "As long as LJ got her to eat."

With nods and orders to take it easy, the two of them left.

Alone for the first time since he opened his eyes, Copper let his mind absorb all that had happened over the past few days. He knew himself, and it'd take some time before he came to terms with the anger over the circumstances of Rusty's death. At some point, he'd have to suck it up and accept the unfulfilled feeling in his gut. Maybe once he saw the lifeless body, he'd finally feel some sense of justice. Now, he just felt cheated. He hadn't asked, but he assumed the club had handled the situation before the cops got involved. They'd hold the body for Copper then determine the best way to dispose of it.

Copper

The door opened, and Shell popped her head in. "Hey, baby," he said.

The tired smile she gave him had warmth filling his chest. As he watched her walk toward the bed, he had a thought that shocked him. Maybe, in some way, it was for the best. Rusty was dead. It was over. He and Shell could begin the process of moving-on the second he was discharged without the looming problem of dealing with Rusty.

He patted the bed next to him and without a word, she climbed in. They both sighed and within seconds, Shell was out cold. He closed his eyes, and instead of feeling anger, he felt pretty damn content.

Took way too much effort, but the next morning Copper convinced the damn doctors he wouldn't hop right back on his bike if they discharged him. He had to sit through a lecture from three physicians and two nurses about taking it easy, letting himself heal, and staying off his bike.

Through all the bullshit, Shell sat by his side looking like a sleepy angel. She'd frowned and nodded at all the lecturers as though it was the first time hearing it. Then she'd promised each doctor she'd make sure he followed orders and acted like a good boy.

Whatever the fuck he had to agree to to get his ass out of the damn hospital he'd do it.

Felt like the doctors were mocking him. Ride his bike...he could barely fucking walk.

Later that evening, he was at Shell's house lounging on the couch while Beth *fixed* him with her doctor kit. In the hours since he'd been released, Beth had *fixed* him no less than five times.

She'd listened to his broken leg with her stethoscope, taken the temperature of the bandages on his stomach, and held the toy pager against his cracked ribs. According to her four-year-old-logic, the shrill beeping would make him all better. She'd frowned and stared at the plastic tools in her kit when he didn't immediately get all better. Only one problem with this little game—Beth wasn't the gentlest of healthcare providers. A few times his eyes had watered with intense pain when she *healed* him. All through it, she beamed with pride at her ability to help.

Made every second of discomfort worth it.

Shell sat on the floor alongside her daughter trying to soften the munchkin's touch. Didn't work. Beth plowed on like a bull in a china shop.

The evening was damn near perfect. Once Beth went to bed, and he could get his woman naked, it would be perfect.

As though she read his mind, Shell stood and hauled her squirming daughter to her feet. "All right, Bethy. Time to brush those teeth and head to bed."

"Can I fix Copper one more time? Please, Mommy!" she whined.

"Not tonight, honey."

"But, Mom—"

"Hey, come here, princess." Copper crooked a finger at her.

Her face lit up, and she scrambled onto the couch. "What?"

He cupped his hand and whispered in her ear. "If you go brush your teeth and get into bed without giving Mommy trouble, we'll go get ice cream tomorrow."

"Yes!" Beth shouted then shot off toward the bathroom.

Shell cocked her head. Hair pulled back in a messy bun, face make-up free, and wearing sweatpants and a T-shirt, she was the most beautiful woman he'd ever seen. "What'd you say to her?"

He winked. "Secret."

With a roll of her eyes, Shell followed her daughter into the bathroom. It took almost half an hour, but she eventually returned. "Phew," she said, gently wedging herself on the couch next to him.

His arm immediately went around her shoulders. "Tired?"

"Bedtime is a process."

"Isn't everything a process with a kiddo?"

"You have a point." She fell silent. "You okay? I don't know exactly what happened, but I know you seem frustrated with the outcome. I've been worried about you. I know how things had to end with Rusty, but you still lost a brother, the one you used to know. The one you raised. You lost him the day you found out what he did to me. It has to be hard for you."

It was true. And all the grief of it would probably hit one day soon. And his ol' lady would be there to help him through it. But for now, he just felt relief Rusty was gone. "Hey," he lifted a finger to her lips. "All you need to know is that you never have to worry about Rusty again. And I wasn't the one to do the job." She didn't need those details. Just the outcome.

Shell visibly relaxed before his eyes. Had he known how much this was eating at her, he'd have told her earlier he wasn't going to off Rusty himself. "Good," she whispered. "It's all over."

"You ready to put it behind us? Move forward?"

Her face softened, and she stared at him, love shining in her eyes. "Yes. That's exactly what I want."

"Good." Copper captured a stray curl and rubbed it between his thumb and forefinger. "You can start by planning the wedding. Doc says I'll be fully functional in three to four months. "So let's plan it for the end of July. Yeah?"

Her mouth flapped open and closed, making him laugh.

"What? You thought I forgot?"

"Um, well, yeah. Well, not forgot, but I thought you were rambling from blood loss or something." Her face had paled a little.

Copper snorted. "Nope. And you agreed. You gonna tell me you lied to me?"

Shell shook her head. More curls fell from the loose pile. "No. I just...are you sure?"

"Michelle Ward, I can't get down on one knee for the next few months, but I can still tell you how I feel. I've wasted so much time. Should have tied you to me years ago. I don't want to spend another day without you by my side. I love you. I want to marry you and adopt that adorable girl back there."

Shell was openly crying now. "You want to adopt Beth?"

"Yeah, baby. I want to adopt Beth."

"And you want to marry me?"

"I want to marry you so fucking bad. So, what do you say? Will you make an honest man outta me?"

Shell threw her arms around him and squeezed. When he winced, she said, "Sorry! Sorry! I forgot you were hurt. Oh, my God, how did I forget?"

He mock scowled at her. He'd take pain any day if it meant having her in his arms. "You gonna put me out of my misery?"

"Oh! Yes," she said. "Yes, Copper, I'll marry you. It's all I've wanted for more than ten years. Of course, I'll marry you."

He gripped her by the back of the head and crushed their mouths together, split lip be damned. There was no way he wasn't tasting that mouth.

She'd agreed to be his wife.

His kingdom was complete now that he had his queen.

EPILOGUE

Six months later

"Say it again," Copper said as he drew his hips back.

"Copper, come on, you're killing me. Just let me come."

Killing her? She had no freaking idea. The slow, sucking grasp of her pussy as he pulled out nearly did him in. "Say it."

She rolled her eyes but gave him a soft smile. "I'm yours."

"My what?" He jerked back farther leaving only the very tip of his dick inside her.

Shell groaned. She looked fucking delectable. Lacy white bra that did nothing to hide the hardened state of her nipples. White garters attached to thigh high white stockings. There'd been a thread she called a thong to match, but he'd done away with that long ago. Her face, with just enough makeup to set the day apart from a regular day, was flush with passion. The hair she'd forbade him to muss before the ceremony was a scattered mess of sweaty curls.

"Your wife."

"Damn straight." He peered down at his cock, glistening with the proof of her arousal. Didn't seem to matter when or how often he wanted her, Shell was always wet and ready for him. "For how long?"

The smile he loved widened. "Forever."

Best. Thing. Ever.

"Forever," he breathed. Then he snapped his hips forward burying as deep as possible in his wife's pussy.

Shell cried out and arched her back. Her perfectly manicured nails dug into his sides as she held on. He paused, absorbing the sensation of his wife holding him deep inside her body. In the months since Rusty's demise, they'd grown closer than he thought was possible for two people to be. Copper couldn't imagine a day, hell, an hour without her in his life.

His recovery had gone as well as could be expected, though the limitations of his body nearly drove him fucking nuts. But as of a week ago, he was free and clear of any braces, crutches, and medical restrictions.

As of an hour ago, they were officially married. The moment they entered the clubhouse for the reception, he'd yanked her into his office, divested her of that sexy as fuck white dress and feasted on her.

"I'm gonna come, Copper," she said on a moan, and he pounded into her harder.

"Give it to me, gorgeous." He sucked a nipple into her mouth, lace and all and Shell shattered, coming on his cock. "Fuck!" He didn't stand a chance once she started clenching all over him like that. The orgasm slammed into him like a charging bull.

"Wow," Shell said with a giggle. "Not bad for a married couple."

Copper grunted. It would take another minute for his brain to kick back in.

Trapped between his heavy body and the wall, Shell wiggled. "Think anyone heard us?"

The reception was at the clubhouse and should be in full swing without them. "Pretty sure you woke your pops in his grave. Expecting his ghost to show up with a shotgun anytime now."

She giggled again as he let her body slide to the floor. "Nah, you made an honest woman outta me."

Copper

"Smartest thing I ever did." Kissing her mouth, he righted his clothes. Not a hard task since all he did was loosen his pants to free his dick.

Shell, on the other hand, had the more arduous task of slipping back into her wedding dress. He propped his ass on the end of his desk and watched the show. She'd worn a short and sassy white dress that hugged her every curve. When he'd first seen it, he'd been surprised by how conservative the dress was. Not even a hint of cleavage. Then she'd turned, and he came face to face with her bare back. The dress dipped nearly to her ass. All he could think about was running his tongue along her spine.

It was the first thing he did after locking the office door.

Fucking sexy as hell.

"You see my panties?" Shell asked, scanning the floor.

With a smirk, Copper bent and retrieved the tattered fabric from the ground. "Not sure they're gonna be much good to you anymore."

Shell's eyes widened. "How did I not realize you did that?"

He stalked forward, shoving the panties in his pants pocket. "Guess I had you a little distracted."

A sly grin curled her now lipstick-free mouth. "Guess so."

"Ready to head out to our party?" he asked his wife. Damn, that sounded sweet.

Shell nodded, and he tucked her hand in his, exactly where it belonged. The last few months had been the most amazing of his life. And now he had the rest of his days to enjoy the woman who made up his whole world.

"Let's do it," she said, rising up on her toes for a kiss.

Fuck yeah.

THE MOMENT COPPER opened the door, a few hundred bikers broke out into raucous cheers and hollers.

"Yeah, Copper, that's how you get it done."

"You bent her over that desk, Prez?"

"Hope you gave her an inch for every year you made her wait for you." That was Izzy's voice.

Shell's face burned.

It'd been nice knowing Izzy. Too bad Shell would never be able to face her again.

She peeked up at her husband who had the smuggest damn look on his face. He glanced down at her with a wink. All she could do was roll her eyes and laugh.

The most fantastic day of her life was topped off by the most wonderful party she could have asked for. Family, friends, good food, plenty of booze, Shell had never had a better time. Even her mother showed up. She didn't smile much, but she was there.

She was also clueless as to what happened in her house while she was out of town a few months ago.

And it would stay that way forever.

Exhausted from dancing with every man associated with the club, Shell walked over toward the bar. Thunder, who'd volunteered to manage the bar, had a bottle of water ready for her. "Looking parched, Mrs. President," he said with a wink.

"Oh, Thunder, you're perfect." She snatched the water and guzzled half the bottle. When her tongue wasn't so dry, she turned and watched her guests. A minute later, her husband spotted her and stalked her way.

Shell shivered. That gaze was so damn potent it was practically a caress.

"Hey, baby," he whispered against her mouth.

"Hi, handsome. Relax with me a moment. See how much fun our family is having." She pulled him in next to her so his back was to the bar as well.

Immediately, his arm slipped around her shoulders, tucking her close. The man didn't believe in personal space.

Not that she was complaining. Being touched by him was hands down her favorite pastime.

"Does look like a pretty successful party, huh?"

Copper

"Yep." She smiled. Music blared through the clubhouse. Everyone was drinking, dancing and having a fabulous time.

"Got a surprise for you," her husband said, pulling a folded paper from his pocket. He unfolded it and handed it over, an almost misty look on his face.

That couldn't be right. Copper didn't do misty.

"What is this?"

He laughed. "Read it, Miss Impatient."

As Shell scanned the document, tears came to her eyes. "Oh, my God," she whispered. "It's official."

He kissed the top of her head. "Yeah, as of yesterday I'm officially Beth's father."

Shell swallowed the golf ball lodged in her throat. "Thank you for this," she said. "Thank you for loving Beth and me. And thank you for wanting to adopt her. I'm not sure I can express to you what this means to me, Aiden," she said, staring up at the man she loved so much it seemed like it couldn't be real.

But it was. And he loved her just the same. She felt it every second of every day.

"Shit, baby, I'm the one who should be thanking you. You and that princess are the best things in my life."

Was it possible for a heart to actually burst with love?

She glanced back at the happy partiers. "Quite the kingdom you have here."

"Your kingdom too, now." He gave a gentle tug on her hair so she looked back up at him. "You're my queen, Shell. This family, this kingdom is as much yours as it is mine. You ready to rule it with me?"

She'd never been readier for anything in her life. Taking her place by her husband's side was her destiny. "Never been more ready for anything, except to marry you."

"Damn good answer, baby," he said before he kissed her.

Shell gave herself over to her husband's passion.

It'd been a long, hard road, finding her way to her man, but she'd come to value the lessons and strength she'd gained along the way. The past was the past, and nothing would change it now. But the future?

Yeah, that was shiny and bright as the sun.

Thank you so much for reading **Copper**. If you enjoyed it, please consider leaving a review on Goodreads or your favorite retailer.

Other books by Lilly Atlas

No Prisoners MC
Hook: A No Prisoners Novella
Striker
Jester
Acer
Lucky
Snake

Trident Ink
Escapades

Hell's Handlers MC
Zach
Maverick
Jigsaw
Copper

Lilly Atlas

Join Lilly's mailing list for a **FREE** No Prisoners short story.

www.lillyatlas.com

Join my Facebook group, **Lilly's Ladies** for book previews, early cover reveals, contests and more!

About the Author

Lilly Atlas is an award-winning contemporary romance author. She's a proud Navy wife and mother of three spunky girls. Every time Lilly downloads a new eBook she expects her Kindle App to tell her it's exhausted and overworked, and to beg for some rest. Thankfully that hasn't happened yet so she can often be found absorbed in a good book.

Made in the USA
Coppell, TX
14 March 2025